Dear Reader,

There are a million different ways to meet people—think about it. And one day you may meet someone who will change your life. No one knows better than Nora Roberts that love can strike at almost any moment! In this very special 2-in-1 collection, join two sets of strangers as they embark on the thrilling journey of finding that special someone and falling in love.

In *From This Day*, B. J. Clark meets her match in Taylor Reynolds—the man who has just purchased the hotel that B.J. manages. It doesn't take long for an attraction to spark between them, but B.J. insists on keeping things professional. Then she realizes the thought of being "just an employee" to Taylor was not at all what she wanted! Now what!?

In *Temptation*, camp owner Eden Carlbough never thought she'd meet the man of her dreams by falling out of an apple tree. But after a group of badly behaved camp girls cause her to take refuge in the treetops, Chase Eliot is right there to catch her when she comes crashing down. And Eden can't help thinking she may have finally found the man who can show her the way to paradise.

We hope you fall in love with these characters the same way they fall in love with each other!

Enjoy!

The Editors
Silhouette Books

NORA ROBERTS

By My Side

Published by Silhouette Books

America's Publisher of Contemporary Romance

SILHOUETTE BOOKS

BY MY SIDE

ISBN-13: 978-0-373-28537-2
ISBN-10:   0-373-28537-X

Copyright © 2006 by Harlequin Books S.A.

The publisher acknowledges the copyright holder of the individual works as follows:

FROM THIS DAY
Copyright © 1983 by Nora Roberts.

TEMPTATION
Copyright © 1987 by Nora Roberts.

This edition published by arrangement with Harlequin Books S.A.

® and TM are trademarks of Harlequin Books S.A., used under license. Trademarks indicated with ® are registered in the United States Patent and Trademark Office, the Canadian Trade Marks Office and in other countries.

Visit Silhouette Books at www.eHarlequin.com

Printed in U.S.A.

CONTENTS

FROM THIS DAY

Chapter One

Spring comes late to New England. Snow lingers in isolated patches. Trees begin their greening hesitantly, tiny closed buds of leaves against naked branches. Early blooms of color burst from the earth's womb. The air is fresh with promise.

B.J. tossed open her window with a flourish and welcomed the early breeze into her room. *Saturday,* she thought with a grin, and began to braid her long, wheat-colored hair. The Lakeside Inn was half-full, the summer season three weeks away, and if all followed her well-ordered plans, her duties as manager would be light for the duration of the weekend.

Her staff was loyal, though somewhat temperamental. Like a large family, they squabbled, sulked, teased and stuck together like mortar and brick when the need arose. *And I,* she mused with a rueful grin, *am head counselor.*

Pulling on faded jeans, B.J. did not pause to consider the incongruity of the title. A small, childlike woman reflected in her glass, curves disguised by casual attire, braids hanging impishly astride a heart shaped, elfin face with huge smoky eyes dominant. Her only large feature, they swamped the tip-tilted nose and cupid's bow mouth and were prone to smolder or sparkle with the fluctuations of her mood. After lacing dilapidated sneakers, she jogged from the room, intending to check on breakfast preparations before stealing an hour for a solitary walk.

The main staircase of the inn was wide and uncarpeted, connecting its four sprawling stories without curve or angle, as straight and sturdy as the building itself. She saw with satisfaction the lobby was both tidy and deserted. The curtains were drawn to welcome the sun, needlepoint pillows plumped, and a vase of fresh wildflowers adorned the high, well-polished registration desk. The clatter of cutlery carried from the dining room as she passed through the downstairs hall, and she heard, with a long suffering sigh, the running argument between her two waitresses.

"If you really like a man with small, pig eyes, you should be very happy."

B.J. watched Dot shrug her thin shoulders with the words as she rolled a place setting in white linen.

"Wally does not have pig eyes," Maggie insisted. "They're very intelligent. You're just jealous," she added with grim relish as she filled the sugar dispensers.

"Jealous! Ha! The day I'm jealous of a squinty-eyed little runt... Oh, hello, B.J."

"Good morning, Dot, Maggie. You rolled two spoons and a knife at that setting, Dot. I think a fork might be a nice touch."

Accompanied by her companion's snickers, Dot unrolled the linen. "Wally's taking me to a double feature at the drive-in tonight." Maggie's smug statement followed B.J. into the kitchen, and she allowed the door to swing shut on the ensuing retort.

Unlike the casual, old fashioned atmosphere of the remainder of the inn, the kitchen sparkled with twentieth century efficiency. Stainless steel glimmered everywhere in the oversized room, the huge stove attesting that the inn's main attraction was its menu. Cupboards and cabinets stood like veteran soldiers, walls and linoleum gleaming with fresh cleaning. B.J. smiled, pleased with the room's perfection and the drifting scent of coffee.

"Morning, Elsie." She received an absent mutter from the round woman working at a long, well-scrubbed counter. "If everything's under control, I'm going out for a couple of hours."

"Betty Jackson won't send any blackberry jelly."

"What? Well, for goodness sake why not?" Annoyed by the complication, B.J. plucked a fresh muffin from a basket and began to devour it. "Mr. Conners always asks for her jelly, and we're down to the last jar."

"She said if you couldn't be bothered to pay a lonely old woman a visit, she couldn't be bothered to part with any jelly."

"Lonely old woman?" B.J.'s exclamation was hampered by a mouthful of muffin. "She runs more news items through that house of hers than the Associated Press. Blast it, Elsie, I really need that jelly. I was too busy last week to go listen to the latest special bulletins."

"The new owner coming Monday got you worried?"

"Who's worried? I'm not worried." Scowling, she confiscated another muffin. "It's simply that as manager of the inn, I want everything to be in order."

"Eddie said you were muttering and slamming around your office after you got the letter saying he was coming."

"I was not…muttering…." Moving to the refrigerator, B.J. poured a glass of juice and spoke to Elsie's wide back. "Taylor

Reynolds has a perfect right to inspect his property. It's just, blast it, Elsie, it was all those vague comments about modernizing. Mr. Taylor Reynolds better keep his hands off the Lakeside Inn and play with his other hotels. We don't need to be modernized," she continued, rapidly working herself up into a temper. "We're perfectly fine just the way we are. There's not a thing wrong with us, we don't need anything." She finished by folding her arms across her chest and glaring at the absent Taylor Reynolds.

"Except blackberry jelly," Elsie said mildly. B.J. blinked and brought herself back to the present.

"Oh, all right," she muttered and stalked toward the door. "I'll go get it. But if she tells me one more time that Howard Beall is a fine boy and good husband material, I'll scream. Right there in her living room with the doilies and chintz, I'll scream!"

Leaving this dire threat hanging in the air, B.J. stepped out into the soothing yellow sunlight.

"Blackberry jelly," she mumbled as she hopped on a battered red bike. "New owners with fancy notions...." Lifting her face to the sky, she tossed a pigtail behind her shoulder.

Pedaling down the maple lined drive, quicksilver temper ebbed, her resilient spirits were lifted with the beauty of the day. The valley was stirring with life. Small clusters of fragile violets and red clover dotted the rolling meadows. Lines of fresh laundry waved in the early breeze. The boundary of mountains was topped by a winter's coat, not yet the soft, lush green it would be in a month's time, but patched with stark black trees and the intermittent color of pines. Clouds scudded thin and white across the sky, chased by the teasing wind which whispered of spring and fresh blossoms.

Good humor restored, B.J. arrived in town with pink cheeks and a smile, waving to familiar faces along the route to Betty Jackson's jelly. It was a small town with tidy lawns, picket fences and old, well-kept homes. The dormers and gables were typical of New England. Nestled like a contented cat in the rolling valley, and the brilliant shimmer of Lake Champlain to the west, Lakeside remained serene and untouched by big city bustle. Having been raised on its outskirts had not dulled its magic for B.J.: she felt, as always when entering its limits, a gratitude that somewhere life remained simple.

Parking her bike in front of a small, green-shuttered house, B.J. swung through the gate and prepared to negotiate for her jelly supply.

"Well, B.J., what a surprise." Betty opened the door and patted her gray permanent. "I thought you'd gone back to New York."

"Things have been a bit hectic at the inn," she returned, striving for the proper humility.

"The new owner." Betty nodded with a fortune teller's wisdom and gestured B.J. inside. "I hear he wants to spruce things up."

Resigned that Betty Jackson's communications system was infallible, B.J. settled herself in the small living room.

"You know Tom Myers is adding another room to his house." Brushing off the seat of an overstuffed chair, Betty shifted her ample posterior and sat. "Seems Lois is in the family way again." She clucked her tongue over the Myers' profligacy. "Three babies in four years. But you like little ones, don't you, B.J.?"

"I've always been fond of children, Miss Jackson," B.J. acknowledged, wondering how to turn the conversation toward preserves.

"My nephew, Howard, just loves children."

B.J. braced herself not to scream and met the bland smile,

calmly. "We've a couple at the inn now. Children do love to eat." Pleased with the maneuver, she pressed on. "They've simply devoured your jellies. I'm down to my last jar. Nobody has the touch you do with jellies, Miss Jackson; you'd put the big manu- facturers out of business if you opened your own line."

"It's all in the timing," Betty preened under the praise, and B.J. tasted the hint of victory.

"I'd just have to close down if you didn't keep me supplied." Gray eyes fluttered ingenuously. "Mr. Conners would be crushed if I had to serve him store-bought goods. He simply raves about your blackberry jelly. *'Ambrosia,'* she added, relishing the word. "He says it's *ambrosia.*"

"Ambrosia." Betty nodded in self-satisfied agreement.

Ten minutes later, B.J. placed a box of a dozen jars of jelly in the basket of her bike and waved a cheerful goodbye.

"I came, I saw, I conquered," she told the sky with audacious pride. "And I did not scream."

"Hey, B.J.!"

She twisted her head at the sound of her name, waving to the group playing sand lot ball as she pedaled to the edge of the field. "What's the score?" she asked the young boy who ran to her bike.

"Five to four. Junior's team's winning."

She glanced over to where Junior stood, tall and gangly on the pitcher's mound, tossing a ball in his glove and grinning.

"Little squirt," she mumbled with reluctant affection. "Let me pinch hit once." Confiscating the boy's battered cap, she secured it over her pigtails and walked onto the field.

"You gonna play, B.J.?" Suddenly surrounded by young bodies and adolescent faces, B.J. lifted a bat and tested it.

"For a minute. I have to get back."

Junior approached, hands on hips, and grinned down from his advantage of three inches. "Wanna bet I strike you out?"

She spared him a brief glance and swung the bat to her shoulder. "I don't want to take your money."

"If I strike you out," he yanked a pigtail with fifteen-year-old audacity, "you gotta kiss me."

"Get on the mound, you apprentice lecher, and come back in ten years."

His grin remained unabashed, as B.J. watched, stifling a smile as he sauntered into position. He squinted, nodded, wound up and pitched. B.J. swung a full circle.

"Strike one!"

She turned and scowled at Wilbur Hayes who stood as umpire. Stepping up to the plate again, the cheers and taunts grew in volume. She stuck out her tongue at Junior's wink.

"Strike two!" Wilbur announced as she watched the pitch sail by.

"Strike?" Turning, she placed her hands on her hips. "You're crazy, that was chin high. I'm going to tell your mother you need glasses."

"Strike two," Wilbur repeated and frowned with adolescent ferocity.

Muttering, B.J. stepped again into the batter's box.

"You might as well put the bat down," Junior shouted, cradling the ball in the mitt. "You're not even coming close to this one."

"Take a good look at the ball, Junior, 'cause it's the last time you'll see it." Shifting the hat lower on her head, B.J. clutched the bat. "It's going clear to New York."

She connected with a solid crack of bat and watched the ball begin its sail before she darted around the bases. Running full steam, head down, she heard the shouts and cheers to slide as she rounded third. Scott Temple crouched at the plate, mitt opened for reception, as she threw herself down, sliding into home in a cloud of dust and frenzied shouts.

"You're out!"

"Out!" Scrambling to her feet, she met Wilbur's bland blue stare, eye to eye and nose to nose. "Out, you little squirt, I was safe by a mile. I'm going to buy you some binoculars."

"Out," he repeated with great dignity, and folded his arms.

"What we need here is an umpire with two working eyes." She turned to her crowd of supporters and threw out her hands. "I demand a second opinion."

"You were out."

Spinning at the unfamiliar voice, B.J. frowned up at the stranger. He stood leaning on the backstop, a small lift to his well-formed mouth and amusement shining from his dark brown eyes. He pushed a lock of curling black hair from his brow and straightened a long, lean frame.

"You should have been content with a triple."

"I was safe," she retorted, rubbing more dirt on her nose. "Absolutely safe."

"Out," Wilbur repeated.

B.J. sent him a withering glance before turning back to the man who approached the heated debate between teams. She studied him with a mixture of resentment and curiosity.

His features were well defined, sculptured with planes and angles, the skin bronzed and smooth, the faintest hint of red in his dark hair where the sun caught it. She saw that though his buff-colored suit was casual, it was obviously well tailored and expensive. His teasing smile widened at her critical survey, and her resentment deepened.

"I've got to get back," she announced, brushing at her jeans. "And don't think I'm not going to mention an eye exam to your mother," she added, giving Wilbur a final glare.

"Hey, kid." She straddled her bike and looked around idly, then smiled as she realized the man had grouped her with the teenagers. Restraining her smile, she looked up with what she hoped was the insolence of youth.

"Yeah?"

"How far is it to the Lakeside Inn?"

"Look, mister, my mother told me not to talk to strange men."

"Very commendable. I'm not offering you candy and a ride."

"Well." She frowned as if debating pros and cons. "O.K. It's about three miles up the road." Making her gesture vague, she finished with the obligatory codicil. "You can't miss it."

He gave a long stare into her wide gray eyes, then shook his head. "That's a big help. Thanks."

"Any time." She watched him wander toward a silver-blue Mercedes and, unable to prevent herself, called after him. "And I was safe. Absolutely safe." Tossing the borrowed hat back to its owner, B.J. cut across the meadow and headed toward the inn.

The four stories of red brick, with their gabled roof and neat shutters, loomed ahead of her. Pedaling up the wide, curving drive, she noted with satisfaction that the short cut had brought her ahead of the Mercedes.

I wonder if he's looking for a room, she thought. Parking her bike, she hauled out her treasure of jellies from the basket. Maybe he's a salesman. No, she contradicted her own thoughts, *that was no salesman.* Well, if he wants a room, we'll oblige him, even if he is an interfering busybody with bad eyes.

"Good morning." B.J. smiled at the newlyweds who strolled across the lawn.

"Oh, good morning, Miss Clark. We're going for a walk by the lake," the groom answered politely.

"It's a lovely day for it," B.J. acknowledged, parking her bike by the entrance. She entered the small lobby, and moving behind the front desk, set down the crate of jelly and reached for the morning mail. Seeing a personal letter from her grandmother, she opened it and began to read with pleasure.

"Get around, don't you?"

Her absorption was rudely broken. Dropping the letter, she lifted her elbows from the counter and stared into dark brown eyes. "I took a short cut." Unwilling to be outmatched by his height or faultless attire, she straightened and lifted her chin. "May I help you?"

"I doubt it, unless you can tell me where to find the manager."

His dismissive tone fueled her annoyance. She struggled to remember her job and remain pleasant. "Is there some problem? There's a room available if you require one."

"Be a good girl and run along." His tone was patronizing. "And fetch the manager for me while you're about it. I'd like to see him."

Drawing herself to her full height she crossed her arms over her chest. "You're looking at her."

His dark brows rose in speculation as his eyes swept over her incredulously. "Do you manage the inn before school and on Saturdays?" he asked sarcastically.

B.J. flushed with anger. "I have been managing the Lakeside Inn for nearly four years. If there's a problem, I shall be delighted to take it up with you here, or in my office. If you require a room," she gestured toward the open register, "we'll be more than happy to oblige you."

"B.J. Clark?" he asked with a deepening frown.

"That's correct."

With a nod, he lifted a pen and signed the register. "I'm sure you'll understand," he began, raising his eyes again in fresh study. "Your morning activity on the baseball diamond and your rather juvenile appearance are deceptive."

"I had the morning free," she said crisply, "and my appearance in no way reflects on the inn's quality. I'm sure you'll see that for yourself during your stay, Mr...." Turning the register to face her, B.J.'s stomach lurched.

"Reynolds," he supplied, smiling at her astonished expression. "Taylor Reynolds."

Struggling for composure, B.J. lifted her face and assumed a businesslike veneer. "I'm afraid we weren't expecting you until Monday, Mr. Reynolds."

"I changed my plans," he countered, dropping the pen back in its holder.

"Yes, well...Welcome to Lakeside Inn," she said belatedly and flicked a pigtail behind her back.

"Thank you. I'll require an office during my stay. Can you arrange it?"

"Our office space is limited, Mr. Reynolds." Cursing Betty Jackson's blackberry jelly, she pulled down the key to the inn's best room and rounded the desk. "However, if you don't mind sharing mine, I'm sure you'll find it adequate."

"Let's take a look. I want to see the books and records anyway."

"Of course," she agreed, gritting her teeth at the stranger's hold over her inn. "If you'll just come with me."

"B.J., B.J." She watched with an inward shudder as Eddie hurtled down the stairs and into the lobby. His glasses were slipping down his nose, his brown hair was flopping around his ears.

"B.J.," he said again, breathless, "Mrs. Pierce-Lowell's T.V. went out right in the middle of her cartoons."

"Oh, blast. Take mine in to her and call Max for the repair."

"He's away for the weekend," Eddie reminded her.

"All right, I'll survive." Giving his shoulder an encouraging pat, she guided him to the door. "Leave me a memo to call him Monday and get mine into her before she misses Bugs Bunny." Feeling the new owner's penetrating stare in the back of her head, B.J. explained apologetically. "I'm sorry, Eddie has a tendency toward the dramatic, and Mrs. Pierce-Lowell is addicted to Saturday morning cartoons. She's one of our regulars, and we make it a policy to provide our guests with what pleases them."

"I see," he replied, but she could find nothing in his expression to indicate that he did.

Moving quickly to the back of the first floor, B.J. opened the door to her office and gestured Taylor inside. "It's not very big," she began as he surveyed the small room with desk and file cabinets and bulletin board, "but I'm sure we can arrange it to suit your needs for the few days you will be here."

"Two weeks," he stated firmly. He strolled across the room, picking up a bronzed paperweight of a grinning turtle.

"Two weeks?" she repeated, and the alarm in her voice caused him to turn toward her.

"That's right, Miss Clark. Is that a problem?"

"No, no, of course not." Finding his direct stare unnerving, she lowered her eyes to the clutter on her desk.

"Do you play ball every Saturday, Miss Clark?" He perched on the edge of the desk. Looking up, B.J. found her face only inches from his.

"No, certainly not," she answered with dignity. "I simply happened to be passing by, and——"

"A very courageous slide," he commented, shocking her by running a finger down her cheek. "And your face proves it."

Somewhat dazed, she glanced at the dust on his finger. "I was safe," she said in defense against a ridiculously speeding pulse. "Wilbur needs an optometrist."

"I wonder if you manage the inn with the same tenacity with which you play ball." He smiled, his eyes very intent on hers. "We'll have a look at the books this afternoon."

"I'm sure you'll find everything in order," she said stiffly. The effect was somewhat spoiled as she backed into the file cabinet. "The inn runs very smoothly, and as you know, makes a nice profit." She continued struggling to maintain her dignity.

"With a few changes, it should make a great deal more."

"Changes?" she echoed, apprehension in her voice. "What sort of changes?"

"I need to look over the place before I make any concrete decisions, but the location is perfect for a resort." Absently, he brushed the dust off his fingers on the windowsill and gazed out. "Pool, tennis courts, health club, a face lift for the building itself."

"There's nothing wrong with this building. We don't cater to the resort set, Mr. Reynolds." Furious, B.J. approached the desk again. "This is an inn, with all the connotations that includes. Family-style meals, comfortable lodgings and a quiet atmosphere. That's why our guests come back."

"The clientele would increase with a few modern attractions," he countered coolly. "Particularly with the proximity to Lake Champlain."

"Keep your hot tubs and disco lounges for your other acquisitions." B.J. bypassed simmer and went straight to boil. "This is Lakeside, Vermont, not L.A. I don't want any plastic surgery on my inn."

Brows rose, and his mouth curved in a grim smile. "Your inn, Miss Clark?"

"That's right," she retorted. "You may hold the purse strings, Mr. Reynolds, but I know this place, and our guests come back year after year because of what we represent. There's no way you're going to change one brick."

"Miss Clark." Taylor stood menacingly over her. "If I choose to tear down this inn brick by brick, that's precisely what I'll do. Whatever alterations I make or don't make, remain my decision, and my decision alone. Your position as manager does not entitle you to a vote."

"And your position as owner doesn't entitle you to brains!" she was unable to choke back as she stomped from the office in a flurry of flying braids.

Chapter Two

With relish, B.J. slammed the door to her room. Arrogant, interfering, insufferable man. Why doesn't he go play Monopoly somewhere else? Doesn't he already have enough hotels to tinker with? There must be a hundred in the Reynolds chain in the States alone, plus all those elegant foreign resorts. Why doesn't he open one in Antarctica?

Abruptly, she caught sight of her reflection in the mirror and stared in disbelief. Her face was smudged. Dust clung to her sweatshirt and jeans. Her braids hung to her shoulders. All in all, she thought grimly, I look like a rather dim-witted ten-year-old. She suddenly noticed a line down her cheek, and lifting her hand, recalled Taylor's finger resting there.

"Oh, blast." Shaking her head, she began to quickly unbind her hair. "I made a mess of it," she muttered and stripped off her morning uniform. "Looking like a grimy teenager and then losing my temper on top of it. Well, he's not going to fire me," she vowed fiercely and stalked to the shower. "I'll quit first! I'm not staying around and watching my inn mutilated."

Thirty minutes later, B.J. pulled a brush through her hair and studied the new reflection with satisfaction. Soft clouds of wheat floated on her shoulders. She wore an ivory dress, nipped at the waist, belted in scarlet to match tiny blazing rubies at her ears. Heels gave her height a slight advantage. She felt confident she could no longer be mistaken for sixteen. Lifting a neatly written page from her dresser, she moved purposefully from the room, prepared to confront the bear in his den.

After a brief excuse for a knock, B.J. pushed open the office door and slowly and purposefully advanced toward the man sitting behind the desk. Shoving the paper under his nose, she waited for his brown eyes to meet hers.

"Ah, B.J. Clark, I presume. This is quite a transfiguration." Leaning back in his chair, Taylor allowed his eyes to travel over the length of her. "Amazing," he smiled into her resentful gray eyes, "what can be concealed under a sweatshirt and baggy pants.... What's this?" He waved the paper idly, his eyes still appraising her.

"My resignation." Placing her palms on the desk, she leaned forward and prepared to give vent to her emotions. "And now that I am no longer in your employ, Mr. Reynolds, it'll give me a great deal of pleasure to tell you what I think. You are," she began as his brow rose at her tone, "a dictatorial, capitalistic opportunist. You've bought an inn which has for generations maintained its reputation for quality and personal service, and in order to make a few more annual dollars, you plan to turn it into a live-in amusement park. In doing so, you will not only have to let the current staff go, some of whom have worked here for twenty years, but you'll succeed in destroying the integrity of the entire district. This is not your average tourist town, it's a quiet, settled community.

People come here for fresh air and quiet, not for a brisk tennis match or to sweat in a sauna, and——"

"Are you finished, Miss Clark?" Taylor questioned. Instinctively she recognized the danger in his lowered tones.

"No." Mustering her last resources of courage, she set her shoulders and sent him a lethal glare. "Go soak in your Jacuzzi!"

On her heel, she spun around and made for the door only to find her back pressed into it as she was whirled back into the room.

"Miss Clark," Taylor began, effectively holding her prisoner by leaning over her, arms at either side of her head. "I permitted you to clear your system for two reasons. First, you're quite a fabulous sight when your temper's in full gear. I noticed that even when I took you for a rude teenager. A lot of it has to do with your eyes going from mist to smoke, it's very impressive. That, of course," he added as she stared up at him, unable to form a sound, "is strictly on a personal level. Now on a professional plane, I am receptive to your opinions, if not to your delivery."

Abruptly, the door swung open, dislodging B.J. and tumbling her into a hard chest. "We found Julius's lunch," Eddie announced cheerfully and disappeared.

"You have a very enthusiastic staff," Taylor commented dryly as his arms propped her up against him. "Who the devil is Julius?"

"He's Mrs. Frank's Great Dane. She doesn't...she won't go anywhere without him."

"Does he have his own room?" His tone was gently mocking.

"No, he has a small run in the back."

Taylor smiled suddenly, his face close to hers. Power shot through her system like a bolt of electricity down a lightning rod. With a jerk, she pulled away and pushed at her tumbled hair.

"Mr. Reynolds," she began, attempting to retrieve her all too elusive dignity. He claimed her hand and pulled her back toward the desk, then pushed her firmly down on the chair.

"Do be quiet, Miss Clark," he told her in easy tones, settling behind the desk. "It's my turn now." She stared with a melding of astonishment and indignation.

"What I ultimately do with this inn is my decision. However, I will consider your opinion as you are intimate with this establishment and with the area and I, as yet, am not." Lifting B.J.'s resignation, Taylor tore it in half and dropped the pieces on the desk.

"You can't do that," she sputtered.

"I have just done it." The mild tone vibrated with authority.

B.J.'s eyes narrowed. "I can easily write another."

"Don't waste your paper," he advised, leaning back in his chair. "I have no intention of accepting your resignation at the moment. Later, I'll let you know. However," he added slowly, shrugging, "if you insist, I shall be forced to close down the inn for the next few months until I've found someone to replace you."

"It couldn't possibly take months to replace me," B.J. protested, but he was looking up at the ceiling as though lost in thought.

"Six months perhaps."

"Six months?" she frowned. "But you can't. We have reservations, it's nearly the summer season. All those people can't be disappointed. And the staff—the staff would be out of work."

"Yes." With an agreeable smile, he nodded and folded his hands on the desk.

Her eyes widened. "But—that's blackmail!"

"I think that term is quite correct." His amusement increased. "You catch on very quickly, Miss Clark."

"You can't be serious. You," she sputtered. "You wouldn't actually close the inn just because I quit."

"You don't know me well enough to be sure, do you?" His eyes were unfathomable and steady. "Do you want to chance it?"

Silence hung for a long moment, each measuring the other. "No," B.J. finally murmured, then repeated with more strength, "No, blast it, I can't! You know that already. But I certainly don't understand why."

"You don't have to know why," he interrupted with an imperious gesture of his hand.

Sighing, B.J. struggled not to permit temper to rule her tongue again. "Mr. Reynolds," she began in what she hoped was a reasonable tone, "I don't know why you find it so important for me to remain as manager of the inn, but——"

"How old are you, Miss Clark?" He cut her off again. She stared in perplexed annoyance.

"I hardly see…"

"Twenty, twenty-one?"

"Twenty-four," B.J. corrected, inexplicably compelled to defend herself. "But I don't see what that has to do with anything."

"Twenty-four," he repeated, obviously concluding she had finished one sentence and that was sufficient. "Chronologically, I have eight years on you, and professionally quite a bit more. I opened my first hotel when you were still leading cheers at Lakeside High."

"I never led cheers at Lakeside High," she said coldly.

"Be that as it may——" he gently inclined his head "——the arithmetic remains the same. My reason for wanting you to remain in your current position at the inn is quite simple. You know the staff, the clientele, the suppliers and so forth…during this transition period I need your particular expertise."

"All right, Mr. Reynolds." B.J. relaxed slightly, feeling the conversation had leveled off to a more professional plane. "But you should be aware, I will give you absolutely no cooperation in changing any aspect which I feel affects the inn's personality. In point of fact, I will do my best to be uncooperative."

"I'm sure you're quite skillful at that," Taylor said easily. B.J. was unsure whether the smile in his eyes was real or in her imagination. "Now that we understand each other, Miss Clark, I'd like to see the place and get an idea of how you run things. I should be fairly well briefed in two weeks."

"You can't possibly understand all I've been trying to tell you in that amount of time."

"I make up my mind quickly," he told her. Smiling, he studied her face. "When something's mine, I know what to do with it." His smile widened at her frown, and he rose. "If you want the inn to remain as is, you'd best stick around and make your sales pitch." Taking her arm, he hauled her up from the chair. "Let's take a look around."

With all the warmth of a January sky, B.J. took Taylor on a tour of the first floor, describing storage closets in minute detail. Throughout, he kept a hand firmly on her arm as if to remind her of his authority. The continued contact made her vaguely uneasy. His scent was musky and essentially male and he moved with a casualness which she felt was deceptive. His voice rolled deep and smooth, and several times, she found herself listening more to its cadence than to his words. Annoyed, she added to the layers of frost coating her tone.

It would be easier, she decided, if he were short and balding with a generous middle, or, perhaps, if he had a sturdy mole on his left cheek and a pair of chins. It's absolutely unfair for a man to look the way he does and have to fight him, she thought resentfully.

"Have I lost you, Miss Clark?"

"What?" Looking up, she collected her wits, inwardly cursing him again for possessing such dark, magnetic eyes. "No, I was thinking perhaps you'd like lunch." A very good improvisation, she congratulated herself.

"Fine." Agreeably, he allowed her to lead the way to the dining room.

It was a basic, rustic room, large and rectangular with beamed ceilings and gently faded wallpaper. Its charm was old and lasting; amber globed lamps, graceful antiques and old silver. Local stone dominated one wall in which a fireplace was set. Brass andirons guarded the empty hearth. Tables had been set to encourage sociability, with a few more secluded for intimate interludes. The air was humming with easy conversation and clattering dishes. A smell of fresh baking drifted toward them. In silence, Taylor studied the room, his eyes roaming from corner to corner until B.J. was certain he had figured the precise square footage.

"Very nice," he said simply.

A large, round man approached, lifting his head with a subtle dramatic flourish.

"'If music be the food of love, play on.'"

"'Give me excess of it, that, surfeiting, the appetite may sicken, and so die.'"

Chuckling at B.J.'s response, he rolled with a regal, if oversized, grace into the dining room.

"Shakespeare at lunch?" Taylor inquired. B.J. laughed; against her will her antagonism dissolved. "That was Mr. Leander. He's been coming to the inn twice a year for the past ten years. He used to tour with a low budget Shakespearean troupe, and he likes to toss lines at me for me to cap."

"And do you always have the correct response?"

"Luckily, I've always been fond of Shakespeare, and as insurance, I cram a bit when he makes his reservation."

"Just part of the service?" Taylor inquired, tilting his head to study her from a new angle.

"You could say that."

Prudently, B.J. scanned the room to see where the young Dobson twins were seated, then steered Taylor to a table as far distant as possible.

"B.J." Dot sidled to her side, eyes lighting on Taylor in pure feminine avarice. "Wilbur brought the eggs, and they're small again. Elsie's threatening to do permanent damage."

"All right, I'll take care of it." Ignoring Taylor's questioning stare, she turned to her waitress. "Dot, see to Mr. Reynold's lunch. Please excuse me, Mr. Reynolds, I'll have to tend to this. Just send for me if you have any questions or if something is not to your satisfaction. Enjoy your meal."

Seeing Wilbur's eggs as a lucky escape hatch, B.J. hurried to the kitchen.

"Wilbur," she said with wicked enjoyment as the door swung shut behind her. "This time, I'm umpire."

A myriad of small demands dominated B.J.'s afternoon. The art of diplomacy as well as the ability to delegate and make decisions was an intricate part of her job, and B.J. had honed her skills. She moved without breaking rhythm from a debate with the Dobson twins on the advisability of keeping a frog in their bathtub to a counseling service with one of the maids who was weeping into the fresh linen supply over the loss of a boyfriend. Through the hours of soothing and listening and laying down verdicts, she was still conscious of the presence of Taylor Reynolds. It was a simple matter to avoid him physically, but his presence seemed to follow her everywhere. He had made himself known, and she could not forget about him. Perversely, she found herself fretting to know where he was and what he was doing. Probably, she thought with a fresh flash of resentment, probably he's even now in my office poring over my books with a microscope, deciding where to put in his silly tennis courts or how to concrete the grove.

The dinner hour came and went. B.J. had decided to forego supervising the dining room to have a few hours of peace. When she came downstairs to the lounge the lighting was muted, the hour late. The three-piece band hired for the benefit of the Saturday crowd had already packed their equipment. The music had been replaced by the murmurs and clinking glasses of the handful of people who remained. It was the quiet time of the evening, just before silence. B.J. allowed her thoughts to drift back to Taylor.

I've got two weeks to make him see reason, she reminded herself, exchanging goodnights as stragglers began to wander from the lounge. That should be plenty of time to make even the most insensitive businessman understand. I simply went about things in the wrong way. Tomorrow, I'll start my campaign with a brand new strategy. I'll keep my temper under control and use a great many smiles. I'm good at smiling when I put my mind to it.

Practicing her talent on the middle-aged occupant in room 224, B.J.'s confidence grew at his rapidly blinking appreciation. Yes, she concluded, smiles are much better than claws at this stage. A few smiles, a more sophisticated appearance, and a brisk, businesslike approach, and I'll defeat the enemy before the war's declared. Rejuvenated, she turned to the bartender who was lackadaisically wiping the counter. "Go on home, Don, I'll clear up the rest."

"Thanks, B.J." Needing no second urging, he dropped his rag and disappeared through the door.

"It's no trouble at all," she told the empty space with a magnanimous gesture of one hand. "I really insist."

Crossing the room, she began to gather half filled baskets of peanuts and empty glasses, switching on the small eye-level television for company. Around her, the inn settled for sleep, the groans and creaks so familiar, they went unnoticed. Now that the day was over, B.J. found the solitude for which she yearned.

Low, eerie music poured out of the television, drifting and floating through the darkened room. Glancing up, B.J. was soon mesmerized by a horror film. Kicking off her shoes, she slid onto a stool. The story was old and well-worn, but she was caught by a shot of clouds drifting over a full moon. She reached one hand absently for a basket of peanuts, settling them into her lap as the fog began to clear on the set to reveal the unknown terror, preceded by the rustle of leaves, and heavy breathing. With a small moan at the stalking monster's distorted face, B.J. covered her eyes and waited for doom to claim the heroine.

"You'd see more without your hand in front of your eyes."

As the voice came, disembodied in the darkness, B.J. shrieked, dislodging a shower of peanuts from her lap. "Don't ever do that again!" she commanded, glaring up at Taylor's grinning face.

"Sorry." The apology lacked conviction. Leaning on the bar, he nodded toward the set. "Why do you have it on if you don't want to watch?"

"I can't help myself, it's an obsession. But I always watch with my eyes closed. Now look, watch this part, I've seen it before." She grabbed his sleeve with one hand and pointed with the other. "She's going to walk right outside like an idiot. I ask you, would anyone with a working brain cell walk out into the pitch darkness when they hear something scraping at the window? Of course not," she answered for him. "A smart person would be huddled under the bed waiting for it to go away. Oh." She pulled him closer, burying her face against his chest as the monster's face loomed in a close-up. "It's horrible, I can't watch. Tell me when it's over."

Slowly, it dawned on her that she was burrowing into his chest, his heartbeat steady against her ear. His fingers tangled in her hair, smoothing and soothing her as though comforting a child. She stiffened and started to pull back, but the hand in her hair kept her still.

"No, wait a minute, he's still stalking about and leering. There." He patted her shoulder and loosened his grip. "Saved by commercial television."

Set free, B.J. fumbled off the stool and began gathering scattered peanuts and composure. "I'm afraid things got rather out of hand this afternoon, Mr. Reynolds." Her voice was not quite steady, but she hoped he would attribute the waver to cowardice. "I must apologize for not completing your tour of the inn."

He watched as she scrambled over the floor on her hands and knees, a curtain of pale hair concealing her face. "That's all right. I wandered a bit on my own. I finally met Eddie when not in motion. He's a very intense young man."

She shifted away from him to search for more far reaching nuts. "He'll be good at hotel management in a couple years. He just needs a little more experience." Keeping her face averted, B.J. waited for the heat to cool from her cheeks.

"I met quite a few of the inn's guests today. Everyone seems very fond of B.J." He closed the distance between them and pushed back the hair which lay across her cheek. "Tell me, what does it stand for?"

"What?" Diverted by the fingers on her skin, she found it hard to concentrate on the conversation.

"B.J." He smiled into bemused eyes. "What does it stand for?"

"Oh." She returned the smile, stepping strategically out of reach. "I'm afraid that's a closely guarded secret. I've never even told my mother."

Behind her, the heroine gave a high-pitched, lilting scream. Scattering nuts again, B.J. threw herself into Taylor's arms.

"Oh, I'm sorry, that caught me off guard." Mortified, she lifted her face and attempted to pull away.

"No, this is the third time in one day you've been in this position." One hand lifted, and traveled down the length of her hair as he held her still. "This time, I'm going to see what you taste like."

Before she could protest, his mouth lowered to hers, at once firm and possessing. His arm around her waist brought her close to mold against him. His tongue found hers, and she was unaware whether he had parted her lips or if they had done so of their own volition. He lingered over her mouth, savoring its softness, deepening the kiss until she clung to him for balance. She told herself the sudden spiraling of her heartbeat was a reaction to the horror movie, the quick dizziness, the result of a missed dinner. Then she told herself nothing and only experienced.

"Very nice." Taylor's murmured approval trailed along her cheekbone, moving back to tease the corner of her mouth. "Why don't we try it again?"

In instinctive defense, she pressed her hand into his chest to ward him off. *Lightly,* she told herself, praying for the earth to stop trembling, *treat it lightly.* "I'm afraid I don't come in thirty-two flavors, Mr. Reynolds, and..."

"Taylor," he interrupted, smiling down at the hand which represented no more of an obstacle than a blade of grass. "I decided this morning, when you stalked me in the office, that we're going to know each other very well."

"Mr. Reynolds..."

"Taylor," he repeated, his eyes close and compelling. "And my decisions are always final."

"Taylor," she agreed, not wanting to debate a minor point when the distance between them was lessening despite the pressure against his chest. "Do you engage in this sort of activity with all the managers of your hotels?" Hoping to wound him with a scathing remark, B.J. was immediately disappointed when he tossed back his head and laughed.

"B.J., this current activity has nothing whatever to do with your position at the inn. I am merely indulging my weakness for women who look good in pigtails."

"Don't you kiss me again!" she ordered, struggling with a sudden desperation which surprised him into loosening his hold.

"You'll have to choose between being demure or being provocative, B.J." His tone was mild, but she saw as she backed away, his eyes had darkened with temper. "Either way we play, I'm going to win, but it would make the game easier to follow."

"I don't play this sort of game," she retorted, "and I am neither demure nor provocative."

"You're a bit of both." His hands slipped into his pockets, and he rocked gently on his heels as he studied her furious face. "It's an intriguing combination." His brow lifted in speculation. An expression of amusement flitted over his features. "But I suppose you already know that or you wouldn't be so good at it."

Forgetting her fears, B.J. took a step toward him. "The only thing I know is that I have absolutely no desire to intrigue you in any way. All that I want you to do is to keep your resort builder's hands off this inn." Her hands balled into tight fists. "I wish you'd go back to New York and sit in your penthouse."

Before he could answer, B.J. turned and darted from the room. She hurried through the darkened lobby without even a backward glance.

Chapter Three

B.J. decided that making a fool of herself the previous evening had been entirely Taylor Reynolds' responsibility. Today, she resolved, slipping a gray blazer over a white silk shirt, I will be astringently businesslike. Nonetheless, she winced at the memory of her naive plea that he not kiss her again, the absurd way her voice had shaken with the words. *Why didn't I come up with some cool, sophisticated retort?* she asked herself. *Because I was too busy throwing peanuts around the room and making a fool of myself,* she answered the question to her frowning mirror image. *Why did a simple kiss cloak my brain with layers of cheesecloth?* The woman in the mirror stared back without answering.

He had caught her off guard, B.J. decided as she arranged her hair in a neat, businesslike roll at her neck's nape. It was so unexpected, she had overreacted. Despite herself, she relived the sensation of his mouth claiming hers, his breath warm on her cheek. The knee trembling, brain spinning feeling never before experienced, washed over her again, and briskly, she shook her head to dispel it. It was simply a matter of the unexpected creating a false intenseness, like pricking your thumb with a needle while sewing.

It was important, she knew, to refrain from thinking of Taylor Reynolds on a personal level, and to remember he held the fate of the Lakeside Inn in his hands.

Dirty pool, her mind muttered, recalling his easy threat to close the inn if she pressed her resignation. Emotional blackmail. He knew he held all the aces, and waited, with that damnably appealing smile, for her to fold or call. *Well*, she decided, and smoothed the charcoal material of her skirt, *I play a pretty mean game of poker myself, Taylor Reynolds*. After trying out several types of smiles in the mirror, polite, condescending, dispassionate, she left the room with brisk steps.

Sunday mornings were usually quiet. Most of the guests slept late, rising in dribbles to wander downstairs for breakfast. Traditionally, B.J. spent these quiet hours closeted in her office with whatever paperwork she felt merited attention. From experience, she had found this particular system worked well, being the least likely time for calamities, minor or major, to befall guests or staff.

She grabbed a quick coffee in the kitchen before plunging into the sea of invoices and account books.

"How providential." She jerked slightly as a hand captured her arm, and she found herself being led to the dining room. "Now, I won't have to have breakfast alone."

The dozens of flaming retorts which sprang to mind at Taylor's presumptuousness were dutifully banked down. B.J. answered with her seasoned polite smile. "How kind of you to ask. I hope you spent a pleasant night."

"As stated in your public relations campaign, the inn is conducive to restful nights."

Waving aside her hostess, B.J. moved through the empty tables to a corner booth. "I think you'll find all my publicity is based on fact, Mr. Reynolds." Sliding in, B.J. struggled to keep her voice light and marginally friendly. Remnants of their argument in her office and their more personal encounter in the lounge clung to her, and she attempted to erase both from her mind.

"So far I find no discrepancies."

Maggie hovered by the table, her smile dreamily absent. No doubt she was thinking of her date last night with Wally, B.J. thought. "Toast and coffee, Maggie," she said kindly, breaking the trance. The waitress scribbled on her pad, her cheeks flushed.

"You know," Taylor observed after giving his order, "you're very good at your job."

B.J. chided herself for her pleasure at the unexpected praise. "Why do you say that?"

"Not only are your books in perfect order, but you know your staff and handle them with unobtrusive deftness. You just managed to convey a five-minute lecture with one brief look."

"It makes it easier when you understand your staff and their habits." Her brows lifted in easy humor. "You see, I happen to know Maggie's mind is still focused on the double feature she and Wally didn't watch last night."

His grin flashed, boyish and quick.

"The staff is very much like a family." B.J. was careful to keep her tone casual, her hands busy pouring coffee. "The guests feel that. They enjoy the informality which is always accompanied by quality service. Our rules are flexible, and the staff is trained to adjust to the individual needs of the guests. The inn is a basic place, not for those who require formal entertainment or unlimited luxury. Fresh air, good food and a pleasant atmosphere are our enticements, and we deliver."

She paused as Maggie placed their breakfast order on the table. "Do you have a moral objection to resorts, B.J.?"

The unexpectedness of Taylor's question put her off. Blinking in confusion at the long, lean fingers as they held a knife, spreading Betty Jackson jelly on toast, she stammered, "No...why of course not." Those fingers, she recalled irrelevantly, had tangled in her hair. "No," she repeated more firmly, meeting his eyes. "Resorts are fine if they are run correctly, as yours are. But their function is entirely different from ours. In a proper resort there's an activity for every minute of the day. Here, the atmosphere is more relaxed, a little fishing or boating, skiing, and above all the menu. The Lakeside Inn is perfect exactly as it is," she concluded more fiercely than she had intended and watched one brow rise, nearly meeting the curling thickness of his hair.

"That's yet to be determined." He lifted his cup to his lips.

His tone was mild, but B.J. recognized traces of anger in the disconcertingly direct eyes. She dropped her eyes to her own cup as if enticed by the rich, black liquid.

"'The gray-eyed morn smiles on the frowning night.'"

The quote brought her head up sharply, and looking into Mr. Leander's smiling, expectant face, B.J. searched her brain. "'Chequering the eastern clouds with streaks of light.'"

Thank goodness I've read *Romeo and Juliet* a dozen times, she thought, watching his pleased saunter as he moved to his table.

"One day, he's going to catch you, and you're going to draw a blank."

"Life's a series of risks," she returned flippantly. "Better to accept its challenges."

Reaching over, he tucked a stray lock behind her ear, and she jerked away from his touch, unexpectedly shy.

"For the most part," he drew the words out with infuriating emphasis, "I believe you do. It should make things very interesting. More coffee?" His question was pleasant and easy as if they had shared the morning meal on a regular basis. B.J. shook her head in refusal.... She felt uneasily inept at parrying words with this domineering, sophisticated man....

Sunlight poured through the many-paned windows, spilling in patchwork patterns on the floor, a lawn mower hummed along the outer edges of lawn, and somewhere close, a bird sang his enjoyment of a golden day. Closeted in the office with Taylor, B.J. tuned even these small pleasures out, keeping her mind firmly on the business at hand. Here, with the impersonal wedges of invoices and account books between them, she felt confident and assured. In discussing the inn's procedure, her feet were on solid ground. Honesty forced her to admit that Taylor Reynolds knew his profession down to the finest detail. He skimmed through her books with the sharp eye of an accountant, shifted and sorted invoices with the ease of a business manager.

At least, B.J. told herself, he doesn't treat me like an empty-headed imbecile who can't tally monthly accounts. Rather, she found him listening to her explanations with attentive respect. Soothed by his obvious appreciation of her intelligence B.J. decided if he did not yet look on the Lakeside Inn as she did, perhaps that too would come.

"I see you deal with a great many small businesses and local farms."

"That's right." She searched the bottom drawer of her desk for an ashtray as he lit a cigarette. "It's advantageous on all sides. We get more personal service and fresher produce, and it boosts local economy." Finding a small ceramic ashtray under a pile of personal correspondence, B.J. placed it on the desk. "The Lakeside Inn is essential to this district. We provide employment and a market for local products and services."

"Umm."

Finding his response less than illuminating, B.J. opened her mouth to continue when the door burst open.

"B.J." Eddie stood, bottom lip trembling. "It's the Bodwins."

"I'll be right there." Suppressing a sigh, she made a mental note to tell Eddie to knock during Taylor's stay.

"Is that a natural disaster or a plague?" Taylor asked, watching Eddie's speedy exit.

"It's nothing, really." She edged toward the door. "Excuse me, I'll just be a minute."

Shutting the door behind her, B.J. hurried to the lobby.

"Hello, Miss Patience, Miss Hope." She greeted the elderly Bodwin sisters with a wary smile.

Tall and lean as two aged willows, the Bodwins were long-standing guests.

"It's so nice to see you both again."

"It's always a pleasure to come back, Miss Clark," Miss Patience announced, and Miss Hope murmured in agreement. Habitually Miss Patience announced, and Miss Hope murmured. It was one of the few things which separated them. Over the years they had melded into mirror images from their identical wire rimmed spectacles to their identical orthopedic shoes.

"Eddie, see that the luggage is taken up, please." Miss Patience flashed a knowing smile which B.J. tried not to notice. B.J. saw her sharp-eyed glance drift over her head. Turning, she spotted Taylor.

"Miss Patience, Miss Hope, this is Taylor Reynolds, the owner of the inn." Miss Patience shot her a meaningful look.

"A pleasure, ladies." Gallantly, he took each thin-boned hand in his. A blush, dormant for twenty-five years, rose to Miss Hope's wrinkled cheek.

"You're a very fortunate young man." Miss Patience gave Taylor a thorough survey, then nodded as if satisfied. "I'm sure you know what a treasure you have in Miss Clark. I hope you appreciate her."

B.J. resisted grinding her teeth for fear the sound would be audible. With a smile, Taylor laid a hand on her shoulder.

"I'm quite convinced Miss Clark is indispensable and my appreciation inadequate."

Satisfied, Miss Patience nodded.

B.J. shook the offending hand from her shoulder and assumed a coolly professional manner. "You have your regular table, number 2."

"Of course." Miss Patience moved her lips into a smile and patted B.J.'s cheek. "You're a good girl, Miss Clark." Smiling vaguely, the two ladies drifted away.

"Surely, B.J.," Taylor turned to B.J. with an infuriating smile, "you're not going to give those two dotty old girls the second table?"

"The Lakeside Inn," she said coldly, turning to precede him to the office, "makes it a habit to please its guests. I see no reason why the Bodwins shouldn't sit wherever they want. Mr. Campbell always seated them at number 2."

"Mr. Campbell," Taylor countered with infuriating calm, "no longer owns the inn. I do."

"I'm well aware of that." Her chin tilted higher in defiance. "Do you want me to turn out the Bodwin sisters and place them at the table near the kitchen? Don't they look fancy enough for you? Why don't you think of them as people rather than little black numbers in the bloody account book?"

Her tirade was sharply cut off as he gripped her shoulders. She found she had swallowed the remaining words before she could prevent herself.

"You have," he began in an ominously low voice, "a very unfortunate temper and some very odd ideas. No one tells me how to run my business. Absolutely no one. Advice is accepted upon request, but I only make the decisions, and I alone give the orders."

He moved toward her. She could only stare, fascinated and faintly terrified.

"Do we understand each other?"

B.J. nodded, wide-eyed, then gathered courage to answer audibly. "Yes, perfectly. What would you like me to do about the Bodwins?"

"You've already done it. When you do something which displeases me, B.J., I'll let you know." The underlying threat brought storm warnings to her eyes. "Of course you know," Taylor continued, his tone softening, "you're a very ingenious lady. You've managed to share my breakfast table and work with me throughout the morning without once using my name. You've skirted around it, jumped over it and crawled under it, fascinating me with the acrobatics."

"That's ridiculous." She attempted to shrug, but his hands were firm on her shoulders. "Your imagination needs re-oiling."

"Then perhaps..." His arms moved to capture her waist. She

arched away only to be brought steadily closer. "You'd say it now." His mouth hovered above hers. She felt the unfamiliar sweet flow of weakness, the trembling warmth just under her skin.

"Taylor." She failed to bring her voice above a whisper.

"Very good, you'll use it more often." His mouth curved, but she saw the smile only in his eyes. "Do I frighten you, B.J.?"

"No." Her denial was faint. "No," she repeated with more firmness.

"Liar." His laugh was both amused and pleased as his mouth teased hers. It rubbed lightly, holding back the promise until with a moan she drew him closer and took it.

Her breasts crushed against his chest, her lips instinctively found his. She felt herself tumbling in helpless cartwheels down an endless shaft where lights whirled in speeding colors. His hands moved from her waist to her hips, his strong fingers discovering the secrets of subtle curves as his mouth took everything she offered. Craving more, she strained against him until her sharpened senses began to dim, and the world spun hazily around her and vanished.

Fear rose like a phoenix from the flames of passion, and she struggled away, stunned and confused. "I...I need to check how lunch is going." She fumbled behind for the doorknob.

His hands in his pockets, Taylor rocked back on his heels and held her gaze with steady assurance. "Of course.... Now run away to your duties. But you understand, B.J., that I intend to have you sooner or later. I can be patient up to a point."

Her hand connected with the knob. She found her voice. "Of all the appalling nerve! I'm not a piece of property you can have your agent pick up for you."

"No, I'm handling this strictly on my own." He smiled at her. "I know when something's going to be mine. Acquiring it is simply a matter of timing."

"I'm not an it." More outraged than she had thought possible, she took a step toward him. "I have no intention of being acquired and added to your trophies! And timing will get you nowhere!"

His smile was maddeningly confident. B.J. slammed the door full force behind her.

Chapter Four

*M*ondays always kept B.J. busy. She was convinced that if a major calamity were to fall, it would fall on a Monday simply because that would be the time she would be least able to cope with it. Taylor Reynolds' presence in her office was an additional Monday morning burden. His calm statement of the previous day was still fresh in her mind, and she was still seething with resentment. In an icy voice, she explained to him each phone call she made, each letter she wrote, each invoice she filed. He would not, she decided, accuse her of being uncooperative. Frigid perhaps, she thought with wicked pleasure, but not uncooperative.

Taylor's impeccable, businesslike attitude did nothing to endear him to her. She was well aware that her cold politeness bordered on the insulting.

Never had she met a man more in control or more annoying. Briefly, she considered pouring her coffee into his lap just to get a reaction. The thought was satisfying.

"Did I miss a joke?" Taylor asked as an involuntary smile flitted over B.J.'s face.

"What?" Realizing her lapse, B.J. struggled to compose her

features. "No, I'm afraid my mind was wandering. You'll have to excuse me," she went on, "I have to make sure that all the rooms are made up by this time of day. Will you be wanting lunch in here or in the dining room?"

"I'll come to the dining room." Leaning back, Taylor studied her as he tapped his pencil against the corner of the desk. "Are you joining me?"

"Oh, I'm terribly sorry." B.J.'s tone was falsely saccharine. "I'm swamped today. I recommend the roast beef, though. I'm sure you'll find it satisfactory." Satisfied with her delivery, she closed the door quietly behind her.

With ingenuity and luck, B.J. managed to avoid Taylor through-out the afternoon. The inn was nearly empty as most of the guests were outdoors enjoying the mild spring weather. B.J. was able to slip down the quiet corridors without running into Taylor. She kept her antenna tuned for his presence, however. Though she knew it was childish, she found herself enjoying the one-way game of hide and seek. It became a self-imposed challenge that she keep out of his sight until nightfall.

In the pre-dinner lull, the inn was drowsy and silent. Humming to herself, B.J. carefully checked off linens in the third floor supply room. She was confident Taylor would not venture into that area of the inn, and relaxed her guard. Her mind traveled from her task, touching on pictures of boating on the lake, walks in the woods, and long summer evenings. Though her daydreams were pleasant, they were underlined by a nagging dissatisfaction. She tried to shrug it off but found it stubborn. There was something missing from the images, or rather someone. Whom would she be boating with on the lake? Whom would she be walking with in the woods? Who would be there to make the long summer evenings special? A distressing image began to form in B.J.'s brain, and she squeezed her eyes tight until it faded.

"I don't need him," she muttered, giving a pile of freshly laundered sheets a pat. "Absolutely not." B.J. backed from the tiny room and quietly pulled the door shut. When she backed into a solid object, she shrieked and fell forward against the closed door.

"Jumpy, aren't you?" Taylor took her shoulders and turned her to face him. His expression was amused. "Muttering to yourself, too. Maybe you need a vacation."

"I...I..."

"A long vacation," he concluded, giving her cheek a fatherly pat.

Finding her tongue, B.J. responded with reasonable calm. "You startled me, sneaking around that way."

"I thought it was a rule of the house," he countered as his grin broke out. "You've been doing it all afternoon."

Furious that her cunning had fallen short of the mark, she spoke with frosty dignity. "I have no idea what you're talking about. Now, if you'll excuse me..."

"Did you know you get a half-inch vertical line between your eyebrows when you're annoyed?"

"I'm very busy." She kept her voice cool as she did her best to keep the space between her brows smooth. *Blast the man!* she thought as his engaging smile began to have its effect on her. "Taylor, if there is something specific you want..." She stopped as she saw his grin widen until it nearly split his face. "If there's some business you want to discuss—" she amended.

"I took a message for you," he informed her, then lifted a

finger to smooth away the crease between her brows. "A very intriguing message."

"Oh?" she said casually, wishing he would back up so that she did not feel so imprisoned between his body and the closed store-room door.

"Yes, I wrote it down so there'd be no mistake." He took a slip of paper from his pocket and read. "It's from a Miss Peabody. She wanted you to know that Cassandra had her babies. Four girls and two boys. Sextuplets." Taylor lowered the paper and shook his head. "Quite an amazing feat."

"Not if you're a cat." B.J. felt the color lacing her cheeks. *Why would he have to be the one to take the message? Why couldn't Cassandra have waited?* "Miss Peabody is one of our oldest guests. She stays here twice a year."

"I see," said Taylor, his mouth twitching. "Well, now that I've done my duty, it's your turn to do yours." Taking her hand, Taylor began to lead her down the corridor. "This country air gives me quite an appetite. You know the menu, what do you recommend we have?"

"I can't possibly," she began.

"Of course you can," he interrupted mildly. "Just think of me as a guest. Inn policy is to give the guests what pleases them. It pleases me to have dinner with you."

Cornered by her own words, B.J. offered no argument. Within minutes, she found herself seated across from the man she had so successfully avoided during the afternoon.

B.J. thought dinner a relatively painless affair. She felt too, as it neared an end, that she had done her duty and done it superbly. It was, however, difficult to resist the pull of Taylor's charm when he chose to put it into use. The charm itself was so natural and understated that she often found herself captivated before she realized what was happening. Whenever she felt her walls of indifference crumbling, she retreated a step and shored up the holes. *What a shame he isn't someone else,* she mused as he recounted an anecdote. *It would be so nice to enjoy a quiet dinner with him if there weren't any boundaries. But there are,* she reminded herself, quickly pulling out of the range of his charm. *Very definite, very important boundaries. This is war,* she reflected, thinking of their conversation of the previous day. *I can't afford to get caught behind enemy lines.* As Taylor raised his glass and smiled at her, B.J. wondered if Mata Hari had ever been faced with a tougher assignment.

They had reached the coffee stage when Eddie approached their table. "Mr. Reynolds?" B.J. looked on with approval as Eddie neither fidgeted nor seemed ready to burst with the tidings he bore. "There's a phone call for you from New York."

"Thank you, Eddie. I'll take it in the office. I shouldn't be long," Taylor told her as he rose.

"Please, don't rush on my account." B.J. gave him a careful smile, resigning herself to the fact she was a coward. "I still have several things to see to this evening."

"I'll see you later," Taylor returned in a tone that brooked no argument. Their eyes met in a quick clash of wills. In a swift change of mood, Taylor laughed and bent down to kiss B.J. on the forehead before he strolled away.

Mouth agape, B.J. rubbed the spot with her fingertips, wondering why she suddenly felt lightheaded. Forcing herself back to earth, she drank her coffee and hurried off to the lounge.

Monday nights at the inn were an old tradition. The lounge

was the center of activity for the weekly event. As B.J. paused in the doorway, she ran a critical eye over the room. The candles had been lit inside each of the coach lanterns which sat on the huddled tables. The lights flickered against the wood. Scents of polish, old wood and smoke melded. The dance floor was gently lit with amber spotlights. Satisfied that the mood was set, B.J. crossed the room and halted next to an ancient Victrola. The faithful mechanism was housed in a rich mahogany cabinet. With affection, B.J. trailed a finger over the smooth lid before opening it.

People began to wander in as she sorted through the collection of old 78s. The hum of conversation behind her was so familiar, it barely tickled her consciousness. Glasses chinked, ice rattled, and an occasional laugh echoed along the walls. With the absentminded skill of an expert, B.J. wound the Victrola into life and set a thick, black record on the turntable. The music which drifted out was scratchy, tinny and charming. Before the record was half over, three couples were on the dance floor. Another Monday night was launched.

During the next half hour, B.J. played an unbroken stream of nineteen-thirty tunes. Over the years, she had noted that no matter what the mean age of the audience, the response to a trip through the past was positive. *Perhaps,* she mused, *it's because the simplicity of the music suits the simplicity of the inn.* With a shrug, she abandoned her analysis and grinned at a couple fox-trotting over the dance floor to the strains of "Tea For Two."

"What the devil is going on in here?"

B.J. heard the demanding question close to her ear and whirled to find herself face to face with Taylor. "Oh, I see you're finished with your call. I hope there isn't any trouble?"

"Nothing important." He waited until she had switched records before he asked again, "B.J., I asked you what's going on in here?"

"Why, just what it looks like," she answered vaguely, hearing from the tone of the record that it was time to replace the needle. "Sit down, Taylor, I'll have Don mix you a drink. You know I'd swear there hasn't been time for this needle to wear out." Delving into her spares, B.J. began the task of changing needles.

"When you're finished, perhaps you'd take a look at my carburetor."

Engrossed in the intricacies of her job, B.J. remained untouched by Taylor's mockery. "We'll see," she murmured, then carefully placed the new needle on the record. "What would you like, Taylor?" As she straightened, she glanced toward the bar.

"Initially, an explanation."

"An explanation?" she repeated, finally giving him her full attention. "An explanation about what?"

"B.J." Impatience was beginning to thread through his tone. "Are you being deliberately dense?"

Liking neither his tone nor his question, B.J. stiffened. "Perhaps if you would be a bit more specific, I would be a bit less dense."

"I was under the impression that this lounge possessed a functional P.A. system."

"Well, of course it does." As she became more confused, B.J. pushed away the thought that perhaps she actually was dense. "What does that have to do with anything?"

"Why isn't it being used?" He glanced down at the Victrola. "And why are you using this archaic piece of equipment?"

"The P.A. system isn't being used," she explained in calm, reasonable tones, "because it's Monday."

"I see." Taylor glanced toward the dance floor where one couple was instructing another on the proper moves of a two step. "That, of course, explains everything."

His sarcasm caused indignation to flood through her. Clamping her teeth on a stream of unwise remarks, B.J. began to sift rapidly through records. "On Monday nights, we use the Victrola and play old records. And it is not an archaic piece of equipment," she added, unable to prevent herself. "It's an antique, a museum quality antique."

"B.J." Taylor spoke to the top of her head as she bent to change records. "Why?"

"Why what?" she snapped, furious with his ambiguity.

"Why do you use the Victrola and play old records on Monday nights?" He spoke very clearly, spacing his words as if speaking to someone whose brain was not fully operative.

"Because," B.J. began, her eyes flowing, her fists clenching.

Taylor held up a hand to halt the ensuing explanation. "Wait." After the one word command, he crossed the room and spoke to one of the guests. Seething, B.J. watched him use his most charming smile. It faded as he moved back to join her. "You're being relieved of Victrola duty for a bit. Outside." With this, he took her arm and pulled her to the side door. The cool night air did nothing to lower B.J.'s temperature. "Now." Taylor closed the door behind him and leaned back against the side of the building. He made a small gesture with his hand. "Go right ahead."

"Oh, you make me so mad I could scream!" With this dire threat, B.J. began pacing up and down the porch. "Why do you have to be so...so..."

"Officious?" Taylor offered.

"Yes!" B.J. agreed, wishing passionately that she had thought of the word herself. "Everything's moving along just fine, and then you have to come in and look down your superior nose." For some moments, she paced in silence. The romance of the moonlight filtering through the trees seemed sadly out of place. "People are enjoying themselves in there." She swung her hand toward the open window. A Cole Porter number drifted back to her. "You don't have any right to criticize it. Just because we're not using a live band, or playing top forty numbers, doesn't mean we're not entertaining the guests. I really don't see why you have to..." She broke off abruptly as he grabbed her arm.

"O.K., time's up." As he spun her around, the hair fell over B.J.'s face, and she brushed it back impatiently. "Now, suppose we start this from the beginning."

"You know," she said between her teeth, "I really hate it when you're calm and patient."

"Stick around," he invited. It began to sink into her brain that his voice was dangerously low. "You might see the other end of the scale." Glaring at him did not seem to improve her situation, but B.J. continued to do so. "If you'll think back to the beginning of this remarkable conversation, you'll recall that I asked you a very simple question. And, I believe, a very reasonable one."

"And I told you," she tossed out, then faltered. "At least, I think I did." Frustrated, she threw both hands up in the air. "How am I supposed to remember what you said and what I said? It took you ten minutes to come to the point in the first place." She let out a deep breath as she realized she did not yet have control of her temper. "All right, what was your very simple, very reasonable question?"

"B.J., you would try the patience of a saint." She heard the amused exasperation in his voice and tried not to be charmed. "I would like to know why I stepped into nineteen-thirty-five when I came into the lounge."

"Every Monday night," she began in crisp, practical tones, "the inn offers this sort of entertainment. The Victrola was brought here more than fifty years ago, and it's been used every Monday night since. Guests who've been here before expect it. Of course," she went on, too involved in her story to realize she was being drawn closer into Taylor's arms, "the P.A. system was installed years ago. The other six nights of the week, we switch off between it and a live band, depending on the season. The Monday night gathering is almost as old as the inn itself and an important part of our tradition."

The low, bluesy tones of "Embraceable You" were floating through the open window. B.J. was swaying to its rhythm, as yet unaware that Taylor was leading her in a slow dance. "The guests look forward to it. I've found since I've worked here, that's true no matter how old or how young the clientele is." Her voice had lost its crispness. She found her trend of thought slipping away from her as their bodies swayed to the soft music.

"That was a very reasonable answer." Taylor drew her closer, and she tilted back her head, unwilling to break eye contact. "I'm beginning to see the advantages of the idea myself." Their faces were close, so close she could feel the touch of his breath on her lips. "Cold?" he asked, feeling her tremble. Though she shook her head, he gathered her closer until the warmth of his body crept into hers. Their cheeks brushed as they merged into one gently swaying form.

"I should go back in," she murmured, making no effort to move away. She closed her eyes and let his arms and the music guide her.

"Um-hum." His mouth was against her ear.

Small night sounds added to the lull of the music from the lounge; a whisper of leaves, the quiet call of a bird, the flutter of moth wings against window glass. The air was soft and cool on B.J.'s shoulders. It was touched with the light scent of hyacinth. Moonlight sprinkled through the maples, causing the shadows to tremble. She could feel Taylor's heartbeat, a sure, steady rhythm against her own breast. He trailed his mouth along her temple, brushing it through her hair as his hands roamed along her back.

B.J. felt her will dissolving as her senses grew more and more acute. She could hear the sound of his breathing over the music, feel the texture of his skin beneath his shirt, taste the male essence of him on her tongue. Her surroundings were fading like an old photograph with only Taylor remaining sharp and clear. Untapped desire swelled inside her. Suddenly, she felt herself being swallowed by emotions she was not prepared for, by needs she could not understand.

"No, please." Her bid for freedom was so swift and unexpected that she broke from Taylor's arms without a struggle. "I don't want this." She clung to the porch rail and faced him.

Closing the distance between them in one easy motion, Taylor circled the back of her neck with his hand. "Yes, you do." His mouth lowered, claiming hers. B.J. felt the porch tilt under her feet.

Longing, painfully sweet, spread through her until she felt she would suffocate. His hands were bringing her closer and closer. With some unexplained instinct, she knew if she were wrapped in his arms again, she would never find the strength to resist him.

"No!" Lifting both hands, she pushed against his chest and freed herself. "I don't!" she cried in passionate denial. Turning, she streaked down the porch steps. "Don't tell me what I want," she flung back at him before she raced around the side of the building.

She paused before she entered the inn to catch her breath and to allow her pounding heart to slow down. Certainly not the usual Monday evening at Lakeside Inn, she thought, smiling wryly to herself. Unconsciously, she hummed a few bars of "Embraceable You," but caught herself with a self-reprimanding frown before she entered the kitchen to remind Dot about the bud vases on the breakfast tables.

Chapter Five

There are days when nothing goes right. The morning, blue and clear and breezy, looked deceptively promising. Clad in a simple green shirtdress and low heels, B.J. marched down the stairs running the word *businesslike* over and over in her mind. Today, she determined, she would be the manager of the inn conducting business with the owner of the inn. There was no moonlight, no music, and she would not forget her responsibilities again. She strolled into the dining room, prepared to greet Taylor casually, then use the need to oversee breakfast preparations as an excuse not to share the morning meal with him. Taylor, however, was already well into a fluffy mound of scrambled eggs and deep into a conversation with Mr. Leander. Taylor gave B.J. an absent wave as she entered, then returned his full attention to his breakfast companion.

Perversely, B.J. was annoyed that her well-planned excuse was unnecessary. She scowled at the back of Taylor's head before she flounced into the kitchen. Ten minutes later, she was told in no uncertain terms that she was in the way. Banished to her office, she sulked in private.

For the next thirty minutes, B.J. occupied herself with busy work, all the while keeping her ears pricked for Taylor's approach. As the minutes passed, she felt a throbbing tension build at the base of her neck. The stronger the ache became, the deeper became her resentment toward Taylor. She set the reason for her headache and her glum mood at his doorstep, though she could not have answered what he had done to cause either. *He was here,* she decided, then broke the point of her pencil. *That was enough.*

"B.J.!" Eddie swirled into the office as she stood grinding her teeth and sharpening her pencil. "There's trouble."

"You bet there is," she muttered.

"It's the dishwasher." Eddie lowered his eyes as if announcing a death in the family. "It broke down in the middle of breakfast."

B.J. let out her breath in a quick sound of annoyance. "All right, I'll call Max. With any luck it'll be going full swing before lunch."

Luck, B.J. was to find, was a mirage.

An hour later, she stood by as Max the repairman did an exploratory on the dishwasher. She found his continual mutters, tongue cluckings and sighs wearing on her nerves. Time was fleeting, and it seemed to her that Max was working at an impossibly slow pace. Impatient, she leaned over his shoulder and stared at tubes and wires. Bracing one hand on Max's back, she leaned in further and pointed.

"Couldn't you just..."

"B.J." Max sighed and removed another screw. "Go play with the inn and let me do my job."

Straightening, B.J. stuck out her tongue at the back of his head, then flushed scarlet as she spotted Taylor standing inside the doorway.

"Have a problem?" he asked. Though his voice and mouth

were sober, his eyes laughed at her. She found his silent mockery infuriating.

"I can handle it," she snapped, wishing her cheeks were cool and her position dignified. "I'm sure you must be very busy." She cursed herself for hinting at his morning involvement. This time he did smile, and she cursed him as well.

"I'm never too busy for you, B.J." Taylor crossed the room, then took her hand and raised it to his lips before she realized his intent. Max cleared his throat.

"Cut that out." She tore her hand away and whipped it behind her back. "There's no need to concern yourself with this," she continued, struggling to assume the businesslike attitude she had vowed to take. "Max is fixing the dishwasher before the lunch rush."

"No, I'm not." Max sat back on his heels and shook his head. In his hand was a small-toothed wheel.

"What do you mean, no you're not?" B.J. demanded, forgetting Taylor in her amazement. "You've got to. I need..."

"What you need is one of these," Max interrupted, holding up the wheel.

"Well, all right." B.J. plucked the part from his hand and scowled at it. "Put one in. I don't see how a silly little thing like this could cause all this trouble."

"When the silly little thing has a broken tooth, it can cause a lot of trouble," Max explained patiently, and glanced at Taylor for masculine understanding. "B.J., I don't carry things like this in stock. You'll have to get it from Burlington."

"Burlington?" Realizing the situation was desperate B.J. used her most pleading look. "Oh, but, Max."

Though well past his fiftieth birthday, Max was not immune to huge gray eyes. He shifted from one foot to the other, sighed and took the part from B.J.'s palm. "All right, all right, I'll drive into Burlington myself. I'll have the machine fixed before dinner, but lunch is out. I'm not a magician."

"Thank you, Max." Rising on her toes, B.J. pecked his cheek. "What would I do without you?" Mumbling, he packed up his tools and started out of the room. "Bring your wife in for dinner tonight, on the house." Pleased with her success, B.J. smiled as the door swung shut. When she remembered Taylor, she cleared her throat and turned to him.

"You should have those eyes registered with the police department," he advised, tilting his head and studying her. "They're a lethal weapon."

"I don't know what you're talking about." She sniffed with pretended indifference while she wished she could have negotiated with Max in private.

"Of course you do." With a laugh, Taylor cupped her chin in his hand. "That look you aimed at him was beautifully timed."

"I'm sure you're mistaken," she replied, wishing his mere touch would not start her heart pounding. "I simply arranged things in the best interest of the inn. That's my job."

"So it is," he agreed, and leaned on the injured dishwasher. "Do you have any suggestions as to what's to be done until this is fixed?"

"Yes." She glanced at the double stainless steel sink. "Roll up your sleeves."

It did not occur to B.J. to be surprised that she and Taylor washed the dozens of breakfast dishes side by side until it was *fait accompli*. The interlude had been odd, B.J. felt, because of the unusual harmony which existed between them. They had enjoyed a companionable banter, an easy partnership without the tension which habitually entered their encounters. When Elsie returned to begin lunch preparations, they scarcely noticed her.

"Not one casualty," Taylor proclaimed as B.J. set the last plate on its shelf.

"That's only because I saved two of yours from crashing on the floor."

"Slander," Taylor stated and swung an arm over her shoulder as he led her from the room. "You'd better be nice to me. What'll you do if Max doesn't fix the dishwasher before dinner? Think of all those lunch dishes."

"I'd rather not. However, I've already given that possibility some consideration." B.J. found the handiest chair in her office and dropped into it. "I know a couple of kids in town that we could recruit in a pinch. But Max won't let me down."

"You have a lot of faith." Taylor sat behind the desk, then lifted his feet to rest on top of it.

"You don't know Max," B.J. countered. "If he said he'd have it fixed before dinner, he will. Otherwise, he'd have said I'll try, or maybe I can, or something of that sort. When Max says I will, he does. That," she added, seeing the opportunity to score a point, "is an advantage of knowing everyone you deal with personally."

Taylor inclined his head in acknowledgement as the phone rang on the desk. Signaling for Taylor not to bother, B.J. rose and answered it.

"Lakeside Inn. Oh, hello, Marilyn. No, I've been tied up this morning." She eased a hip down on the edge of the desk and shuffled through her papers. "Yes, I have your message here. I'm sorry, I just got back into the office. No, you let me know when you have all your acceptances back, then we'll have a better idea of how to plan the food and so on. There's plenty of time. You've got well over a month before the wedding. Trust me; I've handled receptions before. Yes, I know you're nervous. It's all right, prospective brides are meant to be nervous. Call me when you have a definite number. You're welcome, Marilyn. Yes, yes, you're welcome. 'Bye."

B.J. hung up the phone and stretched her back before she realized Taylor was waiting for an explanation. "That was Marilyn," B.J. informed him. "She was grateful."

"Yes, I rather got that impression."

"She's getting married next month." B.J. lifted a hand to rub at the stiffness in the back of her neck. "If she makes it without a nervous breakdown, it'll be a minor miracle. People should elope and not put themselves through all this."

"I'm sure there are countless fathers-of-the-bride who would agree with you after paying the expenses of the wedding." He rose, moving around the desk until he stood in front of her. "Here, let me." Lifting his hands, he massaged her neck and shoulders. B.J.'s protest became a sigh of pleasure. The word *businesslike* floated quietly out of her mind. "Better?" Taylor asked, smiling at her closed eyes.

"Mmm. It might be in an hour or two." She stretched under his hands like a contented kitten. "Ever since Marilyn set the date, she's been on the phone three times a week to check on the reception. It's hard to believe someone could get that excited about getting married."

"Well, not everyone is as cool and collected as you," Taylor remarked as he ran his thumbs along her jawline, stroking his other fingers along the base of her neck. "And, by the way, I wouldn't spread that eloping idea of yours around if I were you. I imagine the inn makes a good profit doing wedding receptions."

"Profit?" B.J. opened her eyes and tried to concentrate on what they had been saying. It was difficult to think with his hands so warm and strong on her skin. "Profit?" she said again and swallowed as her brain cleared. "Oh well...yes." She scooted off the desk and out of his reach. "Yes, usually...that is...sometimes." She wandered the room wishing the interlude in the kitchen had not made her forget who he was. "It depends, you see, on... Oh boy." She ended on a note of disgust and blew out a long breath.

"Perhaps you'd translate all that into English?" Taylor suggested. With a twinge of uneasiness, B.J. watched him seat himself once more behind the desk. *Owner to manager again,* she thought bitterly.

"Well, you see," she began, striving for nonchalance. "There are occasions when we do wedding receptions or certain parties without charge. That is," she rushed on as his face remained inscrutable, "we charge for the food and supplies, but not for the use of the lounge..."

"Why?" The one word interruption was followed by several seconds of complete silence.

"Why?" B.J. repeated and glanced briefly at the ceiling for assistance. "It depends, of course, and it is the exception rather than the rule." *Why?* she demanded of herself. *Why don't I learn to keep my mouth shut?* "In this case, Marilyn is Dot's cousin. You met Dot, she's one of our waitresses," she continued as Taylor remained unhelpfully silent. "She also works here during the summer season.

We decided, as we do on certain occasions, to give Marilyn the reception as a wedding present."

"We?"

"The staff," B.J. explained. "Marilyn is responsible for the food, entertainment, flowers, but we contribute the lounge and our time, and," she added, dropping her voice to a mumble, "the wedding cake."

"I see." Taylor leaned back in the chair and laced his fingers together. "So, the staff donates their time and talent and the inn."

"Just the lounge." B.J. met his accusatory glance with a glare. "It's something we do only a couple of times a year. And if I must justify it from a business standpoint, it's good public relations. Maybe it's even tax deductible. Ask your C.P.A." She began to storm around the office as her temper rose, but Taylor sat calmly. "I don't see why you have to be so picky. The staff works on their own time. We've been doing it for years. It's…"

"Inn policy," Taylor finished for her. "Perhaps I should have you list all the eccentricities of inn policy for me. But I should remind you, B.J., that the inn's policy is not carved in stone."

"You're not going to drop the axe on Marilyn's reception," B.J. stated, prepared for a fight to the finish.

"I've misplaced my black hood, B.J., so I can't play executioner. However," he continued before the look of satisfaction could be fully formed on her face, "you and I will have to have a more detailed discussion on the inn's public relations."

"Yes, sir," she replied in her most wintry voice, and was saved from further argument by the ringing of the phone.

Taylor motioned for her to answer it. "I'll get us some coffee."

B.J. watched him stroll from the room as she lifted the phone to her ear.

When Taylor returned a few moments later, she was seated behind the desk just replacing the receiver. With a sound of annoyance, she supported her chin on her elbows.

"The florist doesn't have my six dozen daffodils."

"I'm sorry to hear that." Taylor placed her coffee on the desk.

"Well, you should be. It's your inn, and they are actually your daffodils."

"It's kind of you to think of me, B.J.," Taylor said amiably. "But don't you think six dozen is a bit extreme?"

"Very funny," she muttered and picked up her coffee cup. "You won't think it's such a joke when there aren't any flowers on the tables."

"So, order something besides daffodils."

"Do I look like a simpleton?" B.J. demanded. "He won't have anything in that quantity until next week. Some trouble at the greenhouse or something. Blast it!" She swallowed her coffee and scowled at the far wall.

"For heaven's sake, B.J., there must be a dozen florists in Burlington. Have them delivered." Taylor dismissed the matter of daffodils with an airy wave.

B.J. gave him an opened mouth look of astonishment. "Delivered from Burlington? Do you have any idea how much those daffodils would cost?" Rising, she paced the room while she considered her options. "I simply can't tolerate artificial flowers," she muttered while Taylor sipped his coffee and watched her. "They're worse than no flowers at all. I hate to do it," she said with a sigh. "It's bad enough having to beg for her jelly, now I'm going to have to beg for her flowers. There's absolutely nothing else I can do. She's got the only garden in town that can handle it." Making a complete circle of the room, B.J. plopped down behind the desk again.

"Are you finished?"

"No," B.J. answered, picking up the phone. "I still have to talk her out of them." Grimly, she set her teeth. "Wish me luck."

Deciding all would be explained in due time, Taylor sat back to watch. "Luck," he said agreeably and finished off his coffee.

When B.J. had completed her conversation, he shook his head in frank admiration. "That," he said as he toasted her with his empty cup, "was the most blatant con job I've ever witnessed."

"Subtlety doesn't work with Betty Jackson." Smug, B.J. answered his toast, then rose. "I'm going to go pick up those flowers before she changes her mind."

"I'll drive you," Taylor offered, taking her arm before she reached the door.

"Oh, you needn't bother." The contact reminded her how slight was her will when he touched her.

"It's no bother," he countered, leading her through the inn's front door. "I feel I must see the woman who, how did you put it? 'Raises flowers with an angel's touch.'"

"Did I say that?" B.J. struggled to prevent a smile.

"That was one of your milder compliments."

"Desperate circumstances call for desperate measures," B.J. claimed and slid into Taylor's Mercedes. "Besides, Miss Jackson does have an extraordinary garden. Her rosebush won a prize last year. Turn left here," she instructed as he came to a fork in the road. "You know, you should be grateful to me instead of making fun.

If you'd had your way, we'd be eating up a healthy percentage of the inn's profits in delivery fees."

"My dear Miss Clark," Taylor drawled, "if there's one thing I can't deny, it's that you are a top flight manager. Of course, I'm also aware that a raise is in order."

"When I want a raise, I'll ask for one," B.J. snapped. As she gave her attention to the view out the side window, she missed Taylor's glance of speculation. She had not liked his use of her surname, nor had she liked being reminded again so soon of the status of their positions. He was her employer, and there was no escaping it. Closing her eyes, she chewed on her lower lip. The day had not run smoothly, perhaps that was why she had been so acutely annoyed over such a small thing. *And so rude,* she added to herself. Decidedly, it was her responsibility to offer the olive branch. Turning, she gave Taylor a radiant smile.

"What sort of raise?"

He laughed, and reached over to ruffle her hair. "What an odd one you are, B.J."

"Oh, I know," she agreed, wishing she could understand her own feelings. "I know. There's the house." She gestured as they approached. "Third from the corner."

They alighted from opposite sides of the car, but Taylor took her arm as they swung through Betty Jackson's gate. This visit, B.J. decided, thinking of the silver blue Mercedes and Taylor's elegantly simple silk shirt, should keep Miss Jackson in news for six months. The doorbell was answered before it had stopped ringing.

"Hello, Miss Jackson," B.J. began and prepared to launch into her first thank you speech. She closed her mouth as she noticed Betty's attention was focused well over her head. "Oh, Miss

Jackson, this is Taylor Reynolds, the owner of the inn. Taylor, Betty Jackson." B.J. made introductions as Betty simultaneously pulled her apron from her waist and metal clips from her hair.

"Miss Jackson." Taylor took her free hand as Betty held the apron and clips behind her back. "I've heard so much about your talents, I feel we're old friends." Blushing like a teenager, Betty was, for the first time in her sixty odd years, at a loss for words.

"We came by for the flowers," B.J. reminded her, fascinated by Betty's reaction.

"Flowers? Oh, yes, of course. Do come in." She ushered them into the house and into her living room, all the while keeping her hand behind her back.

"Charming," Taylor stated, gazing around at chintz and doilies. Turning, he gave Betty his easy smile. "I must tell you, Miss Jackson, we're very grateful to you for helping us out this way."

"It's nothing, nothing at all," Betty said, fluttering her hand with the words. "Please sit down. I'll fix us a nice pot of tea. Come along, B.J." She scurried from the room, leaving B.J. no choice but to follow. Safely enclosed in the kitchen, Betty began to move at lightning speed. "Why didn't you tell me you were bringing *him?*" she demanded, flourishing a teapot.

"Well, I didn't know until..."

"Goodness, you could have given a person a chance to comb her hair and put her face on." Betty dug out her best china cups and inspected them for chips.

B.J. bit the inside of her lip to keep a grin from forming. "I'm sorry, Betty. I had no idea Mr. Reynolds was coming until I was leaving."

"Never mind, never mind." Betty brushed aside the apology

with the back of her hand. "You did bring him after all. I'm positively dying to talk to him. Why don't you run out and get your flowers now before tea?" She produced a pair of scissors. "Just pick whatever you need." She dismissed B.J. with a hasty wave. "Take your time."

After the back door had closed firmly in her face, B.J. stood for a moment, torn between amusement and exasperation before heading towards Betty's early spring blooms.

When she re-entered the kitchen about twenty minutes later, armed with a selection of daffodils and early tulips, she could hear Betty laughing. Carefully placing her bouquet on the kitchen table, she walked into the living room.

Like old friends, Taylor and Betty sat on the sofa, a rose patterned teapot nestled cozily on the low table. "Oh, Taylor," Betty said, still laughing, "you tell such stories! What's a poor woman to believe?"

B.J. looked on in stunned silence. She was certain Betty Jackson had not flirted this outrageously in thirty years. And, she noted with a shake of her head, Taylor was flirting with equal aplomb. As Betty leaned forward to pour more tea, Taylor glanced over her head and shot B.J. a grin so endearingly boyish it took all her willpower not to cross the room and throw herself into his arms. He was, she thought with a curious catch in her heart, impossible. No female under a hundred and two was safe around him. Unable to do otherwise, B.J. answered his grin.

"Miss Jackson," B.J. said, carefully readjusting her features. "Your garden is lovely as always."

"Thanks, B.J. I really do work hard on it. Did you get all that you wanted?"

"Yes, thank you. I don't know how I would have managed without you."

"Well." Betty sighed as she rose. "I'll just get a box for them."

Some fifteen minutes later, after Betty had exacted a promise from Taylor that he drop by again, B.J. was in the Mercedes beside him. In the back seat were the assortment of flowers and a half a dozen jars of jelly as a gift to Taylor.

"You," B.J. began in the sternest voice she could manage, "should be ashamed."

"I?" Taylor countered, giving her an innocent look. "Whatever for?"

"You know very well what for," B.J. said severely. "You very near had Betty swooning."

"I can't help it if I'm charming and irresistible."

"Oh, yes, you can," she disagreed. "You were deliberately charming and irresistible. If you'd said the word, she'd have ripped up her prize rosebush and planted it at the inn's front door."

"Nonsense," Taylor claimed. "We were simply having an enjoyable conversation."

"Did you enjoy the camomile tea?" B.J. asked sweetly.

"Very refreshing. You didn't get a cup, did you?"

"No." B.J. sniffed and folded her arms across her chest. "I wasn't invited."

"Ah, now I see." Taylor sighed as he pulled in front of the inn. "You're jealous."

"Jealous?" B.J. gave a quick laugh and brushed the dust from her skirt. "Ridiculous."

"Yes, I see it now," he said smugly, repressing a grin. "Silly girl!" With this, he stopped the car, and turning to B.J. lowered his smiling mouth to hers. Imperceptibly, his lips lost their teasing quality, becoming warm and soft on her skin. B.J.'s playful struggles ceased, and she stiffened in his arms.

"Taylor, let me go." She found it was more difficult now to catch her breath than it had been when she had been laughing. A small moan escaped her as his lips trailed to her jawline. "No," she managed, and putting her fingers to his lips, pushed him away. He studied her, his eyes dark and full of knowledge as she fought to control her breathing. "Taylor, I think it's time we established some rules."

"I don't believe in rules between men and women, and I don't follow any." He said this with such blatant arrogance, B.J. was shocked into silence. "I'll let you go now, because I don't think it's wise to make love with you in broad daylight in the front seat of my car. However, the time will come when the circumstances will be more agreeable."

B.J. narrowed her eyes and found her voice. "You seriously don't think I'll agree to that, do you?"

"When the time comes, B.J.," he said with maddening confidence, "you'll be happy to agree."

"Fat chance," she said as she struggled out of the car. "We're never going to agree about anything." Slamming the door gave her some satisfaction.

As she ran up the front steps and into the inn, B.J. decided she never wanted to hear the word *businesslike* again.

Chapter Six

B.J. was standing on the wide lawn enjoying the warmth of the spring sun. She had decided to avoid Taylor Reynolds as much as possible and concentrate on her own myriad responsibilities. Unfortunately, that had not been as easy as she had hoped: she had been forced to deal with him on a daily business basis.

Though the inn was relatively quiet, B.J. knew that in a month's time, when the summer season began, the pace would pick up. Her gaze traveled the length and height of the inn, admiring the mellowed bricks serene against the dark pines, the windows blinking in the bright spring sun. On the back porch, two guests were engaged in an undemanding game of checkers. From where she was standing, B.J. could barely hear the murmur of their conversation without hearing the words.

All too soon, this peace would be shattered by children shouting to each other as they raced across the lawn, by the purr of motorboats as they sped past the inn. Yet, somehow, the inn never lost its informal air of tranquility. Here, she mused, the shade was for relaxing, the grass invited bare feet, the drifting snow for sleigh rides and snow men. Elegance had its place, B.J. acknowledged, but the Lakeside Inn had a charm of its own. *And Taylor Reynolds was not going to destroy it.*

You've only got ten days left. He leaves in ten days, she reminded herself. She sighed.

The sigh was as much for herself as for the inn's fate. *I wish he'd never come. I wish I'd never laid eyes on him.* Scowling, she headed back towards the inn.

"That face is liable to turn guests away." Startled, B.J. stared at Taylor as he blocked the doorway. "I think it's best for business if I get you away from here for a while." Stepping forward, he took her hand and pulled her across the lawn.

"I have to go in," she protested. "I...I have to phone the linen supplier."

"It'll keep. Your duties as guide come first."

"Guide? Would you please let me go? Where are we going?"

"Yes. No. And we're going to enjoy one of Elsie's famous picnics." Taylor held up the hamper he held in his free hand. "I want to see the lake."

"You don't need me for that. You can't miss it. It's the huge body of water you come to at the end of the path."

"B.J." He stopped, turning directly to face her. "For two days you've avoided me. Now, I'm well aware we have differences in our outlook on the inn."

"I hardly see..."

"Be quiet," he said pleasantly. "I am willing to give you my word that no major alterations will be started without your being notified. Whatever changes I decide upon will be brought to your attention before any formal plans are drawn up." His tone was brisk and businesslike even while he ignored her attempts to free her hand. "I respect your dedication and loyalty to the inn." His tone was coolly professional.

"But..."

"However," he cut her off easily, "I do own the inn, and you are in my employ. As of now you have a couple hours off. How do you feel about picnics?"

"Well, I..."

"Good. I'm fond of them myself." Smiling easily, he began to move down the well worn path through the woods.

The undergrowth was still soft from winter. Beneath the filtered sunlight wild flowers were a multicolored carpet, bright against their brown background of decaying leaves. Squirrels darted up the trunks of trees where birds had already begun to nest.

"Do you always shanghai your companions?" B.J. demanded, angry and breathless at keeping pace with Taylor's long strides.

"Only when necessary," he replied curtly.

The path widened, then spread into the grassy banks of the lake. Taylor stopped, surveying the wide expanse of lake with the same absorption that B.J. had observed in him earlier.

The lake was unruffled, reflecting a few clouds above it. The mountains on its opposite edge were gently formed. They were not like the awesome, demanding peaks of the West, but sedate and well behaved. The silence was broken once by the quick call of a chickadee, then lay again like a calming hand on the air.

"Very nice," Taylor said at length, and B.J. listened for but heard no condescension in his tone. "A very lovely view. Do you ever swim here?"

"Only since I was two," B.J. answered, groping for a friendly lightness. She wished he would not continue to hold her hand as if he had done so a thousand times before, wished hers did not fit into his as if molded for the purpose.

"Of course." He turned his head, switching his study from the lake to her face. "I'd forgotten, you were born here, weren't you?"

"I've always lived in Lakeside." Deciding that setting up the picnic things was the most expedient way to break the hand contact, B.J. took the hamper and began spreading Elsie's neatly folded cloth. "My parents moved to New York when I was nineteen, and I lived there for almost a year. I transferred colleges at mid-term and enrolled back here."

"How did you find New York?" Taylor dropped down beside her, and B.J. glimpsed at the bronzed forearms which his casually rolled up sleeves revealed.

"Noisy and confusing," she replied, frowning at a platter of crisp golden chicken. "I don't like to be confused."

"Don't you?" His swift grin appeared at her frown. With one deft motion, he pulled out the ribbon which held her hair neatly behind her back. "It makes you look like my adolescent niece." He tossed it carelessly out of reach as B.J. grabbed for it.

"You are an abominably rude man." Pushing back her newly liberated hair, she glared into his smiling face.

"Often," he agreed and lifted a bottle of wine from the hamper. He drew the cork with the ease of experience while B.J. fumed in silence. "How did you happen to become manager of the Lakeside Inn?"

The question took her off guard. For a moment she watched him pour the inn's best Chablis into Dixie cups. "I sort of gravitated to it." Accepting the offered cup, she met the directness of his gaze and realized he would not be content with the vagueness of her answer. "I worked summers at the inn when I was in high school, sort of filling in here and there at first. By the time I graduated, I was assistant manager. Anyway," she continued, "when I moved back from New York, I just slid back in. Mr. Blakely, the old manager, recommended me when he retired, and I took over." She shrugged and bit into a drumstick.

"Between your education and your dedication to your career, where did you find the time to learn how to swing a bat like Reggie Jackson?"

"I managed to find a few moments to spare. When I was fourteen," she explained, grinning at the memory, "I was madly in love with this older man. He was seventeen." She gave Taylor a sober nod. "Baseball oozed from his pores, so I enthusiastically took up the game. He'd call me shortstop, and my toes would tingle."

Taylor's burst of laughter startled a slumbering blue jay who streaked across the sky with an indignant chatter. "B.J., I don't know anyone like you. What happened to the toe tingler?"

Overcome by the pleasure his laughter had brought her, she fumbled for the thread of the conversation. "Oh…he…uh…he's got two kids and sells used cars."

"His loss," Taylor commented, cutting a thin wedge of cheese.

B.J. broke a fragrant hunk of Elsie's fresh bread and held it out to Taylor for a slice of cheese. "Do you spend much time at your other hotels?" she asked, uncomfortable at the personal tone the conversation seemed to be taking.

"Depends." His eyes roamed over her as she sat cross legged on the grass, her soft hair tumbling over her shoulders, her lips slightly parted.

"Depends?" she inquired. He stared a moment at her and she fought not to fidget under his encompassing gaze.

"I make certain my managers are competent." He broke the silence with a smile. "If there's a specific problem, I'll deal with it. First, I like to get the feel of a new acquisition, determine if a policy change is warranted."

"But you work out of New York?" The trend of the conversation was much more to her liking. The tension eased from her shoulders.

"Primarily. I've seen fields in Kansas that looked less like wheat than your hair." He captured a generous handful. B.J. swallowed in surprise. "The fog in London isn't nearly as gray or mysterious as your eyes."

B.J. swallowed and moistened her lips. "Your chicken's getting cold."

His grin flashed at her feeble defense but his hand relinquished its possession of her hair. "It's supposed to be cold." Lifting the wine bottle, Taylor refilled his cup. "Oh, by the way, there was a call for you."

B.J. took a sip of Chablis with apparent calm. "Oh, was it important?"

"Mmm." Taylor moved his shoulders under his cream colored tailored shirt. "A Howard Beall. He said you had his number."

"Oh." B.J. frowned, recalling it was about time for her duty date with Betty Jackson's nephew. Her sigh was automatic.

"My, you simply reek of enthusiasm."

Taylor's dry comment brought on a smile and a shrug. "He's just a man I know."

Taylor contented himself with a slight raising of his brow.

The sky was now an azure arch, without even a puff of cloud to spoil its perfection. Replete and relaxed, B.J. rolled over on her back to enjoy it. The grass was soft and smelled fresh. Overhead, the maple offered a half-shade. Its black branches were touched with young, tender leaves. Through the spreading cluster of trees, dogwoods bloomed white.

"In the winter," she murmured, half to herself, "it's absolutely still here after a snowfall. Everything's white. Snow hangs and drips from the trees and carpets the earth. The lake's like a mirror. The ice is as clear as rain water. You almost forget there's any place else in the world, or that spring will come. Do you ski, Taylor?" She rolled over on her stomach, her elbows supporting her head to smile at him, all animosity forgotten.

"I've been known to." He returned her smile, studying the soft drowsy face, rosy from the sun and the unaccustomed wine.

"The skiing's marvelous here." She tossed back her hair with a quick movement of her shoulders. "Snow skiing's so much more exciting than water skiing, I think. The food at the inn brings the skiing crowd. There's nothing like Elsie's stew after a day on the slopes." Plucking a blade of grass, she twirled it idly.

Taylor moved to lie down beside her. She was too content to be alarmed at his proximity.

"Dumplings?" he inquired, and she grinned down into his face.

"Of course. Hot buttered rum or steaming chocolate."

"I'm beginning to regret I missed the season."

"Well, you're in time for strawberry shortcake," she offered in consolation. "And the fishing's good year round."

"I've always favored more active sports." His finger ran absently up her arm, and B.J. tried hard to ignore the pleasure it gave her.

"Well." Her brow creased as she considered. "There's a good stable about fifteen miles from here, or boats for rent at the marina, or..."

"Those aren't the sports I had in mind." With a swift movement, he dislodged her elbows and brought her toppling onto his chest. "Are they the best you can do?" His arms held her firmly against him, but she was already captured by the fascination of his eyes.

"There's hiking," she murmured, unaware of the strange husky texture of her own voice.

"Hiking," Taylor murmured, before altering their positions in one fluid motion.

"Yes, hiking's very popular." She felt her consciousness drifting as she gazed up at him and struggled to retain some hold on lucidity. "And...and swimming."

"Mmm." Absently, his fingers traced the delicate line of her cheek.

"And there's...uh...there's camping. A lot of people like camping. We have a lot of parks." Her voice faltered as his thumb ran over her lips.

"Parks?" he repeated, prompting her.

"Yes, a number of parks, quite a number. The facilities are excellent for camping." She gave a small moan as his mouth lowered to tease the curve of her neck.

"Hunting?" Taylor asked conversationally as his lips traveled over her jawline to brush the corner of her mouth.

"I, yes. I think...what did you say?" B.J. closed her eyes on a sigh.

"I wondered about hunting," he murmured, kissing closed lids as his fingers slid under her sweater to trace her waist.

"There's bobcat in the mountains to the north."

"Fascinating." He rubbed his mouth gently over hers as his fingers trailed lightly up her flesh to the curve of her breast. "The chamber of commerce would be proud of you." Lazily, his thumb ran over the satin swell. Pleasure became a need as warmth spread from her stomach to tremble in her veins and cloud her brain.

"Taylor." Unable to bring her voice above a whisper, her hand sought the thick mass of his hair. "Kiss me."

"In a minute," he murmured, obviously enjoying the taste of her neck, until with devastating leisure, he moved his mouth to hers.

Trembling with a new, unfamiliar hunger, B.J. pulled him closer until his mouth was no longer teasing but avid on hers. Warmth exploded into fire. His tongue was searching, demanding all of her sweetness, his body as taut as hers was fluid. He took possession of her curves with authority, molding them with firm, strong hands. His mouth no longer roamed from hers but remained to devour what she offered. The heat grew to an almost unbearable intensity, her soul melting in it to flow into his. For a moment, she was lost in the discovery of merging, feeling it with as much clarity as she felt his hands and mouth. Soaring freedom and the chains of need were interchangeable. As time ceased to flow, she plunged deeper and deeper into the all-enveloping present.

His hands took more, all gentleness abandoned. It flashed across the mists in her brain that beneath the control lay a primitive, volatile force from which she had no defense. She struggled weakly. Her protests were feeble murmurs against the demands of his mouth. Feeling her tense, Taylor lifted his head, and she felt the unsteady rhythm of his breathing on her face.

"Please, let me go." Hating the weak timbre of her own voice, she sank her teeth into the lip still tender from his.

"Why should I do that?" Temper and passion threatened his control. She knew she had neither the strength nor the will to resist him if he chose to take.

"Please."

It seemed an eternity that he studied her, searching the smoky depths of her eyes. She watched the anger fade from his eyes as he took in the fair hair spread across the grass, the vulnerable, soft mouth. Finally, he released her with a brief, muttered oath.

"It appears," he began as she scrambled to sit up, "that pigtails suit you more than I realized." He took out a cigarette and lit it deliberately. "Virginity is a rare commodity in a woman your age."

Color flooded her cheeks as B.J. began to pack up the remains of the picnic. "I hardly see what business that is of yours."

"It doesn't matter," he countered easily and she cursed him for his ability to retain his composure so effortlessly while her entire body still throbbed with need. "It will simply take a bit more time." At her uncomprehending stare, he smiled and folded the cloth. "I told you I always win, B.J. You'd best get used to it."

"You listen to me." Storming, she sprang to her feet. "I am not about to be added to your list. This was…this was…" Her hands spread out to sweep away the incident while her brain searched for the proper words.

"Just the beginning," he supplied. Rising with the hamper, he captured her arm in a firm grip. "We haven't nearly finished yet. I wouldn't argue at the moment, B.J.," he warned as she began to sputter. "I might decide to take what you so recently offered here and now, rather than giving you some time."

"You are the most arrogant—" she began. Her voice sounded hopelessly childish even to her own ears.

"That's enough for now, B.J.," Taylor interrupted pleasantly. "There's no point saying anything you might regret." He leaned down and kissed her firmly before helping her to her feet. With an easy swing, he reached for the hamper. B.J. was too dazed to do anything but meekly follow him as he led the way toward the homeward wooded path.

Chapter Seven

Once back at the inn, B.J. wanted nothing more than to disengage her arm from Taylor's grasp and find a dark, quiet hole in which to hide. She knew all too well that she had responded completely to Taylor's demands. Moreover, she knew she had made demands of her own. She was confused by her own reactions. Never before had she had difficulty in avoiding or controlling a romantic interlude, but she was forced to admit that from the moment Taylor had touched her, her mind had ceased to function.

Biology, she concluded, darting Taylor a sidelong glance as they approached the skirting porch. It was simply a matter of basic biology. Any woman would naturally be attracted to a man like Taylor Reynolds. *He has a way of looking at you,* B.J. mused, *that makes your mind go fuzzy, then blank. He has a way of touching you that makes you feel as though you never had been touched before. He's nothing like any other man I've ever known. And I asked him to kiss me.* Color rose to her cheeks. *I actually asked him to kiss me.* It must have been the wine.

Soothed by this excuse, B.J. turned to Taylor as they entered the side door. "I'll take the basket back to the kitchen. Do you need me for anything else?"

"That's an intriguing question," he drawled.

B.J. shot him a quelling glance. "I have to get back to work now," she said briskly. "Now, if you'll excuse me?"

B.J.'s dignified exit was aborted by a flurry of activity in the lobby. Curiosity outweighing pride, she allowed Taylor to lead her toward the source.

A tall, svelte brunette stood by the desk, surrounded by a clutter of shocking pink luggage. Her pencil-slim form was draped in a teal blue suit of raw silk. The scent of gardenias floated toward B.J.

"If you'll see to my luggage, darling, and tell Mr. Reynolds I'm here, I'd be very grateful." She addressed these requests in a low, husky voice to Eddie who stood gaping beside her.

"Hello, Darla. What are you doing here?"

At Taylor's voice, the dark head turned. B.J. noted the eyes were nearly the same shade as the exquisite suit.

"Taylor." Impossibly graceful on four-inch heels, Darla glided across the lobby to embrace Taylor warmly. "I'm just back from checking on the job in Chicago. I knew you'd want me to look this little place over and give you my ideas."

Disengaging himself, Taylor met Darla's glowing smile with an ironic smile. "How considerate of you. B.J. Clark, Darla Trainor. Darla does the majority of my decorating, B.J. manages the inn."

"How interesting." Darla gave B.J.'s sweater and jeans a brief, despairing glance and patted her own perfectly styled hair. "From what I've seen so far, my work is certainly cut out for me." With a barely perceptible shudder, Darla surveyed the lobby's hand hooked rugs and Tiffany lamps.

"We've had no complaints on our decor." B.J. leaped to the inn's defense.

"Well." She was given a small, pitying smile from deeply colored lips. "It's certainly quaint, isn't it? Rather sweet for Ma and Pa Kettle. You'll have to let me know, Taylor, if you plan to enlarge this room." Transferring her attention, Darla's expression softened and warmed. "But, of course, red's always an eye-catcher. Perhaps red velvet drapes and carpeting."

B.J.'s eyes darkened to flint. "Why don't you take your red velvet drapes and..."

"I believe we'll discuss this later," Taylor said diplomatically, tightening his hold on B.J.'s arm. Struggling to prevent herself from crying with the pain, B.J. found argument impossible.

"I'm sure you'd like to get settled in," she forced out between clenched lips.

"Of course." Darla viewed B.J.'s brief outburst with a fluttering of heavy lashes. "Come up for a drink, Taylor. I assume this place has room service."

"Of course. Have a couple of martinis sent up to Miss Trainor's room," Taylor said to Eddie. "What's your room number, Darla?"

"I don't believe I have one yet." Again using her extensive lashes to advantage, Darla turned to a still dazed Eddie. "There seems to be a small communication problem."

"Give Miss Trainor 314, Eddie, and see to her bags." The sharp command in B.J.'s voice snapped Eddie's daydream, and he scurried to comply. "I hope you find it suitable." B.J. turned her best managerial smile on her new and unwelcome guest. "Please let me know if there's anything you need. I'll see to your drinks."

Taylor's hand held her still another moment. "I'll speak with you later."

"Delighted," B.J. returned, feeling the circulation slowly returning to her arm as he released it. "I'll wait to be summoned at your convenience, Mr. Reynolds. Welcome to the Lakeside Inn, Miss Trainor. Have a nice stay."

It was a simple matter to avoid a private meeting with Taylor as he spent the remainder of the day in Darla Trainor's company. They were closeted in 314 for what seemed to B.J. a lifetime. To boost her ego B.J. decided to phone Howard. They arranged a date for the following evening. *Well, at least Howard doesn't closet himself downing martinis with Miss Glamorpuss,* she thought. Somehow this knowledge was not as comforting as it should have been.

The dress B.J. had chosen for dinner was black and sleek. It molded her subtle curves with a lover's intimacy, falling in a midnight pool around her ankles, with a gentle caress for thighs and calves. Small pearl buttons ran from her throat to her waist. The high, puritanical neckline accentuated her firm, small breasts and emphasized her slender neck. She left her hair loose to float in a pale cloud around her shoulders. She touched her scent behind her ears before leaving her room to descend to the dining room.

The candle-lit, corner table where Taylor sat with Darla was intimate and secluded. Glancing in their direction, B.J. could not suppress a scowl. There was no denying that they were a handsome couple. *Made for each other,* she thought bitterly. Darla's vermilion sheath plunged to reveal the creamy swell of her breasts. Taylor's dark suit was impeccably cut. In spite of herself, B.J.'s eyes were drawn to the breadth of his shoulders. She drew in her breath sharply, recalling the feel of his corded muscles now expertly concealed by the fine tailoring, and shivered involuntarily.

Taylor glanced over, his expression indefinable as he made a slow, exacting survey, his eyes lingering on the gentle curves draped in the simplicity of unrelieved black. Though her skin grew warm, B.J. met his eyes levelly. Examination complete, Taylor lifted one brow, whether in approval or disapproval, she could not determine. With a brief gesture of his hand, he ordered B.J. to his table.

Fuming at the casual insolence of the command, she schooled her features into tranquility. She wove her way through the room, deliberately stopping to speak with diners along the route.

"Good evening." B.J. greeted Taylor and his companion with a professional smile. "I hope you're enjoying your meal."

"As always, the food is excellent." Taylor rose and pulled up a chair expectantly. His eyes narrowed in challenge. It was not the moment to cross him, B.J. decided.

"I trust your room pleases you, Miss Trainor," she said pleasantly, as she sat down.

"It's adequate, Miss Clark. Though I must say, I was rather taken aback by the decorating scheme."

"You'll join us for a drink," Taylor stated, motioning a waitress over without waiting for B.J.'s consent. She glared at him for a moment before she glanced up at Dot.

"My usual," she said, not feeling obliged to explain this was a straight ginger ale. She turned back to Darla, coating her voice with polite interest. "And what is it about the decorating which took you aback, Miss Trainor?"

"Really, Miss Clark," Darla began as though the matter was obvious. "The entire room is *provincial,* don't you agree? There are some rather nice pieces, I admit, if one admires American antiques, but Taylor and I have always preferred a modern approach."

Fighting her annoyance and an all too unwanted spasm of jealousy, B.J. said sarcastically, "I see. Perhaps you'd care to elaborate on the modern approach for this country bumpkin. I so seldom get beyond the local five and dime."

Dot set B.J.'s drink in front of her and scurried away, recognizing storm warnings.

"In the first place," Darla began, immune to her frosty gray eyes, "the lighting is all wrong. Those glass domed lamps with pull chains are archaic. You need wall to wall carpeting. The hand hooked rugs and faded Persians will have to go. And the bathroom...Well, needless to say, the bathroom is hopeless." With a sigh, Darla lifted her champagne cocktail and sipped. "Footed tubs belong in period comedies, not in hotels."

B.J. chewed on a piece of ice to keep her temper from boiling over. "Our guests have always found a certain charm in the baths."

"Perhaps," Darla acknowledged with a depreciating shrug. "But with the proper changes and improvements, you'll be catering to a different type of clientele." She drew out a slim cigarette, giving Taylor a brief flutter of lashes as he lit it.

"Do you have any objections to footed tubs and pull chains?" B.J. asked him, voice precise, eyes stormy.

"They suit the present atmosphere of the inn." His voice was equally precise, his eyes cool.

"Maybe I've got a few fresh ideas for you, Miss Trainor, if and when you pull out your little book of samples." Setting down her glass, B.J. watched from the corner of her eye as Taylor flicked his lighter at the end of his cigarette. "Mirrors should be good on the ceiling in particular. Just a light touch of decadence. Lots of chrome and glass to give the rooms that spacious, symmetrical look. And white, plenty of white as well, perhaps with fuchsia accents. The bed, of course," she continued with fresh inspiration. "A large circular bed with fuchsia coverings. Do you like fuchsia, Taylor?"

"I don't believe I asked for your advice on decorating tonight, B.J." Taylor drew casually on his cigarette. The smoke traveled in a thin column toward the exposed beam ceiling.

"I'm afraid, Miss Clark," Darla commented, spurred on by Taylor's mild reproof, "that your taste runs to the vulgar."

"Oh really?" B.J. blinked as if surprised. "I suppose that's what comes from being a country bumpkin."

"I'm sure whatever I ultimately decide will suit you, Taylor." Darla placed a hand with easy familiarity on his as B.J.'s temper rose. "But it will take a bit longer than usual as the alterations will be so drastic."

"Take all the time you need." B.J. gestured with magnanimity as she rose. "In the meantime, keep your hands off my footed tubs."

The dignity of her exit was spoiled by a near collision with Dot who had been discreetly eavesdropping.

"An order of arsenic for table three...on the house," B.J. muttered, skirting around the wide eyed waitress and sweeping from the room.

B.J.'s intention to stalk straight to her room and cool off was undone by a series of small, irritating jobs. It was after ten when the last had been dealt with and she was able to shut the door to her room and give vent to suppressed temper.

"Country bumpkin," she hissed through clenched teeth. Her eyes rested on a William and Mary table. *She'd* probably prefer plastic cubes in black and white checks. Her eyes moved from the dower chest to the schoolmaster's desk and on to the Bostonian rocker and wing chair in softly faded green. Each room of the inn was distinctive, with its own personality, its own treasures. Closing her eyes, B.J. could clearly see the room which Darla now occupied, the delicate pastel of the flowered wallpaper, the fresh gleam of the oak floor, the charm of the narrow, cushioned window seat. The pride of that particular room was an antique highboy in walnut with exquisite teardrop pulls. B.J. could not recall an occasion when a guest who had stayed in that room had done other than praise its comforts, its quiet charm, its timeless grace.

Darla Trainor, B.J. vowed, *is not getting her hands on my inn.* Walking to the mirrored bureau, she stared at her reflection, then let out a long disgusted breath. She's got a face that belongs on a cameo, and mine belongs on a milk commercial, she thought. Picking up her brush, she told herself that these reflections had nothing to do with the problem at hand.

How am I going to convince Taylor that the inn should stay as it is when she's already rattling off changes and giving him intimate smiles? I suppose, B.J. continued, giving her reflection a fierce scowl, *she's not just his decorator.* The kiss she gave him when she arrived wasn't very businesslike. I don't believe for a moment they spent all that time in her room discussing fabrics.

That's no concern of mine, she decided with a strong tug of the brush. But if they think they're going to start steaming off wallpaper without a fight, they're in for a surprise. She put down her brush and turned just as the door swung open to admit Taylor.

Before her astonished eyes, he closed and locked her door before placing the key in his pocket. As he advanced toward her, she could see that he was obviously angry.

"Being the owner doesn't give you the right to use the master key without cause," she snapped, as she backed against the bureau.

"It appears I haven't made myself clear." Taylor's voice was deceptively gentle. "You have, for the time being, a free hand in the day to day managing of this inn. I have not, nor do I desire to infringe upon your routine. However——" He took a step closer. B.J. discovered her hands were clutching the edge of the bureau in a desperate grip. "All orders, all decisions, all changes in policy come from me, and only me."

"Of all the dictatorial..."

"This isn't a debate," he cut her off sharply. "I won't have you issuing orders over my head. Darla is employed by me. I tell her what to do, and when to do it."

"But surely you don't want her to toss out all these lovely old pieces for gooseneck floor lamps and modular shelving. The server in the dining room is Hepplewhite. There're two Chippendale pieces in your room alone, and..."

The hand which moved from the back of her neck to circle her throat halted B.J.'s furious rush of words. She became uncomfortably aware of the strength of his fingers. No pressure was applied, but the meaning was all too evident.

"Whatever I want Darla to do is my concern, and my concern

only." He tightened his grip, bringing her closer. Now B.J. read the extent of his anger in his eyes. Like two dark suns, they burned into hers. "Keep your opinions to yourself until I ask for them. Don't interfere or you'll pay for it. Is that understood?"

"I understand perfectly. Your relationship with Miss Trainor has overruled any opinion of mine."

"That——" his brow lifted "——is none of your business."

"Whatever concerns the inn is my business," B.J. countered. "I offered you my resignation once, and you refused it. If you want to get rid of me now, you'll have to fire me."

"Don't tempt me." He lowered his hand and rested his fingers on the top button of her bodice. "I have my reasons for wanting you around, but don't push it. I agreed to keep you abreast of any alterations I decide on, but if you persist in being rude to others in my employ, you'll be out on your ear."

"I can't see that Darla Trainor needs protection from me," B.J. remarked resentfully.

"Don't you?" His temper appeared to drift toward amusement as he scanned her face. "A couple of centuries ago, you'd have been burned at the stake for looking as you do at this moment. Hell smoke in your eyes, your mouth soft and defiant, all that pale hair tumbling over a black dress." Deftly, his fingers undid the top button and moved down to the next as his eyes kept hers a prisoner. "That dress is just puritanical enough to be seductive. Was it accident or design that you wore it tonight?"

With casual ease, he unloosed half the range of buttons, continuing his progress as his gaze remained fixed on hers.

"I don't know what you mean." Yet her traitorous feet refused to walk away. B.J. found herself powerless to move. "I want...I want you to go."

"Liar," he accused quietly, his hands slipping inside the opened front of her dress. His fingers traced lightly over her skin. "Tell me again you want me to go." His hands rose, his thumbs moving gently under the curve of her breasts. The room began to sway like the deck of a ship.

"I want you to go." Her voice was husky, her lids felt heavy with a tantalizing languor.

"Your body contradicts you, B.J." His hands claimed her breasts briefly before sliding to the smooth skin of her back. He brought her hard against him. "You want me just as much as I want you." His mouth lowered to prove his point.

Surrendering to a force beyond her understanding, B.J. rested in his arms. His demands increased with her submission, his mouth drawing the response she had no strength to withhold. While her mind screamed no, her arms drew him closer. The warnings to run were lost as his lips moved to the vulnerable skin of her throat, teasing the softness with tongue and teeth. She could only cling and fret for more. Mouth returned to mouth. While his hands roamed, arousing fresh pleasure, hers slipped under his jacket.

With a suddenness that gave her no time for defense, no thought of resistance, he fell deep into her heart. He claimed its untouched regions with the deftness of a seasoned explorer. The emotion brought B.J. to a spinning ecstasy which vied with a crushing, hopeless despair. To love him was certain disaster, to need him, undeniable misery, to be in his arms, both the darkness and the light. Trapped in the cage of her own desire, she would never find escape.

Helpless to do other than answer the hunger of his mouth, submit to the caressing journey of his hands, she felt the sting of emptiness behind her closed lids. Her arms pulled him closer to avert the insidious chill of reason.

"Admit it," he demanded, his lips moving again to savage her throat. "Admit you want me. Tell me you want me to stay."

"Yes, I want you." The words trembled on a sob as she buried her face in his shoulder. "Yes, I want you to stay."

She felt him stiffen and burrowed deeper until his hand forced her face to his. Her eyes were luminous, conquering the darkness with the glimmer of unshed tears. Her mouth was soft and tremulous as she fought the need to throw herself into his arms and weep out her newly discovered love. For eternity, he stared, and she watched without comprehension as his features hardened with fresh temper. When he spoke, however, his voice was calm and composed and struck like a fist on the jaw.

"It appears we've gotten away from the purpose of this meeting." Stepping away, his hands retreated to his pockets. "I believe I've made my wishes clear."

She shook her head in confusion. As her hand lifted to her tousled hair, the opening of her dress shifted in innocent suggestion over creamy skin. "Taylor, I…"

"Tomorrow—" she shivered as the coolness of his voice sapped the warmth from her skin "—I expect you to give Miss Trainor your complete cooperation, and your courtesy. Regardless of your disagreement, she is a guest of the inn and shall be treated as such."

"Of course." The hated tears began to flow as pain and rejection washed over her. "Miss Trainor shall be given every consideration." She sniffed, brushed at tears and continued with dignity. "You have my word."

"Your word!" Taylor muttered, taking a step toward her. B.J. streaked to the bath and locked the door.

"Go away!" No longer able to control the sobs, one small fist pounded impotently against the panel. "Go away and leave me alone. I gave you my promise, now I'm off duty."

"B.J., open this door."

She recognized both anger and exasperation in his tone and wept more desperately. "No, go away! Go keep Miss Perfect company and let me alone. Your orders will be carried out to the letter. Just go. I don't have to answer to you until morning."

Taylor's swearing and storming around the room were quite audible, though to B.J. his muttered oaths and comments made little sense. Finally, the bedroom door slammed with dangerous force. In an undignified huddle on the tiled floor, B.J. wept until she thought her heart would break.

Chapter Eight

"Well, you did it again, didn't you?" B.J. stared at her reflection as the morning sun shone in without mercy. *You made a total fool of yourself.* With a weary sigh, she ran a hand through her hair before turning her back on the accusing face in the mirror. *How could I have known I'd fall in love with him?* she argued as she buttoned a pale green cap-sleeved blouse. *I didn't plan it. I didn't want it.*

"Blast," she muttered and pulled on a matching skirt. *How can I control the way he makes me feel? The minute he puts his hands on me, my brain dissolves. To think that I would have let him stay last night knowing all he wanted from me was a quick affair! How could I be so stupid? And then,* she added, shame warring with injured pride, *he didn't want me after all. I suppose he remembered Darla. Why should he waste his time with me when she's available?*

The next ten minutes were spent in fierce self-flagellation as B.J. secured her hair in a roll at the base of her neck. These tasks completed, she squared her shoulders and went out to meet whatever task the day brought.

A casual question to Eddie informed her Taylor was already closeted in the office, and Darla Trainor had not yet risen. B.J. was determined to avoid them both and succeeded throughout the morning.

The lunch hour found her in the lounge, conducting an inventory on the bar stock. The room was quiet, removed from the luncheon clatter. She found the monotony soothing on her nerves.

"So, this is the lounge."

The intrusion of the silky voice jolted B.J.'s calm absorption. She whirled around, knocking bottles of liquor together.

Darla glided into the room looking elegantly businesslike in an oatmeal colored three piece suit, a pad and pencil in perfectly manicured hands. She surveyed the cluster of white clothed tables, the postage stamp dance floor, the vintage upright Steinway. Flicking a finger down the muted glow of knotty pine paneling, she advanced to the ancient oak bar.

"How incredibly drab."

"Thank you," B.J. returned in her most courteous voice before she turned to replace a bottle on the mirrored shelves.

"Fix me a sweet vermouth," Darla ordered, sliding gracefully onto a stool and dropping her pad on the bar's surface.

B.J.'s mouth opened, furious retorts trembling on her tongue. Recalling her promise to Taylor, she clamped it shut and turned to comply.

"You must remember, Miss Clark," Darla's triumphant smile made B.J.'s hand itch to connect with ivory skin, "I'm merely doing my job. There's nothing personal in my observations."

Attempting to overcome her instinctive dislike, B.J. conceded. "Perhaps that's true. But, I have a very personal feeling about the

Lakeside Inn. It's more home than a place of business to me." She set the glass of vermouth at Darla's fingertips before turning back to count bottles.

"Yes, Taylor told me you're quite attached to this little place. He found it amusing."

"Did he?" Feeling her hand tremble, B.J. gripped the shelves until her knuckles whitened. "What a strange sense of humor Taylor must have."

"Well, when one knows Taylor as I do, one knows what to expect." Their eyes met in the mirror. Darla smiled and lifted her glass. "He seems to think you're a valuable employee. What did he say...rather adept at making people comfortable." She smiled again and sipped. "Taylor demands value from his employees as well as obedience. At times, he uses unorthodox methods to keep them satisfied."

"I'm sure you'd know all about that." B.J. turned slowly, deciding wars should be fought face to face.

"Darling, Taylor and I are much more than business associates. And I, of course, understand his...ah...distractions with business."

"How magnanimous of you."

"It would never do to allow emotion to rule a relationship with Taylor Reynolds." Drawing a long, enameled nail over the rim of her glass, Darla gave B.J. a knowledgeable look. "He has no patience with emotional scenes or complications."

The memory of her weeping spell and Taylor's angry swearing played back in B.J.'s mind. "Perhaps we've at last reached a point of agreement."

"The first warning is always friendly, Miss Clark." Abruptly,

Darla's voice hardened, throwing B.J. momentarily off balance. "Don't get too close. I don't allow anyone to infringe on my territory for long."

"Are we still talking about Taylor?" B.J. inquired. "Or did I lose part of this conversation?"

"Just take my advice." Leaning over the bar, Darla took B.J.'s arm in a surprisingly strong grip. "If you don't, the next place you manage will be a dog kennel."

"Take your hand off me." B.J.'s tone was soft and ominous, as the well-shaped nails dug into her flesh.

"As long as we understand each other." With a pleasant smile, Darla released B.J.'s arm and finished her drink.

"We understand each other very well." Taking the empty glass, B.J. placed it under the bar. "Bar's closed, Miss Trainor." She turned her back to recount already counted bottles.

"Ladies." B.J. stiffened and watched Taylor's reflection enter the room. "I hadn't expected to find you at the bar at this time of day." His voice was light, but the eyes which met B.J.'s in the glass did not smile.

"I've been wandering around making notes," Darla told him. B.J. watched her hand rub lightly over the back of his. "I'm afraid the only thing this lounge has going for it is its size. It's quite roomy, and you could easily fit in double the tables. But then, you'll have to let me know if you want to go moody, or modern. Actually, it might be an idea to add another lounge and do both, along the lines of your place in San Francisco."

His murmur was absent as he watched B.J. move to the next shelf.

"I thought I'd get a good look at the dining room if the luncheon crowd is gone." Darla's smile was coaxing. "Why don't you come with me, Taylor, and you can give me a clearer picture of what you have in mind?"

"Hmm?" His attention shifted, but the imperceptible frown remained. "No, I haven't decided on anything yet. Go ahead and take a look, I'll get back to you."

Well arched brows rose at the dismissive tone, but Darla remained cool and composed. "Of course. I'll bring my notes to your office later and we can discuss it."

Her heels echoed faintly on the wooden floor. Her heavy perfume scent lingered in the air after she faded from view.

"Do you want a drink?" B.J. questioned, keeping her back to him and her voice remote.

"No, I want to talk to you."

With great care, B.J. avoided meeting his eyes in the mirror. She lifted a bottle, carefully examining the extent of its contents. "Haven't we covered everything?"

"No, we haven't covered everything. Turn around B.J., I'm not going to talk to your back."

"Very well, you're the boss." As she faced him, she caught a flash of anger in his eyes.

"Do you provoke me purposely, B.J., or is it just an accidental talent?"

"I have no idea. Take your choice." Suddenly, she was struck by inspiration. "Taylor," she said urgently. "I *would* like to talk to you. I'd like to talk to you about buying the inn. It can't be as important to you as it is to me. You could build a resort farther south that would suit you better. I could raise the money if you gave me some time."

"Don't be ridiculous." His abrupt words cooled her enthusiasm. "Where would you come up with the kind of money required to buy a property like this?"

"I don't know." She paced back and forth behind the bar. "Somewhere. I could get a loan for part of it, and you could hold a note for the rest. I've some money saved…"

"No." Standing, he skirted the bar and closed the distance between them. "I have no intention of selling."

"But, Taylor…"

"I said no. Drop it."

"Why are you being so stubborn? You won't even consider changing your mind? I might even be able to come up with a good offer if you gave me time——" Her voice trailed off uncertainly.

"I said I wanted to *talk* to you. At the moment I don't care to discuss the inn or any part of it."

He gripped her arm to spin her around, connecting with the flesh tender from Darla's nails. B.J. gave a cry of pain and jerked away. Taylor loosened his hold immediately, and she fell into the shelves, knocking glasses in a crashing heap on the floor.

"What the devil's got into you?" he demanded as her hand went automatically to nurse her bruised arm. "I barely touched you. Listen, B.J., I'm not tolerating you jumping like a scared rabbit every time I get close. I haven't hurt you. Stop that!" He pulled her hand away, then stared in confusion at the marks on her arm. "Good Lord. I didn't…I'd swear I barely touched you." Astonished, his eyes lifted to hers, darkened with emotions she could not understand. For a moment, she merely stared back, fascinated by seeing his habitual assurance rattled.

"No, I did it before." Dropping her eyes, B.J. busied herself by resecuring the pins in her hair. "It's just a bit sore. You startled me when you grabbed it."

"How did you do that?" He moved to take her arm for a closer examination, but B.J. stepped away quickly.

"I bumped into something. I've got to start looking where I'm going." She began to gather shards of broken glass, fresh resentment causing her head to ache.

"Don't do that," Taylor commanded. "You'll cut yourself."

Like an echo to his words, B.J. jerked as a piece of glass sliced her thumb. Moaning in pain and disgust, she dropped the offending glass back into the heap.

"Let me see." Taylor pulled her to her feet, ignoring her struggles for release. "Ah, B.J." With a sigh of exasperation, he drew a spotless white handkerchief from his pocket, dabbing at the cut. "I'm beginning to think I have to keep you on a very short leash."

"It's nothing," she mumbled, fighting the warmth of his fingers on her wrist. "Let me go, you'll have blood all over you."

"Scourges of war." He brought the wounded thumb briefly to his lips, then wrapped the cloth around it. "You will continue to bind up your hair, won't you?" With his free hand, he dislodged pins, clattering them among broken glass. Studying the flushed face and tumbled hair, his mouth lifted in a smile which brought B.J. new pain. "What is it about you that constantly pulls at my temper? At the moment, you look as harmless as a frazzled kitten."

His fingers combed lightly through her hair, then rested on her shoulders. She felt the sweet, drawing weakness seeping through her limbs. "Do you know how close I came to kicking in that foolish bathroom door last night? You should be careful with tears, B.J., they affect men in strange ways."

"I hate to cry." She lifted her chin, terrified she would do so again. "It was your fault."

"Yes, I suppose it was. I'm sorry."

She stared, stunned by the unexpected apology. In a featherlight caress, he lowered his mouth to brush hers. "It's all right... It doesn't matter." She backed away, frightened by her own need to respond, but found herself trapped against the bar. Taylor made no move toward her, but merely said, "Have dinner with me tonight. Up in my room where we can talk privately."

Her head shook before her lips could form a refusal. He closed the space between them before she could calculate an escape.

"B.J., I'm not going to let you run away. We need to talk somewhere where we won't be interrupted. You know that I want you, and..."

"You should be satisfied with your other acquisitions," she retorted, battling the creeping warmth.

"I beg your pardon?" At her tone, his face hardened. The hand which had lifted to brush through her hair dropped back to his side.

"I'm sure you'll understand if you give it a bit of thought." She lifted her own hand to the sore flesh of her arm as if to keep the memory fresh. His eyes followed her gesture in puzzlement.

"It would be simpler if you elaborated."

"No, I don't think so. Just don't let your ego get out of hand, Taylor. I'm not running from you, I simply have a date tonight."

"A date?" He slipped his hands into his pockets as he rocked back on his heels. His voice was hard.

"That's right. I'm entitled to a personal life. I don't think it's included in my job contract that I have to spend twenty-four hours at your beck and call." Adding salt to her own wound, she continued, "I'm sure Miss Trainor will fill your requirements for the evening very well."

"Undoubtedly," he agreed with a slow nod. Stung by the ease of his answer, B.J.'s ice became fire.

"Well then, that's all decided, isn't it? Have a delightful evening, Taylor. I assure you, I intend to. If you'll excuse me, I've work to do." She brushed by him, only to be brought up short by a hand on her hair.

"Since we're both going to be otherwise engaged this evening, perhaps we can get this out of the way now."

His mouth took hers swiftly, and she could taste his smoldering fury. She made a futile attempt to clamp her lips tightly against his. Ruthlessly, his hand jerked her hair. As she gasped in pained surprise he invaded her mouth, conquering her senses one by one. Just as she had abandoned all semblance of resistance, he drew back, his hands moving with slow insistence from her waist to her shoulders.

"Are you through?" Her voice was husky. Despising the longing to feel his mouth again, she forced herself rigid, keeping her eyes level.

"Oh no, B.J." The tone was confident. "I'm a long way from through. But for now," he continued as she braced herself for another assault, "you'd best tend to that cut."

Too unnerved to answer, B.J. rushed from the lounge. She had left dignity to lay with the scattered pieces of glass.

She felt the kitchen would be the quietest sanctuary at that time of day and entered on the pretext of wanting a cup of coffee.

"What did you do to your hand?" Elsie's question was off-handed as she completed the assembly line production of apple cobblers.

"Just a scratch." Frowning down at Taylor's handkerchief, B.J. shrugged and advanced on the coffee pot.

"Better put some iodine on it."

"Iodine stings."

Tongue clucking, Elsie wiped her hands on her full apron before foraging in a small cabinet for medical supplies. "Sit down and don't be a baby."

"It's just a scratch. It's not even bleeding now." Helplessly, B.J. dropped into a chair as Elsie flourished a small bottle and a bandage. "It's nothing at all. Ouch! Blast it, Elsie! I told you that wretched stuff stings."

"There." Elsie secured the bandage with a satisfied smile. "Out of sight, out of mind."

"So you say." B.J. rested her chin on her hand and stared into the depth of her coffee cup.

"Miss Snooty tried to get into my kitchen," Elsie announced with an indignant sniff.

"Who? Oh, Miss Trainor." Throbbing thumb momentarily forgotten, B.J. gave her cook her full attention. "What happened?"

"I tossed her out, of course." Elsie flicked flour from her abundant bosom and looked pleased.

"Oh." Leaning back in her chair, B.J. laughed at the picture of Elsie ordering sophisticated Darla out of her kitchen. "Was she furious?"

"Fit to be tied," Elsie returned pleasantly. B.J.'s grin widened before she could prevent it. "Going out with Howard tonight?"

"Yes." Her answer was automatic, not even vaguely surprised that communications had delivered this information to Elsie's ears. "To the movies, I think."

"Don't know why you're wasting your time going off with him when Mr. Reynolds is around."

"Well, it keeps Betty Jackson happy, and..." B.J. stopped and frowned as the complete sentence seeped through. "What does Taylor...Mr. Reynolds have to do with it?"

"I don't see why you're going out with Howard Beall when you're in love with Taylor Reynolds." Elsie's statement was matter-of-factly delivered as she poured herself a cup of coffee.

"I am not in love with Taylor Reynolds," B.J. declared, gulping down coffee and scalding both tongue and throat.

"Yes, you are," Elsie corrected, adding cooling cream to her own cup.

"I am not."

"Are too."

"I am not. I am absolutely not! Just what makes you so smart?" she added nastily.

"Fifty years of living, and twenty-four of knowing you." The reply was smug.

"La de da." B.J. attempted to appear sublimely unconcerned.

"Be real nice if you got married and settled down right here." Ignoring B.J.'s fit of choking, Elsie calmly sipped her coffee. "You could keep right on managing the inn."

"Stick to chicken and dumplings, Elsie," B.J. advised when she had recovered. "As a fortune teller, you're a complete failure. Taylor Reynolds would no more marry me and settle here than he would marry a porcupine and live on the moon. I'm a bit too coun-trified and inexperienced for his taste."

"Hmph." Elsie sniffed again and shook her head. "Sure does a lot of looking in your direction."

"I'm sure in the vast wisdom you've amassed in your famous fifty years, you know the difference between a physical attraction and the urge to marry and settle down. Even in our sheltered little town, we learn the difference between love and lust."

"My, my, aren't we all grown up and sassy," Elsie observed with the mild tolerance of an adult watching a child's tantrum. "Finish your coffee and scoot, I've got a prime rib that needs tending. And don't worry that bandage off your thumb," she ordered as B.J. swung through the door.

Obviously, B.J. decided as she prepared for her date that evening, I don't project an imposing enough authority figure. She frowned again as she recalled Elsie dismissing her like a bad tempered child. A breeze wafted through her opened window, billowing the curtains and wafting in the smell of freshly mowed grass. B.J. shrugged off her black mood. I'll simply change my image a bit.

She rooted through her closet and pulled out her birthday present from her grandmother. The blouse was pure white silk and plunged deep to cling provocatively to every curve and plane before it tapered to the narrow waist of sleek black pants. The slacks continued a loving embrace over hips and down the length of shapely legs, molding her shape with the accuracy of a second skin.

"I'm not sure I'm ready for a new image," she muttered, turning sideways in front of her mirror. "I'm not sure Howard's ready either." The thought brought an irrepressible giggle as Howard's pleasantly homely face loomed in her mind.

He had the eyes of a faithful puppy, made all the more soulful by the attempt of a moustache which hung apologetically over his top lip. The main problem, B.J. decided, concentrating on his image, is that he lacks a chin. His face seemed to melt into his neck.

But he's a nice man, B.J. reminded herself. A nice, uncomplicated, predictable, undemanding man. Easing her feet into leather slides, she grabbed her bag and scurried from the room.

Her hopes to slip unseen outside to await Howard's arrival were shattered by a panic-stricken Eddie.

"B.J. Hey, B.J.!" He loped across the lobby and cornered her before she could reach the door.

"Eddie, if the place isn't burning down, hold it until tomorrow. I'm just leaving."

"But, B.J.," he continued, grabbing her hand and ignoring her unconscious search of the room for a tall, dark man. "Dot told Maggie that Miss Trainor is going to redecorate the inn, and that Mr. Reynolds plans to make it into a resort with saunas in every room and an illegal casino in the back." Horrified, his hand clung to hers for reassurance, his eyes pleading behind the thickness of his glasses.

"In the first place," B.J. began patiently, "Mr. Reynolds has no intention of running an illegal casino."

"He has one in Las Vegas," Eddie whispered in confidence.

"Gambling is a prerequisite in Las Vegas, it's not illegal."

"But, B.J., Maggie said the lounge is going to be done in red and gold plush with nude paintings on the walls."

"Nonsense." She patted his hand in amusement as color rose to his cheeks. "Mr. Reynolds hasn't decided anything yet. When he does, I'm sure it won't run to red and gold plush, and nudes!"

"Thank you," Taylor said at her back. B.J. jumped. "Eddie, I believe the Bodwin sisters are looking for you," he added.

"Oh, yes, sir." Face flaming, Eddie shot off, leaving B.J. in the very position she had sought to avoid.

"Well, well." Taylor surveyed her, an encompassing, thoroughly male examination, lingering on the point where her blouse joined above her breasts. "I trust your date has a high boiling point."

She started to snap that Howard had no boiling point at all, but changed her mind. "Do you really like it?" Tossing clouds of hair over her shoulder, B.J. gave Taylor the benefit of a melting, sultry smile.

"Let's say I might find it appealing under different circumstances," he said dryly.

Pleased to observe he was annoyed, B.J. recklessly gave his cheek a brief pat and glided to the door. "Good night, Taylor. Don't wait up now." Triumphant, she stepped out into the pink-clouded evening.

Howard's reaction to her appearance caused her ego to soar yet higher. He swallowed, eyes blinking rapidly, and stammered in small, incoherent sentences the entire distance to town. Finding this a pleasant change from self-assured amusement, B.J. basked in his admiration as she watched the hazy sun sink beyond the hills through the car window.

In town, the streets were already quiet with the mid-week, mid-evening hush which isolates small towns from the outside world. A few windows glowed like cats' eyes in the dark, but most of the houses had bedded down for the night like so many contented domestic pets.

At the far end of town where the theater was, there were more signs of activity. Howard pulled into the parking lot with his usual, plodding precision. The neon sign glowed somewhat ludicrously against the quiet sky. The *L* in PLAZA had been retired for the past six months.

"I wonder," B.J. mused as she alighted from Howard's sensible Buick, "if Mr. Jarvis will ever get that sign fixed or if each of the letters will die a quiet death." Howard's answer was muffled by the car door slam. She was faintly surprised as he took her arm with a possessive air and led her into the theater.

An hour through the feature, B.J decided Howard was not at all himself. He did not consume his popcorn with his usual voracity, nor did he shift throughout the film on the undeniably uncomfortable seats the Plaza offered. Rather, he sat in a glazed-eyed state that seemed almost catatonic.

"Howard." Keeping her voice low, B.J. placed her hand on his. To her surprise he jumped as though she had pinched him. "Howard, are you all right?"

Her astonishment changed to stunned disbelief when he grabbed her, scattering popcorn, and pressed a passionate if fumbling kiss to her mouth. At first, B.J. sat stunned. All other advances by Howard had consisted of a brotherly embrace at the door of the inn. Then, hearing a few snickers from the back of the theater, she wiggled from his arms and pushed against his stocky chest.

"Howard, behave yourself!" She gave an exasperated sigh and straightened in her seat.

Abruptly, Howard gripped her arm and pulled her to her feet, dragging her up the aisle and out of the theater.

"Howard, have you lost your mind?"

"I couldn't sit in there any more," he muttered, bundling her into his car. "It's too crowded."

"Crowded?" She blew an errant curl from her eyes. "Howard, there couldn't have been more than twenty people in there. I think you should see a doctor." She patted his shoulder then tested his brow for signs of fever. "You're a bit warm and not at all yourself. I can get a ride back, you'd better just go home."

"No!" There was no mistaking the vehemence of his tone.

B.J. gave Howard a long, searching stare before settling back uneasily into her seat. Though it was too dark to tell much, he appeared to be concentrating on his driving. He drove rapidly over the winding country road. Soon B.J. was able to distinguish the blinking lights of the hotel.

Suddenly, Howard pulled off the road and seized her. In the beginning, B.J. was more surprised than angry. "Stop it! Stop this, Howard! What in the world has gotten into you?"

"B.J." His mouth searched for hers, and this time his kiss was neither fumbling nor brotherly. "You're so beautiful." His groping hand reached for her blouse.

"Howard Beall, I'm ashamed of you!" B.J. remonstrated, pushing Howard firmly away and sliding toward the car door. "You get home right now and take a cold shower and go to bed!"

"But, B.J.—"

"I mean it." She wrenched open the car door and jumped out. Standing by the road, she tossed back her hair and adjusted her clothes. "I'm walking right back to the inn before you grow fangs again. Consider yourself lucky if I don't say something to your aunt about your temporary bout of insanity." Turning, she began the half-mile hike to the hotel.

* * *

Ten minutes later, shoes in hand and muttering disjointed imprecations toward the entire male sex, B.J. panted up the steep hill. The shadowy trees sighed softly in the moonlight. A lone owl hooted above her. But B.J. was in no mood for the beauties of the evening. "You be quiet," she commanded, glaring up at the bundle of feathers.

"I haven't said anything yet," a deep voice answered.

On the verge of screaming, B.J. found a hand over her mouth. Struggling to escape, she found a hard arm gripping her around the waist. "What the——?"

"Out for a stroll?" Taylor inquired mildly, releasing her. "It does seem an odd place to take a walk," he commented.

"Very funny." She managed two outraged steps before he caught her wrist.

"What's the matter? Your friend run out of gas?"

"Listen, I don't need this right now." Realizing she had dropped her shoes in her fright, B.J. searched the ground. "I've just walked a hundred miles after wrestling with a crazy man."

"Did he hurt you?" The grip on her wrist increased, as Taylor examined her more closely.

"Of course not." Tossing back her hair, B.J. let out a sigh of exasperation. "Howard wouldn't hurt a fly. I don't know what came over him. He's never acted like that before."

"Are you really that artless, or am I watching the second feature?" At her baffled expression, Taylor took her shoulders and administered a brief shake. "Grow up, B.J.! Look at yourself, the poor guy didn't have a chance."

"Don't be ridiculous." She shrugged out of his hold.

"Howard's known me forever. He's never behaved like this before. He's just been reading too many romances or something. Good grief, I used to go skinny dipping with him when I was ten years old."

"Has anyone bothered to point out that you're no longer ten years old?"

Something in his voice made her raise her eyes to his.

"Stand still, B.J." He spoke in quiet command, and she felt her knees tremble. "I feel like a mountain lion stalking a house kitten."

For a moment, they stood apart, the stars glimmering above their heads, the moon a pale white guardian. Somewhere, a nightbird called to its mate, a plaintive sound. It echoed into silence as she melted in his arms.

She rose on her toes to offer him the gift of her mouth, her sigh of surrender merging with the wind's murmur. Her breasts crushed against his chest as his hands molded her hips closer. For this moment, she was his. Her heart sought no past or future but only the warmth and knowledge of now—the eternity of the present. She moaned with pleasure as his mouth sought the curve of her neck. Her fingers tangled with his dark hair as his mouth met hers again and she opened her lips to his kiss.

Locked together, they were oblivious to the sounds of night; the sigh of wind, the mellow call of an owl and the chirp of crickets. With a harsh suddenness, the inn door opened, pooling them in artificial light.

"Oh, Taylor, I've been waiting for you."

B.J. pulled away in humiliation as Darla leaned against the doorway, draped in a flowing black negligee. Her ivory skin gleamed against the lace. Her smooth, raven hair fell loose and full down her back.

"What for?" Taylor's question was abrupt.

Darla pouted and moved lace clad shoulders. "Taylor, darling, don't be a bear."

Devastated that he should have used her so blatantly while he had another woman waiting, B.J. stooped to retrieve her shoes.

"Where do you think you're going?" Taylor captured her wrist and aborted her quick escape.

"To my room," B.J. informed him with her last vestige of calm. "It appears you have a previous engagement."

"Just a minute."

"Please, let me go. I've done my quota of wrestling for one evening."

His fingers tightened on her flesh. "I'm tempted to wring your neck." Taylor tossed her wrist away as though the small contact was abhorrent.

Turning on bare heels, B.J. rushed up the steps and past a sweetly smiling Darla.

Chapter Nine

B.J. moved her files to her room. There, she determined, she could work in peace without Taylor's disturbing presence. She immersed herself in paperwork and tried to block all else from her mind. The gray, drizzling rain which hissed at her windows set the stage for her mood. Thick, low hanging clouds allowed no breath of sun. Still, her eyes were drawn to the misty curtain, her mind floating with the clear rivulets which ran down the glass. Shaking her head to bring herself to order, B.J. concentrated on her linen supply.

Her door swung open, and she turned from the slant top desk. With sinking heart, she watched Taylor enter.

"Hiding out?"

It was apparent from the set of his mouth that his mood had not mellowed since her departure the previous evening.

"No." The lifting of her chin was instinctive. "It's simply more convenient for me to work out of my room while you need the office."

"I see." He towered menacingly over her desk, making her feel small and insignificant. "Darla tells me you two had quite a session yesterday in the lounge."

B.J.'s mouth opened in surprise. She could not believe Darla would have disclosed her own behavior so readily.

"I warned you, B.J., that as long as Darla is a guest at the inn, you're to treat her with the same courtesy you show all other guests."

B.J. was astonished. "I'm sorry, Taylor, perhaps I'm dim. Would you mind explaining that?"

"She told me you were inexcusably rude, that you made some comments on her relationship with me, refused to serve her a drink, made yourself generally unpleasant, and told the staff not to cooperate with her."

"She said that, did she?" B.J.'s eyes darkened with rage. She set her pen down carefully and rose despite Taylor's proximity. "Isn't it odd how two people can view the same scene from entirely different perspectives! Well." She stuck her hand in her pockets and planted her feet firmly. "I have news for you—"

"If you've another version," Taylor returned evenly, "I'd like to hear it."

"Oh!" Unable to prevent herself, she lifted her fist to give his chest a small, inadequate punch. His eyes dropped to it in amused indulgence. "How generous of you. The condemned man is given a fair trial." Whirling, she paced the room in a swirl of agitation, debating whether to give him a verbatim account of her meeting with Darla. Finally, her pride won over her desire to clear herself in Taylor's eyes. "No thanks, your honor. I'll just take the fifth."

"B.J." Taylor took her shoulders and spun her to face him. "Must you constantly provoke me?"

"Must you constantly pick on me?" she countered.

"I wouldn't have said I was doing that." His tone had changed from anger to consideration.

"That's your opinion. I'm the one who's constantly in the position of justifying myself. I'm tired of having to explain my every move, of trying to cope with your moods. I never know from one minute to the next if you're going to kiss me or sit me in the corner with a dunce hat. I'm tired of feeling inadequate, naive and stupid. I never felt like any of those things before, and I don't like it."

Her words tumbled out in a furious rush while Taylor merely looked on, politely attentive.

"And I'm sick of your precious Darla altogether. Sick of her criticizing every aspect of the inn, sick of her looking at me as though I were some straw-chewing hick from Dogpatch. And, I resent her running to you with fabricated stories, and, I detest your using me to boost your over-inflated ego while she's floating around half naked waiting to warm your bed. And... Oh, blast!"

Her torrent of complaints was interrupted by the shrill ringing of the phone. Ripping the receiver from its cradle, B.J. snapped into it.

"What is it? No, nothing's wrong. What is it, Eddie?" Pausing, she listened, her hand lifting to soothe the back of her neck where tension lodged. "Yes, he's here." She turned back to Taylor and held out the phone. "It's for you, a Mr. Paul Bailey."

He took the receiver in silence, his eyes still on her face. As she turned to leave the room, his hand caught her wrist. "Stay here." Waiting for her nod of agreement, he released her. B.J. moved to the far side of the room and stared out at the insistent rain.

Taylor's conversation consisted of monosyllabic replies which B.J. blocked from her mind. Frustrated by the inability to complete her outburst, she now felt the impetus fading. Just as well, she admitted with a sigh of weary resignation. I've already said enough to insure the job at that dog kennel Darla mentioned. Blast! She rested her forehead on the cool glass. *Why did I have to fall in love with an impossible man?*

"B.J." She started at the sound of her name, then twisted her head to watch Taylor cradle the phone. "Pack," he said simply and moved to the door.

Closing her eyes, she tried to tell herself it was better that she leave, better not to be connected with him even as an employee. Nodding mutely, she turned back to the window.

"Enough for three days," he added in afterthought as his hand closed over the knob.

"What?" Thrown into confusion, she turned, staring with a mixture of grief and bewilderment.

"We'll be gone for three days. Be ready in fifteen minutes." Halting, Taylor's features softened suddenly at her clouded expression. "B.J., I'm not firing you. Give me credit for a bit more class than that."

She shook her head, washed with relief and the knowledge of the inevitable. He started to cross the room, then paused and merely leaned against the closed door.

"That was a call from the manager of one of my resorts. There's a bit of a problem, and I've got to see to it. You're coming with me."

"Coming with you?" Her fingers lifted to her temple as if she could smooth in understanding. "What on earth for?"

"In the first place, because I say so." He folded his arms across his chest and became the complete employer. "And secondly, because I like my managers well rounded. No pun intended," he added, smiling as her color rose. "This is a good opportunity for you to see how my other hotels are run."

"But I can't just leave at a moment's notice," she objected, as her mind struggled to cope with the new development. "Who'll take care of things here?"

"Eddie will. It's about time he had a bit more responsibility. You let him lean on you too much. You let all of them lean on you too much."

"But we have five new reservations over the weekend, and..."

"You're down to ten minutes, B.J.," he informed her with a glance at his watch. "If you don't stop arguing, you'll only have the clothes on your back to take with you."

Seeing all of her objections would be overruled, she tried not to think of what going away with Taylor would do to her nervous system. *Business,* she reminded herself. *Just business.*

Somewhat annoyed that he was already walking through the door, having taken it for granted that she was going with him, she called after him, "I can't simply pack because you say to."

He turned back, his temper fraying. "B.J."

"You never said where," she reminded him. "I don't know if I need mukluks or bikinis."

A ghost of a smile played on his lips before he answered. "Bikinis. We're going to Palm Beach."

B.J. was to find her surprises were not yet over for the morning. First, her last minute flurry of instructions was cut off by Taylor's order as she was bundled out of the dripping rain and into his car. On the drive to the airport, she mentally reviewed every possible disaster which could occur during her absence. She opened her mouth to enlighten Taylor only to be given a quelling look which had her suffering in silence.

At the airport, she found herself confronted not with a commercial jet, but with Taylor's private one, already primed for take-off. B.J. stood motionless staring at the small trim plane as he retrieved their luggage.

"B.J., don't stand in the rain. Go on up."

"Taylor." Unmindful of the rain which pelted her, B.J. turned to him. "I think there's something you should know. I'm not very good at flying."

"That's all right." He secured cases under his arm and grabbed her hand. "The plane does most of the work."

"Taylor, I'm serious," she objected, as he dragged her inside the plane.

"Do you get air sick? You can take a pill."

"No." She swallowed and lifted her shoulders. "I get paralyzed. Stewardesses have been known to stow me in the baggage compartment so I don't panic the other passengers."

He rubbed his hands briskly through her hair, scattering rain drops. "So, I've found your weakness. What are you afraid of?"

"Mostly of crashing."

"It's all in your head," he said easily as he helped her off with her jacket. "There's a term for it."

"Dying," she supplied, causing him to laugh again. Miffed by his amusement, she turned away to examine the plush luxury of the cabin. "This looks more like an apartment than a plane." She ran a hand over the soft maroon of a chair. "Everyone's entitled to a phobia," she muttered.

"You're absolutely right." His voice trembled on the edge of laughter. B.J. turned to snap at him but found his smile too appealing.

"You won't think it's so funny when I'm lying in a moaning heap on your shag carpet."

"Possibly not." He moved toward her and she stiffened in defense. Brooding down at her a moment, he searched her wary gray eyes. "B.J.," he began, "shall we call a moratorium on our disagreements? At least for the duration of the trip?"

"Well, I..." His voice was soft and persuasive, and she lowered her eyes to study the buttons of his shirt.

"An armed truce?" he suggested, capturing her chin between his thumb and forefinger and lifting her face. "With negotiations to follow?" He was smiling, his charming, utterly disarming smile. She knew resistance was hopeless.

"All right, Taylor." Unable to prevent her own smile from blossoming, she remained still as his finger lifted to trace it.

"Sit down and fasten your seat belt." He kissed her brow with an easy friendliness which left her weak.

B.J. found that the easy flow of his conversation from the moment of take off eased her tension. Incredibly, she felt no fear as the plane soared into the air.

"It's so flat and so warm!" B.J. exclaimed as she stepped off the plane steps and looked around her.

Taylor chuckled as he led the way to a sleek black Porsche. He exchanged a few words with a waiting attendant, accepted the keys, unlocked the door, and motioned B.J. inside.

"Where is your hotel?" she asked.

"In Palm Beach. This is West Palm Beach. We have to cross Lake Worth to get to the island."

"Oh!" Enchanted by roadside palms, she lapsed into silence.

The white, sandy soil and splashes of brilliant blossoms were so far removed from the scenery of her native New England, she felt as though she had entered another world. The waters of Lake Worth, separating Palm Beach from the mainland, sparkled blue and white under the afternoon sun. The oceanside was lined with resort hotels. B.J. recognized the elaborate initials *T.R.* atop a sleek white building which rose twelve stories over the Atlantic. Hundreds of windows winked back at her. Taylor pulled into the semi-circular macadam drive and stopped the car. B.J. narrowed her eyes against the streaming rays of the sun. The archway which formed the entrance was guarded by palms and semi-tropical plants, their tangle of color obviously well planned and scrupulously tended. The lawn spread, perfectly level and unbelievably green.

"Come," said Taylor, coming around to open the door for her. He helped her out of the car and led her inside.

To B.J. the lobby was a tropical paradise. The floor was flagstoned, the walls a half-circle of windows at the front. A center fountain played over a rocky garden, dotted with lush plants and ferns. B.J. saw that the interior was round, an open circle spiraling to the ceiling where a mural emulating the sky had been painted. The effect was one of limitless space. *How different from the cozy familiarity of the Lakeside Inn!* she thought.

"Ah, Mr. Reynolds." Her meditation was interrupted by the appearance of a slender, well dressed man with a shock of steel gray hair and a lean, bronzed face. "So good to see you."

"Paul." Taylor accepted the proffered hand and returned the

smile of greeting. "B.J., this is Paul Bailey, the manager. Paul, B.J. Clark."

"A pleasure, Miss Clark." B.J.'s hand was engulfed by a smooth, warm grasp. His eyes surveyed her fresh, slender beauty with approval. She found herself smiling back.

"See to our bags and I'll take Miss Clark up. After we've settled in a bit, I'll get back to you."

"Of course. Everything's quite ready." With another flash of teeth, he led the way to the registration desk and secured a key. "Your bags will be right up, Mr. Reynolds. Is there anything else you'd like?"

"Not at the moment. B.J.?"

"What?" B.J. was still admiring the luxurious lobby.

"Would you like anything?" Taylor smiled at her and brushed a curl from her cheek.

"Oh…no, nothing. Thank you."

With a final nod for Bailey, Taylor secured her hand in his and led her to one of the three elevators. They glided up in a cage of octagon glass high above the cluster of greenery.

When they reached the top floor, Taylor moved along the thick carpeting to unlock the door. B.J. entered and crossing the silent plush of ivory carpet, stared down from the dizzying height at the white beach which jutted out into an azure span of sea. In the distance, she could see the churning whitecaps and the flowing grace of gulls as they circled and dove.

"What an incredible view. I'm tempted to dive straight off the balcony." Turning, she caught Taylor watching her from the center of the room. She could not decipher the expression in his eyes. "This is lovely," she said to break the long silence.

She ran a finger over the smooth surface of an ebony bar and wondered if Darla had decorated the room. Grudgingly, she admitted to herself if this were the case, Darla had done a good job.

"Would you like a drink?" Taylor pushed a button cunningly concealed in the mirror tiles on the wall behind the bar. A panel slid open to reveal a fully stocked bar.

"Very clever," B.J. smiled. "Some club soda would be nice," she said, leaning elbows on the bar.

"Nothing stronger?" he asked as he poured the soda over crackling ice. "Come in," he responded to the quiet knock on the door.

"Your luggage, Mr. Reynolds." A red-and-black-uniformed bellboy carried in the cases. B.J. was conscious of his curious gaze and blushed self-consciously.

"Fine, just leave them there." He accepted the tip from Taylor and vanished, closing the door with quiet respect.

B.J. eyed the cases. Taylor's elegant gray sat neatly beside her practical brown. "Why did he bring it all in here?" Setting down her glass, she lifted her eyes. "Shouldn't he have just taken mine to my room?"

"He did." Taylor secured another bottle and poured himself a portion of Scotch.

"But, I thought this was your suite." B.J. glanced around the luxurious room again.

"It is."

"But you just said..." She faltered, as her color rose. "Surely you don't think I'm going to—to..."

"What did you have in mind?" Taylor inquired with infuriating amusement.

"You said you wanted me to see how one of your other hotels was run, you never said anything about...about..."

"You really must learn to complete a sentence, B.J."

"I'm not sleeping with you," she stated very positively, her eyes like two summer storm clouds.

"I don't believe I asked you to," he said lazily before he took an easy sip of Scotch. "There are two very adequate bedrooms in this suite. I'm sure you'll find yours comfortable."

Embarrassment flooded her cheeks. "I'm not staying in here with you. Everyone will think that I'm...that we're..."

"I've never known you to be quite so coherent." His mockery increased her wrath, and her eyes narrowed to dangerous slits. "In any case," he continued unperturbed, "the purity of your reputation is already in question. As you're traveling with me, it will naturally be assumed that we're lovers. As we know differently," he went on as her mouth dropped open, "that hardly matters. Of course, if you'd like to make rumor fact, I might be persuaded."

"Oh, you insufferable, egotistical, conceited..."

"Name calling can hardly be considered persuasion," Taylor admonished, patting her head in an infuriating manner. "I assume, therefore, you'll want your own bedroom?"

"As this is off season," B.J. began, gaining a tenuous grip on her temper, "I'm sure there are a surplus of available rooms."

Smiling, he ran a finger down her arm. "Afraid you won't be able to resist temptation, B.J.?"

"Of course not," she said though her senses tingled at his touch.

"Then that's settled," he said, finishing off his drink. "If you're harboring the notion that I'll be overcome by lust, there's a perfectly sturdy lock on your bedroom door. I'm going down to see Bailey; why don't you change and grab some time at the beach? Your room's the second door on your left down the hall." He pointed as he moved to the door and slipped through before she had time to frame a response.

Before lifting her case and beginning to unpack, B.J. thought of at least a half a dozen withering remarks she should have made. However, she soon regained her sense of proportion.

After all, it wasn't every day that she had the opportunity to indulge in such luxury. She might as well enjoy it. Besides, the suite was certainly large enough for both of them.

Slipping into brief tan shorts and a lime green halter, B.J. decided to finish her unpacking later and head for the beach.

Taylor had certainly made the most of nature's gift, offering a luxury playground with an ocean and sky backdrop. B.J. had seen the huge mosaic tiled pool for those who preferred its filtered water to the sea. On her way to the beach, she glimpsed at the expanse of tennis courts with palms and flowering shrubs skirting about the entrance gate. She had seen enough of the hotel's interior to be certain that Taylor left his guests wanting for nothing.

From the beach B.J. shaded her eyes and studied again the perfection of the imposing resort. It was, she admitted with a sigh, elegantly appealing. As far out of her realm as its owner. *Egg noodles and caviar,* she thought ruefully, reflecting both on the comparison between inn and resort and Taylor and herself. They simply don't belong on the same plate.

"Hello."

Startled, B.J. turned, blinked against the brilliant sun and stared at an even white smile in a bronzed face.

"Hello." Returning the smile with a bit more caution, B.J. studied the attractive face surrounded by thick masses of light, sun bleached hair.

"Aren't you going to give the ocean a try?"

"Not today."

"That's very unusual." He fell into step beside her as she began to cross the sand. "Usually everyone spends their first day roasting and splashing."

"How did you know it was my first day?" B.J. asked.

"Because I haven't noticed you here before, and I would have." He gave her an encompassing and intensely male survey. "And because you're still peaches and cream instead of parboiled."

"Hardly the time of year," B.J. commented, admiring the deep, even tan as he shrugged on his shirt. "I'd say you've been here for some time."

"Two years," he returned, with an appealing grin. "I'm the tennis pro, Chad Hardy."

"B.J. Clark." She paused on the tiled walkway which led to the hotel's beach entrance. "How come you're on the beach instead of the courts?"

"My day off," he explained and surprised her by winding the tips of her hair around his finger. "But if you'd like a private lesson, it could be arranged."

"No, thanks," she declined lightly and turned again toward the door.

"How about dinner?" Chad captured her hand, gently but insistently bringing her back to face him.

"I don't think so."

"A drink?"

She smiled at his persistence. "No, sorry, it's a bit early."

"I'll wait."

Laughing, she shook her head and disengaged her hand. "No, but I appreciate the offer. Goodbye, Mr. Hardy."

"Chad." He moved with her through the archway into the hotel's coolness. "What about tomorrow? Breakfast, lunch, a weekend in Vegas?"

B.J. laughed; such ingenuous charm was hard to resist. "I don't think you'll have any trouble finding a companion."

"I'm having a great deal of trouble securing the one I want," he countered. "If you had any compassion, you'd take pity on me."

With a rueful smile, B.J. surrendered. "All right, I wouldn't mind an orange juice."

In short order, B.J. found herself seated at an umbrella table beside the pool.

"It's not really that early," Chad objected when she adhered to her choice of fruit juice. "Most of the crowd is straggling in to wash off the sand and change for dinner."

"This hits the spot." She sipped from the frosted glass. Then, gesturing with one slender hand, she glanced around at green fan palms and scarlet blooms. "You must find it easy to work here."

"It suits me," Chad agreed, swirling his own drink. "I like the work, the sun." He lifted his glass and smiled with the half toast. "And the benefits." His smile widened. Before she had the opportunity to draw them away, his hand captured her fingers. "How long will you be here?"

"A couple of days." She let her hand lie limp, feeling a struggle would make her appear foolish. "This was actually a spur-of-the-moment trip rather than a vacation."

"Then I'll drink to spur-of-the-moment trip," said Chad.

The friendly, polished charm was potent, and B.J. could not resist beaming him a smile. "Is that your best serve?"

"Just a warm-up." Returning the smile, his grip on her hand tightened slightly. "Watch out for my ace."

"B.J."

Twisting her head, she stared up at Taylor, frowning above her. "Hello, Taylor. Are you finished with Mr. Bailey?"

"For the moment." His glance shifted to Chad, drifted over their joined hands and returned to her face. "I've been looking for you."

"Oh?" Feeling unaccountably guilty, B.J. nibbled her lip in a tell-tale sign of agitation. "I'm sorry, this is Chad Hardy," she began.

"Yes, I know. Hello, Hardy."

"Mr. Reynolds," Chad returned with a polite nod. "I didn't know you were in the hotel."

"For a day or two. When you've finished," he continued, giving B.J. the full benefit of a cold disapproving stare, "I suggest you come up and change for dinner. I don't think that outfit's suitable for the dining room." With a curt nod, he turned on his heel and stalked away.

"Well, well." Releasing her hand, Chad leaned back in his chair and studied B.J. with new interest. "You might have told me you were the big man's lady. I'm rather fond of my job here."

Her mouth opened and closed twice. "I am not Taylor's lady," B.J. spurted on her third try.

Chad's lips twisted in a wry grin. "You'd better tell him that. A pity." He sighed with exaggerated regret. "I was working on some interesting fantasies, but I steer clear of treading on dangerous ground."

Standing, he lifted her chin and gave her a rather wistful smile. "If you find yourself down here again without complications, look me up."

Chapter Ten

The emphatic slamming of the suite's door gave B.J. small satisfaction. Advancing with purpose on Taylor's bedroom, she pounded on his door.

"Looking for me?" The voice was dry.

She whirled around. For a moment, she could only gape at the sight of Taylor leaning against the bathroom door, clad only in a dark green towel tied low over lean hips. His hair fell in tendrils over the lean planes of his face.

"Yes, I..." She faltered and swallowed. "Yes," she repeated with more firmness as she recalled Chad's comments. "That was an uncalled for exhibition out there. You deliberately left Chad with the impression that I was your..." She hesitated, eyes darkening with outraged impotence, as she searched for the right word.

"Mistress?" Taylor suggested amiably.

B.J.'s pupils dilated with fury. "He at least used the term lady." Forgetting the corded arms and dark mat of hair covering his chest, she stalked forward until she stood toe to toe. "You did it on purpose, and I won't tolerate it."

"Oh really?" Had she not been so involved venting her own

anger, B.J. might have recognized the dangerous pitch of his voice. "It appears by the speed with which Hardy lured you into his corner, you're remarkably easy prey. I feel it's my obligation to look out for you."

"Find someone else to protect," she retorted. "I'm not putting up with it."

"Just what do you intend to do about it?" The simple arrogance of the question was accompanied by a like smile which robbed B.J. of all coherency. "If giving Hardy and others of his type the impression that you're my property keeps you from making a fool of yourself, that's precisely what I'll do. Actually," he continued, "you should be grateful."

"Grateful?" B.J. repeated, her voice rising. "Your property? *A fool of myself?* Of all the arrogant, unspeakable gall!"

Her arm pulled back with the intention of connecting her fist with his midsection, but she found it twisted behind her back with astonishing speed. Her body was crushed against the hard undraped lines of his.

"I wouldn't try that again." The warning was soft. "You wouldn't like the consequences." His free hand lowered to her hip, bringing her closer as she tried to back away. "Don't do that," he ordered, holding her still and trapped against him. "You'll just hurt yourself. It seems we've broken our truce." His words were light, though she saw the signs of lingering temper in his eyes.

"You started it." Her declaration was half-defiant, half-defensive. She kept her eyes level with sheer determination.

"Did I?" he murmured before he took her mouth.

She was washed by the familiar flood of need. Offering no struggle, she went willingly into the uncharted world where only the senses ruled. His hand released her arm in order to roam over the bareness of her back, and she circled his neck, wanting only to remain in the drifting heat and velvet darkness.

Abruptly, he set her free. She stumbled back against the wall, thrown off balance by the swiftness of her liberation.

"Go change." He turned and gripped the knob of his door.

B.J. reached out to touch his arm.

"Taylor..."

"Go change!" he shouted. She stumbled back again, eyes round and wide at the swift flare of violence. He slammed the door behind him.

B.J. retreated to her room to sort out her feelings. Was it injured pride? Or was it rage? She could not for the life of her tell.

The early sky lightened slowly from black to misty blue. The stars faded, then died as the sun still lay hidden beneath the horizon. B.J. rose, grateful the restless night was behind her.

She had shared an uncomfortably polite dinner with Taylor, the elegance of the dining room only adding to the sensation that she had stood aside and watched two strangers go through the motions of dining. Taylor's solicitous and unfamiliar formality had disturbed her more than his sudden seething fury. Her own responses had been stilted and cool. Immediately after dinner she pleaded fatigue and crept off unescorted to pass the evening hours alone and miserably awake in her room.

It had been late when she had heard Taylor's key in the lock, his footsteps striding down the hall to pause outside her room. She had held her breath as if he might sense her wakefulness through the panel. Not until she had heard the muffled sound of his door closing had she let it out again.

* * *

B.J. felt no better the next morning. The events of the day before had left her with a lingering sense of loss and sorrow. Though she knew that there was little hope, she had finally acknowledged to herself that she was in love with Taylor. But there was no point thinking about it.

She slipped on her bikini, grabbed a terry robe, and tiptoed from her room.

The view from the wide window in the living room drew her. With a sigh of pleasure, she moved closer to watch the birth of day. The sun had tinted the edge of sea and sky with rose-gold streaks. Pinks and mauves shot through the dawning sky.

"Quite a view."

With a gasp, B.J. spun around, nearly colliding with Taylor whose footsteps had been hidden by the thickness of carpet. "Yes," she returned as their hands lifted simultaneously to brush back the fall of her hair which tumbled to her cheek. "There's nothing so beautiful as a sunrise." Disturbed by his closeness, she found her own words silly.

He was clad only in short denim cut-offs, frayed at the cuffs.

"How did you sleep?" His voice was politely concerned.

She shrugged off his question, evading a direct lie. "I thought I'd take an early swim before the beach gets crowded."

Deliberately, he turned her to face him, while he searched her face with habitual thoroughness. "Your eyes are shadowed." His finger traced the mauve smudges as a frown deepened the angles of his face. "I don't believe I've ever seen you look tired before. You seem to have some inner vitality that continually feeds itself. You look pale and fragile, quite unlike the pigtailed brat I watched sliding into home plate."

His touch was radiating the weakness through her so she stepped back in defense. "I... It's just the first night in a strange bed."

"Is it?" His brow lifted. "You're a generous creature, B.J. You don't even expect an apology, do you?"

Charmed by his smile, her weariness evaporated. "Taylor, I want...I'd like it if we could be friends." She finished in an impulsive rush.

"Friends?" he repeated as the sudden boyish grin split his face. "Oh, B.J., you're sweet, if a bit slow." Taking both hands in his, he lifted them to his lips before speaking again. "All right, friend, let's go for a swim."

But for gulls, the beach was deserted, a stretch of white pure and welcoming. The air already glowed with the promise of heat and light. B.J. stopped and gazed around, pleased with the quiet and the solitude.

"It's like everyone went away."

"You're not much for crowds, are you, B.J.?"

"No, I suppose not." She turned to him with a lift of bare shoulders. "I enjoy people, but more on a one to one level. When I'm around people, I like to know who they are, what they need. I'm good with small problems. I can shore up a brick here, hammer a nail there. I don't think I'm equipped to construct an entire building the way you are."

"One can't keep a building standing without someone shoring up bricks and hammering nails."

She smiled, so obviously pleased and surprised by his observation that he laughed and tousled her hair. "I'll race you to the water."

Giving him a considering look, B.J. shook her head in reluctance. "You're a lot taller than I am. You have an advantage."

"You forget, I've seen you run. And——" His eyes dropped to the length of shapely legs. "For a small woman, you have amazingly long legs."

"Well." She drew the word out, lips pursed. "O.K." Without waiting for his assent, she streaked across the sand and plunged into the sea, striking out with long strokes.

She was brought up short by hands on her waist. Laughing, she struggled away, only to be caught and submerged in the ensuing tussle.

"Taylor, you're going to drown me," she protested as her legs tangled with his.

"That is not my intention," he informed her as he drew her closer. "Hold still a minute or you'll take yourself under again."

Relaxing in his hold, B.J. allowed him to keep them both afloat. She permitted herself a few moments of ecstasy cradled in his arms as the water pooled around them like a cool satin blanket. The change began like a gradual drizzle as she became more aware of his shoulder beneath her cheek, the possessive hold of the arm which banded her bare waist. Powerless to resist, she floated with him as his lips descended to the sleek cap of her hair, then wandered to tease the lobe of her ear with tongue and teeth before moving to the curve of her neck. His fingers traced the low line of the bikini snug at her hips as his mouth roamed her cheek in its journey to hers.

Her lips parted before he requested it, but his kiss remained gentle, the passion simmering just below the surface. His hand touched and fondled, slipping easily under the barrier of her brief top to trail over the curve of her breast. The water sighed gently as flesh met flesh.

What with gentle caresses, the drifting buoyancy of the sea, and the growing heat of the ascending sun B.J. fell into a trancelike state. Perhaps, she thought, mind and limbs lethargic, she was meant to float forever in his arms. She shivered with pleasure.

"You're getting cold," Taylor murmured, drawing her away to study her face. "Come on." He released her, leaving her without support in the sighing sea. The magic shattered. "We'll sit in the sun."

B.J. started for the shore with Taylor swimming easily beside her.

On the beach, she fanned her hair in the sun while Taylor stretched negligently beside her. She tried not to look at the strong planes of his face, his bronzed, glistening skin.

He told me how it would be, she reminded herself. Right from the beginning. I don't seem to be able to do anything about it and if I don't, I'll end up being just another Darla in his life. Bringing her knees to her chest, she rested her chin on them and stared at the distant horizon. He's attracted to me for some reason, perhaps because I'm different from other women in his life. I haven't their sophistication or experience and I suppose he finds that appealing and amusing. I don't know how to fight both loving him and wanting him. If it were just physical, I could avoid being hurt. If it were only an attraction, I could resist him.

She recalled suddenly his quick violence of the previous day and realized he was a man capable of employing whatever means necessary to gain an objective. At the moment, she knew he was playing her like a patient fisherman casting his line into calm waters. But ultimately, they both knew she would be captured in

his net. Though it might be silk, it would still lead to eventual disaster.

"You're very far away." Sitting up, Taylor tangled his fingers in her damp hair and turned her to face him.

Silently, she studied every plane and angle of his face, engraving them on both heart and mind. *There is too much strength there,* she thought, rocked by a surge of love. Too much virility, too much knowledge. She scrambled to her feet, needing to postpone the inevitable.

"I'm starving," she claimed. "Are you going to spring for breakfast? After all, I did win the race."

"Did you?" He rose as she pulled the short robe over the briefness of her bikini.

"Yes," she said, "positively." Picking up Taylor's light blue pullover, she held it out. "I was the undisputed winner." She watched as he dragged the snug, crew necked shirt over his head then bent to retrieve the towels.

"Then you should buy my breakfast." Smiling, he held out his hand. After a brief hesitation, she accepted.

"How do you feel about corn flakes?"

"Unenthusiastic."

"Well." Her shoulders moved in regret. "I'm afraid my funds are rather limited as I was hauled to Florida without ceremony."

"Your credit's good." He released her hand and swung a friendly arm around her shoulders. They moved away from the sea.

By mid afternoon, B.J. felt euphoric. There was a new, charming friendliness about Taylor that made her realize she liked him every bit as much as she loved him.

She was given a thorough if belated tour of the hotel, allowed to wander through the silver and cobalt lounge, linger in the two elegantly stocked boutiques and examine the enormous expanse of the steel and white kitchen. In the game room, she was provided with an endless supply of change as Taylor watched her reckless enthusiasm with tolerance.

Leaning against a machine, he looked on as she steered her computer car to another horrendous wreck. "You know," he commented as she held her hand for another quarter, "by the time you've finished, you'll have spent every bit as much as that dress in the boutique cost. Why is it, you'll take the money for these noisy machines, but you refuse to let me buy you that very appealing dress?"

"This is different," she said vaguely, maneuvering the car around obstructions.

"How?" He grimaced as she narrowly missed an unwary pedestrian and skidded around a corner.

"You never said if you worked out the problem," B.J. murmured as she twisted the wheel to avoid a slow moving vehicle.

"Problem?"

"Yes, the one you came down here to see to."

"Oh, yes." He smiled and brushed an insistent wisp from her cheek. "It's working out nicely."

"Oh, blast!" B.J. frowned as her car careened into a telephone pole, flipped through the air and landed with an impressive show of computer color and sound.

"Come on." Taylor grabbed her hand as she looked up hopefully. "Let's have some lunch before I go bankrupt."

On the sundeck above the pool, they enjoyed quiche Lorraine

and Chablis. A handful of people splashed and romped in the pale blue water. Toying with the remains of her meal, B.J. stared down at the swimmers and sun bathers. Her gaze swept to include the curve of beach before returning to Taylor. He was watching her, a small secret smile on his lips and in his eyes. She blinked in confused embarrassment.

"Is something wrong?" Battling the urge to wipe her cheek to see if it was smudged, she lifted her glass and sipped the cool wine.

"No, I just enjoy looking at you. Your eyes are constantly changing hues. One minute they're like peat smoke, and the next clear as a lake. You'll never be able to keep secrets; they say too much." His smile spread as her color rose. Her eyes shifted to the golden lights in her glass. "You're an incredibly beautiful creature, B.J."

She lifted her head, her eyes wide in surprise.

With a light chuckle, he captured her hand and brought it to his lips. "I don't suppose I should tell you that too often. You'll begin to see how true it is and lose that appealing air of innocence."

Rising, he maintained possession of her hand, pulling her to her feet. "I'm going to take you to the Health Club. You can get a first hand impression of how this place works."

"All right, but…"

"I'm leaving instructions that you're to have the complete routine," he interrupted. "And when I meet you at seven for dinner, I don't want to see any shadows under your eyes."

Transferred from Taylor's authority to a perfectly shaped brunette, B.J. was whirlpooled, saunaed, pummeled and massaged. For three hours, she was alternately steamed and sprayed, plied with iced fruit juice and submerged in churning water. Her first instinct was to retrieve her clothes and quietly slip out. After finding they had been conveniently cached out of sight, she submitted, and soon found tensions she had been unaware of possessing seeping out of her.

Stomach down on a high table, she sighed under the magic hands of the masseuse and allowed her mind to float in the twilight world of half sleep. Dimly, the conversation of two women enjoying the same wonder drifted across to her.

"I happened to be staying here two years ago...so incredibly handsome...what a marvelous catch... All that lovely money as well... The Reynolds empire."

At Taylor's name, B.J.'s eyes opened and her inadvertent eaves-dropping became deliberate.

"It's a wonder some smart woman hasn't snagged him yet." An auburn haired woman tucked a bright strand behind her ear and folded her arms under her chin.

"Darling, you can be sure scores have tried." Her brunette companion stifled a yawn and smiled with wry humor. "I don't imagine he's averse to the chase. A man like that thrives on feminine adulation."

"He's got mine."

"Did you see his companion? I caught a glimpse last night and again today by the pool."

"Mmm, I saw them when they arrived, but I was too busy looking at him to take much notice. A blonde, wasn't she?"

"Um-hum, though I don't think that pale wheat shade was a gift of nature."

B.J.'s first surge of outrage was almost immediately replaced by amusement. So, she decided, if I'm to be Taylor's temporary, if fictional mistress, I might as well hear the opinion of the masses.

"Do you think this one will get her hooks in? Who is she anyway?"

"That's precisely what I attempted to find out." The brunette grimaced and mirrored her companion's position of chin on arms. "It cost me twenty dollars to learn her name is B.J. Clark of all things. Beyond that, not even dear Paul Bailey knows anything. She just popped up out of the blue. She's never been here before. As for getting her hooks in." Elegantly tanned shoulders shrugged. "I wouldn't bet either way. His eyes simply devour her; it's enough to make you drool with envy."

B.J. raised a skeptical eyebrow.

"I suppose," the brunette went on, "huge gray eyes and masses of blond hair are appealing. And she is rather attractive in a whole-some, peaches and cream sort of way."

B.J. rose on her elbows and smiled across the room. "Thank you," she said simply, then lowered her head and grinned into the ensuing silence.

Chapter Eleven

*R*efreshed and pleased with herself, B.J. entered Taylor's suite, carrying a dress box under her arm. Though she had lost the minor tussle with the sales clerk in the boutique, she remained in high spirits. After her session in the spa, she had returned to the shop. Pointing to the gown of silver silk which Taylor had admired, she was prepared to surrender a large hunk of her bank account only to be told Mr. Reynolds had left instructions that any purchases she made were to be billed to him.

Annoyed by his arrogance, however generous, B.J. had argued with the implacable salesgirl. Ultimately, she had left the shop with the dress in hand vowing to see to the monetary details later.

If, she decided, pouring a substantial stream of bath salts under the rushing water of the tub, she was to portray the image of the mysterious lady from nowhere she was going to dress the part. She lowered herself into hot, frothy water and had just begun to relax when the door swung open.

"So, you're back," Taylor said easily, leaning against the door, "Did you enjoy yourself?"

"Taylor!" B.J. slid down in the tub, attempting to cover herself with the blanket of bubbles. "I'm having a bath!"

"Yes. I can see that, and little else. There's no need to drown yourself. Would you like a drink?" The question was pleasant and impersonal.

Recalling the overheard conversation in the spa, B.J.'s pride rallied. It's time, she decided, to give him back a bit of his own.

"That would be lovely." Fluttering her lashes, she hoped her expression was unconcerned. "Some sherry would be nice, if it's no bother."

Watching his brow lift in surprise, B.J. felt decidedly smug. "It's no trouble," he said as he retreated, leaving the door ajar. She prayed fervently the bubbles would not burst until she had a chance to leave the tub and slip into her robe.

"Here you are." Reentering, Taylor handed her a small glass shimmering with golden liquid.

B.J. gave him a smile and sipped. "Thanks. I'll be finished soon if you want the bath."

"Don't rush," he returned, delighted to see her coolness had somewhat rattled him, "I'll use the other."

"Suit yourself," she said agreeably, making sure her shrug was mild and did little to disturb her peaceful waters. Relieved that the door closed behind him, B.J. expelled a long breath and set the remains of her drink on the edge of the tub.

For a full five minutes, B.J. stared at her reflection in the full-length mirror. Silver silk draped crossways over the curve of each breast, narrowing to thin straps over her shoulders before continuing down her sides to leave her back bare to the waist. The skirt fell straight over her slender hips and legs, one side slit to mid-thigh. She had piled her hair in a loose knot on top of her head, allowing a few curling tendrils to escape and frame her face.

B.J. found the stranger in the mirror intimidating. With a flash of intuition, she knew B.J. Clark could not live up to the promises hinted at by the woman in the glass.

"Almost ready?" Taylor's knock and question jolted her out of her reverie.

"Yes, just coming." Shaking her head, she gave the reflection a reassuring smile. "It's just a dress," she reminded both B.J. Clarks and turned from the mirror.

Taylor's hand paused midway in the action of pouring pre-dinner drinks. He lifted his cigarette to his lips, inhaling slowly as he surveyed B.J.'s entrance. "Well," he said as she hesitated, "I see you bought it after all."

"Yes." With a surge of confidence, she crossed the room to join him. "As a woman of ill fame I felt my wardrobe inadequate."

"Care to elaborate?" He handed B.J. a delicate glass.

She accepted automatically. "Just a conversation I overheard in the spa." Her eyes lit with amusement, she set her glass on the bar. "Oh, Taylor, it was funny. I'm sure you have no idea how ardently your...ah...affairs are monitored." Describing her afternoon at the spa, she was unable to suppress her giggles.

"I can't tell you how it boosts the ego to be envied and touted as a woman of mystery! I certainly hope it's not discovered that I'm a hotel manager from Lakeside, Vermont. It would spoil it."

"No one would believe it anyway." He did not appear to be amused by her story as, frowning, he sipped at his drink.

Confused by his expression, B.J. asked, "Don't you like the dress after all?"

"I like it." He took her hand, the smile at last taking command of his mouth. "Obviously, we'll have to have champagne. You look much too elegant for anything else."

They began their meal with oysters Rockefeller and champagne. Their table sat high in the double level dining room, in front of a wide wall aquarium. As the London broil was served, B.J. sipped her wine and glanced around the room.

"This is a lovely place, Taylor." She gestured with a fine-boned hand to encompass the entire resort.

"It does the job." He spoke with the smooth confidence of one who knew the worth of his possessions.

"Yes, it certainly does. It runs beautifully. The staff is efficient and discreet, almost to the point of being invisible. You hardly know they're there, yet everything's perfect. I suppose it's elbow to elbow in here during the winter."

With a movement of his shoulders, he followed her gaze. "I try to avoid hitting the resorts during the heavy season."

"Our summer season will begin in a few weeks," she began, only to find her hand captured and her glass replenished with champagne.

"I've managed to keep you from bringing up the inn all day; let's see if we can finish the evening without it. When we get back tomorrow, we can talk about vacancies and cancellations. I don't discuss business when I'm having dinner with a beautiful woman."

B.J. smiled and surrendered. If only one evening remained of the interlude, she wanted to savor each moment.

"What do you discuss over dinner with a beautiful woman?" she countered, buoyed by the wine.

"More personal matters." His finger traced the back of her hand. "The way her voice flows like an easy river, the way her smile touches her eyes before it moves her mouth, the way her skin warms under my hand." With a low laugh, he lifted her hand, lips brushing the inside of her wrist.

Glancing up warily, B.J. asked, "Taylor, are you making fun of me?"

"No." His voice was gentle. "I have no intention of making fun of you, B.J."

Satisfied with his answer, she smiled and allowed him to lead the conversation into a lighter vein.

Flickering candles, the muted chink of crystal and silver, the low murmur of voices, Taylor's eyes meeting hers—it was an evening B.J. knew she would always remember.

"Let's go for a walk." Taylor rose and pulled back her chair. "Before you fall asleep in your champagne." Hand in hand they walked to the beach.

They walked in silence, enjoying each other and the night. Merging with the aroma of the sea and the night was the tenuous scent of orange blossoms. B.J. knew the fragrance would be forever melded with her memory of the man whose hand lay warm and firm over hers. Would she ever look at the moon again without thinking of him? Ever walk beneath the stars without remembering? Ever draw a breath without longing for him?

Tomorrow, she reflected, it would be business as usual, and a handful of days after, he would be gone. Only a name on a letterhead. Still, she would have the inn, she reminded herself. He'd said no more about changes. She'd have her home and her work and her memories, and that was much more than some ever had.

"Cold?" Taylor asked, and she shivered, afraid he had read her mind. "You're trembling." His arm slipped around her shoulders, bringing aching warmth. "We'd better go back."

Mutely, she nodded and forced tomorrows out of her mind. Relaxing, she felt the remnants of champagne mist pleasurably in her head.

"Oh, Taylor," she whispered as they crossed the lobby. "That's one of the women from the spa this afternoon." She inclined her head toward the brunette watching them with avid interest.

"Hmm." Taylor pushed the button for the glass enclosed elevator.

"Do you think I should wave?" B.J. asked before Taylor pulled her inside.

"No, I've a better idea."

Before she realized his intent, he had her gathered into his arms, silencing her protest with a mind-spinning kiss. Releasing her, he grinned down at the openly staring brunette.

B.J. turned to Taylor as the door of the suite shut behind him. "Really, Taylor, it's a crime I haven't a lurid past she could dig up."

"It's perfectly all right, she'll invent one for you. Want a brandy?" He moved to the bar and released the concealing panel.

"No, my nose is already numb."

"I see; is that a congenial condition?"

"It is," she stated, sliding onto a bar stool, "my gauge for the cautious consumption of liquor. When my nose gets numb, I've already had one more than my limit."

"I see." Turning, he poured amber liquid into a solitary snifter. "Obviously, my plans to ply you with liquor is doomed to fail."

"I'm afraid so."

"What's your weakness, B.J.?" The question was so unexpected she was caught unaware. *You,* she almost answered but caught herself in time. "I'm a pushover for soft lights and quiet music."

"Is that so?"

Magically, the lights lowered and music whispered through the room.

"How did you do that?"

He rounded the bar and stood in front of her. "There's a panel in back of the bar."

"The wonders of technology." Nerves prickling, she tensed like a cornered cat when his hand took her arm.

"I want to dance with you." He drew her to her feet. "Take the pins out of your hair. It smells like wildflowers; I want to feel it in my hands."

"Taylor, I..."

"Ssh." Slowly, he took out the pins until her hair tumbled free over her shoulders. Then, his fingers combed through the length of it before he gathered her close in his arms.

He moved gently to the music, keeping her molded against him. Her tension flowed away, replaced by a sleepy excitement. Her cheek rested naturally in the curve of his shoulder, as if they had danced countless times before, would dance countless times again.

"Are you going to tell me what B.J. stands for?" he murmured against her ear.

"No one knows," she responded hazily as his fingers followed the tingling delight along her bare skin. "Even the F.B.I. is baffled."

"I suppose I'll have to get it from your mother."

"She doesn't remember." She sighed and snuggled closer.

"How do you sign official papers?" His hand caressed the small of her back.

"Just B.J., I always use B.J."

"On a passport?"

She shrugged, her lips unconsciously brushing his neck, her cheek nuzzling the masculine roughness of his chin. "I haven't got one. I've never needed one."

"You need one to fly to Rome."

"Yes, I'll make sure I have one the next time I do. But I'd sign it Bea Jay." She grinned, knowing he would not realize she had just answered his question. She lifted her face to smile at him and found her lips captured in a gentle, teasing kiss.

"B.J.," he murmured and drew her away before her lips were satisfied. "I want…"

"Kiss me again, Taylor." Sweet and heavy, love lay on her. "Really kiss me," she whispered, shutting out the voice of reason. Her eyes fluttered closed as she urged his mouth back to hers.

He said her name again, the words soft on the lips which clung to his in silent request. With a low groan, he crushed her against him.

He swept her feet off the floor as his mouth took hers with unbridled hunger. In dizzying circles, the room whirled as she felt herself lowered to the thick plush of carpet. Unrestrained, his mouth savaged the yielding softness of hers, tongue claiming the sweet moistness. His hand pushed aside the thin silk of her bodice, seeking and finding the smooth promise for more, his mouth and hands roaming over her, finding heat beneath the cool silk, fingers trailing up the slit of her skirt until they captured the firm flesh of her thigh.

Tossed on the turbulent waves of love and need, B.J. responded with a burst of fire. His possession of her mouth and flesh was desperate. She answered by instinct, moving with a woman's hidden knowledge as he took with insatiable appetite the fruits she offered. Her own hands, no longer shy, found their way under his jacket to explore the hard ripple of muscles of his back and shoulders, half-terrified, half-delighting in their strength. From the swell and valley of her breasts, his mouth traveled, burning, tantalizing, to burrow against her neck. Her own lips sought to discover his taste and texture, to assuage her new and throbbing hunger.

His loving had lost all gentleness, his mouth and hands now bringing painful excitement. Her fragile innocence began to dissolve with the ancient cravings of womanhood. B.J. began to tremble with fear and anticipation.

Taylor's mouth lifted from the curve of her neck, and he stared into the eyes cloudy with desire and uncertainty. Abruptly he rose and pulled her to her feet. "Go to bed," he commanded shortly. Turning to the bar, he poured himself another brandy.

Dazed by the abruptness of the rejection, B.J. stood frozen.

"Didn't you hear me? I said go to bed." Downing half his brandy, Taylor pulled out a cigarette.

"Taylor, I don't understand. I thought..." A hand lifted to push at her hair, her eyes liquid and pleading. "I thought you wanted me."

"I do." He drew deep on his cigarette. "Now, go to bed."

"Taylor." The fury in his eyes caused her to flinch.

"Just get out of here before I forget all the rules."

B.J. straightened her shoulders and swallowed her tears. "You're the boss." She ignored the swift flame of temper in his eyes and plunged on. "But I want you to know, what I offered you tonight was a one-time deal. I'll never willingly go into your arms again. From now on, the only thing between you and me is the Lakeside Inn."

"We'll leave it at that for now," he said in curt agreement as he turned away and poured another drink. "Just go to bed."

B.J. ran from the room and turned the lock on her door with an audible click.

Chapter Twelve

$\mathcal{B.J.}$ threw herself into the inn's routine like a bruised child returning to a mother's arms. She and Taylor had flown from Florida to Vermont in almost total silence, he working on his papers while she had buried herself in a magazine. Avoiding Taylor for the next two days was easy. He made no effort to see her. Annoyance made hurt more tolerable. B.J. worked with dedication to construct a wall of resentment to shield the emptiness she would experience when he left both the inn and her.

Furthering her resentment was the stubborn presence of Darla Trainor. Although B.J. observed Taylor was not often in her company, her mere existence rubbed the sore of wounded pride. Seeing Darla was a constant reminder of B.J.'s uncomfortable and confusing relationship with Taylor.

B.J. knew she could not have mistaken the desire he had felt for her the last night in Florida. She concluded, watching Darla's sensuous elegance, that he had ultimately been disappointed in her lack of experience in the physical demands of love.

Wanting to avoid any unnecessary contact with Taylor, B.J. established her office in her room for the duration of his stay. Buried to her elbows in paperwork one afternoon, she jumped and scattered receipts as the quiet afternoon was shattered by screams and scrambling feet above her head. Racing to the third floor, B.J. followed the sounds into 314. For a moment she could only stand in the doorway and gape at the tableau. In the center of the braid rug, Darla Trainor was engaged in a major battle with one of the housemaids. A helpless Eddie was caught in the middle, his pleas for peace ignored.

"Ladies, ladies, please." Taking her life in her hands, B.J. plunged into the thick of battle and attempted to restore order. Hands and mixed accusations flew. "Louise, Miss Trainor is a guest! What's gotten into you?" She tugged, without success, on the housemaid's arm, then switched her attention to Darla. "Please, stop shouting, I can't understand." Frustrated because she was shouting herself, B.J. lowered her voice and tried to pull Darla away. "Please, Miss Trainor, she's half your size and twice your age. You'll hurt her."

"Take your hands off me!" Darla flung out an arm, and by accident or design, her fist connected, sending B.J. sprawling against the bedpost. The light shattered into fragments, then smothered with darkness as she slid gently to the floor.

"B.J." A voice called from down a long tunnel. B.J. responded with a moan and allowed her eyes to open into slits. "Lie still," Taylor ordered. Gingerly, she permitted her eyes to open further and focused on his lean features. He was leaning over her, his face lined with concern while he stroked the hair away from her forehead.

"What happened?" She ignored his command and attempted to sit up. Taylor pushed her back against the pillow.

"That's precisely what I want to know." As he glanced around, B.J. followed his gaze. Eddie sat on a small settee with his arm around a sniffling Louise. Darla stood by the window, her profile etched in indignation.

"Oh." Memory clearing, B.J. let out a long breath and shut her eyes. Unconsciousness, she decided, had its advantages. "The three of them were wrestling in the middle of the room. I'm afraid I got in the path of Miss Trainor's left hook."

The hand stroking her cheek stopped as Taylor's fingers tensed against her skin. "She hit you?"

"It was an accident, Taylor." Darla interrupted B.J.'s response, her eyes shining with regret and persecution. "I was simply trying to take these tacky curtains down when this…this maid—" she gestured regally toward Louise "—this maid comes in and begins shouting and pulling on me. Then he's shouting—" She fluttered a hand toward Eddie before passing it across her eyes. "Then Miss Clark appears from nowhere, and she begins pulling and shouting. It was a dreadful experience." With a long, shuddering sigh, Darla appeared to collect herself. "I only tried to push her away. She had no business coming into my room in the first place. None of these people belong in my room."

"She had no business trying to take down those curtains," Louise chimed in, wringing Eddie's handkerchief. She waved the soggy linen until all eyes shifted to the window in question. The white chintz hung drunkenly against the frame. "She said they were out-of-date and impractical like everything else in this place. I washed those curtains myself two weeks ago." Louise placed a hand on her trembling bosom. "I was not going to have her soiling them. I asked her very nicely to stop."

"Nicely?" Darla exploded. "You attacked me."

"I only attacked her," Louise countered with dignity, "when she wouldn't come down. B.J., she was standing on the Bentwood chair. Standing on it!" Louise buried her face in Eddie's shoulder, unable to go on.

"Taylor." Tucking an errant lock behind her ear, Darla moved toward him, blinking moist eyes. "You aren't going to allow her to speak to me that way, are you? I want her fired. She might have injured me. She's unstable." Darla placed a hand on his arm as the first tear trembled on her lashes.

Infuriated by the display of helpless femininity, B.J. rose. She ignored both Taylor's restraining hand and the throbbing in her head. "Mr. Reynolds, am I still manager of this inn?"

"Yes, Miss Clark."

B.J. heard the annoyance in his voice and added it to her list of things to ignore. "Very well. Miss Trainor, it falls under my jurisdiction as manager of the inn to oversee all hirings and firings. If you wish to lodge a formal complaint, please do so in writing to my attention. In the meantime, I should warn you that you will be held responsible for any damages done to the furnishings of your room. You should know, as well, that the inn will stand behind Louise in this matter."

"Taylor." Nearly sputtering with anger, Darla turned back to him. "You're not going to allow this?"

"Mr. Reynolds," B.J. interrupted, wishing for a bottle of aspirin and oblivion. "Perhaps you'll take Miss Trainor to the lounge for a drink, and we can discuss this matter later."

After a brief study, Taylor nodded. "All right, we'll talk later. Rest in your room for the remainder of the day. I'll see you're not disturbed."

B.J. accepted the display of gratitude and sympathy by both Eddie and Louise before trudging down to her room. Stepping over scattered papers, she secured much needed aspirin then curled up on the quilt of her bed. Dimly, she heard the door open and felt a hand brush through her hair. The grip of sleep was too strong, and she could not tell if the elusive kiss on her mouth was dream or reality.

When she woke up the throbbing had decreased to a negligible ache. Sitting up, B.J. stared at the neat stack of papers on her desk. Maybe it was a dream, she mused, confused by the lack of disorder on her floor. She touched the back of her head and winced as her fingers contacted with a small lump. Maybe I picked them up and don't remember. It's always the mediator who gets clobbered, she thought in disgust, and prepared to go downstairs to confront Taylor. In the lobby, she came upon Eddie, Maggie and Louise in a heated, low-voiced debate. With a sigh, she moved toward them to restore order.

"Oh, B.J." Maggie started with comical guilt. "Mr. Reynolds said you weren't to be disturbed. How are you feeling? Louise said that Miss Trainor gave you a nasty lump."

"It's nothing." She glanced from one solemn face to the next. She moved her shoulders in resignation. "All right, what's the problem?"

The question produced a jumble of words from three different tongues. Pampering her still aching head, B.J. held up a hand for silence. "Eddie," she decided, choosing at random.

"It's about the architect," he began, and she raised her brows in puzzlement.

"What architect?"

"The one who was here when you were in Florida. Only we didn't know he was an architect. Dot thought he was an artist because he was always walking around with a pad and pencil and making drawings."

Resigning herself to a partially coherent story, B.J. prompted, "Drawings of what?"

"Of the inn," Eddie announced with a flourish. "But he wasn't an artist."

"He was an architect," Maggie interrupted, unable to maintain her silence. Eddie shot her a narrow-eyed frown.

"And how do you know he was an architect?" After asking, B.J. wondered why it mattered. Her wandering attention was soon drawn back with a jolt.

"Because Louise heard Mr. Reynolds talking to him on the phone."

B.J.'s gaze shifted to the housemaid as a hollow feeling grew in the pit of her stomach. "How did you hear, Louise?"

"I wasn't eavesdropping," she claimed with dignity, then amended as B.J. raised her brows. "Well, not really, until I heard him talking about the inn. I was going to dust the office, and since Mr. Reynolds was on the phone, I waited outside. When I heard him say something about a new building, and he said the man's name, Fletcher, I remembered Dot talking about this man named

Fletcher making sketches of the inn." She gave the group a small smile in self-reward for her memory. "Anyway, they talked awhile, technical sort of things about dimensions and timber. Then Mr. Reynolds said how he appreciated the Fletcher person not letting on he was an architect until he had everything settled."

"B.J.," Eddie began urgently, grabbing her arm. "Do you think he's going to remodel the inn after all? Do you think he's going to let us all go?"

"No." Feeling her head increase its throbbing, B.J. repeated more emphatically, "No, it's just some mix up, I'll see about it. Now, you all go back to work and don't spread this around anymore."

"It's no mix up." Darla glided over to the group.

"I told you three to go back to work," B.J. ordered in a voice which they recognized as indisputable. They dispersed, waiting until a safe distance before murmuring among themselves. "If you'll pardon me, Miss Trainor, I'm busy."

"Yes, Taylor's quite anxious to see you."

Cursing herself, B.J. nibbled at the bait. "Is he?"

"Oh, yes. He's ready to tell you about his plans for this little place. It's quite a challenge." She surveyed the lobby with the air of one planning a siege.

"What exactly do you know of his plans?" B.J. demanded.

"You didn't really think he intended to leave this place in this condition simply because you want him to?" With a light laugh, Darla brushed away a fictional speck of dust from her vivid blue blouse. "Taylor is much too practical for grand gestures. Though, he might keep you on in some minor capacity once the alterations are complete. You're hardly qualified to manage one of his resorts, but he does seem to think you have some ability. Of course, if I were you, I'd pack up and bow out now to spare myself the humiliation."

"Are you saying," B.J. began, spacing words with great care, "that Taylor has made definite plans to convert the inn into a resort?"

"Well, of course." Darla smiled indulgently. "He'd hardly need me and an architect otherwise, would he? I wouldn't worry. I'm sure he'll keep the bulk of your staff on, at least temporarily."

With a final smile, Darla turned and left B.J. staring at her retreating back.

After the first flow of despair, fury bubbled. She took the steps two at a time and slammed into her room. Minutes later, she sped out again, taking stairs in a headlong flight and stomping into the office unannounced.

"B.J." Rising from the desk, Taylor studied her furious face. "What are you doing out of bed?"

For an answer, she slammed the paper on his desk. He lifted it, scanning her resignation. "It seems we've been through this before."

"You gave me your word." Her voice trembled at the breach of trust but she lifted her chin. "You can tear that one up too, but it won't change anything. Find yourself a new patsy, Mr. Reynolds. I quit!"

Streaking from the room, she collided bodily with Eddie, brushed him aside and rushed up the stairs. In her room, she pulled out her cases and began to toss articles in them at random.

Clothing, cosmetics, knick-knacks, whatever was close at hand was dumped, until the first case overflowed.

She stopped her frantic activities to whirl around at the metallic click of the lock. The door opened to admit Taylor.

"Get out!" she commanded, wishing fleetingly she was big enough to toss him out. "This is my room until I leave."

"You're making one beautiful mess," he observed calmly. "You might as well stop that, you're not going anywhere."

"Yes, I am." She caught herself before she tossed her asparagus fern among her lingerie. "I'm leaving just as fast as I can pack. Not only is working for you intolerable, but being under the same roof is more than I can stand. You promised!" She spun to face him, cursing the mist which clouded her eyes. "I believed you. I trusted you. How could I have been so stupid! There's no way I could have prevented you once you'd made your decision, and I would have adjusted somehow. You could have been honest with me."

Tears were spilling over with more speed than she could blink them away, and impatiently she brushed at them with the back of her hand. "Oh!" She spun away to pull pictures from the wall. "I wish I were a man!"

"If you were a man, we'd have had no problem to begin with. If you don't stop tearing up the room, I'll have to stop you. I think you've been battered enough for one day."

She heard it in his voice, the calm control, the half-amused exasperation. Despair for her abiding love merged with fury at his betrayal.

"Just leave me alone!"

"Lie down, B.J., and we'll talk later."

"No, don't you touch me," she ordered as he made to take her arm. "I mean it, Taylor, don't touch me!"

At the desperation in her voice, he dropped his hand to his side. "All right then." The first warning signals of anger touched his face. In the cool precision of his voice, she could hear the danger. "Suppose you tell me what exactly it is I've done?"

"You know very well."

"Spell it out for me," he interrupted, moving away and lighting a cigarette.

"That architect you brought here while we were in Florida."

"Fletcher?" Taylor cut her off again, but this time he gave her his full attention. "What about him?"

"What about him?" B.J. repeated incredulously. "You brought him here behind my back, making all his little drawings and plans. You probably took me to Florida just to get me out of the way while he was here."

"That was a consideration."

His easy admission left her speechless. A wave of pain washed over her, reflecting in her eyes.

"B.J." Taylor's expression became more curious than angry. "Suppose you tell me precisely what you know."

"Darla was only too happy to enlighten me." Turning away, she assuaged the hurt with more furious packing. "Go talk to her."

"She's gone by now. I told her to leave, B.J., did you think I'd let her stay after she hit you?" The soft texture of his voice caused her hands to falter a moment. Quickly, she forced them to move again. "What did she say to you?"

"She told me everything. How you'd brought in the architect

to draw up plans for turning the inn into a resort. That you're going to bring in someone to manage it, how…" Her voice broke. "It's bad enough you've been lying to me, Taylor, bad enough you broke your word, but that's personal. What is more important is that you're going to change the whole structure of this community, alter dozens of lives for a few more dollars you don't even need. Your resort in Palm Beach is beautiful and perfect for where and what it is, but the inn…"

"Be quiet, B.J." He crushed out his cigarette then thrust his hands in his pockets. "I told you before, I make my own decisions. I called Fletcher in for two reasons." A swift gesture of his hand haltered her furious retort. "One, to design a house for a piece of property my agent picked up for me last week. It's about ten miles outside of town, five acres on a hill overlooking the lake. You probably know it."

"Why do you need…"

"The second purpose," he continued, ignoring her, "was to design an addition to the inn, adhering to its present architecture. The office space is just too limited. Since I plan to move my base from New York to the inn after we're married, I require larger accommodations."

"I don't see…" Her words stumbled to a halt, as she stared into calm brown eyes. A medley of emotions played through her, eradicating the ache in her head. "I never agreed to marry you," she managed at length.

"But you will," he countered and leaned against her desk. "In the meantime, you can ease the various minds downstairs that the inn will remain as is, and you'll remain in the position of manager with some adjustments."

"Adjustments?" She could only parrot his last word and sink into a chair.

"I have no problem basing my business in Vermont, but I won't base my marriage in a hotel. Therefore, we'll live in the house when it's completed, and Eddie can take over some of your duties. You'll also have to be free to travel from time to time. We leave for Rome in three weeks."

"Rome?" she echoed him again, dimly remembering his speaking of Rome and passports.

"Yes, your mother's sending your birth certificate so you can see to getting a passport."

"My mother?" Unable to sit, B.J. rose and paced to the window, trying to clear the fog which covered her brain. "You seem to have everything worked out very neatly." She struggled for control. "I don't suppose it occurred to you to ask my feelings on the matter?"

"I know your feelings." His hands descended to her shoulders, and she stiffened. "I told you once, you can't keep secrets with those eyes."

"I guess it's very convenient for you that I happen to be in love with you." She swallowed, focusing on the gleam of the sun as it filtered through the pines on the hillside.

"It makes things less complicated." His fingers worked at the tension in her shoulders but she held herself rigid.

"Why do you want to marry me, Taylor?"

"Why do you think?" She felt his lips in her hair and squeezed her eyes shut.

"You don't have to marry me for that, and we both know it."

Taking a deep breath, she gripped the windowsill tighter. "That first night you came to my room, you'd already won."

"It wasn't enough." His arms circled her waist and brought her back against him. She struggled to keep her mind clear. "The minute you swaggered into the office with invisible six guns at your hips, I made up my mind to marry you. I knew I could make you want me, I'd felt that the first time I held you, but the night in your room, you looked up at me, and I knew making you want me wasn't enough. I wanted you to love me."

"So——" she moved her shoulders as if it was of little consequence "——you comforted yourself with Darla in the meantime."

She was spun around so quickly, her hair flew out to fall over her face, obscuring vision. "I never touched Darla or anyone from the first minute I saw you. That little charade in the nightgown was strictly for your benefit, and you were stupid enough to fall for it. Do you think I could touch another woman when I had you on my mind?"

Without giving her time to answer, his mouth closed over hers, commanding and possessive. His arms banded her waist, dragging her against him. "You've been driving me crazy for nearly two weeks." Allowing her time to draw a quick breath, his mouth crushed hers again. Slowly, the kiss altered in texture, softening, sweetening, his hand moving with a tender lightness which drugged her reason.

"B.J.," he murmured, resting his chin on her hair. "It would be less intimidating if you owned a few more pounds and inches. I've had a devil of a time fighting my natural instincts. I don't want to hurt you, and you're too small and much too innocent." Lifting her chin, he framed her face with his hands. "Have I told you yet that I love you?"

Her eyes grew wide, her mouth opening, but powerless to form sound. She shook her head briskly and swallowed the obstruction in her throat.

"I didn't think I had. Actually, I think I was hit the minute you stood up from home plate, turned those eyes on me and claimed you were absolutely safe." He bent down and brushed her lips.

She threw her arms around his neck as though he might vanish in a puff of smoke. "Taylor, why have you waited so long?"

Drawing her away, he lifted a brow in amusement, reminding her of the brevity of their relationship.

"It's been years," she claimed, burying her face in his shoulder as joy washed over her. "Decades, centuries."

"And during the millennium," he replied, stroking fingers through her hair, "you've been more exasperating than receptive. The day I came into the lounge and found you ticking off bourbon bottles, I had hoped to start things along a smooth road, but you turned on the ice very effectively. The next day in your room, when you switched to fire, it was very illuminating. The things you said made a great deal of sense, so I decided a change of setting and attitude were in order. Providentially, Bailey called from Florida."

"You said you had to go to Palm Beach to help him with a problem."

"I lied," he said simply, then laughed with great enjoyment at her astonishment. "I had planned," he began, dropping into a chair and pulling her into his lap, "to get you away from the inn for a couple of days. More important to have you to myself. I wanted you relaxed and perhaps a bit off guard." He laughed again and nuzzled her ear. "Of course, then I had to see you sitting with Hardy and looking like a fresh peach ripe for picking."

"You were jealous." Indescribably pleased, she sighed and burrowed closer.

"That's a mild word for it."

They spent the next few minutes in mutually agreeable silence. Taylor lingered over the taste of her mouth, his hand sliding beneath the barrier of her shirt. "I was quite determined to do things properly, hence the dinner and wine and soft music. I had fully intended to tell you I loved you and ask you to marry me that last night in Florida."

"Why didn't you?"

"You distracted me." His lips trailed along her cheek, reminding her of the power of their last night together. "I had no intention of allowing things to progress the way they did, but you have a habit of stretching my willpower. That night it snapped. Then, I felt you trembling, and your eyes were so young." He sighed and rested his cheek on her hair. "I was furious with myself for losing control of the situation."

"I thought you were furious with me."

"It was better that you did. If I had told you then how I felt about you, nothing would have stopped me from taking you. I was in no frame of mind to introduce you gently to the ways of love. I've never needed anyone so much in my life as I needed you that night."

Round and liquid with love, her eyes lifted to his. "Do you need me, Taylor?"

His hand lifted to brush back her hair. The arm cradling her shifted her closer. "You look like a child," he murmured, tracing her lips with his finger. "A child's mouth, and I can't seem to do without the taste of it. Yes, B.J., I need you."

His mouth lowered, featherlight, but her arm circled his neck and demanded more. The pressure increased, and the door opened to the world of heat and passion. She felt his hand on her breast, never aware that the buttons of her shirt had been loosened. Her fingers tightened in his hair, willing him to prolong the ecstasy.

His mouth moved to her brow, then rested on her hair, his fingers tracing lightly over her bare skin. "You can see why I've been keeping away from you the last day or so."

With a soft sound of agreement, she buried her face against his shoulder.

"I wanted to get everything set up before I got near you again. I could have done with one more day; we still need a marriage license."

"I'll talk to Judge Walker," she murmured, "if you want one quickly. He's Eddie's uncle."

"Small towns are the backbone of America," Taylor decided. He pulled her close to cover her mouth again when a frantic knock sounded on the door.

"B.J." Eddie's voice drifted through the panel. "Mrs. Frank wants to feed Julius, and I can't find his dinner. And the Bodwin sisters are out of sunflower seeds for Horatio."

"Who's Horatio?" Taylor demanded.

"The Bodwin's parakeet."

"Tell him to feed Horatio to Julius," he suggested, giving the door a scowl.

"It's a thought." Lingering on it briefly, B.J. cast it aside. "Julius's dinner is on the third shelf right hand side of the fridge," she called out. "Send someone into town for a package of sunflower seeds. Now, go away, Eddie, I'm very busy. Mr. Reynolds and I are in conference." With a smile, she circled Taylor's neck again. "Now, Mr. Reynolds, perhaps you'd like my views on the construction of this house you're planning as well as my educated opinion on the structure of your office space."

"Be quiet, B.J."

"You're the boss," she agreed the moment before their lips met.

TEMPTATION

This book is dedicated with gratitude
and affection to Nancy Jackson.

Chapter One

"If there's one thing I hate," Eden mumbled, "it's six o'clock in the morning."

Sunlight poured through the thinly screened windows of the cabin and fell on the wooden floor, the metal bars of her bunk, and her face. The sound of the morning bell echoed dully in her head. Though she'd known that long, clanging ring for only three days, Eden already hated it.

For one fanciful moment, she buried her face under the pillow, imagining herself cuddled in her big four-poster. The Irish-linen sheets would smell ever-so-slightly of lemon. In her airy pastel bedroom, the curtains would be drawn against the morning, the scent of fresh flowers sweetening the air.

The pillowcase smelled of feathers and detergent.

With a grunt, Eden tossed the pillow to the floor, then struggled to sit up. Now that the morning bell had stopped, she could hear the cries of a couple of excited crows. From the cabin directly across the compound came a happy blast of rock music. With glazed eyes, she watched Candice Bartholomew bound out of the adjoining bunk. Her sharp-featured pixie's face was split by a grin.

"Morning." Candy's long, clever fingers ran through her thatch of red hair like scoops, causing it to bounce into further disarray. Candy was, Eden had always thought, all bounce. "It's a beautiful day," she announced, in a voice as cheerful as the rest of her. Watching her friend stretch in frilly baby-doll pajamas, Eden gave another noncommittal grunt. She swung her bare legs off the mattress and contemplated the accomplishment of putting her feet on the floor.

"I could grow to hate you." Eden's voice, still husky with sleep, carried the rounded tones of her finishing-school education. Eyes shut, she pushed her own tousled blond hair away from her face.

Grinning, Candy tossed open the cabin door so that she could breathe in the fresh morning air while she studied her friend. The strong summer sunlight shot through Eden's pale hair, making it look fragile where it lay against her forehead and cheeks. Her eyes remained shut. Her slender shoulders slumped, she let out an enormous yawn. Candy wisely said nothing, knowing Eden didn't share her enthusiasm for sunrise.

"It can't be morning," Eden grumbled. "I swear I only lay down five minutes ago." Resting her elbows on her knees, she dropped her face into her hands. Her complexion was creamy, with just a suggestion of rose on the crest of her cheekbones. Her nose was small, with a hint of an upward tilt at the tip. What might have been a coolly aristocratic face was gentled by a full, generous mouth.

Candy took in one last breath of air, then shut the door. "All you need is a shower and some coffee. The first week of camp's the toughest, remember?"

Eden opened wide, lake-blue eyes. "Easy for you to say. You're not the one who fell in the poison ivy."

"Still itching?"

"A little." Because her own foul mood was making her feel guilty, Eden managed a smile. Everything softened, eyes, mouth, voice. "In any case, this is the first time we're the campees instead of the campers." Letting out another fierce yawn, she rose and tugged on a robe. The air coming through the screens was fresh as a daisy, and chilly enough to make Eden's toes curl. She wished she could remember what she'd done with her slippers.

"Try under the bunk," Candy suggested.

Eden bent down and found them. They were embroidered pink silk, hardly practical, but it hadn't seemed worthwhile to invest in another pair. Putting them on gave her an excuse to sit down again. "Do you really think five consecutive summers at Camp Forden for Girls prepared us for this?"

Haunted by her own doubts, Candy clasped her hands together. "Eden, are you having second thoughts?"

Because she recognized distress in the bubbly voice, Eden buried her own doubts. She had both a financial and emotional interest in the newly formed Camp Liberty. Complaining wasn't going to put her on the road to success. With a shake of her head, she walked over to squeeze Candy's shoulder. "What I have is a terminal case of morning crankiness. Let me get that shower, then I'll be ready to face our twenty-seven tenants."

"Eden." Candy stopped her before she closed the bathroom door. "It's going to work, for both of us. I know it."

"I know it, too." Eden closed the bathroom door and leaned against it. She could admit it now, while she was alone. She was scared to death. Her last dime, and her last ray of hope, were tied up in the six cabins, the stables and the cafeteria that were Camp Liberty. What did Eden Carlbough, former Philadelphia socialite, know about managing a girls' summer camp? Just enough to terrify her.

If she failed now, with this, could she pick up the pieces and go on? Would there be any pieces left? Confidence was what was needed, she told herself as she turned the taps on. Once inside the narrow shower stall, she gave the tap optimistically marked HOT another twist. Water, lukewarm, dripped out halfheartedly. Confidence, Eden thought again as she shivered under the miserly spray. Plus some cold hard cash and a whole barrel of luck.

She found the soap and began to lather with the soft-scented French milled she still allowed herself to indulge in. A year ago she would never have considered something as lowly as soap an indulgence.

A year ago.

Eden turned so that the rapidly cooling water hit her back. A year ago she would have risen at eight, had a leisurely, steaming shower, then breakfasted on toast and coffee, perhaps some shirred eggs. Sometime before ten, she would have driven to the library for her volunteer morning. There would have been lunch with Eric, perhaps at the Deux Cheminées before she gave her afternoon to the museum or one of Aunt Dottie's charities.

The biggest decision she might have made was whether to wear her rose silk suit or her ivory linen. Her evening might have been spent quietly at home, or at one of Philadelphia's elegant dinner parties.

No pressure. No problems. But then, Papa had been alive.

Eden sighed as she rinsed away the last of the lather. The light

French scent clung to her even as she dried her skin with the serviceable camp-issue towel. When her father had been alive, she had thought that money was simply something to spend and that time was forever. She had been raised to plan a menu, but not to cook; to run a home, but not to clean it.

Throughout her childhood, she had been carelessly happy with her widowed father in the ageless elegance of their Philadelphia home. There had always been party dresses and cotillions, afternoon teas and riding lessons. The Carlbough name was an old and respected one. The Carlbough money had been a simple fact of life.

How quickly and finally things could change.

Now she was giving riding instructions and juggling columns in a ledger with the vain hope that one and one didn't always make two.

Because the tiny mirror over the tiny sink was dripping with condensation, Eden rubbed it with the towel. She took a miserly dab of the half pot of imported face cream she had left. She was going to make it last through the summer. If *she* lasted through the summer herself, another pot would be her reward.

Eden found the cabin empty when she opened the bathroom door. If she knew Candy, and after twenty years she certainly did, the redhead would be down with the girls already. How easily she became acclimatized, Eden thought; then she reminded herself it was time she did the same. She took her jeans and her red T-shirt with CAMP LIBERTY emblazoned on the chest, and began to dress. Even as a teenager, Eden had rarely dressed so casually.

She had enjoyed her social life—the parties, the well-chaperoned ski trips to Vermont, the trips to New York for shopping or the theater, the vacations in Europe. The prospect of earning a living had never been considered, by her, or her father. Carlbough women didn't work, they chaired committees.

College years had been spent with the idea of rounding out her education rather than focusing on a career. At twenty-three, Eden was forced to admit she was qualified to do absolutely nothing.

She could have blamed her father. But how could she blame a man who had been so indulgent and loving? She had adored him. She could blame herself for being naive and shortsighted, but she could never blame her father. Even now, a year after his sudden death, she still felt pangs of grief.

She could deal with that. The one thing she had been taught to do, the one thing she felt herself fully qualified to accomplish, was to cover emotion with poise, with control, or with disdain. She could go day after day, week after week through the summer, surrounded by the girls at camp and the counselors Candy had hired, and none of them would know she still mourned her father. Or that her pride had been shattered by Eric Keeton.

Eric, the promising young banker with her father's firm. Eric, always so charming, so attentive, so suitable. It had been during her last year of college that she had accepted his ring and made her promises to him. And he had made promises to her.

When she discovered the hurt was still there, Eden coated it, layer by layer, with anger. Facing the mirror, she tugged her hair back in a short ponytail, a style her hairdresser would have shuddered at.

It was more practical, Eden told her reflection. She was a practical woman now, and hair waving softly to the shoulders would just have got in the way during the riding lessons she was to give that morning.

For a moment, she pressed her fingers against her eyes. Why were the mornings always the worst? She would wake, expecting to come out of some bad dream and find herself at home again. But it wasn't her home any longer. There were strangers living in it now. Brian Carlbough's death had not been a bad dream, but a horrible, horrible reality.

A sudden heart attack had taken him overnight, leaving Eden stunned with shock and grief. Even before the grief could fade, Eden had been struck with another shock.

There had been lawyers, black-vested lawyers with long, technical monologues. They had had offices that had smelled of old leather and fresh polish. With solemn faces and politely folded hands, they had shattered her world.

Poor investments, she had been told, bad market trends, mortgages, second mortgages, short-term loans. The simple fact had been, once the details had been sifted through, there had been no money.

Brian Carlbough had been a gambler. At the time of his death, his luck had turned, and he hadn't had time to recoup his losses. His daughter had been forced to liquidate his assets in order to pay off the debts. The house she had grown up in and loved was gone. She had still been numbed by grief when she had found herself without a home or an income. Crashing down on top of that had been Eric's betrayal.

Eden yanked open the cabin door and was met by the balmy morning air of the mountains. The breathtaking view of greening hills and blue sky didn't affect her. She was back in Philadelphia, hearing Eric's calm, reasonable voice.

The scandal, she remembered and began marching toward the

big cabin where mess would be served. *His* reputation. *His* career. Everything she had loved had been taken away, but he had only been concerned with how he might be affected.

He had never loved her. Eden jammed her hands into her pockets and kept walking. She'd been a fool not to see it from the beginning. But she'd learned, Eden reminded herself. How she'd learned. It had simply been a merger to Eric, the Carlbough name, the Carlbough money and reputation. When they had been destroyed, he had cut his losses.

Eden slowed her quick pace, realizing she was out of breath, not from exertion but from temper. It would never do to walk into breakfast with her face flushed and her eyes gleaming. Giving herself a moment, she took a few deep breaths and looked around her.

The air was still cool, but by midmorning the sun would be warm and strong. Summer had barely begun.

And it was beautiful. Lining the compound were a half-dozen small cabins with their window flaps open to the morning. The sound of girlish laughter floated through the windows. Along the pathway between cabins four and five was a scattering of anemones. A dogwood, with a few stubborn blooms clinging to it, stood nearby. Above cabin two, a mockingbird chattered.

Beyond the main camp to the west were rolling hills, deeply green. Grazing horses and trees dotted them. There was an openness here, a sense of space which Eden found incredible. Her life had always been focused on the city. Streets, buildings, traffic, people, those had been the familiar. There were times when she felt a quick pang of need for what had been. It was still possible for her to have all that. Aunt Dottie had offered her home and her love. No one would ever know how long and hard Eden had wrestled with the temptation to accept the invitation and let her life drift.

Perhaps gambling was in Eden's blood, too. Why else would she have sunk what ready cash she had had left into a fledgling camp for girls in the hills?

Because she had had to try, Eden reminded herself. She had had to take the risk on her own. She could never go back into the shell of the fragile porcelain doll she had been. Here, centered in such open space, she would take the time to learn about herself. What was inside Eden Carlbough? Maybe, just maybe, by expanding her horizons, she would find her place.

Candy was right. Eden took a long last breath. It was going to work. They were going to make it work.

"Hungry?" Her hair damp from whatever shower she'd popped into, Candy cut across Eden's path.

"Starved." Content, Eden swung a friendly arm around Candy's shoulder. "Where did you run off to?"

"You know me, I can't let any part of this place run by itself." Like Eden, Candy swept her gaze over the camp. Her expression reflected everything inside her—the love, the fear, the fierce pride. "I was worried about you."

"Candy, I told you, I was just cranky this morning." Eden watched a group of girls rush out of a cabin and head for breakfast.

"Eden, we've been friends since we were six months old. No one knows better than I what you're going through."

No, no one did, and since Candy was the person she loved best, Eden determined to do a better job of concealing the wounds that were still open. "I've put it behind me, Candy."

"Maybe. But I know that the camp was initially my venture, and that I roped you in."

"You didn't rope me in. I wanted to invest. We both know it was a pitifully small amount."

"Not to me. The extra money made it possible for me to include the equestrian program. Then, when you agreed to come in and give riding lessons…"

"Just keeping a close eye on my investment," Eden said lightly. "Next year I won't be a part-time riding instructor and book-keeper. I'll be a full-fledged counselor. No regrets, Candy." This time she meant it. "It's ours."

"And the bank's."

Eden shrugged that away. "We need this place. You, because it's what you've always wanted to do, always worked and studied toward. Me…" She hesitated, then sighed. "Let's face it, I haven't got anything else. The camp's putting a roof over my head, giving me three meals a day and a goal. I need to prove I can make it."

"People think we're crazy."

The pride came back, with a feeling of recklessness Eden was just learning to savor. "Let them."

With a laugh, Candy tugged at Eden's hair. "Let's eat."

Two hours later, Eden was winding up the day's first riding lesson. This was her specialty, her contribution to the partnership she and Candy had made. It had also been decided to trust Eden with the books, mainly because no one could have been more inept with figures than Candice Bartholomew.

Candy had interviewed and hired a staff of counselors, a nutritionist and a nurse. They hoped to have a pool and a swimming instructor one day, but for now there was supervised swimming and rowing on the lake, arts and crafts, hiking and archery. Candy had spent months refining a program for the summer, while Eden had juggled the profit-and-loss statements. She prayed the money would hold out while Candy ordered supplies.

Unlike Candy, Eden wasn't certain the first week of camp would be the toughest. Her partner had all the training, all the qualifications for running the camp, but Candy also had an optimist's flair for overlooking details like red ink on the books.

Pushing those thoughts aside, Eden signaled from the center of the corral. "That's all for today." She scanned the six young faces under their black riding hats. "You're doing very well."

"When can we gallop, Miss Carlbough?"

"After you learn to trot." She patted one of the horses' flanks. Wouldn't it be lovely, she thought, to gallop off into the hills, riding so fast even memories couldn't follow? Foolish, Eden told herself; she gave her attention back to the girls. "Dismount, then cool down your horses. Remember, they depend on you." The breeze tossed her bangs, and she brushed at them absently. "Remember to put all the tack in its proper place for the next class."

This caused the groans she expected. Riding and playing with the horses was one thing, tidying up afterward was another. Eden considered exerting discipline without causing resentment another accomplishment. Over the past week, she'd learned to link the girls' faces and names. The eleven- and twelve-year-olds in her group had an enthusiasm that kept her on her toes. She'd already separated in her mind the two or three she instructed who had the kind of horse fever she recognized from her own adolescence. It was rewarding, after an hour on her feet in the sun, to answer the rapid-fire questions. Ultimately, one by one, she nudged them toward the stables.

"Eden!" Turning, she spotted Candy hustling toward her. Even from a distance, Eden recognized concern.

"What's happened?"

"We're missing three kids."

"What?" Panic came first, and quickly. Years of training had her pulling it back. "What do you mean, missing?"

"I mean they're nowhere in camp. Roberta Snow, Linda Hopkins and Marcie Jamison." Candy dragged a hand through her hair, a habitual gesture of tension. "Barbara was lining up her group for rowing, and they didn't show. We've looked every-where."

"We can't panic," Eden said, as much to warn herself as Candy. "Roberta Snow? Isn't she the little brunette who stuck a lizard down one of the other girls' shirts? And the one who set off the morning bell at 3:00 a.m.?"

"Yes, that's her." Candy set her teeth. "The little darling. Judge Harper Snow's granddaughter. If she's skinned her knee, we'll probably face a lawsuit." With a shake of her head, Candy switched to an undertone. "The last anyone saw of her this morning, she was walking east." She pointed a finger, paint-spattered from her early art class. "No one noticed the other girls, but my bet is that they're with her. Darling Roberta is an inveterate leader."

"If she's walking that way, wouldn't she run into that apple orchard?"

"Yeah." Candy shut her eyes. "Oh, yeah. I'm going to have six girls up to their wrists in modeling clay in ten minutes, or I'd go off myself. Eden, I'm almost sure they headed for the orchard. One of the other girls admitted she heard Roberta planning to sneak over there for a few samples. We don't want any trouble with the owner. He's letting us use his lake only because I begged, shamelessly. He wasn't thrilled about having a girls' summer camp for a neighbor."

"Well, he has one," Eden pointed out. "So we'll all have to deal with it. I'm the one most easily spared around here, so I'll go after them."

"I was hoping you'd say that. Seriously, Eden, if they've snuck into that orchard, which I'd bet my last dime they have, we could be in for it. The man made no bones about how he feels about his land and his privacy."

"Three little girls are hardly going to do any damage to a bunch of apple trees." Eden began to walk, with Candy scurrying to keep pace.

"He's Chase Elliot. You know, Elliot Apples? Juice, cider, sauce, jelly, chocolate-covered apple seeds, whatever can be made from an apple, they do it. He made it abundantly clear that he didn't want to find any little girls climbing his trees."

"He won't find them, I will." Leaving Candy behind, Eden swung over a fence.

"Put Roberta on a leash when you catch up to her." Candy watched her disappear through the trees.

Eden followed the path from the camp, pleased when she found a crumpled candy wrapper. Roberta. With a grim smile, Eden picked it up and stuffed it in her pocket. Judge Snow's granddaughter had already earned a reputation for her stash of sweets.

It was warm now, but the path veered through a cool grove of aspens. Sunlight dappled the ground, making the walk, if not her errand, pleasant. Squirrels dashed here and there, confident enough in their own speed not to be alarmed at Eden's intrusion. Once a rabbit darted across her path, and disappeared into the brush with a frantic rustle. Overhead a woodpecker drummed, sending out an echo.

It occurred to Eden that she was more completely alone than she had ever been before. No civilization here. She bent down for another candy wrapper. Well, very little of it.

There were new scents here, earth, animal, vegetation, to be discovered. Wildflowers sprang up, tougher and more resilient than hothouse roses. It pleased her that she was even beginning to be able to recognize a few. They came back, year after year, without pampering, taking what came and thriving on it. They gave her hope. She could find a place here. Had found a place, she corrected herself. Her friends in Philadelphia might think her mad, but she was beginning to enjoy it.

The grove of aspens thinned abruptly, and the sunlight was strong again. She blinked against it, then shielded her eyes as she scanned the Elliot orchards.

Apple trees stretched ahead of her as far as she could see, to the north, south and east. Row after row after row of trees lined the slopes. Some of them were old and gnarled, some young and straight. Instantly she thought of early spring and the overwhelming scent of apple blossoms.

It would be magnificent, she thought as she stepped up to the fence that separated the properties. The fragrance, the pretty white-and-pink blossoms, the freshly green leaves, would be a marvelous sight. Now the leaves were dark and thick, and instead of blossoms, she could see fruit in the trees closest to her. Small, shiny, and green they hung, waiting for the sun to ripen them.

How many times had she eaten applesauce that had begun right here? The idea made her smile as she began to climb the fence.

Her vision of an orchard had been a lazy little grove guarded by an old man in overalls. A quaint picture, but nothing as huge and impressive as the reality.

The sound of giggling took her by surprise. Shifting toward the direction of the sound, Eden watched an apple fall from a tree and roll toward her feet. Bending, she picked it up, tossing it away as she walked closer. When she looked up, she spotted three pairs of sneakers beneath the cover of leaves and branches.

"Ladies." Eden spoke coolly and was rewarded by three startled gasps. "Apparently you took a wrong turn on your way to the lake."

Roberta's triangular, freckled face appeared through the leaves. "Hi, Miss Carlbough. Would you like an apple?"

The devil. But even as she thought it, Eden had to tighten her lips against a smile. "Down," she said simply, then stepped closer to the trunk to assist.

They didn't need her. Three agile little bodies scrambled down and dropped lightly onto the ground. In a gesture she knew could be intimidating, Eden lifted her left eyebrow.

"I'm sure you're aware that leaving camp property unsupervised and without permission is against the rules."

"Yes, Miss Carlbough." The response would have been humble if it hadn't been for the gleam in Roberta's eye.

"Since none of you seem interested in rowing today, Mrs. Petrie has a great deal of washing up to be done in the kitchen." Pleased by her own inspiration, Eden decided Candy would approve. "You're to report to Miss Bartholomew, then to Mrs. Petrie for kitchen detail."

Only two of the girls dropped their heads and looked down at the ground.

"Miss Carlbough, do you think it's fair to give us extra kitchen detail?" Roberta, one half-eaten apple still in hand, tilted her pointed chin. "After all, our parents are paying for the camp."

Eden felt her palms grow damp. Judge Snow was a wealthy and powerful man with a reputation for indulging his granddaughter. If the little monster complained... No. Eden took a deep breath and not by a flicker showed her anxiety. She wouldn't be intimidated or blackmailed by a pint-size con artist with apple juice on her chin.

"Yes, your parents are paying for you to be entertained, instructed and disciplined. When they signed you up for Camp Liberty, it was with the understanding that you would obey the rules. But if you prefer, I'd be glad to call your parents and discuss this incident with them."

"No, ma'am." Knowing when to retreat, Roberta smiled charmingly. "We'll be glad to help Mrs. Petrie, and we're sorry for breaking the rules."

And I'm sure you have a bridge I could buy, Eden thought, but she kept her face impassive. "Fine. It's time to start back."

"My hat!" Roberta would have darted back up the tree if Eden hadn't made a lucky grab for her. "I left my hat up there. Please, Miss Carlbough, it's my Phillies cap, and it's autographed and everything."

"You start back. I'll get it. I don't want Miss Bartholomew to worry any longer than necessary."

"We'll apologize."

"See that you do." Eden watched them scramble over the fence. "And no detours," she called out. "Or I keep the cap." One look at Roberta assured her that that bit of blackmail was all that was needed. "Monsters," she murmured as they jogged back into the grove, but the smile finally escaped. Turning back, she studied the tree.

All she had to do was climb up. It had looked simple enough when Roberta and her partners-in-crime had done it. Somehow, it didn't look as simple now. Squaring her shoulders, Eden stepped forward to grab a low-hanging branch. She'd done a little mountain-climbing in Switzerland; how much harder could this be? Pulling herself up, she hooked her foot in the first vee she found. The bark was rough against her palm. Concentrating on her goal, she ignored the scrapes. With both feet secured, she reached for the next branch and began to work her way up. Leaves brushed her cheeks.

She spotted the cap hanging on a short branch, two arms' lengths out of reach. When she made the mistake of looking down, her stomach clenched. So don't look, Eden ordered herself. What you can't see can't hurt you. She hoped.

Eden cautiously inched her way out to the cap. When her fingers made contact with it, she let out a low breath of relief. After setting it on her own head, she found herself looking out, beyond the tree, over the orchard.

Now it was the symmetry that caught her admiration. From her bird's height, she could see the order as well as the beauty. She could just barely glimpse a slice of the lake beyond the aspens. It winked blue in the distance. There were barnlike buildings, and what appeared to be a greenhouse, far off to the right. About a quarter of a mile away, there was a truck, apparently abandoned, on a wide dirt path. In the quiet, birds began to sing again. Turning her head, she saw the bright yellow flash of a butterfly.

The scent of leaves and fruit and earth was tangy, basic. Unable to resist, Eden reached out and plucked a sun-warmed apple.

He'd never miss it, she decided as she bit into the skin. The tart flavor, not quite ripe, shot into her mouth. She shivered at the shock of it, the sensual appeal, then bit again. Delicious, she thought. Exciting. Forbidden fruit usually was, she remembered, but she grinned as she took a third bite.

"What in the devil are you doing?"

She started, almost unseating herself, as the voice boomed up from below. She swallowed the bite of apple quickly before peering down through the leaves.

He stood with his hands on his hips, narrow, lean, spare. A faded denim workshirt was rolled up past the elbows to show tan and muscle. Warily, Eden brought her eyes to his face. It was tanned like his arms, with the skin drawn tight over bone. His nose was long and not quite straight, his mouth full and firm and frowning. Jet-black and unruly, his hair fell over his brow and curled just beyond the collar of his shirt. Pale, almost translucent green eyes scowled up at her.

An apple, Eden, and now the serpent. The idea ran through her head before she drew herself back.

Wonderful, she thought. She'd been caught pinching apples by the foreman. Since disappearing wasn't an option, she opened her mouth to start a plausible explanation.

"Young lady, do you belong at the camp next door?"

The tone brought on a frown. She might be penniless, she might be scrambling to make a living, but she was still a Carlbough. And a Carlbough could certainly handle an apple foreman. "Yes, that's right. I'd like to—"

"Are you aware that this is private property, and that you're trespassing?"

The color of her eyes deepened, the only outward sign of her embarrassed fury. "Yes, but I—"

"These trees weren't planted for little girls to climb."

"I hardly think——"

"Come down." There was absolute command in his tone. "I'll have to take you back to the camp director."

The temper she had always gently controlled bubbled up until she gave serious consideration to throwing what was left of the apple down on his head. No one, absolutely no one, gave her orders. "That won't be necessary."

"I'll decide what's necessary. Come down here."

She'd come down all right, Eden thought. Then, with a few well-chosen words, he'd be put precisely in his place. Annoyance carried her from branch to branch, leaving no room for thoughts of height or inexperience. The two scrapes she picked up on the trip were hardly felt. Her back was to him as she lowered herself into a vee of the trunk. The pleasure of demolishing him with icy manners would be well worth the embarrassment of having been caught in the wrong place at the wrong time. She imagined him cringing and babbling an incoherent apology.

Then her foot slipped, and her frantic grab for a limb was an inch short of the mark. With a shriek that was equal parts surprise and dismay, she fell backward into space.

The breath whooshed back out of her as she connected with something solid. The tanned, muscled arms she'd seen from above wrapped around her. Momentum carried them both to the ground and, like the apple, they rolled. When the world stopped spinning, Eden found herself beneath a very firm, very long body.

Roberta's cap had flown off and Eden's face, no longer shadowed by the brim, was left unguarded in the sunlight. Chase stared down at her and felt soft breasts yield under him.

"You're not twelve years old," he murmured.

"Certainly not."

Amused now, he shifted his weight, but didn't remove it. "I didn't get a good look at you when you were in the tree." He had time to make up for that now, he decided, and he looked his fill. "You're quite a windfall." Carelessly, he brushed stray strands of hair away from her face. His fingertips were as rough against her skin as the bark had been to her palms. "What are you doing in a girls' summer camp?"

"Running it," she said coldly. It wasn't a complete lie. Because it would have bruised her dignity even more to squirm, she settled on sending him an icy look. "Would you mind?"

"Running it?" Since she had dropped out of one of his trees, he had no qualms about ignoring her request. "I met someone. Bartholomew—red hair, appealing face." He scanned Eden's classic features. "You're not her."

"Obviously not." Because his body was too warm, too male, and too close, she sacrificed some dignity by putting her hands to his shoulders. He didn't budge. "I'm her partner. Eden Carlbough."

"Ah, of the Philadelphia Carlboughs."

The humor in his voice was another blow to her pride. Eden combated it with a withering stare. "That's correct."

Intriguing little package, he thought. All manners and breeding. "A pleasure, Miss Carlbough. I'm Chase Elliot of the South Mountain Elliots."

Chapter Two

*P*erfect, just perfect, Eden thought as she stared up at him. Not the foreman, but the bloody owner. Caught stealing apples by, falling out of trees on and pinned to the ground under, the owner. She took a deep breath.

"How do you do, Mr. Elliot."

She might have been in the front parlor pouring tea, Chase thought; he had to admire her. Then he burst out laughing. "I do just fine, Miss Carlbough. And you?"

He was laughing at her. Even after the scandal and shame she had faced, no one had dared laugh at her. Not to her face. Her lips trembled once before she managed to control them. She wouldn't give the oaf the pleasure of knowing how much he infuriated her.

"I'm quite well, thank you, or will be when you let me up."

City manners, he thought. Socially correct and absolutely meaningless. His own were a bit cruder, but more honest. "In a minute. I'm finding this conversation fascinating."

"Then perhaps we could continue it standing up."

"I'm very comfortable." That wasn't precisely true. The soft, slender lines of her body were causing him some problems. Rather than alleviate them, Chase decided to enjoy them. And her. "So, how are you finding life in the rough?"

He was still laughing at her, without troubling to pretend otherwise. Eden tasted the fury bubbling up in her throat. She swallowed it. "Mr. Elliot——"

"Chase," he interrupted. "I think, under the circumstances, we should dispense with formalities."

Control teetered long enough for her to shove against his shoulders again. It was like pushing rock. "This is ridiculous. You *have* to let me up."

"I rarely have to do anything." His voice was a drawl now, and insolent, but no less imposing than the bellow that had first greeted her. "I've heard a lot about you, Eden Carlbough." And he'd seen the newspaper pictures that he now realized had been just shy of the mark. It was difficult to capture that cool sexuality in two dimensions. "I never expected a Carlbough of Philadelphia to fall out of one of my trees."

Her breathing became unsteady. All the training, the years she'd spent being taught how to coat every emotion with politeness, began to crack. "It was hardly my intention to fall out of one of your trees."

"Wouldn't have fallen out if you hadn't climbed up." He smiled, realizing how glad he was that he'd decided to check this section of the orchard himself.

This couldn't be happening. Eden closed her eyes a moment and waited for things to fall back into their proper places. She couldn't be lying flat on her back under a stranger. "Mr. Elliot." Her voice was calm and reasonable when she tried it again. "I'd be more than happy to give you a complete explanation if you'd let me up."

"Explanation first."

Her mouth quite simply fell open. "You are the most unbelievably rude and boorish man I have ever met."

"My property," he said simply. "My rules. Let's hear your explanation."

She almost shuddered with the effort to hold back the torrent of abuse that leaped to her tongue. Because of her position, she had to squint up at him. Already a headache was collecting behind her eyes. "Three of my girls wandered away from camp. Unfortunately, they climbed over the fence and onto your property. I found them, ordered them down and sent them back to the camp, where they are being properly disciplined."

"Tar and feathers?"

"I'm sure you'd prefer that, but we settled on extra kitchen detail."

"Seems fair. But that doesn't explain you falling out of my tree and into my arms. Though I've about decided not to complain about that. You smell like Paris." To Eden's amazement, he leaned down and buried his face in her hair. "Wicked nights in Paris."

"Stop it." Now her voice wasn't calm, wasn't disciplined.

Chase felt her heart begin to thud against his own. It ran through his mind that he wanted to do more than sample her scent. But when he lifted his head, her eyes were wide. Along with the awareness in them was a trace of fear.

"Explanation," he said lightly. "That's all I intend to take at the moment."

She could hear her own pulse hammering in her throat. Of its own accord, her gaze fell upon his mouth. Was she mad, or could she almost taste the surge of masculine flavor that would certainly be on his lips? She felt her muscles softening, then instantly stiff-

ened. She might very well be mad. If an explanation was what it
took, she'd give it to him and get away. Far away.

"One of the girls…" Her mind veered vengefully to Roberta.
"One of them left her cap in the tree."

"So you went up after it." He nodded, accepting her explanation. "That doesn't explain why you were helping yourself to one
of my apples."

"It was mealy."

Grinning again, he ran a hand along her jawline. "I doubt that.
I'd imagine it was hard and tart and delicious. I had my share of
stomachaches from green apples years ago. The pleasure's usually
worth the pain."

Something uncomfortably like need was spreading through her.
The fear of it chilled both her eyes and voice. "You have your explanation, and your apology."

"I never heard an apology."

She'd be damned, she'd be twice damned if she'd give him one
now. Glaring at him, she nearly managed to look regal. "I want
you to let me up this instant. You're perfectly free to prosecute
if you feel the need for compensation for a couple of worm-
filled apples, but for now, I'm tired of your ridiculous backwoods arrogance."

His apples were the best in the state, the best in the country.
But at the moment, he relished the idea of her sinking her pretty
white teeth into a worm. "You haven't had a taste of backwoods
arrogance yet. Maybe you should."

"You wouldn't dare," she began, only to have the last word
muffled by his mouth.

The kiss caught her completely off guard. It was rough and demanding and as tart as the apple had been. Forbidden fruit. To a woman accustomed to coaxing, to requesting, the hard demand left her limp, unable to respond or protest. Then his hands were on her face, his thumbs tracing her jawline. Like the kiss, his palms were hard and thrilling.

He didn't regret it. Though he wasn't a man used to taking from a woman what wasn't offered, he didn't regret it. Not when the fruit was this sweet. Even though she lay very still, he could taste the panicked excitement on her lips. Yes, very sweet, he thought. Very innocent. Very dangerous. He lifted his head the moment she began to struggle.

"Easy," he murmured, still stroking her chin with his thumb. Her eyes were more frantic than furious. "It seems you're not the woman of the world you're reputed to be."

"Let me up." Her voice was shaking now, but she was beyond caring.

Getting to his feet, Chase brought her with him. "Want some help brushing off?"

"You are the most offensive man I've ever met."

"I can believe it. A pity you've been spoiled and pampered for so long." She started to turn away, but he caught her shoulders for one last look. "It should be interesting to see how long you last here without the basics—like hairdressers and butlers."

He's just like everyone else, she thought; she coated her hurt and doubt with disdain. "I'm very late for my next class, Mr. Elliot. If you'll excuse me?"

He lifted his hands from her shoulders, holding the palms out a moment before dropping them. "Try to keep the kids out of the trees," he warned. "A fall can be dangerous."

His smile had insults trembling on her lips. Clamping her tongue between her teeth, Eden scrambled over the fence.

He watched her, enjoying the view until she was swallowed up by the aspens. Glimpsing the cap at his feet, he bent down for it. As good as a calling card, he decided, tucking it into his back pocket.

Eden went through the rest of the day struggling not to think. About anything. She had deliberately avoided telling Candy about her meeting with Chase. In telling of it, she would have to think about it.

The humiliation of being caught up a tree was hard enough to swallow. Still, under other circumstances, she and Candy might have shared a laugh over it. Under any other circumstances.

But more than the humiliation, even more than the anger, were the sensations. She wasn't sure what they were, but each separate sensation she had experienced in the orchard remained fresh and vibrant throughout the day. She couldn't shake them off or cover them over, and she certainly couldn't ignore them. If she understood anything, she understood how important it was for her to close off her feelings before they could grow.

Ridiculous. Eden interrupted her own thoughts. She didn't know Chase Elliot. Moreover, she didn't want to know him. It was true that she couldn't block out what had happened, but she could certainly see that it never happened again.

Over the past year, she had taken control of the reins for the first time in her life. She knew what it was to fumble, what it was to fail, but she also knew she would never fully release those reins again. Disillusionment had toughened her. Perhaps that was the one snatch of silver lining in the cloud.

Because of it, she recognized Chase Elliot as a man who held his own reins, and tightly. She had found him rude and overbearing, but she had also seen his power and authority. She'd had her fill of dominating men. Rough-edged or polished, they were all the same underneath. Since her experience with Eric, Eden's opinion of men in general had reached a low ebb. Her encounter with Chase had done nothing to raise it.

It was annoying that she had to remind herself continually to forget about him.

Learning the camp's routine was enough to occupy her mind. Since she didn't have Candy's years of training and experience in counseling, her responsibilities were relatively few and often mundane, but at least she had the satisfaction of knowing she was more than a spectator. Ambition had become a new vice. If her role as apprentice meant she mucked out stalls and groomed horses, then Eden was determined to have the cleanest stables and the glossiest horses in Pennsylvania. She considered her first blister a badge of accomplishment.

The rush after the dinner bell still intimidated Eden. Twenty-seven girls aged ten to fourteen swarmed the cafeteria. It was one of Eden's new duties to help keep order. Voices were raised on topics that usually ranged from boys to rock stars, then back to boys. With a little luck, there was no jostling or shoving in line. But luck usually required an eagle eye.

Camp Liberty's glossy brochures had promised wholesome food. Tonight's menu included crispy chicken, whipped potatoes and steamed broccoli. Flatware rattled on trays as the girls shuffled, cafeteria-style, down the serving line.

"It's been a good day." Candy stood beside Eden, her eyes

shifting back and forth as she managed to watch the entire room at once.

"And nearly over." Even as she said it, Eden realized her back didn't ache quite as much as it had the first couple of days. "I've got two girls in the morning riding session who show real promise. I was hoping I could give them a little extra time a couple of days a week."

"Great, we'll check the schedule." Candy watched one of the counselors convince a camper to put a stem of broccoli on her plate. "I wanted to tell you that you handled Roberta and company beautifully. Kitchen detail was an inspiration."

"Thanks." Eden realized how low her pride had fallen when such a small thing made her glow. "I did have a twinge of guilt about dumping them on Mrs. Petrie."

"The report is they behaved like troopers."

"Roberta?"

"I know." Candy's smile was wry. Both women turned to see the girl in question, already seated and eating daintily. "It's like waiting for the other shoe to drop. Eden, do you remember Marcia Delacroix from Camp Forden?"

"How could I forget?" With the bulk of the campers seated, Eden and Candy joined the line. "She was the one who put the garter snake in Miss Forden's lingerie drawer."

"Yeah." She turned to give Roberta another look. "Do you believe in reincarnation?"

With a laugh, Eden accepted a scoop of potatoes. "Let's just say I'll be checking my underwear." Hefting the tray, she started forward. "You know, Candy, I—" She saw it as if in slow motion. Roberta, the devil's own gleam in her eyes, held her fork vertically, a thick blob of potatoes clinging to the tines. Aim was taken as Roberta pulled back the business end of the fork with an expert flick. Even as Eden opened her mouth, Roberta sent the blob sailing into the hair of the girl across from her. Pandemonium.

Globs of potatoes flew. Girls screamed. More retaliated. In a matter of seconds, floors, tables, chairs and adolescents were coated in a messy layer of white. Like a general leading the way into battle, Candy stepped into the chaos and lifted her whistle. Before she had the chance to blow it, she was hit, right between the eyes.

A shocked silence fell.

With her tray still in her hands, Eden stood, afraid to breathe. One breath, one little breath, she thought, and she would dissolve into helpless laughter. She felt the pressure of a giggle in her lungs as Candy slowly wiped the dollop of potato from the bridge of her nose.

"Young ladies." The two words, delivered in Candy's most ferocious voice, had Eden's breath catching in her throat. "You will finish your meal in silence. Absolute silence. As you finish, you will line up against this wall. When the dinner hour is over, you will be issued rags, mops and buckets. The mess area will shine tonight."

"Yes, Miss Bartholomew." The acknowledgment came in murmured unison. Only Roberta, her hands folded neatly, her face a picture of innocence, responded in clear tones.

After a long ten seconds of silent staring, Candy walked back to Eden and picked up her tray. "If you laugh," she said in an undertone, "I'll tie your tongue into a square knot."

"Who's laughing?" Eden desperately cleared her throat. "I'm not laughing."

"Yes, you are." Candy sailed, like a steamship, to the head table. "You're just clever enough to do it discreetly."

Eden sat, then carefully smoothed her napkin on her lap. "You've got mashed potatoes in your eyebrows." Candy glared at her, and she lifted her coffee cup to hide a grin behind it. "Actually, it's very becoming. You may have found an alternative to hair gel."

Candy glanced down at the cooling potatoes on her own plate. "Would you like to try some?"

"Now, darling, you're the one who's always telling me we have to set an example." Eden took a satisfying bite of her chicken. "Mrs. Petrie's a gem, isn't she?"

It took the better part of two hours to clean the mess area and to mop up the puddles of water spilled by the inexperienced janitorial crew. By lights-out most of the girls were too tired to loiter. A pleasant late-evening hush covered the camp.

If the mornings were the worst for Eden, the evenings were invariably the best. A long day of physical activity left her comfortably tired and relaxed. The sounds of night birds and insects were becoming familiar. More and more, she looked forward to an hour of solitude with a sky full of stars. There was no theater to dress for, no party to attend. The longer she was away from her former life-style, the less she missed it.

She was growing up, she reflected, and she liked the idea. She supposed maturity meant recognizing what was really important. The camp was important, her friendship with Candy vital. The girls under their care for the summer, even the dastardly Roberta Snow, were what really mattered. She came to realize that even if everything she had once had was handed back to her, she would no longer be able to treat it in the same way.

She had changed. And even though she was certain there were still more changes to come, she liked the new Eden Carlbough. This Eden was independent, not financially, but internally. She'd never realized how dependent she had been on her father, her fiancé, the servants. The new Eden could cope with problems, large ones, small ones. Her hands were no longer elegantly manicured. The nails were neat, but short and rounded, unpainted. Practical, Eden thought as she held one up for inspection. Useful. She liked what she saw.

She continued her nightly ritual by walking to the stables. Inside it was cool and dark, smelling of leather, hay and horses. Just stepping inside helped to cement her confidence. This was her contribution. In most other areas, she still relied on pride and nerve, but here she had skill and knowledge.

She would check each of the six horses, then the tack, before she would consider her duties over for the day. Candy might be able to build a cathedral out of papier-mâché, but she knew nothing about strained tendons or split hooves.

Eden stopped at the first stall to stroke the roan gelding she called Courage. In her hand was a paper bag with six apple halves. It was a nightly ritual the horses had caught on to quickly. Courage leaned his head over the stall door and nuzzled her palm.

"Such a good boy," she murmured as she reached into the bag. "Some of the girls still don't know a bit from a stirrup, but we're going to change that." She held the apple in her palm and let him take it. While he chewed contentedly, Eden stepped into the stall to check him over. He'd been a bargain because of his age and his slight swayback. She hadn't been looking for thoroughbreds, but for dependability and gentleness. Satisfied that his grooming had been thorough, she latched the stall door behind her and went to the next.

Next summer they'd have at least three more mounts. Eden smiled as she worked her way from stall to stall. She wasn't going to question whether there would be a Camp Liberty next summer. There would be, and she'd be part of it. A real part.

She realized that she'd brought little with her other than money and a flair for horses. It was Candy who had the training, Candy who had had the three younger sisters and a family that had possessed more tradition than money. Unlike Eden, Candy had always known she would have to earn her own way and had prepared for it. But Eden was a quick learner. By Camp Liberty's second season, she would be a partner in more than name.

Her ambition was already spiraling upward. In a few years, Camp Liberty would be renowned for its equestrian program. The name Carlbough would be respected again. There might even come a time when her Philadelphia contemporaries would send their children to her. The irony of it pleased her.

After the fifth apple had been devoured, Eden moved to the last stall. Here was Patience, a sweet-tempered, aging mare who would tolerate any kind of ineptitude in a rider as long as she received affection. Sympathetic to old bones and muscles, Eden often spent an extra hour rubbing the mare down with liniment.

"Here you are, sweetheart." As the horse gnawed the apple, Eden lifted each hoof for inspection. "A pretty sketchy job," she mumbled before drawing a hoof pick out of her back pocket. "Let's see, wasn't it little Marcie who rode you last? I suppose this means we have to have a discussion on responsibility." With a sigh, Eden switched to another hoof. "I hate discussions on responsibility. Especially when I'm giving them." Patience snorted sympathetically. "Well, I can't leave all the dirty work to Candy, can I? In any case, I don't think Marcie meant to be inconsiderate. She's still a bit nervous around horses. We'll have to show her what a nice lady you are. There. Want a rubdown?" After sticking the pick back in her pocket, Eden rested her cheek against the mare's neck. "Oh, me too, Patience. A nice long massage with some scented oil. You can just lie there with your eyes closed while all the kinks are worked out, then your skin feels so soft, your muscles so supple." With a quick laugh, Eden drew away. "Well, since you can't oblige me, I'll oblige you. Just let me get the liniment."

Giving the mare a final pat, she turned. Her breath caught on a gasp.

Chase Elliot leaned against the open stall door. Shadows fell across his face, deepening its hollows. In the dim light, his eyes were like sea foam. She would have taken a step backward in retreat, but the mare blocked her way. He smiled at her predicament.

That triggered her pride. She could be grateful for that. It had thrown her that, in the shadowed light, he was even more attractive, more...compelling than he had been in the sun. Not handsome, she amended quickly. Certainly not in the smooth, conventional sense, the sense she had always gauged men's looks by before. Everything about him was fundamental. Not simple, she thought. No, not simple, but basic. Basic, like his kiss that morning. Warmth prickled along her skin.

"I'd be happy to help you with the massage." He smiled again. "Yours, or the mare's."

"No, thank you." She became aware that she was even more disheveled than she had been at their first meeting, and that she smelled, all too obviously, of horse. "Is there something I can do for you, Mr. Elliot?"

He liked her style, Chase decided. She might be standing in a stall that could use a bit of cleaning, but she was still the lady of the drawing room. "You've got a good stock here. A bit on the mature side, but solid."

Eden had to ward off a surge of pleasure. His opinion hardly mattered. "Thank you. I'm sure you didn't come to look over the horses."

"No." But he stepped inside the stall. The mare shifted to accommodate him. "Apparently you know your way around them." He lifted a hand to run it down the mare's neck. There was a simple gold ring on his right hand. Eden recognized its age and value, as well as the strength of the man who wore it.

"Apparently." There was no way past him, so she linked her fingers together and waited. "Mr. Elliot, you haven't told me what you're doing here."

Chase's lips twitched as he continued to stroke the mare. Miss Philadelphia was nervous, he thought. She covered it well enough with frigid manners, but her nerves were jumping. It pleased him to know that she hadn't been able to brush off that quick, impulsive kiss any more than he had. "No, I haven't." Before she could avoid it, he reached down for her hand. An opal gleamed dully in the shadowed light, nestled in a circle of diamond chips that promised to catch heat and fire.

"Wrong hand for an engagement ring." He discovered that the

fact pleased him, perhaps more than it should have. "I'd heard you and Eric Keeton were to be married last spring. Apparently it didn't come off."

She would like to have sworn, shouted, yelled. That's what *he* wanted, Eden told herself, letting her hand lie passive in his. "No, it didn't. Mr. Elliot, for a, let's say, country squire, you have boundless curiosity about Philadelphia gossip. Don't your apples keep you busy enough?"

He had to admire anyone who could shoot straight and smile. "I manage to eke out a bit of free time. Actually, I was interested because Keeton's a family connection."

"He is not."

There, he'd ruffled her. For the first time since her initial surprise, she was really looking at him. Take a good look, Chase thought. You won't see any resemblance. "Distant, certainly." Capturing her other hand, he turned the palms up. "My grandmother was a Winthrop, and a cousin of his grandmother. Your Philadelphia hands have a couple of blisters. You should take care."

"A Winthrop?" Eden was surprised enough at the name to forget her hands.

"We've thinned the blood a bit in the last few generations." She should be wearing gloves, he thought, as he touched a blister with his thumb. "Still, I'd expected an invitation and was curious why you dumped him."

"I didn't dump him." The words came out like poisoned honey. "But to satisfy your curiosity, and to use your own crude phrase, he dumped me. Now if you'd give me back my hands, I could finish for the day."

Chase obliged, but continued to block her way out of the stall. "I'd never considered Eric bright, but I'd never thought him stupid."

"What a delightful compliment. Please excuse me, Mr. Elliot."

"Not a compliment." Chase brushed at the bangs over her forehead. "Just an observation."

"Stop touching me."

"Touching's a habit of mine. I like your hair, Eden. It's soft, but it goes its own way."

"A veritable bouquet of compliments." She managed one small step backward. He had her pulse thudding again. She didn't want to be touched, not physically, not emotionally, not by anyone. Instinct warned her how easily he could do both. "Mr. Elliot—"

"Chase."

"Chase." She acknowledged this with a regal nod. "The morning bell goes off at six. I still have several things to do tonight, so if there's a purpose in your being here, could we get to it?"

"I came to bring you back your hat." Reaching in his back pocket, he pulled out the Phillies cap.

"I see." One more black mark against Roberta. "It's not mine, but I'd be happy to return it to its owner. Thank you for troubling."

"You were wearing it when you fell out of my tree." Chase ignored her outstretched hand and dropped the cap on her head. "Fits, too."

"As I've already explained—"

Eden's frigid retort was interrupted by the sound of running feet. "Miss Carlbough! Miss Carlbough!" Roberta, in an angelic pink nightgown and bare feet, skidded to a halt at the open stall.

Beaming, she stared up at Chase. Her adolescent heart melted. "Hi."

"Hi."

"Roberta." Voice stern, teeth nearly clenched, Eden stepped forward. "It's almost an hour past lights-out."

"I know, Miss Carlbough. I'm sorry." When she smiled, Eden thought you could almost believe it. "I just couldn't get to sleep because I kept thinking about my cap. You promised I could have it back, but you never gave it to me. I helped Mrs. Petrie. Honest, you can ask. There were millions of pans, too. I even peeled potatoes, and——"

"Roberta!" The sharp tone was enough for the moment. "Mr. Elliot was kind enough to return your hat." Whipping it off her own head, Eden thrust it into the girl's hands. "I believe you should thank him, as well as apologize for trespassing."

"Gee, thanks." She treated him to a dazzling smile. "Are those your trees, really?"

"Yeah." With a fingertip, Chase adjusted the brim of her hat. He had a weakness for black sheep and recognized a kindred soul in Roberta.

"I think they're great. Your apples tasted a whole lot better than the ones we get at home."

"Roberta."

The quiet warning had the girl rolling her eyes, which only Chase could see. "I'm sorry I didn't show the proper respect for your property." Roberta turned her head to see whether Eden approved of the apology.

"Very nice, Roberta. Now straight back to bed."

"Yes, ma'am." She shot a last look at Chase. Her little heart fluttered. Crushing the cap down on her head, she raced to the door.

"Roberta." She whipped back around at the sound of Chase's voice. He grinned at her. "See you around."

"Yeah, see you." In love, Roberta floated off to her cabin. When the stable door slammed at her back, all Eden could manage was a sigh.

"It's no use," Chase commented.

"What isn't?"

"Pretending you don't get a kick out of her. A kid like that makes you feel good."

"You wouldn't be so sure of that if you'd seen what she can do with mashed potatoes." But Eden gave in enough to smile. "She's a monster, but an appealing one. Still, I have to admit, if we had twenty-seven Robertas in camp this summer, I'd end up in a padded room."

"Certain people just breed excitement."

Eden remembered the dinner hour. "Some call it chaos."

"Life flattens out quickly without a little chaos."

She looked at him, realizing she'd dropped her guard enough to have an actual conversation. And realizing as well that they'd stopped talking about Roberta. The stables suddenly seemed very quiet. "Well, now that we've gotten that settled, I think—"

He took a step forward. She took a step back. A smile played around his lips again as he reached for her hand. Eden bumped solidly into the mare before she managed to raise her free hand to his chest.

"What do you want?" Why was she whispering, and why was the whisper so tremulous?

He wasn't sure what he wanted. Once, quickly, he scanned her face before bringing his gaze back to hers with a jolt. Or perhaps he was. "To walk with you in the moonlight, I think. To listen to the owls hoot and wait for the nightingale."

The shadows had merged. The mare stood quietly, breathing softly. His hand was in Eden's hair now, as if it belonged there. "I have to go in." But she didn't move.

"Eden and the apple," he murmured. "I can't tell you how tempting I've found that combination. Come with me. We'll walk."

"No." Something was building inside her, too quickly. She knew he was touching more than her hand, more than her hair. He was reaching for something he should not have known existed.

"Sooner or later." He'd always been a patient man. He could wait for her the way he waited for a new tree to bear fruit. His fingers slid down to her throat, stroking once. He felt her quick shudder, heard the unsteady indrawn breath. "I'll be back, Eden."

"It won't make any difference."

Smiling, he brought her hand to his lips, turning it palm up. "I'll still be back."

She listened to his footsteps, to the creak of the door as he opened it, then shut it again.

Chapter Three

The camp was developing its own routine. Eden adjusted hers to it. Early hours, long, physical days and basic food were both a solace and a challenge. The confidence she'd once had to work at became real.

There were nights during the first month of summer that she fell into her bunk certain she would never be able to get up in the morning. Her muscles ached from rowing, riding and endless hiking. Her head spun from weekly encounters with ledgers and account books. But in the morning the sun would rise, and so would she.

Every day it became easier. She was young and healthy. The daily regimented exercise hardened muscles only touched on by occasional games of tennis. The weight she had lost over the months since her father's death gradually came back, so that her look of fragility faded.

To her surprise, she developed a genuine affection for the girls. They became individuals, not simply a group to be coped with or income on the books. It surprised her more to find that same affection returned.

Right from the start, Eden had been certain the girls would love Candy. Everyone did. She was warm, funny, talented. The most Eden had hoped for, for herself, was to be tolerated and respected. The day Marcie had brought her a clutch of wildflowers, Eden had been too stunned to do more than stammer a thank-you. Then there had been the afternoon she had given Linda Hopkins an extra half hour in the corral. After her first gallop, Linda had thrown herself into Eden's arms for a fierce and delightful hug.

So the camp had changed her life, in so many more ways than she'd expected.

The summer grew hot with July. Girls darted around the compound in shorts. Dips in the lake became a glorious luxury. Doors and windows stayed open at night to catch even the slightest breeze. Roberta found a garter snake and terrorized her cabin mates. Bees buzzed around the wildflowers and stings became common.

Days merged together, content, but never dull, so that it seemed possible that summer could last forever. As the time passed, Eden began to believe that Chase had forgotten his promise, or threat, to come back. She'd been careful to stay well within the borders of the camp herself. Though once or twice she'd been tempted to wander toward the orchards, she stayed away.

It didn't make sense for her to still be tense and uneasy. She could tell herself he'd only been a brief annoyance. Yet every time she went into the stables in the evening, she caught herself listening. And waiting.

Late in the evening, with the heat still shimmering, Eden stretched out on her bunk, fully dressed. Bribed by the promise of a bonfire the following night, the campers had quieted down early. Relaxed and pleasantly weary, Eden pictured it. Hot dogs flaming on sharpened sticks, marshmallows toasting, the blaze flickering heat over her face and sending smoke billowing skyward. Eden found herself looking forward to the evening every bit as much as the youngest camper. With her head pillowed on her folded arms, she stared up at the ceiling while Candy paced.

"I'm sure we could do it, Eden."

"Hmm?"

"The dance." Gesturing with the clipboard she was carrying, Candy stopped at the foot of the bunk. "The dance I've been talking about having for the girls. Remember?"

"Of course." Eden forced her mind back to business. "What about it?"

"I think we should go ahead with it. In fact, if it works out, I think it should be an annual event." Even after she plopped herself down on Eden's bed, her enthusiasm continued to bounce around the room. "The boys' camp is only twenty miles from here. I'm sure they'd go for it."

"Probably." A dance. That would mean refreshments for somewhere close to a hundred, not to mention music, decorations. She thought first of the red ink in the ledger, then about how much the girls would enjoy it. There had to be a way around the red ink. "I guess there'd be room in the mess area if we moved the tables."

"Exactly. And most of the girls have records with them. We could have the boys bring some, too." She began to scrawl on her clipboard. "We can make the decorations ourselves."

"We'd have to keep the refreshments simple," Eden put in before

Candy's enthusiasm could run away with her. "Cookies, punch, that sort of thing."

"We can plan it for the last week of camp. Kind of a celebrational send-off."

The last week of camp. How strange, when the first week had been so wearing, that the thought of it ending brought on both panic and regret. No, summer wouldn't last forever. In September there would be the challenge of finding a new job, a new goal. She wouldn't be going back to a teaching job as Candy was, but to want ads and résumés.

"Eden? Eden, what do you think?"

"About what?"

"About planning the dance for the last week of camp?"

"I think we'd better clear it with the boys' camp first."

"Honey, are you okay?" Leaning forward, Candy took Eden's hand. "Are you worried about going back home in a few weeks?"

"No. Concerned." She gave Candy's hand a squeeze. "Just concerned."

"I meant it when I told you not to worry about a job right away. My salary takes care of the rent on the apartment, and I still have a little piece of the nest egg my grandmother left me."

"I love you, Candy. You're the best friend I've ever had."

"The reverse holds true, Eden."

"For that reason, there's no way I'm going to sit around while you work to pay the rent and put dinner on the table. It's enough that you've let me move in with you."

"Eden, you know I'm a lot happier sharing my apartment with you than I was living alone. If you look at it as a favor, you're going to feel pressured, and that's ridiculous. Besides, for the past few months, you were taking care of fixing all the meals."

"Only a small portion of which were edible."

"True." Candy grinned. "But I didn't have to cook. Listen, give yourself a little space. You'll need some time to find out what it is you want to do."

"What I want to do is work." With a laugh, Eden lay back on the bed again. "Surprise. I really want to work, to keep busy, to earn a living. The past few weeks have shown me how much I enjoy taking care of myself. I'm banking on getting a job at a riding stable. Maybe even the one I used to board my horse at. And if that doesn't pan out——" She shrugged her shoulders. "I'll find something else."

"You will." Candy set the clipboard aside. "And next year, we'll have more girls, a bigger staff and maybe even a profit."

"Next year, I'm going to know how to make a hurricane lamp out of a tuna can."

"And a pillow out of two washcloths."

"And pot holders."

Candy remembered Eden's one mangled attempt. "Well, maybe you should take it slow."

"There's going to be no stopping me. In the meantime, I'll contact the camp director over at—what's the name, Hawk's Nest?"

"Eagle Rock," Candy corrected her, laughing. "It'll be fun for us, too, Eden. They have counselors. *Male* counselors." Sighing, she stretched her arms to the ceiling. "Do you know how long it's been since I've spoken with a man?"

"You talked to the electrician just last week."

"He was a hundred and two. I'm talking about a man who still has all his hair and teeth." She touched her tongue to her upper lip. "Not all of us have passed the time holding hands with a man in the stables."

Eden plumped up her excuse for a pillow. "I wasn't holding hands. I explained to you."

"Roberta Snow, master spy, gave an entirely different story. With her, it appears to be love at first sight."

Eden examined the pad of callus on the ridge of her palm. "I'm sure she'll survive."

"Well, what about you?"

"I'll survive, too."

"No, I mean, aren't you interested?" After folding her legs under her, Candy leaned forward. "Remember, darling, I got a good look at the man when I was negotiating for the use of his lake. I don't think there's a woman alive who wouldn't sweat a bit after a look at those spooky green eyes."

"I never sweat."

Chuckling, Candy leaned back. "Eden, you're talking to the one who loves you best. The man was interested enough to track you down in the stables. Think of the possibilities."

"It's possible that he was returning Roberta's cap."

"And it's possible that pigs fly. Haven't you been tempted to wander over by the orchard, just once?"

"No." Only a hundred times. "Seen one apple tree, you've seen them all."

"The same doesn't hold true for an apple grower who's about six-two, with a hundred and ninety well-placed pounds and one of the most fascinating faces this side of the Mississippi." Concern edged into her voice. She had watched her friend suffer and had been helpless to do more than offer emotional support. "Have fun, Eden. You deserve it."

"I don't think Chase Elliot falls into the category of fun." Danger, she thought. Excitement, sexuality and, oh yes, temptation. Tossing her legs over the bunk, Eden walked to the window. Moths were flapping at the screen.

"You're gun-shy."

"Maybe."

"Honey, you can't use Eric as a yardstick."

"I'm not." With a sigh, she turned back. "I'm not pining or brooding over him, either."

The quick shrug was Candy's way of dismissing someone she considered a weasel. "That's because you were never really in love with him."

"I was going to marry him."

"Because it seemed the proper thing to do. I know you, Eden, like no one else. Everything was very simple and easy with Eric. It all fit—click, click, click."

Amused, Eden shook her head. "Is something wrong with that?"

"Everything's wrong with that. Love makes you giddy and foolish and achy. You never felt any of that with Eric." She spoke from the experience of a woman who'd fallen in love, and out again, a dozen times before she'd hit twenty. "You would have married him, and maybe you would even have been content. His tastes were compatible with yours. His family mixed well with yours."

Amusement fled. "You make it sound so cold."

"It was. But you're not." Candy raised her hands, hoping she hadn't gone too far. "Eden, you were raised a certain way, to be a certain way; then the roof collapsed. I can only guess at how traumatic that was. You've picked yourself up, but still you've closed pieces of yourself off. Isn't it time you put the past behind you, really behind you?"

"I've been trying."

"I know, and you've made a good start, with the camp, with your outlook. Maybe it's time you started looking for a little more, just for yourself."

"A man?"

"Some companionship, some sharing, some affection. You're too smart to think that you need a man to make things work, but to cut them off because one acted like a weasel isn't the answer, either." She rubbed at a streak of red paint on her fingernail. "I guess I still believe that everyone needs someone."

"Maybe you're right. Right now I'm too busy pasting myself back together and enjoying the results. I'm not ready for complications. Especially when they're six foot two."

"You were always the romantic one, Eden. Remember the poetry you used to write?"

"We were children." Restless, Eden moved her shoulders. "I had to grow up."

"Growing up doesn't mean you have to stop dreaming." Candy rose. "We've started one dream here, together. I want to see you have other dreams."

"When the time's right." Touched, Eden kissed Candy's cheek. "We'll have your dance and charm your counselors."

"We could invite some neighbors, just to round things out."

"Don't press your luck." Laughing, Eden turned toward the door. "I'm going for a walk before I check on the horses. Leave the light on low, will you?"

The air was still, but not quiet. The first nights Eden had spent in the hills, the country quiet had disturbed her. Now, she could hear and appreciate the night music. The chorus of crickets in soprano, the tenor crying of an owl, the occasional bass lowing of the cows on a farm half a mile away all merged into a symphony accompanied by the rustling of small animals in the brush. The three-quarter moon and a galaxy of stars added soft light and dramatic shadows. The erratic yellow beams of an army of fire-flies was a nightly light show.

As she strolled toward the lake, she heard the rushing song of peepers over the softer sound of lapping water. The air smelled as steamy as it felt, so she rounded the edge of the lake toward the cooler cover of trees.

With her mind on her conversation with Candy, Eden bent to pluck a black-eyed Susan. Twisting the stem between her fingers, she watched the petals revolve around the dark center.

Had she been a romantic? There had been poetry, dreamy, op-timistic poetry, often revolving around love. Troubadour love, she thought now. The sort that meant long, wistful glances, sterling sacrifices and purity. Romantic, but unrealistic, Eden admitted. She hadn't written any poetry in a long time.

Not since she had met Eric, Eden realized. She had gone from dreamy young girl to proper young woman, exchanging verses for silver patterns. Now both the dreamy girl and the proper woman were gone.

That was for the best, Eden decided, and she tossed her flower onto the surface of the lake. She watched it float lazily.

Candy had been right. It had not been a matter of love with Eric, but of fulfilling expectations. When he had turned his back on her, he had broken not her heart, but her pride. She was still repairing it.

Eric had given her a suitable diamond, sent her roses at the proper times and had never been at a loss for a clever compliment. That wasn't romance, Eden mused, and it certainly wasn't love. Perhaps she'd never really understood either.

Was romance white knights and pure maidens? Was it Chopin and soft lights? Was it the top of the Ferris wheel? Maybe she'd prefer the last after all. With a quiet laugh, Eden wrapped her arms around herself and held her face up to the stars.

"You should do that more often."

She whirled, one hand pressing against her throat. Chase stood a few feet away at the edge of the trees, the edge of the shadows. It flashed through her mind that this was the third time she had seen him and the third time he had taken her by surprise. It was a habit she wanted to break.

"Do you practice startling people, or is it a natural gift?"

"I can't remember it happening much before you." The fact was, he hadn't come up on her, but she on him. He'd been walking since dusk, and had stopped on the banks of the lake to watch the water and to think of her. "You've been getting some sun." Her hair seemed lighter, more fragile against the honeyed tone of her skin. He wanted to touch it, to see if it was still as soft and fragrant.

"Most of the work is outdoors." It amazed her that she had to fight the urge to turn and run. There was something mystical, even fanciful, about meeting him here in the moonlight, by the water. Almost as if it had been fated.

"You should wear a hat." He said it absently, distracted by the pounding of his own heart. She might have been an illusion, long slender arms and legs gleaming in the moonlight, her hair loose and drenched with it. She wore white. Even the simple shorts and shirt seemed to glimmer. "I'd wondered if you walked here."

He stepped out of the shadows. The monotonous song of the crickets seemed to reach a crescendo. "I thought it might be cooler."

"Some." He moved closer. "I've always been fond of hot nights."

"The cabins tend to get stuffy." Uneasy, she glanced back and discovered she had walked farther than she'd intended. The camp, with its comforting lights and company, was very far away. "I didn't realize I'd crossed over onto your property."

"I'm only a tyrant about my trees." She was less of an illusion up close, more of a woman. "You were laughing before. What were you thinking of?"

Her mouth was dry. Even as she backed away, he seemed to be closer. "Ferris wheels."

"Ferris wheels? Do you like the drop?" Satisfying his own need, he reached for her hair. "Or the climb?"

At his touch, her stomach shot down to her knees. "I have to get back."

"Let's walk."

To walk with you in the moonlight. Eden thought of his words, and of fate. "No, I can't. It's late."

"Must be all of nine-thirty." Amused, he took her hand, then immediately turned it over. There was a hardening ridge of calluses on the pad beneath her fingers. "You've been working."

"Some people make a living that way."

"Don't get testy." He turned her hand back to run a thumb over her knuckles. Was it a talent of his, Eden wondered, to touch a woman in the most casual of ways and send her blood pounding? "You could wear gloves," Chase went on, "and keep your Philadelphia hands."

"I'm not in Philadelphia." She drew her hand away. Chase simply took her other one. "And since I'm pitching hay rather than serving tea, it hardly seems to matter."

"You'll be serving tea again." He could see her, seated in some fussy parlor, wearing pink silk and holding a china pot. But, for the moment, her hand was warm in his. "The moon's on the water. Look."

Compelled, she turned her head. There were such things as moonbeams. They gilded the dark water of the lake and silvered the trees. She remembered some old legend about three women, the moonspinners, who spun the moon on spindles. More romance. But even the new, practical Eden couldn't resist.

"It's lovely. The moon seems so close."

"Some things aren't as close as they seem; others aren't so far away."

He began to walk. Because he still had her hand, and because he intrigued her, Eden walked with him. "I suppose you've always lived here." Just small talk, she told herself. She didn't really care.

"For the most part. This has always been headquarters for the business." He turned to look down at her. "The house is over a hundred years old. You might find it interesting."

She thought of her home and of the generations of Carlboughs who had lived there. And of the strangers who lived there now. "I like old houses."

"Are things going well at camp?"

She wouldn't think of the books. "The girls keep us busy." Her laugh came again, low and easy. "That's an understatement. We'll just say their energy level is amazing."

"How's Roberta?"

"Incorrigible."

"I'm glad to hear it."

"Last night she painted one of the girls while the girl was asleep."

"Painted?"

Eden's laugh came again, low and easy. "The little darling must have copped a couple of pots of paint from the art area. When Marcie woke up, she looked like an Indian preparing to attack a wagon train."

"Our Roberta's inventive."

"To say the least. She told me she thought it might be interesting to be the first woman chief justice."

He smiled at that. Imagination and ambition were the qualities he most admired. "She'll probably do it."

"I know. It's terrifying."

"Let's sit. You can see the stars better."

Stars? She'd nearly forgotten who she was with and why she had wanted to avoid being with him. "I don't think I——" Before she'd gotten the sentence out, he'd tugged her down on a soft, grassy rise. "One wonders why you bother to ask."

"Manners," he said easily as he slipped an arm around her shoulders. Even as she stiffened, he relaxed. "Look at the sky. How often do you notice it in the city?"

Unable to resist, she tilted her face up. The sky was an inky black backdrop for countless pinpoints of lights. They spread, winking, shivering, overhead with a glory that made Eden's throat ache just in the looking. "It isn't the same sky that's over the city."

"Same sky, Eden. It's people who change." He stretched out on his back, crossing his legs. "There's Cassiopeia."

"Where?" Curious, Eden searched, but saw only stars without pattern.

"You can see her better from here." He pulled her down beside him, and before she could protest, he was pointing. "There she is. Looks like a W this time of year."

"Yes!" Delighted, she reached for his wrist and outlined the constellation herself. "I've never been able to find anything in the sky."

"You have to look first. There's Pegasus." Chase shifted his arm. "He has a hundred and sixty-six stars you can view with the naked eye. See? He's flying straight up."

Eyes narrowed, she concentrated on finding the pattern. Moonlight splashed on her face. "Oh yes, I see." She shifted a bit closer to guide his hand again. "I named my first pony Pegasus. Sometimes I'd imagine he sprouted wings and flew. Show me another."

He was looking at her, at the way the stars reflected in her eyes, at the way her mouth softened so generously with a smile. "Orion," he murmured.

"Where?"

"He stands with his sword behind him and his shield lifted in front. And a red star, thousands of times brighter than the sun, is the shoulder of his sword arm."

"Where is he? I—" Eden turned her head and looked directly into Chase's eyes. She forgot the stars and the moonlight and the soft, sweet grass beneath her. The hand on his wrist tightened until the rhythm of his pulse was the rhythm of hers.

Her muscles contracted and held as she braced for the kiss. But his lips merely brushed against her temple. Warmth spread through her as softly as the scent of honeysuckle spread through the air. She heard an owl call out to the night, to the stars, or to a lover.

"What are we doing here?" she managed.

"Enjoying each other." Without rushing, his lips moved over her face.

Enjoying? That was much too mild a word for what was burning through her. No one had ever made her feel like this, so weak and hot, so strong and desperate. His lips were soft, the hand that rested on the side of her face was hard. Beneath his, her heart began to gallop uncontrolled. Eden's fingers slipped off the reins.

She turned her head with a moan and found his mouth with hers. Her arms went around him, holding him close as her lips parted in demand. In all her life she had never known true hunger, not until now. This was breathless, painful, glorious.

He'd never expected such unchecked passion. He'd been prepared to go slowly, gently, as the innocence he'd felt in her required. Now she was moving under him, her fingers pressing and kneading the muscles of his back, her mouth hot and willing on his. The patience that was so much a part of him drowned in need.

Such new, such exciting sensations. Her body gave as his pressed hard against it. Gods and goddesses of the sky guarded them. He smelled of the grass and the earth, and he tasted of fire. Night sounds roared in her head, and her own sigh was only a dim echo when his lips slid down to her throat.

Murmuring his name, Eden combed her fingers through his

hair. He wanted to touch her, all of her. He wanted to take her now. When her hand came to rest on his face, he covered it with his own and felt the smooth stone of her ring.

There was so much more he needed to know. So little he was sure of. Desire, for the moment, couldn't be enough. Who was she? He lifted his head to look down at her. Who the hell was she, and why was she driving him mad?

Pulling himself back, he tried to find solid ground. "You're full of surprises, Eden Carlbough of the Philadelphia Carlboughs."

For a moment, she could only stare. She'd had her ride on the Ferris wheel, a wild, dizzying ride. Somewhere along the line, she'd been tossed off to spiral madly in the air. Now she'd hit the ground, hard. "Let me up."

"I can't figure you, Eden."

"You aren't required to." She wanted to weep, to curl up into a ball and weep, but she couldn't focus on the reason. Anger was clearer. "I asked you to let me up."

He rose, holding out a hand to help her. Ignoring it, Eden got to her feet. "I've always felt it was more constructive to shout when you're angry."

She shot him one glittering look. Humiliation. It was something she'd sworn she would never feel again. "I'm sure you do. If you'll excuse me."

"Damn it." He caught her arm and swung her back to face him. "Something was happening here tonight. I'm not fool enough to deny that, but I want to know what I'm getting into."

"We were enjoying each other. Wasn't that your term?" Nothing more, Eden repeated over and over in her head. Nothing more than a moment's enjoyment. "We've finished now, so good night."

"We're far from finished. That's what worries me."

"I'd say that's your problem, Chase." But a ripple of fear—of anticipation—raced through her, because she knew he was right.

"Yeah, it's my problem." My God, how had he passed so quickly from curiosity to attraction to blazing need? "And because it is, I've got a question. I want to know why Eden Carlbough is playing at camp for the summer rather than cruising the Greek Isles. I want to know why she's cleaning out stables instead of matching silver patterns and planning dinner parties as Mrs. Eric Keeton."

"My business." Her voice rose. The new Eden wasn't as good as the old one at controlling emotion. "But if you're so curious, why don't you call one of your family connections? I'm sure any of them would be delighted to give you all the details."

"I'm asking you."

"I don't owe you any explanations." She jerked her arm away and stood trembling with rage. "I don't owe you a damn thing."

"Maybe not." His temper had cooled his passion and cleared his head. "But I want to know who I'm making love with."

"That won't be an issue, I promise you."

"We're going to finish what we started here, Eden." Without stepping closer, he had her arm again. The touch was far from gentle, far from patient. "That I promise you."

"Consider it finished."

To her surprise and fury, he only smiled. His hand eased on her arm to one lingering caress. Helpless against her response, she shivered. "We both know better than that." He touched a finger to her lips, as if reminding her what tastes he'd left there. "Think of me."

He slipped back into the shadows.

Chapter Four

It was a perfect night for a bonfire. Only a few wispy clouds dragged across the moon, shadowing it, then freeing it. The heat of the day eased with sunset, and the air was balmy, freshened by a calm, steady breeze.

The pile of twigs and sticks that had been gathered throughout the day had been stacked, tepeelike, in a field to the east of the main compound. In the clearing, it rose from a wide base to the height of a man. Every one of the girls had contributed to the making of it, just as every one of them circled around the bonfire now, waiting for the fire to catch and blaze. An army of hot dogs and marshmallows was laid out on a picnic table. Stacked like swords were dozens of cleaned and sharpened sticks. Nearby was the garden hose with a tub full of water, for safety's sake.

Candy held up a long kitchen match, drawing out the drama as the girls began to cheer. "The first annual bonfire at Camp Liberty is about to begin. Secure your hot dogs to your sticks, ladies, and prepare to roast."

Amid the giggles and gasps, Candy struck the match, then held it to the dry kindling at the base. Wood crackled. Flames licked, searched for more fuel, and spread around and around, following the circle of starter fluid. As they watched, fire began its journey up and up. Eden applauded with the rest.

"Fabulous!" Even as she watched, smoke began to billow. Its scent was the scent of autumn, and that was still a summer away. "I was terrified we wouldn't get it started."

"You're looking at an expert." Catching her tongue between her teeth, Candy speared a hot dog with a sharpened stick. Behind her, the bonfire glowed red at the center. "The only thing I was worried about was rain. But just look at those stars. It's perfect."

Eden tilted her head back. Without effort, without thought, she found Pegasus. He was riding the night sky just as he'd been riding it twenty-four hours before. One day, one night. How could so much have happened? Standing with her face lifted to the breeze and her hands growing warm from the fire, she wondered if she had really experienced that wild, turbulent moment with Chase.

She had. The memories were too ripe, too real for dreams. The moment had happened, and all the feelings and sensations that had grown from it. Deliberately she turned her gaze to a riot of patternless stars.

It didn't change what she remembered, or what she still felt. The moment had happened, she thought again, and it had passed. Yet, somehow, she wasn't certain it was over.

"Why does everything seem different here, Candy?"

"Everything *is* different here." Candy took a deep breath, drawing in the scents of smoke, drying grass and roasting meat. "Isn't it marvelous? No stuffy parlors, no boring dinner parties, no endless piano recitals. Want a hot dog?"

Because her mouth was watering, Eden accepted the partially

blackened wiener. "You simplify things, Candy." Eden ran a thin line of ketchup along the meat and stuck it in a bun. "I wish I could."

"You will once you stop thinking you're letting down the Carlbough name by enjoying a hot dog by a bonfire." When Eden's mouth dropped open, Candy gave her a friendly pat. "You ought to try the marshmallows," she advised before she wandered off to find another stick.

Is that what she was doing? Eden wondered, chewing automatically. Maybe, in a way that wasn't quite as basic as Candy had said, it was. After all, she had been the one who had sold the house that had been in the family for four generations. In the end, it had been she who had inventoried the silver and china, the paintings and the jewelry for auction. So, in the end, it had been she who had liquidated the Carlbough tradition to pay off debts and to start a new life.

Necessary. No matter how the practical Eden accepted the necessity, the grieving Eden still felt the loss, and the guilt.

With a sigh, Eden stepped back. The scene that played out in front of her was like a memory from her own childhood. She could see the column of gray smoke rising toward the sky, twirling and curling. At the core of the tower of wood, the fire was fiercely gold and greedy. The smell of outdoor cooking was strong and summery, as it had been during her own weeks at Camp Forden for Girls. For a moment, there was regret that she couldn't step back into those memories of a time when life was simple and problems were things for parents to fix.

"Miss Carlbough."

Brought out of a half-formed dream, Eden glanced down at Roberta. "Hello, Roberta. Are you having fun?"

Nora Roberts

"It's super!" Roberta's enthusiasm was evident from the smear of ketchup on her chin. "Don't you like bonfires?"

"Yes, I do." Smiling, she looked back at the crackling wood, one hand dropping automatically to Roberta's shoulder. "I like them a lot."

"I thought you looked sort of sad, so I made you a marshmallow."

The offering dripped, black and shriveled, from the end of a stick. Eden felt her throat close up the same way it had when another girl had offered her a clutch of wildflowers. "Thanks, Roberta. I wasn't sad really, I was just remembering." Gingerly, Eden pulled the melted, mangled marshmallow from the stick. Half of it plopped to the ground on the way to her mouth.

"They're tricky," Roberta observed. "I'll make you another one."

Left with the charred outer hull, Eden swallowed valiantly. "You don't have to bother, Roberta."

"Oh, I don't mind." She looked up at Eden with a glowing, generous grin. Somehow, all her past crimes didn't seem so important. "I like to do it. I thought camp was going to be boring, but it's not. Especially the horses. Miss Carlbough..." Roberta looked down at the ground and seemed to draw her courage out of her toes. "I guess I'm not as good as Linda with the horses, but I wondered if maybe you could—well, if I could spend some more time at the stables."

"Of course you can, Roberta." Eden rubbed her thumb and forefinger together, trying fruitlessly to rid herself of the goo. "And you don't even have to bribe me with marshmallows."

"Really?"

"Yes, really." Attracted despite herself, Eden ruffled Roberta's hair. "Miss Bartholomew and I will work it into your schedule."

"Gee, thanks, Miss Carlbough."

"But you'll have to work on your posting."

Roberta's nose wrinkled only a little. "Okay. But I wish we could do stuff like barrel racing. I've seen it on TV."

"Well, I don't know about that, but you might progress to small jumps before the end of camp."

Eden had the pleasure of seeing Roberta's eyes saucer with pleasure. "No fooling?"

"No fooling. As long as you work on your posting."

"I will. And I'll be better than Linda, too. Wow, jumps." She spun in an awkward pirouette. "Thanks a lot, Miss Carlbough. Thanks a lot."

She was off in a streak, undoubtedly to spread the word. If Eden knew Roberta, and she was beginning to, she was certain the girl would soon have talked herself into a gold medal for equestrian prowess at the next Olympic Games.

But, as she watched Roberta spin from group to group, Eden realized she wasn't thinking of the past any longer; nor was she regretting. She was smiling. As one of the counselors began to strum a guitar, Eden licked marshmallow goop from her fingers.

"Need some help with that?"

With her fingers still in her mouth, Eden turned. She should have known he'd come. Perhaps, in her secret thoughts, she had hoped he would. Now she found herself thrusting her still-sticky fingers behind her back.

He wondered if she knew how lovely she looked, with the fire at her back and her hair loose on her shoulders. There was a frown on her face now, but he hadn't missed that one quick flash of pleasure. If he kissed her now, would he taste that sweet, sugary flavor she had been licking from her fingers? Through it would he find that simmering, waiting heat he'd tasted once before? The muscles in his stomach tightened, even as he dipped his thumbs into his pockets and looked away from her toward the fire.

"Nice night for a bonfire."

"Candy claims she arranged it that way." Confident there was enough distance between them, and that there were enough people around them, Eden allowed herself to relax. "We weren't expecting any company."

"I spotted your smoke."

That made her glance up and realize how far the smoke might travel. "I hope it didn't worry you. We notified the fire department." Three girls streaked by behind them. Chase glanced their way and had them lapsing into giggles. Eden caught her tongue in her cheek. "How long did it take you to perfect it?"

With a half smile, Chase turned back to her. "What?"

"The deadly charm that has females crumpling at your feet?"

"Oh, that." He grinned at her. "I was born with it."

The laugh came out before she could stop it. To cover her lapse, Eden crossed her arms and took a step backward. "It's getting warm."

"We used to have a bonfire on the farm every Halloween. My father would carve the biggest pumpkin in the patch and stuff some overalls and a flannel shirt with straw. One year he dressed himself up as the Headless Horseman and gave every kid in the neighborhood a thrill." Watching the fire, he remembered and wondered why until tonight he hadn't thought of continuing the tradition. "My mother would give each of the kids a caramel apple, then we'd sit around the fire and tell ghost stories until we'd scared ourselves silly. Looking back, I think my father got a bigger kick out of it than any of us kids."

She could see it, just as he described, and had to smile again. For her, Halloween had been tidy costume parties where she'd dressed as a princess or ballerina. Though the memories were still lovely, she couldn't help wishing she'd seen one of the bonfires and the Headless Horseman.

"When we were planning tonight, I was as excited as any of the girls. I guess that sounds foolish."

"No, it sounds promising." He put a hand to her cheek, turning her slightly toward him. Though she stiffened, her skin was warm and soft. "Did you think of me?"

There it was again—that feeling of drowning, of floating, of going under for the third time. "I've been busy." She told herself to move away, but her legs didn't respond. The sound of singing and strumming seemed to be coming from off in the distance, with melody and lyrics she couldn't quite remember. The only thing that was close and real was his hand on her cheek.

"I-it was nice of you to drop by," she began, struggling to find solid ground again.

"Am I being dismissed?" He moved his hand casually from her cheek to her hair.

"I'm sure you have better things to do." His fingertip skimmed the back of her neck and set every nerve end trembling. "Stop."

The smoke billowed up over her head. Light and shadow created by the fire danced over her face and in her eyes. He'd thought of her, Chase reminded himself. Too much. Now he could only think what it would be like to make love with her near the heat of the fire, with the scent of smoke, and night closing in.

"You haven't walked by the lake."

"I told you, I've been busy." Why couldn't she make her voice firm and cool? "I have a responsibility to the girls, and the camp, and—"

"Yourself?" How badly he wanted to walk with her again, to study the stars and talk. How badly he wanted to taste that passion and that innocence again. "I'm a very patient man, Eden. You can only avoid me for so long."

"Longer than you think," she murmured, letting out a sigh of relief as she spotted Roberta making a beeline for them.

"Hi!" Delighted with the quick fluttering of her heart, Roberta beamed up at Chase.

"Hi, Roberta," he said. She was thrilled that he'd remembered her name. He gave her a smile, and his attention, without releasing Eden's hair. "You're taking better care of your cap, I see."

She laughed and pushed up the brim. "Miss Carlbough said if I wandered into your orchard again, she'd hold my cap for ransom. But if you invited us to come on a tour, that would be educational, wouldn't it?"

"Roberta." Why was it the child was always one step ahead of everyone else? Eden lifted her brow in a quelling look.

"Well, Miss Bartholomew said we should think of interesting things." Roberta put her most innocent look to good use. "And I think the apple trees are interesting."

"Thanks." Chase thought he heard Eden's teeth clench. "We'll give it some thought."

"Okay." Satisfied, Roberta stuck out a wrinkled black tube. "I made you a hot dog. You have to have a hot dog at a bonfire."

"Looks terrific." Accepting it, he pleased Roberta by taking a generous bite. "Thanks." Only Chase and his stomach knew that the meat was still cold on the inside.

"I got some marshmallows and sticks, too." She handed them over. "It's more fun to do it yourself, I guess." Because she was on the border between childhood and womanhood, Roberta picked up easily on the vibrations around her. "If you two want to be alone, you know, to kiss and stuff, no one's in the stables."

"Roberta!" Eden pulled out her best camp director's voice. "That will do."

"Well, my parents like to be alone sometimes." Undaunted, she grinned at Chase. "Maybe I'll see you around."

"You can count on it, kid." As Roberta danced off toward a group of girls, Chase turned back. The moment he took a step toward her, Eden extended her skewered marshmallow toward the fire. "Want to go kiss and stuff?"

It was the heat of the fire that stung her cheeks with color, Eden assured herself. "I suppose you think it would be terribly amusing for Roberta to go home and report that one of the camp directors spent her time in the stables with a man. That would do a lot for Camp Liberty's reputation."

"You're right. You should come to my place."

"Go away, Chase."

"I haven't finished my hot dog. Have dinner with me."

"I've had a hot dog already, thank you."

"I'll make sure hot dogs aren't on the menu. We can talk about it tomorrow."

"We will not talk about it tomorrow." It was anger that made her breathless, just as it was anger that made her unwise enough to turn toward him. "We will not talk about anything tomorrow."

"Okay. We won't talk." To show how reasonable he was, he bent down and closed the conversation, his mouth covering hers. He wasn't holding her, but it took her brain several long, lazy seconds before it accepted the order to back away.

"Don't you have any sense of propriety?" she managed in a strangled voice.

"Not much." He made up his mind, looking down at her eyes, dazed and as blue as his lake, that he wasn't going to take no for an answer—to any question. "We'll make it about nine tomorrow morning at the entrance to the orchard."

"Make what?"

"The tour." He grinned and handed her his stick. "It'll be educational."

Though she was in an open field, Eden felt her back press into a corner. "We have no intention of disrupting your routine."

"No problem. I'll pass it on to your co-director before I go back. That way, you'll be sure to be coordinated."

Eden took a long breath. "You think you're very clever, don't you?"

"Thorough, just thorough, Eden. By the way, your marshmallow's on fire."

With his hands in his pockets, he strolled off while she blew furiously on the flaming ball.

She'd hoped for rain but was disappointed. The morning dawned warm and sunny. She'd hoped for support but was faced with Candy's enthusiasm for a field trip through one of the most prestigious apple orchards in the country. The girls were naturally delighted with any shift in schedule, so as they walked as a group the short distance to the Elliot farm, Eden found herself separated from the excitement.

"You could try not to look as though you're walking to the guillotine." Candy plucked a scrawny blue flower from the side of the road and stuck it in her hair. "This is a wonderful opportunity— for the girls," she added quickly.

"You managed to convince me of that, or else I wouldn't be here."

"Grumpy."

"I'm not grumpy," Eden countered. "I'm annoyed at being manipulated."

"Just a small piece of advice." Picking another flower, Candy twirled it. "If I'd been manipulated by a man, I'd make certain he believed it was my idea in the first place. Don't you think it would throw him off if you walked up to the gates with a cheery smile and boundless enthusiasm?"

"Maybe." Eden mulled the idea over until her lips began to curve. "Yes, maybe."

"There now. With a little practice, you'll find out that deviousness is much better in some cases than dignity."

"I wouldn't have needed either if you'd let me stay behind."

"Darling, unless I miss my guess, a certain apple baron would have plucked you up from whatever corner you'd chosen to hide in, tossed you over his wonderfully broad shoulder and dragged you along on our little tour, like it or not." Pausing, Candy let a sigh escape. "Now that I think about it, that would have been more exciting."

Because she was well able to picture it herself, Eden's mood hardened again. "At least I thought I could count on support from my best friend."

"And you can. Absolutely." With easy affection, Candy draped an arm over Eden's shoulder. "Though why you think you need my support when you have a gorgeous man giving you smoldering kisses, I can't imagine."

"That's just it!" Because several young heads turned when she raised her voice, Eden fought for calm again. "He had no business pulling something like that in front of everyone."

"I suppose it is more fun in private."

"Keep this up, and you may find that garter snake in your underwear yet."

"Just ask him if he's got a brother, or a cousin. Even an uncle. Ah, here we are," she continued before Eden could reply. "Now smile and be charming, just like you were taught."

"You're going to pay for this," Eden promised her in an undertone. "I don't know how, I don't know when, but you'll pay."

They brought the group to a halt when the road forked. On the left were stone pillars topped with an arching wrought-iron sign that read ELLIOT. Sloping away from the pillars was a wall a foot thick and high as a man. It was old and sturdy, proving to Eden that the penchant for privacy hadn't begun with Chase.

The entrance road, smooth and well-maintained, ribboned back over the crest of a hill before it disappeared. Along the road were trees, not apple but oak, older and sturdier than the wall.

It was the continuity that drew her, the same symmetry she had seen and admired in the groves. The stone, the trees, even the road, had been there for generations. Looking, Eden understood his pride in them. She, too, had once had a legacy.

Then he strode from behind the wall and she fought back even that small sense of a common ground.

In a T-shirt and jeans, he looked lean and capable. There was a faint sheen of sweat on his arms that made her realize he'd already been working that morning. Drawn against her will, she dropped her gaze to his hands, hands that were hard and competent and unbearably gentle on a woman's skin.

"Morning, ladies." He swung the gates open for them.

"Oh Lord, he's something," Eden heard one of the counselors mumble. Remembering Candy's advice, she straightened her shoulders and fixed on her most cheerful smile.

"This is Mr. Elliot, girls. He owns the orchards we'll tour today. Thank you for inviting us, Mr. Elliot."

"My pleasure—Miss Carlbough."

The girlish murmurs of agreement became babbles of excitement as a dog sauntered to Chase's side. His fur was the color of apricots and glistened as though it had been polished in the sunlight. The big, sad eyes studied the group of girls before the dog pressed against Chase's leg. Eden had time to think that a smaller man might have been toppled. The dog was no less than three feet high at the shoulder. More of a young lion than a house pet, she thought. When he settled to sit at Chase's feet, Chase didn't have to bend to lay a hand on the dog's head.

"This is Squat. Believe it or not, he was the runt of his litter. He's a little shy."

Candy gave a sigh of relief when she saw the enormous tail thump the ground. "But friendly, right?"

"Squat's a pushover for females." His gaze circled the group. "Especially so many pretty ones. He was hoping he could join the tour."

"He's neat." Roberta made up her mind instantly. Walking forward, she gave the dog's head a casual pat. "I'll walk with you, Squat."

Agreeable, the dog rose to lead the way.

There was more to the business of apples than Eden had imagined. It wasn't all trees and plump fruit to be plucked and piled into baskets for market. Harvesting wasn't limited to autumn with the variety of types that were planted. The season, Chase explained, had been extended into months, from early summer to late fall.

They weren't just used for eating and baking. Even cores and peelings were put to use for cider, or dried and shipped to Europe for certain champagnes. As they walked, the scent of ripening fruit filled the air, making more than one mouth water.

The Tree of Life, Eden thought as the scent tempted her. Forbidden fruit. She kept herself surrounded by girls and tried to remember that the tour was educational.

He explained that the quick-maturing trees were planted in the forty-foot spaces between the slow growers, then cut out when the space was needed. A practical business, she remembered, organized, with a high level of utility and little waste. Still, it had the romance of apple blossoms in spring.

Masses of laborers harvested the summer fruit. While they watched the men and machines at work, Chase answered questions.

"They don't look ripe," Roberta commented.

"They're full-size." Chase rested a hand on her shoulder as he chose an apple. "The changes that take place after the fruit's reached maturity are mainly chemical. It goes on without the tree. The fruit's hard, but the seeds are brown. Look." Using a pocketknife with casual skill, he cut the fruit in half. "The apples we harvest now are superior to the ones that hang longer." Reading

Roberta's expression correctly, Chase tossed her half the fruit. The other half Squat took in one yawning bite.

"Maybe you'd like to pick some yourself." The reaction was positive, and Chase reached up to demonstrate. "Twist the fruit off the stem. You don't want to break the twig and lose bearing wood."

Before Eden could react, the girls had scattered to nearby trees. She was facing Chase. Perhaps it was the way his lips curved. Perhaps it was the way his eyes seemed so content to rest on hers, but her mind went instantly and completely blank.

"You have a fascinating business." She could have kicked herself for the inanity of it.

"I like it."

"I, ah…" There must be a question, an intelligent question, she could ask. "I suppose you ship the fruit quickly to avoid spoilage."

He doubted that either of them gave two hoots about apples at the moment, but he was willing to play the game. "It's stored right after picking at thirty-two degrees Fahrenheit. I like your hair pulled back like that. It makes me want to tug on the string and watch it fall all over your shoulders."

Her pulse began to sing, but she pretended she hadn't heard. "I'm sure you have various tests to determine quality."

"We look for richness." Slowly, he turned the fruit over in his hand, but his gaze roamed to her mouth. "Flavor." He watched her lips part as if to taste. "Firmness," he murmured, as he circled her throat with his free hand. "Tenderness."

Her breath seemed to concentrate, to sweeten into the sound of a sigh. It was almost too late when she bit it off. "It would be best if we stuck to the subject at hand."

"Which subject?" His thumb traced along her jawline.

"Apples."

"I'd like to make love with you in the orchards, Eden, with the sun warm on your face and the grass soft at your back."

It terrified her that she could almost taste what it would be like, to be with him, alone. "If you'll excuse me."

"Eden." He took her hand, knowing he was pushing too hard, too fast, but unable to stop himself. "I want you. Maybe too much."

Though his voice was low, hardly more than a whisper, she felt her nerves jangling. "You should know you can't say those things to me here, now. If the children—"

"Have dinner with me."

"No." On this, she told herself she would stand firm. She would not be manipulated. She would not be maneuvered. "I have a job, Chase, one that runs virtually twenty-four hours a day for the next few weeks. Even if I wanted to have dinner with you, which I don't, it would be impossible."

He considered all this reasonable. But then, a great many smoke screens were. "Are you afraid to be alone with me? Really alone."

The truth was plain and simple. She ignored it. "You flatter yourself."

"I doubt a couple hours out of an evening would disrupt the camp's routine, or yours."

"You don't know anything about the camp's routine."

"I know that between your partner and the counselors, the girls are more than adequately supervised. And I know that your last riding lesson is at four o'clock."

"How did you—"

"I asked Roberta," he said easily. "She told me you have supper at six, then a planned activity or free time from seven to nine. Lights-out is at ten. You usually spend your time after supper with the horses. And sometimes you ride out at night when you think everyone's asleep."

She opened her mouth, then shut it again, having no idea what to say. She had thought those rides exclusively hers, exclusively private.

"Why do you ride out alone at night, Eden?"

"Because I enjoy it."

"Then tonight you can enjoy having dinner with me."

She tried to remember there were girls beneath the trees around them. She tried to remember that a display of temper was most embarrassing for the person who lost control. "Perhaps you have some difficulty understanding a polite refusal. Why don't we try this? The last place I want to be tonight, or at any other time, is with you."

He moved his shoulders before he took a step closer. "I guess we can just settle all this now. Here."

"You wouldn't..." She didn't bother to finish the thought. By now she knew very well what he would dare. One quick look around showed her that Roberta and Marcie were leaning against the trunk of a tree, happily munching apples and enjoying the show. "All right, stop it." So much for not being manipulated. "I have no idea why you insist on having dinner with someone who finds you so annoying."

"Me, either. We'll discuss it tonight. Seven-thirty." Tossing Eden the apple, he strolled over toward Roberta.

Eden hefted the fruit. She even went so far as to draw a mental bull's-eye on the back of his head. With a sound of disgust, she took a hefty bite instead.

Chapter Five

Vengefully, Eden dragged a brush through her hair. Despite the harsh treatment, it sprang back softly to wisp around her face and wave to her shoulders. She wouldn't go to any trouble as she had for other dates and dinners, but leave it loose and unstyled. Though he was undoubtedly too hardheaded to notice that sort of female subtlety.

She didn't bother with jewelry, except for the simple pearl studs she often wore around camp. In an effort to look cool, even prim, she wore a high-necked white blouse, regretting only the lace at the cuffs. Matching it with a white skirt, she tried for an icy look. The result was an innocent fragility she couldn't detect in the one small mirror on the wall.

Intending on making it plain that she had gone to no trouble for Chase's benefit, she almost ignored makeup. Grumbling to herself, Eden picked up her blusher. Basic feminine vanity, she admitted; then she added a touch of clear gloss to her lips. There was, after all, a giant step between not fussing and looking like a hag. She was reaching for her bottle of perfume before she stopped herself. No, that was definitely fussing. He would get soap, and soap only. She turned away from the mirror just as Candy swung through the cabin door.

"Wow." Stopping in the doorway, Candy took a long, critical look. "You look terrific."

"I do?" Brow creased, Eden turned back to the mirror. "Terrific wasn't exactly what I was shooting for. I wanted something along the lines of prim."

"You couldn't look prim if you wore sackcloth and ashes, any more than I could look delicate even with lace at my wrists."

With a sound of disgust, Eden tugged at the offending lace. "I knew it. I just knew it was a mistake. Maybe I can rip it off."

"Don't you dare." Laughing, Candy bounded into the room to stop Eden from destroying her blouse. "Besides, it isn't the clothes that are important. It's the attitude, right?"

Eden gave the lace a last tug. "Right. Candy, are you sure everything's going to be under control here? I could still make excuses."

"Everything's already under control." Candy flopped down on her bunk, then began to peel the banana she held. "In fact, things are great. I've just taken a five-minute break to see you off and stuff my face." She took a big bite to prove her point. "Then," she continued over a mouthful of banana, "we're getting together in the mess area to take an inventory of our record collection for the dance. The girls want some practice time before the big night."

"You could probably use extra supervision."

Candy waved her half-eaten banana. "Everyone's going to be in the same four walls for the next couple of hours. You go enjoy your dinner and stop worrying. Where are you going?"

"I don't know." She stuffed some tissue in her bag. "And I really don't care."

"Come on, after nearly six weeks of wholesome but god-awful boring food, aren't you just a little excited about the prospect of oysters Rockefeller or escargots?"

"No." She began to clasp and unclasp her bag. "I'm only going because it was simpler than creating a scene."

Candy broke off a last bite of banana. "Certainly knows how to get his own way, doesn't he?"

"That's about to end." Eden closed her purse with a snap. "Tonight."

At the sound of an approaching car, Candy propped herself up on an elbow. She noticed Eden nervously biting her lower lip, but she only gestured toward the door with her banana peel. "Well, good luck."

Eden caught the grin and paused, her hand on the screen door. "Whose side are you on, anyway?"

"Yours, Eden." Candy stretched, and prepared to go rock and roll. "Always."

"I'll be back early."

Candy grinned, wisely saying nothing as the screen door slammed shut.

However hard Eden might have tried to look remote, icy, disinterested, the breath clogged up in Chase's lungs the moment she stepped outside. They were still an hour from twilight, and the sun's last rays shot through her hair. Her skirt swirled around bare legs honey-toned after long days outdoors. Her chin was lifted, perhaps in anger, perhaps in defiance. He could only see the elegant line of her throat.

The same slowly drumming need rose up inside him the moment she stepped onto the grass.

She'd expected him to look less...dangerous in more formal attire. Eden discovered she had underestimated him again. The muscles in his arms and shoulders weren't so much restricted as enhanced by the sports jacket. The shirt, either by design or good fortune, matched his eyes and was left open at the throat. Slowly and easily he smiled at her, and her lips curved in automatic response.

"I imagined you looking like this." In truth, he hadn't been sure she would come, or what he might have done if she had locked herself away in one of the cabins and refused to see him. "I'm glad you didn't disappoint me."

Feeling her resolve weaken, Eden made an effort to draw back. "I made a bargain," she began, only to fall silent when he handed her a bunch of anemones freshly picked from the side of the road. He wasn't supposed to be sweet, she reminded herself. She wasn't supposed to be vulnerable to sweetness. Still, unable to resist, she buried her face in the flowers.

That was a picture he would carry with him forever, Chase realized. Eden, with wildflowers clutched in both hands; her eyes, touched with both pleasure and confusion, watching him over the petals.

"Thank you."

"You're welcome." Taking one of her hands, he brought it to his lips. She should have pulled away. She knew she should. Yet there was something so simple, so right in the moment—as if she recognized it from some long-ago dream. Bemused, Eden took a step closer, but the sound of giggling brought her out of the spell.

Immediately she tried to pull her hand away. "The girls." She glanced around quickly enough to catch the fielder's cap as it disappeared around the corner of the building.

"Well, then, we wouldn't want to disappoint them?" Turning her hand over, Chase pressed a kiss to her palm. Eden felt the heat spread.

"You're being deliberately difficult." But she closed her hand as if to capture the sensation and hold it.

"Yes." He smiled, but resisted the impulse to draw her into his arms and enjoy the promise he'd seen so briefly in her eyes.

"If you'd let me go, I'd like to put the flowers in water."

"I'll do it." Candy left her post by the door and came outside. Even Eden's glare didn't wipe the smile from her face. "They're lovely, aren't they? Have a good time."

"We'll do that." Chase linked his fingers with Eden's and drew her toward his car. She told herself the sun had been in her eyes. Why else would she have missed the low-slung white Lamborghini parked beside the cabin. She settled herself in the passenger's seat with a warning to herself not to relax.

The moment the engine sprang to life, there was a chorus of goodbyes. Every girl and counselor had lined up to wave them off. Eden disguised a chuckle with a cough.

"It seems this is one of the camp's highlights this summer."

Chase lifted a hand out of the open window to wave back. "Let's see if we can make it one of ours."

Something in his tone made her glance over just long enough to catch that devil of a smile. Eden made up her mind then and there. No, she wouldn't relax, but she'd be damned if she'd be intimidated either. "All right." She leaned back in her seat, prepared to make the best of a bad deal. "I haven't had a meal that wasn't served on a tray in weeks."

"I'll cancel the trays."

"I'd appreciate it." She laughed, then assured herself that laughing wasn't really relaxing. "Stop me if I start stacking the silverware." The breeze blowing in the open window was warm and as fresh as the flowers Chase had brought her. Eden allowed herself the pleasure of lifting her face to it. "This is nice, especially when I was expecting a pickup truck."

"Even country bumpkins can appreciate a well-made machine."

"That's not what I meant." Ready with an apology, she turned, but saw he was smiling. "I suppose you wouldn't care if it was."

"I know what I am, what I want and what I can do." As he took a curve he slowed. His eyes met hers briefly. "But the opinions of certain people always matter. In any case, I prefer the mountains to traffic jams. What do you prefer, Eden?"

"I haven't decided." That was true, she realized with a jolt. In a matter of weeks her priorities, and her hopes, had changed direction. Musing on that, she almost missed the arching ELLIOT sign when Chase turned between the columns. "Where are we going?"

"To dinner."

"In the orchard?"

"In my house." With that he changed gears and had the car cruising up the gravel drive.

Eden tried to ignore the little twist of apprehension she felt. True, this wasn't the crowded, and safe, restaurant she had imagined. She'd shared private dinners before, hadn't she? She'd been raised from the cradle to know how to handle any social situation. But the apprehension remained. Dinner alone with Chase wouldn't be, couldn't possibly be, like any other experience.

Even as she was working out a polite protest, the car crested the hill. The house rose into view.

It was stone. She couldn't know it was local stone, quarried from the mountains. She saw only that it was old, beautifully weathered. At first glance, it gave the appearance of being gray, but on a closer look colors glimmered through. Amber, russet, tints of green and umber. The sun was still high enough to make the chips of mica and quartz glisten. There were three stories, with the second overhanging the first by a skirting balcony. Eden could see flashes of red and buttercup yellow from the pots of geraniums and marigolds. She caught the scent of lavender even before she saw the rock garden.

A wide, sweeping stone stairway, worn slightly in the center, led to double glass doors of diamond panes. A redwood barrel was filled with pansies that nodded in the early evening breeze.

It was nothing like what she had expected, and yet…the house, and everything about it, was instantly recognizable.

His own nervousness caught Chase off guard. Eden said nothing when he stopped the car, still nothing when he got out to round the hood and open her door. It mattered, more than he had ever imagined it could, what she thought, what she said, what she felt about his home.

She held her hand out for his in a gesture he knew was automatic. Then she stood beside him, looking at what was his, what had been his even before his birth. Tension lodged in the back of his neck.

"Oh, Chase, it's beautiful." She lifted her free hand to shield her eyes from the sun behind the house. "No wonder you love it."

"My great-grandfather built it." The tension had dissolved without his being aware of it. "He even helped quarry the stone. He wanted something that would last and that would carry a piece of him as long as it did."

She thought of the home that had been her family's for generations, feeling the too-familiar burning behind her eyes. She'd lost
that. Sold it. The need to tell him was almost stronger than pride,
because in that moment she thought he might understand.

He felt her change in mood even before he glanced down and
saw the glint of tears in her eyes. "What is it, Eden?"

"Nothing." No, she couldn't tell him. Some wounds were best
left hidden. Private. "I was just thinking how important some tra-
ditions are."

"You still miss your father."

"Yes." Her eyes were dry now, the moment past. "I'd love to
see inside."

He hesitated a moment, knowing there had been more and that
she'd been close to sharing it with him. He could wait, Chase told
himself, though his patience was beginning to fray. He would have to
wait until she took that step toward him rather than away from him.

With her hand still in his, he climbed the steps to the door. On
the other side lay a mountain of apricot fur known as Squat. Even
after Chase opened the door, the mound continued to snore.

"Are you sure you should have such a vicious watchdog unchained?"

"My theory is most burglars wouldn't have the nerve to step over
him." Catching Eden around the waist, Chase lifted her up and over.

The stone insulated well against the heat, so the hall was cool
and comfortable. High, beamed ceilings gave the illusion of unlimited space. A Monet landscape caught her eye, but before she
could comment on it, Chase was leading her through a set of
mahogany doors.

The room was cozily square, with window seats recessed into
the east and west walls. Instantly Eden could imagine the charm

of watching the sun rise or set. Comfort was the theme of the room, with its range of blues from the palest aqua to the deepest indigo. Hand-hooked rugs set off the American antiques. There were fresh flowers here, too, spilling out of a Revere Ware bowl. It was a touch she hadn't expected from a bachelor, particularly one who worked with his hands.

Thoughtful, she crossed the room to the west window. The slanting sun cast long shadows over the buildings he had taken them through that morning. She remembered the conveyor belts, the busy sorters and packers, the noise. Behind her was a small, elegant room with pewter bowls and wild roses.

Peace and challenge, she realized, and she sighed without knowing why. "I imagine it's lovely when the sun starts to drop."

"It's my favorite view." His voice came from directly behind her, but for once she didn't stiffen when he rested his hands on her shoulders. He tried to tell himself it was just coincidence that she had chosen to look out that window, but he could almost believe that his own need for her to see and understand had guided her there. It wouldn't be wise to forget who she was and how she chose to live. "There's no Symphony Hall or Rodin Museum."

His fingers gently massaged the curve of her shoulders. But his voice wasn't as patient. Curious, she turned. His hands shifted to let her slide through, then settled on her shoulders again. "I don't imagine they're missed. If they were, you could visit, then come back to this." Without thinking, she lifted her hand to brush the hair from his forehead. Even as she caught herself, his hand closed around her wrist. "Chase, I—"

"Too late," he murmured; then he kissed each of her fingers, one by one. "Too late for you. Too late for me."

She couldn't allow herself to believe that. She couldn't accept the softening and opening of her emotions. How badly she wanted to let him in, to trust again, to need again. How terrifying it was to be vulnerable. "Please don't do this. It's a mistake for both of us."

"You're probably right." He was almost sure of it himself. But he brushed his lips over the pulse that hammered in her wrist. He didn't give a damn. "Everyone's entitled to one enormous mistake."

"Don't kiss me now." She lifted a hand but only curled her fingers into his shirt. "I can't think."

"One has nothing to do with the other."

When his mouth touched hers, it was soft, seeking. *Too late.* The words echoed in her head even as she lifted her hands to his face and let herself go. This is what she had wanted, no matter how many arguments she had posed, no matter how many defenses she had built. She wanted to be held against him, to sink into a dream that had no end.

He felt her fingers stream through his hair and had to force himself not to rush her. Desire, tensed and hungry, had to be held back until it was tempered with acceptance and trust. In his heart he had already acknowledged that she was more than the challenge he had first considered her. She was more than the summer fling he might have preferred. But as her slim, soft body pressed against his, as her warm, willing mouth opened for him, he could only think of how he wanted her, now, when the sun was beginning to sink toward the distant peaks to the west.

"Chase." It was the wild, drumming beat of her heart that frightened her most. She was trembling. Eden could feel it start somewhere deep inside and spread out until it became a stunning combination of panic and excitement. How could she fight the first and give in to the second? "Chase, please."

He had to draw himself back, inch by painful inch. He hadn't meant to take either of them so far, so fast. Yet perhaps he had, he thought as he ran a hand down her hair. Perhaps he had wanted to push them both toward an answer that still seemed just out of reach.

"The sun's going down." His hands weren't quite steady when he turned her toward the window again. "Before long, the lights will change."

She could only be grateful that he was giving her time to regain her composure. Later she would realize how much it probably had cost him.

They stood a moment in silence, watching the first tints of rose spread above the mountains. A loud, rasping cough had her already-tense nerves jolting.

"S'cuze me."

The man in the doorway had a grizzled beard that trailed down to the first button of his red checked shirt. Though he was hardly taller than Eden, his bulk gave the impression of power. The folds and lines in his face all but obscured his dark eyes. Then he grinned, and she caught the glint of a gold tooth.

So this was the little lady who had the boss running around in circles. Deciding she was prettier than a barrelful of prime apples, he nodded to her by way of greeting. "Supper's ready. Unless you want to eat it cold, you best be moving along."

"Eden Carlbough, Delaney." Chase only lifted a brow, knowing Delaney had already sized up the situation. "He cooks and I don't, which is why I haven't fired him yet."

This brought on a cackle. "He hasn't fired me because I wiped his nose and tied his shoes."

"We could add that that was close to thirty years ago."

She recognized both affection and exasperation. It pleased her to know someone could exasperate Chase Elliot. "It's nice to meet you, Mr. Delaney."

"Delaney, ma'am. Just Delaney." Still grinning, he pulled on his beard. "Mighty pretty," he said to Chase. "It's smarter to think of settling down with someone who isn't an eyesore at breakfast. Supper's going to get cold," he added. Then he was gone.

Though Eden had remained politely silent during Delaney's statement, it took only one look at Chase's face to engender a stream of laughter. The sound made Chase think more seriously about gagging Delaney with his own beard.

"I'm glad you're amused."

"Delighted. It's the first time I've ever seen you speechless. And I can't help be pleased not to be considered an eyesore." Then she disarmed him by offering him her hand. "Supper's going to get cold."

Instead of the dining room, Chase led her out to a jalousied porch. Two paddle fans circled overhead, making the most of the breeze that crept in the slanted windows. A wind chime jingled cheerfully between baskets of fuchsia.

"Your home is one surprise after another," Eden commented as she studied the plump love seats and the glass-and-wicker table. "Every room seems fashioned for relaxation and stunning views."

The table was set with colorful stoneware. Though the sun had yet to drop behind the peaks, two tapers were already burning. There was a single wild rose beside her plate.

Romance, she thought. This was the romance she had once dreamed of. This was the romance she must now be very wary of.

But, wary or not, she picked up the flower and smiled at him. "Thank you."

"Did you want one, too?" As she laughed, Chase drew back her chair.

"Sit down. Sit down. Eat while it's hot." Despite his bulk, Delaney bustled into the room. In his large hands was an enormous tray. Because she realized how easily she could be mowed down, Eden obeyed. "Hope you got an appetite. You could use a little plumping up, missy. Then, I've always preferred a bit of healthy meat on female bones."

As he spoke, he began to serve an exquisite seafood salad. "Made my special, Chicken Delaney. It'll keep under the covers if you two don't dawdle over the salad. Apple pie's on the hot plate, biscuits in the warmer." He stuck a bottle of wine unceremoniously in an ice bucket. "That's the fancy wine you wanted." Standing back, he took a narrowed-eyed glance around before snorting with satisfaction. "I'm going home. Don't let my chicken get cold." Wiping his hands on his jeans, he marched to the door and let it swing shut behind him.

"Delaney has amazing style, doesn't he?" Chase took the wine from the bucket to pour two glasses.

"Amazing," Eden agreed, finding it amazing enough that those gnarled hands had created anything as lovely as the salad in front of her.

"He makes the best biscuits in Pennsylvania." Chase lifted his glass and toasted her. "And I'd put his Beef Wellington up against anyone's."

"Beef Wellington?" With a shake of her head, Eden sipped her wine. It was cool, just a shade tart. "I hope you'll take it the right way when I say he looks more like the type who could charcoal a steak over a backyard grill." She dipped her fork in the salad and sampled it. "But..."

"Appearances can be deceiving," Chase finished for her, pleased with the way her eyes half shut as she tasted. "Delaney's been cooking here as long as I can remember. He lives in a little cottage my grandfather helped him build about forty years ago. Nose-wiping and shoe-tying aside, he's part of the family."

She only nodded, looking down at her plate for a moment as she remembered how difficult it had been to tell her longtime servants she was selling out. Perhaps they had never been as familiar or as informal as Chase's Delaney, but they, too, had been part of the family.

It was there again, that dim candle glow of grief he'd seen in her eyes before. Wanting only to help, he reached over to touch her hand. "Eden?"

Quickly, almost too quickly, she moved her hand and began to eat again. "This is wonderful. I have an aunt back home who would shanghai your Delaney after the first forkful."

Home, he thought, backing off automatically. Philadelphia was still home.

The Chicken Delaney lived up to its name. As the sun set, the meal passed easily, even though they disagreed on almost every subject.

She read Keats and he read Christie. She preferred Bach and he Haggard, but it didn't seem to matter as the glass walls filtered the rosy light of approaching twilight. The candles burned lower. The wine shimmered in crystal, inviting one more sip. Close and clear and quick came the two-tone call of a quail.

"That's a lovely sound." Her sigh was easy and content. "If things are quiet at camp, we can hear the birds in the evening. There's a whippoorwill who's taken to singing right outside the cabin window. You can almost set your watch by her."

"Most of us are creatures of habit," he murmured. He wondered about her, what habits she had, what habits she had changed. Taking her hand, he turned it up. The ridge of callus had hardened. "You didn't take my advice."

"About what?"

"Wearing gloves."

"It didn't seem worth it. Besides…" Letting the words trail off, she lifted her wine.

"Besides?"

"Having calluses means I did something to earn them." She blurted it out, then sat swearing at herself and waiting for him to laugh.

He didn't. Instead he sat silently, passing his thumb over the toughened skin and watching her. "Will you go back?"

"Go back?"

"To Philadelphia."

It was foolish to tell him how hard she'd tried not to think about that. Instead, she answered as the practical Eden was supposed to. "The camp closes down the last week in August. Where else would I go?"

"Where else?" he agreed, but when he released her hand she felt a sense of loss rather than relief. "Maybe there comes a time in everyone's life when they have to take a hard look at the options." He rose, and her hands balled into fists. He took a step toward her, and her heart rose up to her throat. "I'll be back."

Alone, she let out a long, shaky breath. What had she been expecting? she asked herself. What had she been hoping for? Her legs weren't quite steady when she rose, but it could have been the wine. But wine would have made her warm, and she felt a chill. To ward it off, she rubbed her arms with her hands. The sky was a quiet, deepening blue but for a halo of scarlet along the horizon. She concentrated on that, trying not to imagine how it would look when the stars came out.

Maybe they would look at the stars together again. They could look, picking out the patterns, and she would again feel that click that meant her needs and dreams were meshing. With his.

Pressing a hand to her lips, she struggled to block off that train of thought. It was only that the evening had been lovelier than she had imagined. It was only that they had more in common than she had believed possible. It was only that he had a gentleness inside him that softened parts of her when she least expected it. And when he kissed her, she felt as though she had the world pulsing in the palm of her hand.

No. Uneasy, she wrapped her hands around her forearms and squeezed. She was romanticizing again, spinning daydreams when she had no business dreaming at all. She was just beginning to sort out her life, to make her own place. It wasn't possible that she was looking to him to be any part of it.

She heard the music then, something low and unfamiliar that nonetheless had tiny shivers working their way up her spine. She had to leave, she thought quickly. And right away. She had let the atmosphere get to her. The house, the sunset, the wine. Him. Hearing his footsteps, she turned. She would tell him she had to get back. She would thank him for the evening, and…escape.

When he came back into the room, she was standing beside the table so that the candlelight flickered over her skin. Dusk swirled behind her with its smoky magic. The scent of wild roses from the bush outside the window seemed to sigh into the room. He wondered, if he touched her now, if she would simply dissolve in his hands.

"Chase, I think I'd better——"

"Shh." She wouldn't dissolve, he told himself as he went to her. She was real, and so was he. One hand captured hers, the other slipping around her waist. After one moment of resistance, she began to move with him. "One of the pleasures of country music is dancing to it."

"I, ah, I don't know the song." But it felt so good, so very good, to sway with him while darkness fell.

"It's about a man, a woman and passion. The best songs are."

She shut her eyes. She could feel the brush of his jacket against her cheek, the firm press of his hand at her waist. He smelled of soap, but nothing a woman would use. This had a tang that was essentially masculine. Wanting to taste, she moved her head so that her lips rested against his neck.

His pulse beat there, quick, surprising her. Forgetting caution, she nestled closer and felt its sudden rise in speed. As her own raced to match it, she gave a murmur of pleasure and traced it with the tip of her tongue.

He started to draw her away. He meant to. When he'd left her, he'd promised himself that he would slow the pace to one they could both handle. But now she was cuddled against him, her body swaying, her fingers straying to his neck, and her mouth… With an oath, Chase dragged her closer and gave in to hunger.

The kiss was instantly torrid, instantly urgent. And somehow, though she had never experienced anything like it, instantly familiar.

Her head tilted back in surrender. Her lips parted. Here and now, she wanted the fire and passion that had only been hinted at.

Perhaps he lowered her to the love seat, perhaps she drew him to it, but they were wrapped together, pressed against the cushions. An owl hooted once, then twice, then gave them silence.

He'd wanted to believe she could be this generous. He'd wanted to believe his lips would touch hers and find unrestricted sweetness. Now his mind spun with it. Whatever he had wanted, whatever he had dreamed of, was less, so much less than what he now held in his arms.

He stroked a hand down her body and met trembling response. With a moan, she arched against him. Through the sheer fabric of her blouse, he could feel the heat rising to her skin, enticing him to touch again and yet again.

He released the first button of her blouse, then the second, following the course with his lips. She shivered with anticipation. Her lace cuffs brushed against his cheeks as she lifted her hands to his hair. It seemed her body was filling, flooding with sensations she'd once only imagined. Now they were so real and so clear that she could feel each one as it layered over the next.

The pillows at her back were soft. His body was hard and hot. The breeze that jingled the wind chime overhead was freshened with flowers. Behind her closed eyes came the flicker and glow of candlelight. In teams of thousands, the cicadas began to sing. But more thrilling, more intense, was the sound of her name whispering from him as he pressed his lips against her skin.

Suddenly, searing, his mouth took hers again. In the kiss she could taste everything, his need, his desire, the passion that teetered on the edge of sanity. As her own madness hovered, she felt her senses swimming with him. And she moaned with the ecstasy of falling in love.

For one brief moment, she rose on it, thrilled with the knowledge that she had found him. The dream and the reality were both here. She had only to close them both in her arms and watch them become one.

Then the terror of it fell on her. She couldn't let it be real. How could she risk it? Once she had given her trust and her promise, if not her heart. And she had been betrayed. If it happened again, she would never recover. If it happened with Chase, she wouldn't want to.

"Chase, no more." She turned her face away and tried to clear her head. "Please, this has to stop."

Her taste was still exploding in his mouth. Beneath his, her body was trembling with a need he knew matched his own. "Eden, for God's sake." With an effort that all but drained him, he lifted his head to look down at her. She was afraid. He recognized her fear immediately and struggled to hold back his own needs. "I won't hurt you."

That almost undid her. He meant it, she was sure, but that didn't mean it wouldn't happen. "Chase, this isn't right for me. For either of us."

"Isn't it?" Tension knotted in his stomach as he drew her toward him. "Can you tell me you didn't feel how right it was a minute ago?"

"No." It was both confusion and fear that had her dragging her hands through her hair. "But this isn't what I want. I need you to understand that this can't be what I want. Not now."

"You're asking a hell of a lot."

"Maybe. But there isn't any choice."

That infuriated him. She was the one who had taken his choice away, simply by existing. He hadn't asked her to fall into his life. He hadn't asked her to become the focus of it before he had a chance for a second breath. She'd given in to him to the point where he was half-mad for her. Now she was drawing away. And asking him to understand.

"We'll play it your way." His tone chilled as he drew away from her.

She shuddered, recognizing instantly that his anger could be lethal. "It's not a game."

"No? Well, in any case, you play it well."

She pressed her lips together, understanding that she deserved at least a part of the lash. "Please, don't spoil what happened."

He walked to the table and, lifting his glass, studied the wine. "What did happen?"

I fell in love with you. Rather than answer him, she began to button her blouse with nerveless fingers.

"I'll tell you." He tossed back the remaining wine, but it didn't soothe him. "Not for the first time in our fascinating relationship, you blew hot and cold without any apparent reason. It makes me wonder if Eric backed out of the marriage out of self-defense."

He saw her fingers freeze on the top button of her blouse. Even in the dim light, he could watch the color wash out of her face. Very carefully, he set his glass down again. "I'm sorry, Eden. That was uncalled-for."

The fight for control and composure was a hard war, but she won. She made her fingers move until the button was in place, then, slowly, she rose. "Since you're so interested, I'll tell you that

Eric jilted me for more practical reasons. I appreciate the meal, Chase. It was lovely. Please thank Delaney for me."

"Damn it, Eden."

When he started forward, her body tightened like a bow. "If you could do one thing for me, it would be to take me back now and say nothing. Absolutely nothing."

Turning, she walked away from the candlelight.

Chapter Six

During the first weeks of August, the camp was plagued with one calamity after another. The first was an epidemic of poison ivy. Within twenty-four hours, ten of the girls and three of the counselors were coated with calamine lotion. The sticky heat did nothing to make the itching more bearable.

Just as the rashes started to fade came three solid days of rain. As the camp was transformed into a muddy mire, outdoor activities were canceled. Tempers soared. Eden broke up two hair-pulling battles in one day. Then, as luck would have it, lightning hit one of the trees and distracted the girls from their boredom.

By the time the sun came out, they had enough pot holders, key chains, wallets and pillows to open their own craft shop.

Men with Jeeps and chain saws came to clear away the debris from the tree. Eden wrote out a check and prayed the last crisis was over.

It was doubtful the check had even been cashed when the secondhand restaurant stove she and Candy had bought stopped working. In the three days the parts were on order, cooking was done in true camp style—around an open fire.

The gelding, Courage, developed an infection that settled in his lungs. Everyone in camp worried about him and fussed over him and pampered him. The vet dosed him with penicillin. Eden spent three sleepless nights in the stables, nursing him and waiting for the crisis to pass.

Eventually the horse's appetite improved, the mud in the compound dried and the stove was back in working order. Eden told herself that the worst had to be over as the camp's routine picked up again.

Yet oddly, the lull brought out a restlessness she'd been able to ignore while the worst was happening. At dusk, she wandered to the stables with her sackful of apples. It wasn't hard to give a little extra attention to Courage. He'd gotten used to being pampered during his illness. Eden slipped him a carrot to go with the apple.

Still, as she worked her way down the stalls, she found the old routine didn't keep her mind occupied. The emergencies over the past couple of weeks had kept her too busy to take a second breath, much less think. Now, with calm settling again, thinking was unavoidable.

She could remember her evening with Chase as if it had been the night before. Every word spoken, every touch, every gesture, was locked in her mind as it had been when it had been happening. The rushing, tumbling sensation of falling in love was just as vital now, and just as frightening.

She hadn't been prepared for it. Her life had always been a series of preparations and resulting actions. Even her engagement had been a quiet step along a well-paved road. Since then, she'd learned to handle the detours and the roadblocks. But Chase was a sudden one-way street that hadn't been on any map.

It didn't matter, she told herself as she finished Patience's rubdown. She would navigate this and swing herself back in the proper direction. Having her choices taken away at this point in her life wasn't something she would tolerate. Not even when the lack of choice seemed so alluring and so right.

"I thought I'd find you here." Candy leaned against the stall door to give the mare a pat. "How was Courage tonight?"

"Good." Eden walked to the little sink in the corner to wash liniment from her hands. "I don't think we have to worry about him anymore."

"I'm glad to know that you'll be using your bunk instead of a pile of hay."

Eden pressed both hands to the small of her back and stretched. No demanding set of tennis had ever brought on this kind of ache. Strangely enough, she liked it. "I never thought I'd actually look forward to sleeping in that bunk."

"Well, now that you're not worried about the gelding, I can tell you I'm worried about you."

"Me?" Eden looked for a towel and, not finding one, dried her hands on her jeans. "Why?"

"You're pushing yourself too hard."

"Don't be silly. I'm barely pulling my weight."

"That stopped being even close to the truth the second week of camp." Now that she'd decided to speak up, Candy took a deep breath. "Damn it, Eden, you're exhausted."

"Tired," Eden corrected her. "Which is nothing a few hours on that miserable bunk won't cure."

"Look, it's okay if you want to avoid the issue with everyone else, even with yourself. But don't do it with me."

It wasn't often Candy's voice took on that firm, no-nonsense tone. Eden lifted a brow and nodded. "All right, what is the issue?"

"Chase Elliot," Candy stated, and she saw Eden freeze up. "I didn't hound you with questions the night you came back from dinner."

"And I appreciate that."

"Well, don't, because I'm asking now."

"We had dinner, talked a bit about books and music, then he brought me back."

Candy closed the stall door with a creak. "I thought I was your friend."

"Oh, Candy, you know you are." With a sigh, Eden closed her eyes a moment. "All right, we did exactly what I said we did, but somewhere between the talk and the ride home, things got a little out of hand."

"What sort of things?"

Eden found she didn't even have the energy to laugh. "I've never known you to pry."

"I've never known you to settle comfortably into depression."

"Am I?" Eden blew her bangs out of her eyes. "God, maybe I am."

"Let's just say that you've jumped from one problem to the next in order to avoid fixing one of your own." Taking a step closer, Candy drew Eden down on a small bench. "So let's talk."

"I'm not sure I can." Linking her hands, Eden looked down at them. The opal ring that had once been her mother's winked back at her. "I promised myself after Papa died and everything was in such a mess that I would handle things and find the best way to solve the problems. I've needed to solve them myself."

"That doesn't mean you can't lean on a friend."

"I've leaned on you so much I'm surprised you can walk upright."

"I'll let you know when I start limping. Eden, unless my memory's faulty, we've taken turns leaning on each other since before either of us could walk. Tell me about Chase."

"He scares me." With a long breath, Eden leaned back against the wall. "Everything's happening so fast, and everything I feel seems so intense." Dropping the last of her guard, she turned her face to Candy's. "If things had worked out differently, I'd be married to another man right now. How can I even think I might be in love with someone else so soon?"

"You're not going to tell me you think you're fickle." The last thing Eden had expected was Candy's bright, bubbling laughter, but that was what echoed off the stable walls. "Eden, I'm the fickle one, remember? You've always been loyal to a fault. Wait, I can see you're getting annoyed, so let's take this logically." Candy crossed her ankles and began to count off on her fingers.

"First, you were engaged to Eric—the slime—because of all the reasons we've discussed before. It seemed the proper thing to do. Were you in love with him?"

"No, but I thought——"

"Irrelevant. No is the answer. Second, he showed his true colors, the engagement's been off for months, and you've met a fascinating, attractive man. Now, let's even take it a step further." Warming up to the subject, Candy shifted on the bench. "Suppose—God forbid—that you had actually been madly in love with Eric. After he had shown himself to be a snake, your heart would have been broken. With time and effort, you would have pulled yourself back together. Right?"

"I certainly like to think so."

"So we agree."

"Marginally."

That was enough for Candy. "Then, heart restored, if you'd met a fascinating and attractive man, you would have been equally free to fall for him. Either way, you're in the clear." Satisfied, Candy rose and dusted her palms on her jeans. "So what's the problem?"

Not certain she could explain, or even make sense of it herself, Eden looked down at her hands. "Because I've learned something. Love is a commitment, it's total involvement, promises, compromises. I'm not sure I can give those things to anyone yet. And if I were, I don't know if Chase feels at all the same way."

"Eden, your instincts must tell you he does."

With a shake of her head, she rose. She did feel better having said it all out loud, but that didn't change the bottom line. "I've learned not to trust my instincts, but to be realistic. Which is why I'm going to go hit the account books."

"Oh, Eden, give it a break."

"Unfortunately, I had to give it a break during the poison ivy, the lightning, the stove breakdown and the vet visits." Hooking her arm through Candy's, she started to walk toward the door. "You were right, and talking it out helped, but practicality is still the order of the day."

"Meaning checks and balances."

"Right. I'd really like to get to it. The advantage is I can frazzle my brain until the bunk really does feel like a feather bed."

Candy pushed open the door, then squared her shoulders. "I'll help."

"Thanks, but I'd like to finish them before Christmas."

"Oh, low blow, Eden."

"But true." She latched the door behind them. "Don't worry about me, Candy. Talking about it cleared my head a bit."

"Doing something about it would be better, but it's a start. Don't work too late."

"A couple of hours," Eden promised.

The office, as Eden arrogantly called it, was a small side room off the kitchen. After switching on the gooseneck lamp on the metal army-surplus desk, she adjusted the screen, flap up. As an afterthought, she switched the transistor radio on the corner of the desk to a classical station. The quiet, familiar melodies would go a long way toward calming her.

Still, as always, she drew in a deep breath as she took her seat behind the desk. Here, she knew too well, things were black-and-white. There were no multiple choices, no softening the rules as there could be in other areas of the camp. Figures were figures and facts were facts. It was up to her to tally them.

Opening the drawers, she pulled out invoices, the business checkbook and the ledger. She began systematically sorting and entering as the tape spilled out of the adding machine at her elbow.

Within twenty minutes, she knew the worst. The additional expenses of the past two weeks had stretched their capital to the limit. No matter how many ways Eden worked the numbers, the answer was the same. They weren't dead broke, but painfully close to it. Wearily, she rubbed the bridge of her nose between her thumb and forefinger.

They could still make it, she told herself. She pressed her hand down on the pile of papers, letting her palm cover the checks and balances. By the skin of their teeth, she thought, but they could still make it. If there were no more unexpected expenses. And if, she continued, the pile seeming to grow under her hand, she and Candy lived frugally over the winter. She imagined the pile growing another six inches under her restraining hand. If they got the necessary enrollments for the next season, everything would turn around.

Curling her fingers around the papers, she let out a long breath. If one of those *if*s fell through, she still had some jewelry that could be sold.

The lamplight fell across her opal-and-diamond ring, but she looked away, feeling guilty at even considering selling it. But she would. If her other choices were taken away, she would. What she wouldn't do was give up.

The tears began so unexpectedly that they fell onto the blotter before she knew she had shed them. Even as she wiped them away, new ones formed. There was no one to see, no one to hear. Giving in, Eden laid her head on the piles of bills and let the tears come.

They wouldn't change anything. With tears would come no fresh ideas or brilliant answers, but she let them come anyway. Quite simply, her strength had run out.

He found her like that, weeping almost soundlessly over the neat stacks of paper. At first Chase only stood there, with the door not quite shut at his back. She looked so helpless, so utterly spent. He wanted to go to her, but held himself back. He understood that the tears would be private. She wouldn't want to share them, particularly not with him. And yet, even as he told himself to step back, he moved toward her.

"Eden."

Her head shot up at the sound of her name. Her eyes were drenched, but he saw both shock and humiliation in them before she began to dry her cheeks with the backs of her hands.

"What are you doing here?"

"I wanted to see you." It sounded simple enough, but didn't come close to what was moving inside him. He wanted to go to her, to gather her close and fix whatever was wrong. He stuck his hands in his pockets and remained standing just inside the door. "I just heard about the gelding this morning. Is he worse?"

She shook her head, then struggled to keep her voice calm. "No, he's better. It wasn't as serious as we thought it might be."

"That's good." Frustrated by his inability to think of something less inane, he began to pace. How could he offer comfort when she wouldn't share the problem? Her eyes were dry now, but he knew it was pride, and pride alone, that held her together. The hell with her pride, he thought. He needed to help.

When he turned back, he saw she had risen from the desk. "Why don't you tell me about it?"

The need to confide in him was so painfully strong that she automatically threw up the customary shield. "There's nothing to tell. It's been a rough couple of weeks. I suppose I'm overtired."

It was more than that, he thought, though she did look exhausted. "The girls getting to you?"

"No, really, the girls are fine."

Frustrated, he looked for another answer. The radio was playing something slow and romantic. Glancing toward it, Chase noticed the open ledger. The tail of adding-machine tape was spilling onto the floor. "Is it money? I could help."

Eden closed the book with a snap. Humiliation was a bitter taste at the back of her throat. At least it dried the last of her tears. "We're fine," she told him in a voice that was even and cool. "If you'd excuse me, I still have some work to do."

Rejection was something Chase had never fully understood until he'd met her. He didn't care for it. Nodding slowly, he searched for patience. "It was meant as an offer, not an insult." He would have turned and left her then, but the marks of weeping and sleeplessness gave her a pale, wounded look. "I'm sorry about the trouble you've been having the past year, Eden. I knew you'd lost your father, but I didn't know about the estate."

She wanted, oh so badly, to reach out, to let him gather her close and give her all the comfort she needed. She wanted to ask him what she should do, and have him give her the answers. But wouldn't that mean that all the months of struggling for self-sufficiency had been for nothing? She straightened her shoulders. "It isn't necessary to be sorry."

"If you had told me yourself, it would have been simpler."

"It didn't concern you."

He didn't so much ignore the stab of hurt as turn it into annoyance. "Didn't it? I felt differently—feel differently. Are you going to stand there and tell me there's nothing between us, Eden?"

She couldn't deny it, but she was far too confused, far too afraid, to try to define the truth. "I don't know how I feel about you, except that I don't want to feel anything. Most of all, I don't want your pity."

The hands in his pockets curled into fists. He didn't know how to handle his own feelings, his own needs. Now she was treating them as though they didn't matter. He could leave, or he could beg. At the moment, Chase saw no choice between the two. "Understanding and pity are different things, Eden. If you don't know that, there's nothing else to say."

Turning, he left her. The screen door swished quietly behind him.

For the next two days, Eden functioned. She gave riding instructions, supervised meals and hiked the hills with groups of girls. She talked and laughed and listened, but the hollowness that had spread inside her when the door had closed at Chase's back remained.

Guilt and regret. Those were the feelings she couldn't shake, no matter how enthusiastically she threw herself into her routine. She'd been wrong. She'd known it even as it was happening, but pride had boxed her in. He had offered to help. He had offered to care, and she'd refused him. If there was a worse kind of selfishness, she couldn't name it.

She'd started to phone him, but hadn't been able to dial the number. It hadn't been pride that had held her back this time. Every apology that formed in her mind was neat and tidy and meaningless. She couldn't bear to give him a stilted apology, nor could she bear the possibility that he wouldn't care.

Whatever had started to grow between them, she had squashed. Whatever might have been, she had cut off before it had begun to flower. How could she explain to Chase that she'd been afraid of being hurt again? How could she tell him that when he'd offered help and understanding she'd been afraid to accept it because it was so easy to be dependent?

She began to ride out alone at night again. Solitude didn't soothe her as it once had; it only reminded her that she had taken steps to insure that she would remain alone. The nights were warm, with the lingering scent of honeysuckle bringing back memories of a night where there had been pictures in the sky. She couldn't look at the stars without thinking of him.

Perhaps that was why she rode to the lake, where the grass was soft and thick. Here she could smell the water and wild blossoms. The horse's hooves were muffled, and she could just hear the rustle of wings in flight—some unseen bird in search of prey or a mate.

Then she saw him.

The moon was on the wane, so he was only a shadow, but she knew he was watching her. Just as she had known, somehow, that she would find him there tonight. Reining in, she let the magic take her. For the moment, even if it were only a moment, she would forget everything but that she loved him. Tomorrow would take care of itself.

She slid from the horse and went to him.

He said nothing. Until she touched him, he wasn't sure she wasn't a dream. In silence, she framed his face in her hands and pressed her lips to his. No dream had ever tasted so warm. No illusion had ever felt so soft.

"Eden—"

With a shake of her head, she cut off his words. There were weeks of emptiness to fill, and no questions that needed answering. Rising on her toes, she kissed him again. The only sound was her sigh as his arms finally came around her. She discovered a bottomless well of giving inside her. Something beyond passion, something beyond desire. Here was comfort, strength and the understanding she had been afraid to accept.

His fingers trailed up to her hair, as if each touch reassured him she was indeed real. When he opened his eyes again, his arms wouldn't be empty, but filled with her. Her cheek rubbed his, smooth skin against a day's growth of beard. With her head nestled in a curve of his shoulder, she watched the wink and blink of fireflies and thought of stars.

They stood in silence while an owl hooted and the horse whinnied in response.

"Why did you come?" He needed an answer, one he could take back with him when she had left him again.

"To see you." She drew away, wanting to see his face. "To be with you."

"Why?"

The magic shimmered and began to dim. With a sigh, she drew back. Dreams were for sleeping, Eden reminded herself. And questions had to be answered. "I wanted to apologize for the way I behaved before. You were being kind." Searching for words, she turned to pluck a leaf from the tree that shadowed them. "I know how I must have seemed, how I sounded, and I am sorry. It's difficult, still difficult for me to…" Restless, she moved her shoulders. "We were able to muffle most of the publicity after my father died, but there was a great deal of gossip, of speculation and not-so-quiet murmurs."

When he said nothing, she shifted again, uncomfortable. "I suppose I resented all of that more than anything else. It became very important to me to prove myself, that I could manage, even succeed. I realize that I've become sensitive about handling things

myself and that when you offered to help, I reacted badly. I apologize for that."

Silence hung another moment before he took a step toward her.
Eden thought he moved the way the shadows did. Silently. "That's
a nice apology, Eden. Before I accept it, I'd like to ask if the kiss
was part of it."

So he wasn't going to make it easy for her. Her chin lifted. She
didn't need an easy road any longer. "No."

Then he smiled and circled her throat with his hand. "What was
it for then?"

The smile disturbed her more than the touch, though it was the
touch she backed away from. Strange how you could take one step
and find yourself sunk to the hips. "Does there have to be a reason?"
When she walked toward the edge of the lake, she saw an owl
swoop low over the water. That was the way she felt, she realized.
As if she were skimming along the surface of something that could
take her in over her head. "I wanted to kiss you, so I did."

The tension he'd lived with for weeks had vanished, leaving him
almost light-headed. He had to resist the urge to scoop her up and
carry her home, where he'd begun to understand she belonged.
"Do you always do what you want?"

She turned back with a toss of her head. She'd apologized, but
the pride remained. "Always."

He grinned, nudging a smile from her. "So do I."

"Then we should understand each other."

He trailed a finger down her cheek. "Remember that."

"I will." Steady again, she moved past him to the gelding. "We're
having a dance a week from Saturday. Would you like to come?"

His hand closed over hers on the reins. "Are you asking me for a date?"

Amused, she swung her hair back before settling a foot in the stirrup. "Certainly not. We're short of chaperons."

She bent her leg to give herself a boost into the saddle, but found herself caught at the waist. She dangled in midair for a moment before Chase set her on the ground again, turning her to face him. "Will you dance with me?"

She remembered the last time they had danced and saw from the look in his eyes that he did as well. Her heart fluttered in the back of her dry throat, but she lifted a brow and smiled. "Maybe."

His lips curved, then descended slowly to brush against hers. She felt the world tilt, then steady at an angle only lovers understand. "A week from Saturday," he murmured, then lifted her easily into the saddle. His hand remained over hers another moment. "Miss me."

He stayed by the water until she was gone and the night was silent again.

Chapter Seven

The last weeks of summer were hot and long. At night, there was invariably heat lightning and rumbling thunder, but little rain. Eden pushed herself through the days, blocking out the uncertainty of life after September.

She wasn't escaping, she told herself. She was coping with one day at a time. If she had learned one important lesson over the summer, it was that she could indeed make changes, in herself and in her life.

The frightened and defeated woman who had come to Camp Liberty almost as if it were a sanctuary would leave a confident, successful woman who could face the world on her own terms.

Standing in the center of the compound, she ran her hands down her narrow hips before dipping them into the pockets of her shorts. Next summer would be even better, now that they'd faced the pitfalls and learned how to maneuver around them. She knew she was skipping over months of her life, but found she didn't want to dwell on the winter. She didn't want to think of Philadelphia and snowy sidewalks, but of the mountains and what she had made of her life there.

If it had been possible, she would have found a way to stay behind during the off-season. Eden had begun to understand that only necessity and the need for employment were taking her back east. It wasn't her home any longer.

With a shake of her head, Eden pushed away thoughts of December. The sun was hot and bright. She could watch it shimmer on the surface of Chase's lake and think of him.

She wondered what would have happened if she had met him two years earlier when her life had been so ordered and set and mapped-out. Would she have fallen in love with him then? Perhaps it was all a matter of timing; perhaps she would have given him a polite how-do-you-do and forgotten him.

No. Closing her eyes, she could recall vividly every sensation, every emotion he'd brought into her life. Timing had nothing to do with something so overwhelming. No matter when, no matter where, she would have fallen in love with him. Hadn't she fought it all along, only to find her feelings deepening?

But she'd thought herself in love with Eric, too.

She shivered in the bright sun and watched a jay race overhead. Was she so shallow, so cold, that her feelings could shift and change in the blink of an eye? That was what held her back and warned her to be cautious. If Eric hadn't turned his back on her, she would have married him. His ring would be on her finger even now. Eden glanced down at her bare left hand.

But that hadn't been love, she reassured herself. Now she knew what love felt like, what it did to heart and mind and body. And yet... How did he feel? He cared, and he wanted, but she knew enough of love now to understand that wasn't enough. She, too, had once cared and wanted. If Chase was in love with her, there wouldn't be any *before*. Time would begin now.

Don't be a fool, she told herself with a flash of annoyance. That kind of thinking would only make her drift back to dependence. There was a before for both of them, and a future. There was no way of being sure that the future would merge with what she felt today.

But she wanted to be a fool, she realized with a quick, delicious shudder. Even if only for a few weeks, she wanted to absorb and concentrate all those mad feelings. She'd be sensible again. Sensible was for January, when the wind was sharp and the rent had to be paid. In a few days she would dance with him, smile up at him. She would have that one night of the summer to be a fool.

Kicking off her shoes, Eden plucked them up in one hand and ran the rest of the way to the dock. Girls, already separated into groups, were waiting for the signal to row out into the lake.

"Miss Carlbough!" In her camp uniform and her familiar cap, Roberta hopped up and down on the grass near the rowboats. "Watch this." With a quick flurry of motion, she bent over, kicked up her feet and stood on her head. "What do you think?" she demanded through teeth clenched with effort. Her triangular face reddened.

"Incredible."

"I've been practicing." With a grunt, Roberta tumbled onto the grass. "Now, when my mom asks what I did at camp, I can stand on my head and show her."

Eden lifted a brow, hoping Mrs. Snow got a few more details. "I'm sure she'll be impressed."

Still sprawled on the grass, arms splayed out to the sides, Roberta stared up at Eden. She was just old enough to wish that her hair was blond and wavy. "You look real pretty today, Miss Carlbough."

Touched, and more than a little surprised, Eden held out a hand to help Roberta up. "Why, thank you, Roberta. So do you."

"Oh, I'm not pretty, but I'm going to be once I can wear makeup and cover my freckles."

Eden rubbed a thumb over Roberta's cheek. "Lots of boys fall for freckles."

"Maybe." Roberta tucked that away to consider later. "I guess you're soft on Mr. Elliot."

Eden dropped her hand back in her pocket. "Soft on?"

"You know." To demonstrate, Roberta sighed and fluttered her eyes. Eden wasn't sure whether to laugh or give the little monster a shove into the lake.

"That's ridiculous."

"Are you getting married?"

"I haven't the vaguest idea where you come up with such nonsense. Now into the boat. Everyone's ready to go."

"My mom told me people sometimes get married when they're soft on each other."

"I'm sure your mother's quite right." Hoping to close the subject, Eden helped Roberta into their assigned rowboat, where Marcie and Linda were already waiting. "However, in this case, Mr. Elliot and I barely know each other. Everyone hook their life jackets, please."

"Mom said she and Daddy fell in love at first sight." Roberta hooked on the preserver, though she thought it was a pain when she swam so well. "They kiss all the time."

"I'm sure that's nice. Now——"

"I used to think it was kind of gross, but I guess it's okay." Roberta settled into her seat and smiled. "Well, if you decide not to marry Mr. Elliot, maybe I will."

Eden was busy locking in the oars, but she glanced up. "Oh?"

"Yeah. He's got a neat dog and all those apple trees." Roberta adjusted the brim of her cap over her eyes. "And he's kind of pretty." The two girls beside her giggled in agreement.

"That's certainly something to think about." Eden began to row. "Maybe you can discuss the idea with your mother when you get home."

"'Kay. Can I row first?"

Eden could only be grateful that the girl's interest span was as fast-moving as the rest of her. "Fine. You and I will row out. Marcie and Linda can row back."

After a bit of drag and a few grunts, Roberta matched her rhythm to Eden's. As the boat began to glide, it occurred to Eden that she was rowing with the same three girls who had started the adventure in the apple orchard. With a silent chuckle, she settled into sync with Roberta and let her mind drift.

What if she had never gone up in that tree? Absently, she touched her lower lip with her tongue, recalling the taste and feel of Chase. If she had it to do over, would she run in the opposite direction?

Smiling, Eden closed her eyes a moment, so that the sun glowed red under her lids. No, she wouldn't run. Being able to admit it, being able to be sure of it, strengthened her confidence. She wouldn't run from Chase, or from anything else in life.

Perhaps she was soft on him, as Roberta had termed it. Perhaps she could hug that secret to herself for a little while. It would be wonderful if things could be as simple and uncomplicated as Roberta made them. Love equaled marriage, marriage equaled happiness. Sighing, Eden opened her eyes and watched the surface of the lake. For a little while she could believe in poetry and dreams.

Daydreams... They were softer and even more mystical than dreams by night. It had been a long time since Eden had indulged in them. Now the girls were chattering and calling to their friends in the other boats. Someone was singing, deliberately off-key. Eden's arms moved in a steady rhythm as the oars cut smoothly into the water and up into the air again.

So she was floating...dreaming with her eyes open...silk and ivory and lace. The glitter of the sun on water was like candlelight. The call of crows was music to dance by.

She was riding on Pegasus. High in a night sky, his white wings effortlessly cut through the air. She could taste the cool, thin wind that took them through clouds. Her hair was free, flying behind her, twined with flowers. More clouds, castle-like, rose up in the distance, filmy and gray and secret. Their secrets were nothing to her. She had freedom for the first time, full, unlimited freedom.

And he was with her, riding the sky through snatches of light and dark. Higher, still higher they rose, until the earth was only mist beneath them. And the stars were flowers, the white petals of anemones that she could reach out and pick as the whim struck her.

When she turned in his arms, she was his without boundaries. All restrictions, all doubts, had been left behind in the climb.

"Hey, look. It's Squat!"

Eden blinked. The daydream disintegrated. She was in a

rowboat, with muscles that were just beginning to ache from exertion. There were no flowers, no stars, only water and sky.

They'd rowed nearly the width of the lake. A portion of Chase's orchard spread back from the shore, and visible was one of the greenhouses he had taken the camp through on the day of the tour. Delighted with the company, Squat dashed back and forth in the shallow water near the lake's edge. His massive paws scattered a flurry of water that coated him until he was a sopping, shaggy mess.

Smiling as the girls called out greetings to the dog, Eden wondered if Chase was home. What did he do with his Sundays? she thought. Did he laze around the house with the paper and cups of coffee? Did he switch on the ball game, or go out for long, solitary drives? Just then, as if to answer her questions, he and Delaney joined the dog on the shore. Across the water, Eden felt the jolt as their eyes met.

Would it always be like that? Always stunning, always fresh? Always immediate? Inhaling slowly, she coaxed her pulse back to a normal rate.

"Hey, Mr. Elliot!" Without a thought for the consequences, Roberta dropped her oar and jumped up. Excitement had her bouncing up and down as the boat teetered.

"Roberta." Acting by instinct, Eden locked her oars. "Sit down, you'll turn us over." Eden started to grab for her hand as the other girls took Roberta's lead and jumped to their feet.

"Hi, Mr. Elliot!"

The greeting rang out in unison, just before the boat tipped over.

Eden hit the water headfirst. After the heat of the sun it seemed shockingly cold, and she surfaced sputtering with fury. With one hand, she dragged the hair out of her eyes and focused on the three bobbing heads. The girls, buoyed by their life jackets, waved unrepentantly at the trio on shore.

Eden grabbed the edge of the upended boat. "Roberta!"

"Look, Miss Carlbough." Apparently the tone, said through gritted teeth, passed over the girl's head. "Squat's coming out."

"Terrific." Treading water, Eden plucked Roberta by the arm and tried to drag her back to the capsized boat. "Remember the rules of boating safety. Stay here." Eden went for the next girl, but twisted her head to see the dog paddling toward them. Uneasy with his progress, she looked back toward shore.

Her request that Chase call back his dog caught in her throat as she spotted his grin. Though she couldn't hear the words, she saw Delaney turn to him with some remark. It was enough to see Chase throw back his head and laugh. That sound carried.

"Want some help?" he called out.

Eden pulled at the next giggling girl. "Don't put yourself out," she began, then shrieked when Squat laid a wet, friendly nose on her shoulder. Her reaction seemed to amuse everyone, dog included. Squat began to bark enthusiastically in her ear.

Fresh pandemonium broke out as the girls began to splash water at each other and the dog. Eden found herself caught in the crossfire. In the other boats, campers and counselors looked on, grinning or calling out encouraging words. Squat paddled circles around her as she struggled to restore some kind of order.

"All right, ladies. Enough." That earned her a mouthful of lake. "It's time to right the boat."

"Can Squat take a ride with us?" Roberta giggled as he licked water from her face.

"No."

"That hardly seems fair."

Eden nearly submerged before Chase gripped her arm. She'd been too busy trying to restore order and her own dignity to notice that he'd swum the few yards from shore. "He came out to help."

His hair was barely damp, while hers was plastered to her head. Chase hooked an arm around her waist to ease her effort to tread water.

"You'd better right the boat," he said to the girls, who immediately fell to doing so with a vengeance. "Apparently you do better with horses." His voice was soft and amused in Eden's ear.

She started to draw away, but her legs tangled with his. "If you and that monster hadn't been on shore——"

"Delaney?"

"No, not Delaney." Frustrated, Eden pushed at her hair.

"You're beautiful when you're wet. Makes me wonder why I haven't thought of swimming with you before."

"We're not supposed to be swimming, we're supposed to be boating."

"Either way, you're beautiful."

She wouldn't be moved. Even though the girls had already righted the boat, Eden knew she was in over her head. "It's that dog," she began. Even as she said it, the girls were climbing back into the boat and urging Squat to join them.

"Roberta, I said——" Chase gently dunked her. Surfacing, she heard him striking the bargain.

"We'll swim back. You bring Squat. He likes boats."

"I said—" Again, she found herself under water. This time when she came up for air, she gave Chase her full attention. The swing she took at him was slow and sluggish because of the need to tread water.

He caught her fist and kissed it. "Beat you back."

Narrowing her eyes, Eden gave him a shove before striking out after the boat. The water around her ears muffled the sound of Squat's deep barking and the girls' excited cheering. With strong, even strokes, she kept a foot behind the boat and made certain the girls behaved.

Less than twenty feet from shore, Chase caught her by the ankle. Laughing and kicking, Eden found herself tangled in his arms.

"You cheat." As he rose, he swept her off her feet so that her accusation ended in another laugh. His bare chest was cool and wet under her palms. His hair was dripping so that the sunlight was caught in each separate drop of water. "I won."

"Wrong." She should have seen it coming. Without effort, he pitched her back in the lake. Eden landed bottom first. "I won."

Eden stood to shake herself off. Managing to suppress a smile, she nodded toward the whooping girls. "And that, ladies, is a classic example of poor sportsmanship." She reached up to squeeze the water out of her hair, unaware that her shirt clung to every curve. Chase felt his heart stop. She waded toward shore, with the clear lake water clinging to her tanned legs. "Good afternoon, Delaney."

"Ma'am." He gave her a gold, flashing grin. "Nice day for a swim."

"Apparently."

"I was about to pick me some blackberries for jam." He cast his gaze over the three dripping girls. "If I had some help, could be I'd have a jar or so extra for some neighbors."

Before Eden could consent or refuse, all the girls and Squat were jumping circles around her. She had to admit that a ten- or fifteen-minute break would make the row back to camp a little more appealing. "Ten minutes," she told them before turning back to signal to the other boats.

Delaney toddled off, sandwiched between girls who were already barraging him with questions. As they disappeared into a cluster of trees, a startled flock of birds whizzed out. She laughed, turning back to see Chase staring at her.

"You're a strong swimmer."

She had to clear her throat. "I think I've just become more competitive. Maybe I should keep an eye on the girls so——"

"Delaney can handle them." He reached out to brush a bead of water from her jawline. Beneath his gentle touch, she shivered. "Cold?"

More than the sun had taken the lake's chill from her skin. Eden managed to shake her head. "No." But when his hands came to her shoulders, she stepped back.

He wore only cutoffs, faded soft from wear. The shirt he had peeled off before diving into the lake had been tossed carelessly to the ground. "You don't feel cold," he murmured as he stroked his hands down her arms.

"I'm not." She heard the laughter beyond the trees. "I really can't let them stay long. They'll have to change."

Patient, Chase took her hand. "Eden, you're going to end up in the lake again if you keep backing up." He was frightening her. Frustrated, he struggled not to push. It seemed that every time he thought he'd gained her trust, he saw that quick flash of anxiety in her eyes again. He smiled, hoping the need that was roiling inside him didn't show. "Where are your shoes?"

Off-balance, she looked down and stared at her own bare feet. Slowly, her muscles began to relax again. "At the bottom of your lake." Laughing, she shook her wet hair back, nearly destroying him. "Roberta always manages to keep things exciting. Why don't we give them a hand with the berry-picking."

His arm came across her body to take her shoulder before she could move past him. "You're still backing away, Eden." Lifting a hand, he combed his fingers through her sleek, wet hair until they rested at the base of her neck. "It's hard to resist you this way, with your face glowing and your eyes aware and just a bit frightened."

"Chase, don't." She put her hand to his.

"I want to touch you." He shifted so that the full length of her body was against his. "I need to touch you." Through the wet cotton, she could feel the texture of his skin on hers. "Look at me, Eden." The slightest pressure of his fingers brought her face up to his. "How close are you going to let me get?"

She could only shake her head. There weren't any words to describe what she was feeling, what she wanted, what she was still too afraid to need. "Chase, don't do this. Not here, not now." Then she could only moan, as his mouth traveled with a light, lazy touch over her face.

"When?" He had to fight the desire to demand rather than to ask, to take rather than to wait. "Where?" This time the kiss wasn't lazy, but hard, bruising. Eden felt rational thought spiral away even as she groped for an answer. "Don't you think I know what happens to you when we're like this?" His voice thickened as his patience stretched thinner and thinner. "Good God, Eden, I need you. Come with me tonight. Stay with me."

Yes, yes. Oh, yes. How easy it would be to say it, to give in, to give everything without a thought for tomorrow. She clung to him a moment, wanting to believe dreams were possible. He was so solid, so real. But so were her responsibilities.

"Chase, you know I can't." Fighting for rationality, she drew away. "I have to stay at camp."

Before she could move away again, he caught her face in his hands. She thought his eyes had darkened, a stormier green now, with splashes of gold from the sun. "And when summer's over, Eden? What then?"

What then? How could she have the answer, when the answer was so cold, so final? It wasn't what she wanted, but what had to be. If she was to keep her promise to herself, to make her life work, there was only one answer. "Then I'll go back, back to Philadelphia, until next summer."

Only summers? Was that all she was willing to give? It was the panic that surprised him and kept the fury at bay. When she left, his life would be empty. He took her shoulders again, fighting back the panic.

"You'll come to me before you go." It wasn't a question. It wasn't a demand. It was a simple statement. The demand she could have rebelled against; the question she could have refused.

"Chase, what good would it do either of us?"

"You'll come to me before you go," he repeated. Because if she didn't, he'd follow her. There would be no choice.

Chapter Eight

Red and white crepe paper streamed from corner to corner, twined together in elongated snakes of color. Balloons, bulging with air from energetic young lungs, were crowded into every available space. Stacked in three uneven towers were all the records deemed fit to play.

Dance night was only a matter of hours away.

Under Candy's eagle eye, tables were carried outside, while others were grouped strategically around the mess area. This simple chore took twice as long as it should have, as girls had to stop every few feet to discuss the most important aspect of the evening: boys.

Although her skills with paint and glue were slim at best, Eden had volunteered for the decorating committee—on the understanding that her duties were limited to hanging and tacking what was already made. In addition to the crepe paper and balloons, there were banners and paper flowers that the more talented members of campers and staff had put together by hand. The best of these was a ten-foot banner dyed Camp Liberty red and splashed

with bold letters that spelled out WELCOME TO CAMP
LIBERTY'S ANNUAL SUMMER DANCE.

Candy had already taken it for granted that it would be the first
of many. In her better moods, Eden hoped she was right. In her
crankier ones, she wondered if they could swing a deal with the
boys' camp to split the cost of refreshments. For the moment, she
pushed both ideas aside, determined to make this dance the best-
decorated one in Pennsylvania.

Eden let an argument over which records had priority run its
course below her as she climbed a stepladder to secure more
streamers. Already, the record player at the far end of the room
was blaring music.

It was silly. She told herself that yet again as she realized she was
as excited about the evening as any of the girls. She was an adult,
here only to plan, supervise and chaperon. Even as she reminded
herself of this, her thoughts ran forward to the evening, when the
mess area would be filled with people and noise and laughter. Like
the girls below her, her thoughts kept circling back to vital
matters—like what she should wear.

It was fascinating to realize that this simple end-of-the-summer
dance in the mountains was more exciting for her than her own
debutante ball. That she had taken lightly, as the next step along
the path that had been cleared for her before she was born. This
was new, untried and full of possibilities.

It all centered on Chase. Eden was nearly ready to accept that
as a new song blared into life. Since it was one she'd heard dozens
of times before, she began to hum along with it. Her ponytail
swayed with the movement as she attached another streamer.

"We'll ask Miss Carlbough." Eden heard the voices below, but paid little attention, as she had a tack in her mouth and five feet of crepe paper held together by her thumb. "She always knows, and if she doesn't, she finds out."

She had started to secure the tack, but as the statement drifted up to her, she stopped pushing. Was that really the way the girls saw her? Dependable? With a half laugh, she sent the tack home. To her, the statement was the highest of compliments, a sign of faith.

She'd done what she had set out to do. In three short months, she had accomplished something she had never done in all her years of living. She had made something of herself, by herself. And, perhaps more importantly, for herself.

It wasn't going to stop here. Eden dropped the rest of the tacks into her pocket. The summer might be nearly over, but the challenge wasn't. Whether she was in South Mountain or Philadelphia, she wasn't going to forget what it meant to grow. Twisting on the ladder, she started down to find out what it was the girls had wanted to ask her. On the second rung, she stopped, staring.

The tall, striking woman strode into the mess. The tail of her Hermès scarf crossed the neck of a cerise suit and trailed on behind. Her bone-white hair was perfect, as was the double strand of pearls that lay on her bosom. Tucked in the crook of one arm was a small piece of white fluff known as BooBoo.

"Aunt Dottie!" Delighted, Eden scrambled down from the ladder. In seconds she was enveloped by Dottie's personal scent, an elusive combination of Paris and success. "Oh, it's wonderful to see you." Drawing back from the hug, Eden studied the lovely, strong-boned face. Even now, she could see shadows of her father in the eyes and around the mouth. "You're the last person I expected to see here."

"Darling, have you grown thorns in the country?"

"Thorns? I—oh." Laughing, Eden reached in her pocket. "Thumbtacks. Sorry."

"The hug was worth a few holes." Taking Eden's hand, she stepped back to make her own study. Though her face remained passive, she let out a quiet sigh of relief. No one knew how many restless nights she'd spent worrying over her brother's only child. "You look beautiful. A little thin, but with marvelous color." With Eden's hand still in hers, she glanced around the room. "But darling, what an odd place you've chosen to spend the summer."

"Aunt Dottie." Eden just shook her head. Throughout the weeks and months after her father's death, Dottie had stubbornly refused to accept Eden's decision not to use Dottie's money as a buffer, her home as a refuge. "If I have marvelous color, credit the country air."

"Hmm." Far from convinced, Dottie continued to look around as a new record plopped down to continue the unbroken cycle of music. "I've always considered the south of France country enough."

"Aunt Dottie, tell me what you're doing here. I'm amazed you could even find the place."

"It wasn't difficult. The chauffeur reads a map very well." Dottie gave the fluff in her arms a light pat. "BooBoo and I felt an urge for a drive to the country."

"I see." And she did. Like everyone else she had left behind, Eden knew that her aunt considered her camp venture an impulse. It would take more than one summer to convince Dottie, or anyone else, that she was serious. After all, it had taken her most of the summer to convince herself.

"Yes, and since I was in the neighborhood..." Dottie let that trail off. "What a chic outfit," she commented, taking in Eden's paint-spattered smock and tattered sneakers. "Then, perhaps bohemian's coming back. What do you have there?"

"Crepe paper. It goes with the thumbtacks." Eden extended her hand. BooBoo regally allowed her head to be patted.

"Well, give them both to one of these charming young ladies and come see what I've brought you."

"Brought me?" Obeying automatically, Eden handed over the streamers. "Start these around the tables, will you, Lisa?"

"Do you know," Dottie began as she linked her arm through Eden's, "the nearest town is at least twenty miles from here? That is if one could stretch credibility and call what we passed through a town. There, there, BooBoo, I won't set you down on the nasty ground." She cuddled the dog as they stepped outside. "BooBoo's a bit skittish out of the city, you understand."

"Perfectly."

"Where was I? Oh yes, the town. It had one traffic light and a place called Earl's Lunch. I was almost curious enough to stop and see what one did at Earl's Lunch."

Eden laughed, and leaned over to kiss Dottie's cheek. "One eats a small variety of sandwiches and stale potato chips and coffee while exchanging town gossip."

"Marvelous. Do you go often?"

"Unfortunately, my social life's been a bit limited."

"Well, your surprise might just change all that." Turning, Dottie gestured toward the canary-yellow Rolls parked in the main compound. Eden felt every muscle, every emotion freeze as the man straightened from his easy slouch against the hood.

"Eric."

He smiled, and in a familiar gesture, ran one hand lightly over his hair. Around him, a group of girls had gathered to admire the classic lines of the Rolls and the classic looks of Eric Keeton.

His smile was perfectly angled as he walked toward her. His walk was confident, just a shade too conservative for a swagger. As she watched him, Eden saw him in the clear light of disinterest. His hair, several shades darker than her own, was perfectly styled for the boardroom or the country club. Casual attire, which included pleated slacks and a polo shirt, fit neatly over his rather narrow frame. Hazel eyes, which had a tendency to look bored easily, smiled and warmed now. Though she hadn't offered them, he took both her hands.

"Eden, how marvelous you look."

His hands were soft. Strange, she had forgotten that. Though she didn't bother to remove hers, her voice was cool. "Hello, Eric."

"Lovelier than ever, isn't she, Dottie?" Her stiff greeting didn't seem to disturb him. He gave her hands an intimate little squeeze. "Your aunt was worried about you. She expected you to be thin and wan."

"Fortunately, I'm neither." Now, carefully, deliberately, Eden removed her hands. She would have been greatly pleased, though she had no way of knowing it, that her eyes were as cold as her voice. It was so easy to turn away from him. "Whatever possessed you to drive all this way, Aunt Dottie? You weren't really worried?"

"A tad." Concerned with the ice in her niece's voice, Dottie touched Eden's cheek. "And I did want to see the—the place where you spent the summer."

"I'll give you a tour."

A thin left brow arched in a manner identical to Eden's. "How charming."

"Aunt Dottie!" Red curls bouncing, Candy raced around the side of the building. "I knew it had to be you." Out of breath and grinning broadly, Candy accepted Dottie's embrace. "The girls were talking about a yellow Rolls in the compound. Who else could it have been?"

"As enthusiastic as ever." Dottie's smile was all affection. She might not have always understood Candice Bartholomew, but she had always been fond of her. "I hope you don't mind a surprise visit."

"I love it." Candy bent down to the puff of fur. "Hi, BooBoo." Straightening, she let her gaze drift over Eric. "Hello, Eric." Her voice dropped an easy twenty-five degrees. "Long way from home."

"Candy." Unlike Dottie, he had no fondness for Eden's closest friend. "You seem to have paint all over your hands."

"It's dry," she said, carelessly, and somewhat regretfully. If the paint had been wet, she would have greeted him more personally.

"Eden's offered to take us on a tour." Dottie was well aware of the hostility. She'd driven hundreds of miles from Philadelphia for one purpose. To help her niece find happiness. If it meant she had to manipulate...so much the better. "I know Eric's dying to look around, but if I could impose on you——" She laid her hand on Candy's. "I'd really love to sit down with a nice cup of tea. BooBoo, too. The drive was a bit tiring."

"Of course." Manners were their own kind of trap. Candy sent Eden a look meant to fortify her. "We'll use the kitchen, if you don't mind the confusion."

"My dear, I thrive on it." With that she turned to smile at Eden and was surprised by the hard, knowing look in Eden's eyes.

"Go right ahead, Aunt Dottie. I'll show Eric what the camp has to offer."

"Eden, I—"

"Go have your tea, darling." She kissed Dottie's cheek. "We'll talk later." She turned, leaving Eric to follow or not. When he fell into step beside her, she began. "We've six sleeping cabins this season, with plans to add two more for next summer. Each cabin has an Indian name to keep it distinct."

As they passed the cabins, she saw that the anemones were still stubbornly blooming. They gave her strength. "Each week, we have a contest for the neatest cabin. The reward is extra riding time, or swimming time, or whatever the girls prefer. Candy and I have a small shower in our cabin. The girls share facilities at the west end of the compound."

"Eden." Eric cupped her elbow in his palm in the same manner he had used when strolling down Broad Street. She gritted her teeth, but didn't protest.

"Yes?" The cool, impersonal look threw him off. It took him only a moment to decide it meant she was hiding a broken heart.

"What have you been doing with yourself?" He waved his hand in a gesture that took in the compound and the surrounding hills. "Here?"

Holding on to her temper, Eden decided to take the question literally. "We've tried to keep the camp regimented, while still allowing for creativity and fun. Over the past few weeks, we've found that we can adhere fairly tightly to the schedule as long as we make room for fresh ideas and individual needs." Pleased with herself, she dipped her hands into the pockets of her smock. "We're up at six-thirty. Breakfast is at seven sharp. Daily inspection begins at seven-thirty and activities at eight. For the most part, I deal with the horses and stables, but when necessary, I can pitch in and help in other areas."

"Eden." Eric stopped her by gently tightening his fingers on her elbow. Turning to him, she watched the faint breeze ruffle his smooth, fair hair. She thought of the dark confusion of Chase's hair. "It's difficult to believe you've spent your summer camping out in a cabin and overseeing a parade of girls on horseback."

"Is it?" She merely smiled. Of course it was difficult for him. He owned a stable, but he'd never lifted a pitchfork. Rather than resentment, Eden felt a stirring of pity. "Well, there's that, among a few other things such as hiking, smoothing over cases of homesickness and poison ivy, rowing, giving advice on teenage romance and fashion, identifying fifteen different varieties of local wildflowers and seeing that a group of girls has fun. Would you like to see the stables?" She headed off without waiting for his answer.

"Eden." He caught her elbow again. It took all her willpower not to jab it back into his soft stomach. "You're angry. Of course you are, but I—"

"You've always had a fondness for good horseflesh." She swung the stable door open so that he had to back off or get a faceful of wood. "We've two mares and four geldings. One of the mares is past her prime, but I'm thinking of breeding the other. The foals would interest the girls and eventually become part of the riding stock. This is Courage."

"Eden, please. We have to talk."

She stiffened when his hands touched her shoulders. But she was calm, very calm, when she turned and removed them. "I thought we were talking."

He'd heard the ice in her voice before, and he understood it. She was a proud, logical woman. He'd approach her on that level. "We have to talk about us, darling."

"In what context?"

He reached for her hand, giving a small shrug when she drew it away. If she had accepted him without a murmur, he would have been a great deal more surprised. For days now, he'd been planning exactly the proper way to smooth things over. He'd decided on regretful, with a hint of humble thrown in.

"You've every right to be furious with me, every right to want me to suffer."

His tone, soft, quiet, understanding, had her swallowing a ball of heat. Indifference, she reminded herself, disinterest, was the greatest insult she could hand him. "It doesn't really concern me if you suffer or not." That wasn't quite true, she admitted. She wouldn't be averse to seeing him writhe a bit. That was because he had come, she realized. Because he had had the gall to come and assume she'd be waiting.

"Eden, you have to know that I have suffered, suffered a great deal. I would have come before, but I wasn't sure you'd see me."

This was the man she had planned to spend her life with. This was the man she had hoped to have children with. She stared at him now, unsure whether she was in the midst of a comedy or a tragedy. "I'm sorry to hear that, Eric. I don't see any reason why you should have suffered. You were only being practical, after all."

Soothed by her placid attitude, he stepped toward her. "I admit that, rightly or wrongly, I was practical." His hands slid up her arms in an old gesture that made her jaw clench. "These past few months have shown me that there are times when practical matters have to take second place."

"Is that so?" She smiled at him, surprised that he couldn't feel the heat. "What would go first?"

"Personal..." He stroked a finger over her cheek. "Much more personal matters."

"Such as?"

His lips were curved as his mouth lowered. She felt the heat of anger freeze into icy disdain. Did he think her a fool? Could he believe himself so irresistible? Then she nearly did laugh, as she realized the answer to both questions was yes.

She let him kiss her. The touch of his lips left her totally unmoved. It fascinated her that, only a few short months before, his kisses had warmed her. It had been nothing like the volcanic heat she experienced with Chase, but there had been a comfort and an easy pleasure. That was all she had thought there was meant to be.

Now there was nothing. The absence of feeling in itself dulled the edge of her fury. She was in control. Here, as in other areas of her life, she was in control. Though his lips coaxed, she simply stood, waiting for him to finish.

When he lifted his head, Eden put her hands on his arms to draw herself away. It was then she saw Chase just inside the open stable door.

The sun was at his back, silhouetting him, blinding her to the expression on his face. Even so, her mouth was dry as she stared, trying to see through shadow and sun. When he stepped forward, his eyes were on hers.

Explanations sprang to her tongue, but she could only shake her head as his gaze slid over her and onto Eric.

"Keeton." Chase nodded, but didn't extend his hand. He knew if he had the other man's fingers in his he would take pleasure in breaking them, one by one.

"Elliot." Eric returned the nod. "I'd forgotten. You have land around here, don't you?"

"A bit." Chase wanted to murder him, right there in the stables, while Eden watched. Then he would find it just as satisfying to murder her.

"You must know Eden, then." Eric placed a hand on her shoulder in a casually possessive movement. Chase followed the gesture before looking at her again. Her instinctive move to shrug away Eric's hand was stopped by the look. Was it anger she saw there, or was it disgust?

"Yes. Eden and I have run into each other a few times." He dipped his hands into his pockets as they balled into fists.

"Chase was generous enough to allow us to use his lake." Her right hand groped for her left until they were clasped together. "We had a tour of his orchards." Though pride suffered, her eyes pleaded with him.

"Your land must be very near here." Eric hadn't missed the exchange of looks. His hand leaned more heavily on Eden's shoulder.

"Near enough."

Then they were looking at each other, not at her. Somehow that, more than anything, made her feel as though she'd been shifted to the middle. If there was tension and she was the cause of it, she wanted to be able to speak on her own behalf. But the expression in Chase's eyes only brought confusion. The weight of Eric's hand only brought annoyance. Moving away from Eric, she stepped toward Chase.

"Did you want to see me?"

"Yes." But he'd wanted more than that, a great deal more. Seeing her in Eric's arms had left him feeling both murderous and empty. He wasn't ready to deal with either yet. "It wasn't important."

"Chase—"

"Oh, hello." The warmth in Candy's voice came almost as a shock. She stepped through the doorway with Dottie at her side. "Aunt Dottie, I want you to meet our neighbor, Chase Elliot."

Even as Dottie extended her hand, her eyes were narrowed speculatively. "Elliot? I'm sure I know that name. Yes, yes, didn't we meet several years ago? You're Jessie Winthrop's grandson."

Eden watched his lips curve, his eyes warm, but he wasn't looking at her. "Yes, I am, and I remember you very well, Mrs. Norfolk. You haven't changed."

Dottie's laugh was low and quick. "It's been fifteen years if it's been a day. I'd say there's been a change or two. You were about a foot shorter at the time." She sized him up approvingly in a matter of ten seconds. "It's apples, isn't it? Yes, of course, it is. Elliot's."

And, oh my God, she realized almost as quickly, I've brought Eric along and jammed up the works. A person would have to have a three-inch layer of steel coating not to feel the shock waves bouncing around the stables.

What could be done, she told herself, could be undone. Smiling, she looked at her niece. "Candy's been telling me about the social event of the season. Are we all invited?"

"Invited?" Eden struggled to gather her scattered wits. "You mean the dance?" She had to laugh. Her aunt was standing in the stables in Italian shoes and a suit that had cost more than any one of the horses. "Aunt Dottie, you don't intend to stay here?"

"Stay here?" The white brows shot up. "I should say not." She twisted the pearls at her neck as she began to calculate. She didn't intend to bunk down in a cabin, but neither was she about to miss the impending fireworks. "Eric and I are staying at a hotel some miles away, but I'd be heartbroken if you didn't ask us to the party tonight." She put a friendly hand on Chase's arm. "You're coming, aren't you?"

He knew a manipulator when he saw one. "Wouldn't miss it."

"Wonderful." Dottie slid Candy's hand back into the crook of her arm, then patted it. "We're all invited then."

Fumbling, Candy looked from Eric to Eden. "Well, yes, of course, but—"

"Isn't this sweet?" Dottie patted her hand again. "We'll have a delightful time. Don't you think so, Eden?"

"Delightful," Eden agreed, wondering if she could hitch a ride out of town.

Chapter Nine

Eden had problems—big problems. But not the least of them were the sixty adolescents in the mess hall. However she handled Eric, however she managed to explain herself to Chase, sixty young bodies couldn't be put on hold.

The boys arrived in vans at eight o'clock. Unless Eden missed her guess, they were every bit as nervous as the girls. Eden remembered her own cotillion days, the uncertainty and the damp palms. The blaring music helped cover some of the awkwardness as the boys' counselors trooped them in.

The refreshment table was loaded. There was enough punch stored in the kitchen to bathe in. Candy gave a brief welcoming speech to set the tone, the banners and the paper flowers waving at her back. A fresh record was set spinning on the turntable. Girls stood on one side of the room, boys on the other.

The biggest problem, naturally, was that no one wanted to go first. Eden had worked that out by making up two bowls of corresponding numbers. Boys picked from one, girls from another. You matched, you danced. It wasn't imaginative, but it was expedient.

When the first dance was half over, she slipped into the kitchen to check on backup refreshments, leaving Candy to supervise and to mingle with the male counselors.

When she returned, the dance floor wasn't as crowded, but this time the partners had chosen for themselves.

"Miss Carlbough?"

Eden turned her head as she bent to place a bowl of chips in an empty space on the long crowded table. Roberta's face was spotless. Her thatch of wild hair had been tamed into a bushy ponytail and tied with a ribbon. She had little turquoise stars in her ears to match a ruffled and not-too-badly-wrinkled blouse. The dusting of freckles over her face had been partially hidden by a layer of powder. Eden imagined she had conned it out of one of the older girls, but let it pass.

"Hi, Roberta." Plucking two pretzels from a bowl, she handed one over. "Aren't you going to dance?"

"Sure." She glanced over her shoulder, confident and patient. "I wanted to talk to you first."

"Oh?" It didn't appear that she needed a pep talk. Eden had already seen the skinny, dark-haired boy Roberta had set her sights on. If Eden was any judge, he didn't stand a chance. "What about?"

"I saw that guy in the Rolls."

Eden's automatic warning not to speak with her mouth full was postponed. "You mean Mr. Keeton?"

"Some of the girls think he's cute."

"Hmm." Eden nibbled on her own pretzel.

"A couple of them said you were soft on him. They think you had a lovers' quarrel, you know, like Romeo and Juliet or something. Now he's come to beg you to forgive him, and you're going to realize that you can't live without him and go off and get married."

The pretzel hung between two fingers as Eden listened. After a moment, she managed to clear her throat. "Well, that's quite a scenario."

"I said it was baloney."

Trying not to laugh, she bit into the pretzel. "Did you?"

"You're smart, all the girls say so." Reaching behind Eden, she took a handful of chips. "I said you were too smart to be soft on the guy in the Rolls, because he's not nearly as neat as Mr. Elliot." Roberta glanced over her shoulder as if in confirmation. "He's shorter, too."

"Yes." Eden had to bite her lip. "Yes, he is."

"He doesn't look like he'd jump in the lake to fool around."

The last statement had Eden trying to imagine Eric diving into the cool waters of the lake half-dressed. Or bringing her a clutch of wildflowers. Or finding pictures in the sky. Her lips curved dreamily. "No, Eric would never do that."

"That's why I knew it was all baloney." Roberta devoured the chips. "When Mr. Elliot comes, I'm going to dance with him, but now I'm going to dance with Bobby." Shooting Eden a smile, she walked across the room and grabbed the hand of the lanky, dark-haired boy. As Eden had thought, he didn't have a chance.

She watched the dancing, but thought of Chase. It came to her all at once that he was the only man she knew whom she hadn't measured against her father. Comparisons had never occurred to her. She hadn't measured Chase against anyone but had fallen in love with him for himself. Now all she needed was the courage to tell him.

"So this is how young people entertain themselves these days."

Eden turned to find Dottie beside her. For Camp Liberty's summer dance, she had chosen mauve lace. The pearls had been exchanged for a single, sensational ruby. BooBoo had a clip of rhinestones—Eden sincerely hoped they were only rhinestones—secured on top of her head. Feeling a wave of affection, Eden kissed her aunt. "Are you settled into your hotel?"

"So to speak." Accepting a potato chip, Dottie took her own survey. The powder-blue voile was the essence of simplicity with its cap sleeves and high neck, but Dottie approved the way it depended on the wearer for its style. "Thank God you haven't lost your taste."

Laughing, Eden kissed her again. "I've missed you. I'm so glad you came."

"Are you?" Always discreet, Dottie led her toward the screen door. "I was afraid you weren't exactly thrilled to see me here." She let the screen whoosh shut as they stepped onto the porch. "Particularly with the surprise I brought you."

"I was glad to see you, Aunt Dottie."

"But not Eric."

Eden leaned back on the rail. "Did you think I would be?"

"Yes." She sighed, and brushed at the bodice of her lace. "I suppose I did. It only took five minutes to realize what a mistake I'd made. Darling, I hope you understand I was trying to help."

"Of course I do, and I love you for it."

"I thought that whatever had gone wrong between you would have had time to heal over." Forgetting herself, Dottie offered BooBoo the rest of the chip. "To be honest, the way he's been talking to me, I was sure by bringing him to you I'd be doing the next-best thing to saving your life."

"I can imagine," Eden murmured.

"So much for grand gestures." Dottie moved her shoulders so that the ruby winked. "Eden, you never told me why you two called off the wedding. It was so sudden."

Eden opened her mouth, then closed it again. There was no reason to hurt and infuriate her aunt after all these months. If she told her now, it would be for spite or, worse, for sympathy. Eric was worth neither. "We just realized we weren't suited."

"I always thought differently." There was a loud blast of music and a chorus of laughter. Dottie cast a glance over her shoulder. "Eric seems to think differently, too. He's been to see me several times in recent weeks."

Pushing the heavy fall of hair from her shoulders, Eden walked to the edge of the porch. Perhaps Eric had discovered that the Carlbough name wasn't so badly tarnished after all. It gave her no pleasure to be cynical, but it was the only answer that seemed right. It wouldn't have taken him long to realize that eventually she would come into money again, through inheritances. She swallowed her bitterness as she turned back to her aunt.

"He's mistaken, Aunt Dottie. Believe me when I say he doesn't have any genuine feelings for me. Perhaps he thinks he does," she added, when she saw the frown centered between Dottie's brows. "I'd say it's a matter of habit. I didn't love Eric." Her hands outstretched, she went to take her aunt's. "I never did. It's taken me some time to understand that I was going to marry him for all the wrong reasons—because it was expected, because it was easy. And..." She drew in her breath. "Because I mistakenly thought he was like Papa."

"Oh, darling."

"It was my mistake, so most of it was my fault." Now that it was said, and said aloud, she could accept it. "I always compared the men I dated with Papa. He was the kindest, most caring man I've ever known, but even though I loved and admired him, it was wrong of me to judge other men by him."

"We all loved him, Eden." Dottie drew Eden into her arms. "He was a good man, a loving man. A gambler, but—"

"I don't mind that he was a gambler." Now, when she drew back, Eden could smile. "I know if he hadn't died so suddenly, he'd have come out on top again. But it doesn't matter, Aunt Dottie, because I'm a gambler, too." She turned so that her gesture took in the camp. "I've learned how to make my own stake."

"How like him you are." Dottie was forced to draw a tissue out of her bag. "When you insisted on doing this, even when I first came here today, I could only think my poor little Eden's gone mad. Then I looked, really looked, at your camp, at the girls, at you, and I could see you'd made it work." After one inelegant sniff, she stuffed the tissue back in her bag. "I'm proud of you, Eden. Your father would have been proud of you."

Now it was Eden's eyes that dampened. "Aunt Dottie, I can't tell you how much that means to me. After he died and I had to sell everything, I felt I'd betrayed him, you, everyone."

"No." Dottie cupped Eden's chin in her hand. "What you did took tremendous courage, more than I had. You know how badly I wanted to spare you all of that."

"I know, and I appreciate it, but it had to be this way."

"I think I understand that now. I want you to know that I hurt for you, Eden, but I was never ashamed. Even now, knowing you don't need it, I'll tell you that my house is yours whenever you like."

"Knowing that is enough."

"And I expect this to be the finest camp in the east within five years."

Eden laughed again, and all the weight she'd carried with her since her father's death slipped off her shoulders. "It will be."

With a nod, Dottie took a step along the rail and looked out at the compound. "I do believe you should have a pool. Girls should have regulated, regimented swimming lessons. Splashing in the lake doesn't meet those standards. I'm going to donate one."

Eden's back went up immediately. "Aunt Dottie——"

"In your father's name." Dottie paused and cocked a brow. "Yes, I can see you won't argue with that. If I can donate a wing to a hospital, I can certainly donate a swimming pool in my brother's name to my favorite niece's camp. In fact, my accountant's going to be thrilled. Now, would you like Eric and me to go?"

Barely recovered from being so neatly maneuvered, Eden only sighed. "Having Eric here means nothing now. I want you to stay as long as you like."

"Good. BooBoo and I are enjoying ourselves." Dottie bent down to nuzzle in the dog's fur. "The delightful thing about BooBoo is that she's so much more tractable than any of my children were. Eden, one more thing before I go inside and absorb culture. I would swear that I felt, well, how to put it? One might almost say earth tremors when I walked into the stables this afternoon. Are you in love with someone else?"

"Aunt Dottie——"

"Answer enough. I'll just add my complete approval, not that it matters. BooBoo was quite charmed."

"Are you trying to be eccentric?"

With a smile, Dottie shifted the bundle in her arms. "When you can't rely on beauty any longer, you have to fall back on something. Ah, look here." She stepped aside as the Lamborghini cruised up. Lips pursed, Dottie watched Chase climb out. "Hello again," she called. "I admire your taste." She gave Eden a quick pat. "Yes, I do. I think I'll just pop inside and try some punch. It isn't too dreadful, is it?"

"I made it myself."

"Oh." Dottie rolled her eyes. "Well, I've some gambler in me as well."

Bracing herself, Eden turned toward Chase. "Hello. I'm glad you could—"

His mouth covered hers so quickly, so completely, that there wasn't even time for surprise. She might think of the hard possessiveness of the kiss later, but for now she just slid her hands up his back so that she could grip his shoulders. Instantly intense, instantly real, instantly right.

She hadn't felt this with Eric. That was what Chase told himself as she melted against him. She'd never felt this with anyone else. And he was going to be damn sure she didn't. Torn between anger and need, he drew her away.

"What—" She had to stop and try again. "What was that for?"

He gathered her hair in his hand to bring her close again. His lips tarried a breath from hers. "As someone once said to me, I wanted to kiss you. Any objections?"

He was daring her. Her chin angled in acceptance. "I can't think of any."

"Mull it over. Get back to me." With that, he propelled her toward the lights and music.

* * *

She didn't like to admit that cowardice might be part of the reason she carefully divided her time between the girls and the visiting counselors. Eden told herself it was a matter of courtesy and responsibility. But she knew she needed to have her thoughts well in hand before she spoke privately with Chase again.

She watched him dance with Roberta and wanted to throw herself into his arms and tell him how much she loved him. How big a fool would that make her? He hadn't asked about Eric, so how could she explain? It hummed through her mind that if he hadn't asked, it didn't matter to him. If it didn't matter, he wasn't nearly as involved as she was. Still, she told herself that before the evening was over she would find the time to talk it through with him, whether he wanted to hear it or not. She just wanted to wait until she was sure she could do a good job of it.

There was no such confusion about the evening in general. The summer dance was a hit. Plans between the camp coordinators were already under way to make it an annual event. Already Candy was bubbling with ideas for more joint ventures.

As always, Eden would let Candy plan and organize; then she would tidy up the details.

By keeping constantly on the move, Eden avoided any direct confrontation with Eric or Chase. Of course they spoke, even danced, but all in the sanctuary of the crowded mess hall. Eric's conversation had been as mild as hers, but there had been something dangerous in Chase's eyes. It was that, and the memory of that rocketing kiss, that had her postponing the inevitable.

"I guess you like her a lot," Roberta ventured as she saw Chase's gaze wander toward Eden yet again.

"What?" Distracted, Chase looked back at his dance partner.

"Miss Carlbough. You're soft on her. She's so pretty," Roberta added with only the slightest touch of envy. "We voted her the prettiest counselor, even though Miss Allison has more—" She caught herself, realizing suddenly that you didn't discuss certain parts of a woman's anatomy with a man, even with Mr. Elliot. "More, ah…"

"I get the picture." Charmed, as always, Chase swung her in a quick circle.

"Some of the other girls think Mr. Keeton's a honey."

"Oh?" Chase's smile turned into a sneer as he glanced at the man in question.

"I think his nose is skinny."

"It was almost broken," Chase muttered.

"And his eyes are too close together," Roberta added for good measure. "I like you a lot better."

Touched, and remembering his first crush, Chase tugged on her ponytail to tilt her face to his. "I'm pretty soft on you, too."

From her corner, Eden watched the exchange. She saw Chase bend down and saw Roberta's face explode into smiles. A sigh nearly escaped her before she realized she was allowing herself to be envious of a twelve-year-old. With a shake of her head, she told herself that it was the strain of keeping herself unavailable that was beginning to wear on her. The music never played below loud. Uncountable trips to the kitchen kept the refreshment table full. Boys and girls shouted over the music to make themselves heard.

Five minutes, she told herself. She would steal just five quiet, wonderful minutes by herself.

This time, when she slipped back into the kitchen, she kept

going. The moist summer air soothed her the moment she stepped outside. It smelled of grass and honeysuckle. Grateful for the fresh air after the cloying scent of fruit punch, Eden breathed deeply.

Tonight, the moon was only a sliver in the sky. She realized she had seen it change, had watched its waning and waxing more in the past three months than she had in all of her life. This was true of more than the moon. She would never look at anything else exactly the same way again.

She stood for a moment, finding the pictures in the sky that Chase had shown her. With the air warm on her face, she wondered if there would ever be a time when he would show her more.

As she crossed the grass, the light was silvery. From behind her came the steady murmur of music and voices. She found an old hickory tree and leaned against it, enjoying the solitude and the distance.

This was what warm summer nights were for, she thought. For dreams and wishes. No matter how cold it got during the winter, no matter how far away summer seemed, she would be able to take this night out of her memory and live it again.

The creak and swish of the back door cut through her concentration.

"Eric." She straightened, not bothering to disguise the irritation in her voice.

He came to her until he, too, stood under the hickory. Starlight filtered through the leaves to mix with the shadows. "I've never known you to leave a party."

"I've changed."

"Yes." Her eyes were calm and direct. He shifted uncomfortably. "I've noticed." When he reached out to touch her, she didn't step back. She didn't even feel his touch. "We never finished talking."

"Yes, we did. A long time ago."

"Eden." Moving cautiously, he lifted a finger to trace her jawline. "I've come a long way to see you, to make things right between us."

Eden merely tilted her head to the side. "I'm sorry you were inconvenienced, but there's nothing to make right." Oddly, the anger, even the bitterness, had become diluted. It had started weakening, she knew, when he had kissed her that afternoon. Looking at him now, she felt detached, as if he were someone she'd known only vaguely. "Eric, it's foolish for either of us to drag this out. Let's just leave things alone."

"I admit I was a fool." He blocked her exit, as if by simply continuing in the same vein he could put things back in the order he wanted. "Eden, I hurt you, and I'm sorry, but I was thinking of you as well as myself."

She wanted to laugh, but found she didn't even have the energy to give him that much. "Of me, Eric? All right, have it your way. Thank you and goodbye."

"Don't be difficult," he said, displaying a first trace of impatience. "You know how difficult it would have been for you to go through with the wedding while the scandal was still fresh in everyone's mind."

That stopped her, more than his hand had. She leaned back against the tree and waited. Yes, there was still a trace of anger, she discovered. It was mild, and buried quite deep, but it was still there. Perhaps it would be best to purge everything from her system. "Scandal. By that I assume you mean my father's poor investments."

"Eden." He moved closer again to put a comforting hand on her arm. "Your position changed so dramatically, so abruptly, when your father died and left you..."

"To earn my own way," she finished for him. "Yes, we can agree on that. My position changed. Over the past few months I've become grateful for that." There was annoyance now, but only as if he were a pesky fly she had to swat away. "I've learned to expect things from myself and to realize money had very little to do with the way I was living."

She saw by his frown that he didn't understand, would never understand the person who had grown up from the ashes of that old life. "You might find this amazing, Eric, but I don't care what anyone thinks about my altered circumstances. For the first time in my life, I have what I want, and I earned it myself."

"You can't expect me to believe that this little camp is what you want. I know you, Eden." He twined a lock of hair around his finger. "The woman I know would never choose something like this over the life we could have together in Philadelphia."

"You might be right again." Slowly, she reached up to untangle his hand from her hair. "But I'm no longer the woman you knew."

"Don't be ridiculous." For the first time he felt a twinge of panic. The one thing he had never considered was driving hundreds of miles to be humiliated. "Come back to the hotel with me tonight. Tomorrow we can go back to Philadelphia and be married, just as we always planned."

She studied him for a moment, trying to see if there was some lingering affection for her there, some true emotion. No, she decided almost at once. She wished it had been true, for then she could have had some kind of respect for him.

"Why are you doing this? You don't love me. You never did, or you couldn't have turned your back on me when I needed you."

"Eden—"

"No, let me finish. Let's finish this once and for all." She pushed him back a foot with an impatient movement of her hands. "I'm not interested in your apologies or your excuses, Eric. The simple truth is you don't matter to me."

It was said so calmly, so bluntly, that he very nearly believed it. "You know you don't mean that, Eden. We were going to be married."

"Because it was convenient for both of us. For that much, Eric, I'll share the blame with you."

"Let's forget blame, Eden. Let me show you what we can have."

She held him off with a look. "I'm not angry anymore, and I'm not hurt. The simple fact is, Eric, I don't love you, and I don't want you."

For a moment, he was completely silent. When he did speak, Eden was surprised to hear genuine emotion in his voice. "Find someone to replace me so soon, Eden?"

She could almost laugh. He had jilted her almost two steps from the altar, but now he could act out the role of betrayed lover. "This grows more and more absurd, but no, Eric, it wasn't a matter of replacing you, it was a matter of seeing you for what you are. Don't make me explain to you what that is."

"Just how much does Chase Elliot have to do with all of this?"

"How dare you question me?" She started past him, but this time he grabbed her arm, and his grip wasn't gentle. Surprised by his refusal to release her, she stepped back and looked at him again. He was a child, she thought, who had thrown away a toy and was ready to stamp his feet now that he wanted it back and couldn't have it. Because her temper was rising, she fell back on her attitude of icy detachment. "Whatever is or isn't between Chase and me is none of your concern."

This cool, haughty woman was one he recognized. His tone softened. "Everything about you concerns me."

Weary, she could only sigh. "Eric, you're embarrassing yourself."

Before she could rid herself of him again, the screen door opened for a second time.

"Apparently I'm interrupting again." Hands in pockets, Chase stepped down from the porch.

"You seem to be making a habit of it." Eric released Eden, only to step between her and Chase. "You should be able to see that Eden and I are having a private conversation. They do teach manners, even here in the hills, don't they?"

Chase wondered if Eric would appreciate his style of manners. No, he doubted the tidy Philadelphian would appreciate a bloody nose. But then, he didn't give a damn what Eric appreciated. He'd taken two steps forward before Eden realized his intent.

"The conversation's over," she said quickly, stepping between them. She might as well have been invisible. As she had felt herself being shifted to the middle that afternoon, now she felt herself being nudged aside.

"Seems you've had considerable time to say what's on your mind." Chase rocked back on his heels, keeping his eyes on Eric.

"I don't see what business it is of yours how long I speak with my fiancée."

"Fiancée!" Eden's outraged exclamation was also ignored.

"You've let some months slip past you, Keeton." Chase's voice remained mild. His hands remained in his pockets. "Some changes have been made."

"Changes?" This time Eden turned to Chase, with no better results. "What are you talking about?"

Calmly, without giving her a glance, he took her hand. "You promised me a dance."

Instantly, Eric had her other arm. "We haven't finished."

Chase turned back, and for the first time the danger in his eyes was as clear as glass. "Yes, you have. The lady's with me."

Infuriated, Eden yanked herself free of both of them. "Stop it!" She'd had enough of being pulled in two directions without being asked if she wanted to move in either. For the first time in her life, she forgot manners, courtesy and control and did what Chase had once advised. When you're mad, he'd said, yell.

"You are both so *stupid*!" A toss of her head had the hair flying into her eyes to be dragged back impatiently. "How dare you stand here like two half-witted dogs snarling over the same bone? Don't either of you think I'm capable of speaking my own mind, making my own decisions? Well, I've got news for both of you. I can speak my own mind just fine. You." She turned to face Eric. "I meant every word I said to you. Understand? *Every single word.* I tried to phrase things as politely as possible, but if you push, let me warn you, you won't receive the same courtesy again."

"Eden, darling—"

"No, no, no!" She slapped away the hand he held out to her. "You dumped me the moment things got rough. If you think I'll take you back now, after you've shown yourself to be a weak, callous, insensitive——" oh, what was Candy's word? "——weasel," she remembered with relish, "you're crazy. And if you dare, if you *dare* touch me again, I'll knock your caps loose."

God, what a woman, Chase thought. He wondered how soon he could take her into his arms and show her how much he loved her. He'd always thought her beautiful, almost ethereal; now she was a Viking. More than he'd wanted anything in his life, he wanted to hold that passion in his arms and devour it. He was smiling at her when she whirled on him.

"And you." Taking a step closer to Chase, she began to stab him in the chest with her finger. "You go find someone else to start a common brawl over. I'm not flattered by your Neanderthal attempts at playing at the white knight."

It wasn't quite what he'd had in mind. "For God's sake, Eden, I was——"

"Shut up." She gave him another quick jab. "I can take care of myself, Mr. Macho. And if you think I appreciate your interference in my affairs, you're mistaken. If I wanted some—some muscle-flexing he-man to clean up after me, I'd rent one."

Sucking in a deep breath, she turned to face both of them. "The two of you have behaved with less common sense than those children in there. Just for future reference, I don't find it amusing that two grown men should feel it necessary for their egos to use me as a Ping-Pong ball. I make my own choices, and I've got one for you, so listen carefully. I don't want either one of you."

Turning on her heel, she left them standing under the hickory, staring after her.

Chapter Ten

The last day of the session was pandemonium. There was packing and tears and missing shoes. Each cabin gave birth to its own personal crisis. Gear had to be stored until the following summer, and an inventory had to be made of kitchen supplies.

Beds were stripped. Linen was laundered and folded. Eden caught herself sniffling over a pillowcase. Somehow, during the first inventory, they came up short by two blankets and counted five towels more than they'd started with.

Eden decided to leave her personal packing until after the confusion had died down. It even crossed her mind to spend one last night in camp and leave fresh the following morning. She told herself it was more practical, even more responsible, for one of them to stay behind so that a last check could be made of the empty cabins. In truth, she just couldn't let go.

She wasn't ready to admit that. Leaving the laundry area for the stables, she began counting bridles. The only reason she was considering staying behind, she lectured herself, was to make certain all the loose ends were tied up. As she marked numbers on her clipboard, she struggled to block out thoughts of Chase. He certainly had nothing to do with her decision to remain behind. She counted snaffle bits twice, got two different totals, then counted again.

Impossible man. She slashed the pencil over the paper, marking and totaling until she was satisfied. Without pausing, she started a critical study of reins, checking for wear. A good rubbing with saddle soap was in order, she decided. That was one more reason to stay over one more night. But, as it often had during the past week, her confrontation with Chase and Eric ran through her mind.

She had meant everything she'd said. Just reaffirming that satisfied her. Every single word, even though she had shouted it, had come straight from the heart. Even after seven days her indignation, and her resolve, were as fresh as ever.

She had simply been a prize to be fought over, she remembered as indignation began to simmer toward rage. Is that all a woman was to a man, something to yank against his side and stretch his ego on? Well, that wasn't something she would accept. She had only truly forged her own identity in recent months. That wasn't something she was going to give up, or even dilute, for anyone, for any man.

Fury bubbling, Eden crossed over to inspect the saddles. Eric had never loved her. Now, more than ever, that was crystal clear. Even without love, without caring, he'd wanted to lay some sort of claim. My woman. My property. My *fiancée*! She made a sound, somewhere between disgust and derision, that had one of the horses blowing in response.

If her aunt hadn't taken him away, Eden wasn't sure what she might have done. And, at this point, she was equally unsure she wouldn't have enjoyed it immensely.

But worse, a hundred times worse, was Chase. As she stared into space, her pencil drummed a rapid rat-a-tat-tat on the clipboard. He'd never once spoken of love or affection. There had been no promises asked or given, and yet he'd behaved just as abominably as Eric.

That was where the comparison ended, she admitted, as she pressed the heel of her hand to her brows. She was in love with Chase. Desperately in love. If he'd said a word, if he'd given her a chance to speak, how different things might have been. But now she was discovering that leaving him was infinitely more difficult than it had been to leave Philadelphia.

He hadn't spoken; he hadn't asked. The compromises she might have made for him, and only him, would never be needed now. Whatever might have been was over, she told herself, straightening her shoulders. It was time for new adjustments, new plans and, again, a new life. She had done it once, and she could do it again.

"Plans," she muttered to herself as she studied the clipboard again. There were so many plans to make for the following season. It would be summer again before she knew it.

Her fingers clutched the pencil convulsively. Was that how she would live her life, from summer to summer? Would there only be emptiness in between, emptiness and waiting? How many times would she come back and walk along the lake hoping to see him?

No. This was the mourning period. Eden closed her eyes for a moment and waited for the strength to return. You couldn't adjust and go on unless you'd grieved first. That was something else she had learned. So she would grieve for Chase. Then she would build her life.

"Eden. Eden, are you in there?"

"Right here." Eden turned as Candy rushed into the tack room.

"Oh, thank God."

"What now?"

Candy pressed a hand to her heart as if to push her breath back. "Roberta."

"Roberta?" Her stomach muscles balled like a fist. "Is she hurt?"

"She's gone."

"What do you mean, gone? Did her parents come early?"

"I mean gone." Pacing, Candy began to tug on her hair. "Her bags are all packed and stacked in her cabin. She's nowhere in camp."

"Not again." More annoyed than worried now, Eden tossed the clipboard aside. "Hasn't that child learned anything this summer? Every time I turn around she's off on a little field trip of her own."

"Marcie and Linda claim that she said she had something important to take care of before she left." Candy lifted her hands, then let them fall. "She didn't tell them what she was up to, that I'm sure of. You and I both know that she might only have gone to pick some flowers for her mother, but—"

"We can't take any chances," Eden finished.

"I've got three of the counselors out looking, but I thought you might have some idea where she could have gone before we call out the marines." She paused to catch her breath. "What a way to round out the summer."

Eden closed her eyes a minute to concentrate. Conversations with Roberta scattered through her memory until she focused on one in particular. "Oh, no." Her eyes shot open. "I think I know where she's gone." She was already rushing out of the tack room as Candy loped to keep up.

"Where?"

"I'll need to take the car. It'll be quicker." Thinking fast, Eden dashed to the rear of their cabin, where the secondhand compact was parked under a gnarled pear tree. "I'd swear she's gone to say goodbye to Chase, but make sure the orchard gets checked."

"Already done, but—"

"I'll be back in twenty minutes."

"Eden—"

The gunning of the motor drowned out Candy's words. "Don't worry, I'll bring the little darling back." She set her teeth. "If I have to drag her by her hair."

"Okay, but—" Candy stepped back as the compact shot forward. "Gas," she said with a sigh as Eden drove away. "I don't think there's much gas in the tank."

Eden noticed that the sky was darkening and decided to blame Roberta for that as well. She would have sworn an oath that Roberta had gone to see Chase one last time. A three-mile hike would never have deterred a girl of Roberta's determination.

Eden drove under the arching sign, thinking grimly of what she would say to Roberta once she had her. The pleasure she got from that slid away as the car bucked and sputtered. Eden looked down helplessly as it jolted again, then stopped dead. The needle of the gas gauge registered a flat *E*.

"Damn!" She slapped a hand on the steering wheel, then let out a yelp. Padded steering wheels weren't part of the amenities on cars as old as this one. Nursing her aching wrist, she stepped out of the car just as the first blast of thunder shook the air. As if on cue, a torrent of rain poured down.

For a moment, Eden merely stood beside the stalled car, her throbbing hand at her mouth, while water streamed over her. Her clothes were soaked through in seconds. "Perfect," she mumbled; then, on the heels of that: "Roberta." Casting one furious look skyward, she set off at a jogging run.

Lightning cracked across the sky like a whip. Thunder bellowed in response. Each time, Eden's heart leaped toward her throat. As each step brought her closer to Chase's home, her fear mounted.

What if she'd been wrong? What if Roberta wasn't there, but was caught somewhere in the storm, wet and frightened? What if she was lost or hurt? Her breath began to hitch as anxiety ballooned inside her.

She reached Chase's door, soaked to the skin and terrified.

Her pounding at the door sounded weak against the cannoning thunder. Looking back over her shoulder, Eden could see nothing but a solid wall of rain. If Roberta was out there, somewhere... Whirling back, she pounded with both fists, shouting for good measure.

When Chase opened the door, she nearly tumbled over his feet. He took one look at her soaked, bedraggled figure and knew he'd never seen anything more beautiful in his life. "Well, this is a surprise. Get you a towel?"

Eden grabbed his shirt with both hands. "Roberta," she managed, trying to convey everything with one word.

"She's in the front room." Gently, he pushed the hair out of her eyes. "Relax, Eden, she's fine."

"Oh, thank God." Near tears, Eden pressed her fingers to her eyes. But when she lowered them, her eyes were dry and furious. "I'll murder her. Right here, right now. Quickly."

Before she could carry through with her threat, Chase stepped in front of her. Now that he'd had a good taste of her temper, he no longer underestimated it. "I think I have an idea how you feel, but don't be too rough on her. She came by to propose."

"Just move aside, or I'll take you down with her." She shoved him aside and strode past him. The moment she stood in the doorway,

Eden drew a breath. "Roberta." Each syllable was bitten off. The girl on the floor stopped playing with the dog and looked up.

"Oh, hi, Miss Carlbough." She grinned, apparently pleased with the company. After a moment her teeth dropped down to her lower lip. Though perhaps an optimist, Roberta was no fool. "You're all wet, Miss Carlbough."

The low sound deep in Eden's throat had Squat's ears pricking. "Roberta," she said again as she started forward. Squat moved simultaneously. Drawing up short, Eden gave the dog a wary glance. He sat now, his tail thumping, directly between Eden and Roberta. "Call off your dog," she ordered without bothering to look at Chase.

"Oh, Squat wouldn't hurt you." Roberta scurried across the floor to leap lovingly on his neck. Squat's tail thumped even harder. Eden thought for a moment that he was smiling. She was certain she'd gotten a good view of his large white teeth. "He's real friendly," Roberta assured her. "Just hold your hand out and he'll sniff it."

And take it off at the wrist—which was giving her enough trouble as it was. "Roberta," Eden began again, staying where she was. "After all these weeks, aren't you aware of the rules about leaving camp?"

"Yes, ma'am." Roberta hooked an arm around Squat's neck. "But it was important."

"That isn't the point." Eden folded her hands. She was aware of how she looked, how she sounded, and she knew that if she turned her head she would see Chase grinning at her. "Rules have a purpose, Roberta. They aren't made up just to spoil your fun, but to see to order and safety. You've broken one of the most important ones today, and not for the first time. Miss Bartholomew and I are responsible for you. Your parents expect, and rightfully so, that we'll..."

Eden trailed off as Roberta listened, solemn-eyed. She opened her mouth again, prepared to complete the lecture, but only a shuddering breath came out. "Roberta, you scared me to death."

"Gee, I'm sorry, Miss Carlbough." To Eden's surprise, Roberta jumped up and dashed across the room to throw her arms around Eden's waist. "I didn't mean to, really. I guess I didn't think anyone would miss me before I got back."

"Not miss you?" A laugh, a little shaky, whispered out as Eden pressed a kiss to the top of Roberta's head. "You monster, don't you know I've developed radar where you're concerned?"

"Yeah?" Roberta squeezed hard.

"Yeah."

"I am sorry, Miss Carlbough, really I am." She drew back so that her freckled, triangular face was tilted to Eden's. "I just had to see Chase for a minute." She sent Eden an intimate, feminine glance that had Eden looking quickly over at Chase.

"Chase?" Eden repeated, knowing her emphasis on Roberta's use of the first name would get her nowhere.

"We had a personal matter to discuss." Chase dropped down onto the arm of a chair. He wondered if Eden had any idea how protectively she was holding Roberta.

Though it was difficult, Eden managed to display some dignity in her dripping clothes. "I realize it's too much to expect a twelve-year-old to show a consistent sense of responsibility, but I would have expected more from you."

"I called the camp," he said, taking the wind out of her sails. "Apparently I just missed catching you. They know Roberta's safe." Rising, he walked over and grabbed the tail of her T-shirt. A flick of the wrist had water dripping out. "Did you walk over?"

"No." Annoyed that he had done exactly what he should have done, Eden smacked his hand away. "The car..." She hesitated, then decided to lie. "Broke down." She turned to frown at Roberta again. "Right before the storm."

"I'm sorry you got wet," Roberta said again.

"And so you should be."

"Didn't you put gas in the car? It was out, you know."

Before Eden could decide to murder her after all, they were interrupted by the blast of a horn.

"That'll be Delaney." Chase walked to the window to confirm it. "He's going to run Roberta back to camp."

"That's very kind of him." Eden held her hand out for Roberta's. "I appreciate all the trouble."

"Just Roberta." Chase caught Eden's hand before she could get away from him again. Ready and willing, or kicking and screaming, he was holding on to what he needed. "You'd better get out of those wet clothes before you come down with something."

"As soon as I get back to camp."

"My mother says you catch a chill if your feet stay wet." Roberta gave Squat a parting hug. "See you next year," she said to Chase, and for the first time Eden saw a hint of shyness. "You really will write?"

"Yeah." Chase bent down, tilted her head and kissed both cheeks. "I really will write."

Her freckles all but vanished under her blush. Turning, she threw herself into Eden's arms again. "I'll miss you, Miss Carlbough."

"Oh, Roberta, I'll miss you, too."

"I'm coming back next year and bringing my cousin. Everyone says we're so much alike we should be sisters."

"Oh," Eden managed weakly. "Wonderful." She hoped one winter was enough time to recharge.

"This was the best summer ever." Roberta gave one last squeeze as tears began to cloud Eden's eyes. "Bye!"

The front door was slamming behind her before Eden had taken the first step. "Roberta—"

"It was my best summer ever, too." Chase took her free hand before she could try for the door.

"Chase, let me go. I have to get back."

"Dry clothes. Though, as I may have mentioned before, you look wonderful wet and dripping."

"I'm not staying," she said, even as he tugged her toward the stairs.

"Since I just heard Delaney pull off, and your car's out of gas, I'd say you are." Because she was shivering now, he hurried her up. "And you're leaving puddles on the floor."

"Sorry." He propelled her through his bedroom. Eden had a fleeting impression of quiet colors and a brass bed before she was nudged into the adjoining bath. "Chase, this is very nice of you, but if you could just drive me back—"

"After you've had a hot shower and changed."

A hot shower. He could have offered her sable and emeralds and not tempted her half so much. Eden hadn't had a hot shower since the first week of June. "No, I really think I should get back."

But the door was already closing behind him.

Eden stared at it; then, her lower lip caught between her teeth, she looked back at the tub. Nothing she'd ever seen in her life had seemed so beautiful, so desirable. It took her less than ten seconds to give in.

"Since I'm here anyway…" she mumbled, and began to peel out of her clothes.

The first sizzle of hot spray stole her breath. Then, with a sigh of pure greed, she luxuriated in it. It was sinful, she thought as the water sluiced over her head. It was heaven.

Fifteen minutes later, she turned the taps off, but not without regret. On the rack beside the tub was a thick, thirsty bath towel. She wrapped herself in it and decided it was nearly as good as the shower. Then she noticed her clothes were gone.

For a moment, she only frowned at the empty rail where she'd hung them. Then she gripped the towel tighter. He must have come in and taken them while she was in the shower. Lips pursed, Eden studied the frosted glass doors and wondered how opaque they really were.

Be practical, she told herself. Chase had come in and taken her clothes because they needed to be dried. He was simply being a considerate host. Still, her nerves drummed a bit as she lifted the navy-blue robe from the hook on the back of the door.

It was his, of course. His scent clung to the material so that she felt he was all but in the room with her as she drew it on. It was warm and thick, but she shivered once as she secured the belt.

It was practical, she reminded herself. The robe was nothing more than an adequate covering until her clothes were dry again. But she tilted her head so that her chin rubbed along the collar.

Fighting off the mood, she took the towel and rubbed the mist away from the mirror. What she saw was enough to erase any romantic fantasies from her mind. True, the hot water from the shower had brought some color to her cheeks, but she hadn't even a trace of mascara left to darken her lashes. With the color of the robe to enhance them, her eyes dominated her face. She looked as though she'd been saved just before going under for the third time. Her hair was wet, curling in little tendrils around her face.

Eden dragged a hand through it a few times, but couldn't bring it to order without a brush.

Charming, she thought before she pulled the door open. In Chase's bedroom she paused, wanting to look, wanting even more to touch something that belonged to him. With a shake of her head, she hurried through the bedroom and down the stairs. It was only when she stopped in the doorway of the front room and saw him that her nerves returned in full force.

He looked so right, so at ease in his workshirt and jeans as he stood in front of a nineteenth-century cabinet pouring brandy from a crystal decanter. She'd come to realize that it was his contradictions, as much as anything else, that appealed to her. At the moment, reasons didn't matter. She loved him. Now she had to get through this last encounter before burying herself in the winter months.

He turned and saw her. He'd known she was there, had felt her there, but had needed a moment. When he'd come into the bath to take her wet clothes, she'd been humming. He'd only seen a shadow of her behind the glass but had wanted, more than he could remember wanting anything, to push the barrier aside and take her. To hold her with her skin wet and warm, her eyes huge and aware.

He wanted her as much, as sharply, now as she stood in the doorway dwarfed by his robe.

So he'd taken a moment, for the simple reason that he had to be sure he could speak.

"Better?"

"Yes, thanks." Her hand reached automatically for the lapels of the robe and fidgeted there. He crossed the room to offer her a snifter.

"Drink. This should ward off the danger of wet feet."

As she took the glass, Chase closed the doors at her back. Eden found herself gripping the snifter with both hands. She lifted it slowly, hoping the brandy would clear her head.

"I'm sorry about all this." She made certain her tone was as polite and as distant as she could manage. She kept her back to the doors.

"No trouble." He wanted to shake her. "Why don't you sit down?"

"No, I'm fine." But when he continued to stand in front of her, she felt it necessary to move. She walked to the window, where the rain was still pouring from the sky. "I don't suppose this can keep up for long."

"No, it can't." The amusement he was beginning to feel came out in his voice. Wary, Eden turned back to him. "In fact, I'm amazed it's gone on this long." Setting his brandy aside, he went to her. "It's time we stopped it, Eden. Time you stopped backing away."

She gave a quick shake of her head and skirted around him. "I don't know what you mean."

"The hell you don't." He was behind her quickly, and there was nowhere to run. He took the snifter from her nerveless fingers before turning her to face him again. Slowly, deliberately, he gathered her hair in his hands, drawing it back until her face was unframed. There was a flash of fear in her eyes, but beneath it, waiting, was the need he'd wanted to see.

"We stood here once before, and I told you then it was too late."

The sun had been streaming through the glass then. Now the rain was lashing against it. As she stood there, Eden felt past and present overlap. "We stood here once before, and you kissed me."

His mouth found hers. Like the storm, the kiss was fierce and urgent. He'd expected hesitation and found demand. He'd expected fear and found passion. Drawing her closer, he found hunger and need and shimmering desire. What he had yet to find, what he discovered he needed most, was acceptance.

Trust me. He wanted to shout it at her, but her hands were in his hair, entangling him and pulling him to her.

The rain beat against the windowpanes. Thunder walked across the sky. Eden was whirling in her own private storm. She wanted him, wanted to feel him peeling the robe from her shoulders and touching her. She wanted that first delirious sensation of skin meeting skin. She wanted to give her love to him where it could be alive and free, but knew she had to keep it locked inside, secret, lonely.

"Chase. We can't go on like this." She turned her head away. "I can't go on like this. I have to leave. People are waiting for me."

"You're not going anywhere. Not this time." He slid a hand up her throat. His patience was at an end.

She sensed it and backed away. "Candy will be wondering where I am. I'd like to have my clothes now."

"No."

"No?"

"No," he said again as he lifted his brandy. "Candy won't be wondering where you are, because I phoned her and told her you weren't coming back. She said you weren't to worry, that things were under control. And no—" he sipped his brandy "—you can't have your clothes. Can I get you something else?"

"You phoned her?" All the fear, all the anxiety, drained away to make room for temper. Her eyes darkened, losing their fragility. Chase almost smiled. He loved the cool woman, the nervous one, the determined one, but he adored the Viking.

"Yeah. Got a problem with that?"

"Where did you possibly get the idea that you had a right to make my decisions for me?" She pushed a hand, covered by the cuff of his robe, against his chest. "You had no business calling Candy, or anyone else. More, you had no business assuming that I'd stay here with you."

"I'm not assuming anything. You are staying here. With me."

"Guess again." This time, when she shoved, there was enough power behind it to take him back a step. He knew that if he hadn't already been mad about her, he would have fallen in love at that moment. "God, but I'm sick to death of dealing with overbearing, dictatorial men who think all they have to do is want something to have it."

"You're not dealing with Eric now, Eden." His voice was soft, perhaps a shade too soft. "You're not dealing with other men, but with me. Only me."

"Wrong again, because I'm through dealing with you. Give me my clothes."

He set the snifter down very carefully. "No."

Her mouth would have fallen open if her jaw hadn't been clenched so tightly. "All right, I'll walk back in this." Ready to carry out her threat, she marched to the door and yanked it open. Squat lay across the threshold. As they spotted each other, he rose on his haunches with what Eden was certain was a leer. She took one more step, then, cursing herself for a coward, turned back.

"Are you going to call off that beast?"

Chase looked down at Squat, knowing the dog would do nothing more dangerous than slobber on her bare feet. Hooking his thumb in his pocket, he smiled. "He's had his shots."

"Terrific." With her mind set on one purpose, she strode to the window. "I'll go out this way then." Kneeling on the window seat, she began to struggle with the sash. When Chase caught her around the waist, she turned on him.

"Take your hands off me. I said I was leaving, and I meant it." She took a swing, surprising them both when it landed hard in his gut. "Here, you want your robe back. I don't need it. I'll walk the three miles naked." To prove her point, she began fighting the knot at the belt.

"I wouldn't do that." As much for his sake as hers, he caught her hands. "If you do, we won't spend much time talking this through."

"I'm not spending any time at all." She squirmed until they both went down on the cushions of the window seat. "I don't have anything else to say to you." She managed to kick until the robe was hitched up to her thighs. "Except that you have the manners of a pig, and I can't wait until I'm hundreds of miles away from you. I decided the other night, when I was given the choice between a boring fool and a hardheaded clod, that I'd rather join a convent. Now take your hands off me, or I swear, I'll hurt you. No one, but no one, pushes me around."

With that, she put all her energy into one last shove. It sent them both tumbling off the cushions and onto the floor. As he had done once before, Chase rolled with her until he had her pinned beneath him. He stared at her now as he had then, while she fought to get her breath back.

"Oh God, Eden, I love you." Laughing at them both, he crushed his lips to hers.

She didn't fight the kiss. She didn't even move, though her fingers stiffened under his. Each breath took such an effort that she thought her heart had slowed down to nothing. When she could speak again, she did so carefully.

"I'd appreciate it if you'd say that again."

"I love you." He watched her eyes close and felt that quick twinge of panic. "Listen to me, Eden. I know you've been hurt, but you have to trust me. I've watched you take charge of your life this summer. It hasn't been the easiest thing I've ever done to stand back and give you the space you needed to do that."

She opened her eyes again. Her heart wasn't beating at a slow rhythm now, but seemed capable of bursting out of her chest. "Was that what you were doing?"

"I understood that you needed to prove something to yourself. And I think I knew that until you had, you wouldn't be ready to share whatever that was with me."

"Chase—"

"Don't say anything yet." He brought her hand to his lips. "Eden, I know you're used to certain things, a certain way of life. If that's what you need, I'll find a way to give it to you. But if you give me a chance, I can make you happy here."

She swallowed, afraid of misunderstanding. "Chase, are you saying you'd move back to Philadelphia if I asked you to?"

"I'm saying I'd move anywhere if it was important to you, but I'm not letting you go back alone, Eden. Summers aren't enough."

Her breath came out quietly. "What do you want from me?"

"Everything." He pressed his lips to her hand again, but his eyes were no longer calm. "A lifetime, starting now. Love, arguments, children. Marry me, Eden. Give me six months to make you happy here. If I can't, we'll go anywhere you like. Just don't back away."

"I'm not backing away." Her fingers entwined with his. "And I don't want to be anyplace but here."

She saw the change in his eyes even as his fingers tightened on hers. "If I touch you now, there's no going back."

"You've already told me it was too late." She drew him down to her. Passion and promises merged as they strained closer. She felt again that she had the world in the palm of her hand and held it tightly. "Don't ever let me go. Oh, Chase, I could feel my heart breaking when I thought of leaving here today, leaving you when I loved you so much."

"You wouldn't have gotten far."

Her lips curved at that. Perhaps, in some areas, she could accept a trace of arrogance. "You'd have come after me?"

"I'd have come after you so fast I'd have been there before you."

She felt pleasure grow, and glow. "And begged?"

His brow lifted at the glint in her eyes. "Let's just say I'd have left little doubt as to how much I wanted you."

"And crawled," she said, twining her arms around his neck. "I'm almost sorry I missed that. Maybe you could do it now."

He took a quick nip at her ear. "Don't press your luck."

Laughing, she held on. "One day this will be gray," she murmured as she trailed her fingers through his hair. "And I still won't be able to keep my hands out of it." She drew his head back to look at him, and this time there was no laughter, only love. "I've waited for you all my life."

He buried his face in her throat, fighting back the need to make her his, then and there. With Eden it would be perfect, it would be everything dreams were made of. He drew away to trace the line of her cheekbone. "You know, I wanted to murder Eric when I saw him with his hands on you."

"I didn't know how to explain when I saw you there. Then, later..." Her brow arched. "Well, you behaved very badly."

"You were magnificent. You scared Eric to death."

"And you?"

"You only made me want you more." He tasted her again, feeling the wild, sweet thrill only she had ever brought to him. "I had plans to kidnap you from camp. Bless Roberta for making it easy."

"I hope she's not upset you're going to marry me instead. You have a neat dog, and you're kind of cute." She pressed her lips to the sensitive area just below his ear.

"She understood perfectly. In fact, she approves."

Eden stopped her lazy exploration of his throat. "Approves? You mean you told her you were going to marry me?"

"Sure I did."

"Before you asked me?"

Grinning, Chase leaned down to nip at her bottom lip. "I figured Squat and I could convince you."

"And if I'd said no?"

"You didn't."

"There's still time to change my mind." He touched his lips to hers again, letting them linger and warm. "Well," she said with a sigh, "maybe just this once I'll let you get away with it."

ℳℴ RA ROBERTS

21857 THE MacKADE BROTHERS: RAFE AND JARED	___ $14.95 U.S.	___ $18.95 CAN.
21885 THE MacKADE BROTHERS: DEVIN AND SHANE	___ $14.95 U.S.	___ $18.95 CAN.
21876 BORN O'HURLEY	___ $14.95 U.S.	___ $18.95 CAN.
28507 O'HURLEY'S RETURN	___ $14.95 U.S.	___ $18.95 CAN.
28511 RULES OF PLAY	___ $14.95 U.S.	___ $18.95 CAN.
28513 THE MacGREGORS: SERENA ~ CAINE	___ $14.95 U.S.	___ $18.95 CAN.

(limited quantities available)

TOTAL AMOUNT	$ _____
POSTAGE & HANDLING	$ _____
($1.00 FOR 1 BOOK, 50¢ for each additional)	
APPLICABLE TAXES*	$ _____
TOTAL PAYABLE	$ _____

(check or money order—please do not send cash)

To order, complete this form and send it, along with a check or money order for the total above, payable to Harlequin Books, to: **In the U.S.:** 3010 Walden Avenue, P.O. Box 9077, Buffalo, NY 14269-9077; **In Canada:** P.O. Box 636, Fort Erie, Ontario, L2A 5X3.

Name: _____

Address: _____ City: _____

State/Prov.: _____ Zip/Postal Code: _____

Account Number (if applicable): _____

075 CSAS

*New York residents remit applicable sales taxes.
*Canadian residents remit applicable GST and provincial taxes.

▼ Silhouette®
Where love comes alive™